T.A. FORD

Copyright © 2010 T.A. Ford
All rghts reserved.

ISBN: 1439270953
ISBN-13: 9781439270950

For those that offered love and support regardless of my fumbles, I dedicate *Aaren* to you!

Acknowledgement

For those that offered love and support regardless of my fumbles, I dedicate *Aaren* to you!

Read more of TA Ford's work at http://thedivaspen.com.

Chapter One

PENNS POINT

Aaren shifted under the snug fit of her seat belt and tried to focus once more on the journey. The narrow stretch of highway ran two lanes, one north and one south. It divided the dense Kentucky foliage, parting occasionally to reveal wide-open plains. Sleepy farmhouses, just like the one she'd grown up in, sat well back from the road. This road was *the* road she hadn't seen or travelled in over fourteen years.

The darkness thinned under the car's headlights. It was then that the approaching sign on the side of the road made the contents in her stomach pitch.

Welcome to Penns Point, Kentucky! The Salt of the Earth.
She was home.

Aaren closed her eyes for the millisecond needed to release the tightness in her chest. She exhaled slowly and opened her eyes. Her two-seater sports car coasted past the sign. Once, this road had been rutted gravel. The smooth, paved surface under her tires spoke to progress, advancement, and changes that only time could visit. Funny, change she could handle. Except for one: Penns Point without her father in it.

Old Rachette Bridge, the great divider of the haves and have-nots, was just beyond the next curve. Beneath it, the murky waters of Salt River flowed in and out of the Ohio River. Without conscious thought, she eased her foot from the gas pedal. The car slowed. Aaren let her eyes seek more as she rode over the bridge. The familiar dips in the road and rusted beams that formed a ghostly arch above. Her hands tightened on the steering wheel and her breath stilled.

She was home.

On the seat next to the empty bottle of Pepsi, her cell phone beeped. Aaren reached inside her Kate Spade bag, never taking her eyes from the shadows that her headlights fought hard to part. Her fingers grazed lipstick, a comb, and something else solid. Contact. She removed the phone and flipped it open.

"Hello?"

"So you leave town and I have to hear it from your answering service?"

"Hello, Gavin."

"What's your excuse this time? You aren't taking any cases so it can't be work."

Aaren's fingers, riding the top of the steering wheel, parted, then closed around it tightly. She chewed at her bottom lip, tasting the coppery remnants of her fading gloss. She was in no mood to hear again how she'd failed him.

"Aaren? You can't keep refusing to face me."

"I don't owe you an accounting of my whereabouts—"

"I beg to differ. I'm your husband. We owe each other. *Till death do us part* and all those pesky little vows in between."

Her eyelids fell shut briefly, until the urge to the end the call passed. When she refocused on the road, her voice was controlled and exact. "We are separated, Gavin. And we're getting divorced."

"I won't just give up on our life, our marriage."

"You think you can force me somehow?"

"Melodrama doesn't suit you, Aaren. Save it for the courtroom."

She fumed. Gavin was bitter now, and it made him predictable. He'd never lost a case, nor a client. He had no intention of losing a wife.

"What is it you want?"

"For starters, you can answer my question. Where are you?"

"I'm home," she mumbled.

"The hell you are. I went there. We were supposed to have dinner, remember?"

"When I say home, I mean Kentucky," she sighed.

There was a pause. She could see him in his office: nostrils flaring, glasses riding the tip of his regal nose. Her words would have his Nubian skin deepening with each measure of anger. And now he'd make this trip about them. How many times throughout their marriage had he tried to convince her to visit Kentucky? How many times had he asked to meet her father?

"Aaren, six years—"

"Six and a *half*—"

"Six years I've asked to visit your home. We separate, and *then* you decide to go?"

"I don't have time for—"

"Make time, damn it! What's going on with you? We're more than husband and wife. We're partners. We *were* friends. Now I can't reach you, and it's been happening for months."

"All the more reason to end our marriage."

"All the more reason to save it!" he snapped back.

She closed her eyes once more. He'd been a good husband; he did all the things he was supposed to. He'd always provided for her, not that she needed him to, but still. He supported her, kept their lives in neat, tidy order. Nope, it wasn't Gavin, the famous litigator, who had the problem. It was her.

How could she tell him what she rarely admitted to herself? That she'd married him only because she didn't have a good reason not to.

"My father died," she blurted. Then she clenched her teeth, not wanting another unnecessary word to slip. Farmhouses shrouded in darkness zipped by. The speedometer climbed as the engine purred along the empty road. She was getting closer. Soon she'd be there. What would she do when she was actually there, at the house she swore never to return to? She had little time or patience for this tired debate. God help her, she barely had the strength for what lay ahead.

"Oh, Aaren. Baby."

She tensed.

"Aaren?"

He's dead, Pops is dead. Dead. Dead. Dead.

Slowly, she eased the pressure off the gas pedal. She was speeding. The trees had cleared. Her eyes went over to the vacant terrain. There the tall grass swayed under the blue-grey light of the moon. A mist coming in from the river made it ethereal. She'd forgotten the quiet beauty of the country, especially along Route 23. How could she forget that?

"Aaren? Are you still there?"

"Yes."

"What time is the funeral? I'll be there."

"It's not your concern anymore."

"Are you serious? I should be there to support you."

"I'm fine, really. I'm sorry I didn't call. Sorry I was such a horrible wife, sorry for everything, okay? I can't do this now. I don't have the energy."

"You're not alone."

"There's no need for you to come."

"No need? Even now you don't get it. Your needs are my needs. We'll talk more when I get there."

"NO! This is hard enough. Let me deal with Pop's death my way. I can't do that and deal with us, too. Don't you understand?"

"No, I don't understand! Christ, Aaren! What is this? Really!"

"Nothing! And your constant need to 'fix' me is what I can't take anymore!"

"I'm not trying to fix you! I love you!"

She recoiled. He'd spoken those dreaded words again. It chained them together. She was sick of pretending those words held merit.

"Let me go," came her soft plea. Aaren held her breath during the answering silence. Gavin responded, finally, with a sad sigh.

"Fine, you're right. This isn't the time to argue. You're in pain. I understand."

"Thank you. I'll call you in a couple days, okay?"

"Of course. Talk to you then. And Aaren? I'm sorry about your father."

The muted sound of his disconnect left her ear as numb as her heart. But it soon passed. Once again she felt nothing. And that was exactly the way she liked it.

Making a hard turn to the left, she drove off the paved road to a dirt one that stretched 500 feet before veering across the lawn to the front of the house. Aaren shifted into park, then released a deep sigh. She laid her head back into the headrest. Her childhood, her entire world for the first eighteen years of her life, sat before her. The house built by her father for her mother, and treated as shrine to her memory since her death, was not the way Aaren remembered it. Now, it was in a dilapidated, weather-worn state. Everything about the exterior screamed *forgotten*. The white siding that used to have a fresh coat from Fred's Hardware every other year was peeling and covered by growing weeds.

The large front porch swing moved with a slight sway from an unseen push, and Aaren could hear the creak of the chains through the closed-up car windows. Gone were the days of girlish giggles and secret-swapping with her best girlfriend. She and Becca had sat there many an afternoon, blowing large fruity-pink bubblegum bubbles while debating their futures. Ebony and Ivory was what they'd called themselves. Rebecca Treviso was the only white girl who lived on the south side of Rachette. Their friendship went all the way back to the first day of preschool. Together they'd planned their entire lives from that swing. For Aaren, it had been a family and home with the boy of her dreams, not the hope-stealing walls of a New York courtroom.

But that was a long time ago.

Aaren turned the car off. She squeezed the keys from the ignition into her fist, letting the metal bite into her skin. She wasn't Abraham Robinson's baby-girl anymore, hadn't been for fourteen years, and Pop's death made it all the more clear. She considered starting the car again and leaving.

Maybe I should find someplace in town to hole up until the funeral? she thought. *Should it really be so hard to walk through that door, after all these years?*

Her heart answered *no*. Part of her wanted to come home. Part of her had always needed it. A bigger part of her was tired of running. She pushed her car door open, and emerged into the cool night breeze. Kentucky air carried the freshness of soil, new spring leaves, and lemon grass that grew wild wherever there was water nearby. She closed the door and moved toward the porch, hugging herself against the gentle breath of the wind. Each step forward brought memories that broke over her like an incoming tide. Aaren looked up to the second-story window that was once her bedroom, and the tree with branches, even thicker now, that reached the sill. She would climb out that window and swing down from those massive limbs to sprint across their land to the stables where she'd meet Jarrod. *My Jay-bird.* She remembered the grin he'd give her, and the out-of-breath kisses he'd steal, lighting that fire inside her. And then he'd look at her, and—

Aaren caught herself. Those thoughts had no place in her present. And for a long, cold moment, she wished Jarrod Pennington was just as dead as her Pop.

The wooden steps creaked under the soles of her shoes as she climbed to the porch. It was the only sound; the night had gone quiet around her. A check under the weathered welcome mat turned over the key Becca had promised to leave for her. Pop had given her one inside a small mustard-yellow envelope when she'd left home, but somewhere during the years, it had fallen into the forgotten space of things never used. Thanks to Becca, the humiliation of being locked out of her own house was averted. She fingered the silvery metal for a moment, until a soft squeak drew her eyes to the left. The porch swing moved slightly. A ghostly image of her father rocking in it, smoking his pipe, materialized. He stared out at the land he loved. His gaze never moved her way.

"Pop…" she said softly to a now-empty porch swing. She closed her eyes and reopened them. *Gone. Pop is gone. No, dead. Pop is dead.*

Aaren unlocked the screen door, then the next, and pushed it open. The darkness was complete. She reached a hand along the wall for the switch and flicked it up. The foyer brightened underneath the domed globe, but shadows remained in the corners. The house smelled the same, looked the same, and to her surprise felt the same as it did the day she left. The stairwell faced the front door and the hall that ran alongside it led directly to the kitchen in the back of the house. To the left was a bonus room that her father used for his office, and to her right was the entrance to the living area. She closed the door and stepped through. Inside was the same taupe-colored cloth sofa set she wasn't allowed to sit on as a child. Now, seeing how worn it was, she wondered why. A white-and-tan crocheted throw was folded evenly over its rounded back. She smiled and ran her finger over the loops. It was old, something her mother had made years ago. She didn't remember a time when it wasn't there.

Her mother's caretaking touch remained, even long after her image had faded from Aaren's mind. Noelle Robinson's black ceramic figurines, ordered straight from the Sears and Penney's catalogues, were polished and lined up on the coffee table, ready to watch over her daughter. As a girl, Aaren had taken extra care in preserving their shine. In doing so, she'd preserved the mother she'd barely known.

She moved through the living room, her eyes darting from one fixture to the next, landing on the fireplace mantle. Photographs of Aaren and her mother together were crammed in between her school photos, one for every year from grade-school to high school. Her fingers closed around a cool silver frame. This one had always been her favorite: it was a close-up of Aaren as a new baby, gentle in her mother's arms. Noelle's hair was styled into a single, large afro puff that had always reminded Aaren of a halo. Pops had told her that the photo was taken three days after she was born, right here in this very house. She put the frame back and looked at the others, documenting her evolution into pre-adulthood. He hadn't put her pictures away. She'd just assumed he would. From their placement, it was obvious he looked upon them every day.

Aaren stepped away, forcing down the knot in her throat. The back of her leg bumped the piano bench. Turning, she found more of her mom's collectible figurines. A sad smile tipped the corner of her mouth as remembered music filled her ears. Most nights, she'd sit here after supper, playing tunes she thought her Pop would like. *Blessed Assurance.* And *Sweet Hour of Prayer.* And out of the corner of her eye, she'd see him nod, smiling, with his eyes closed. Those times were the only ones Aaren knew she'd made him happy.

She flipped up the key cover then sat on the cranberry cushion that covered the wooden bench. Running her fingers over the ivories, she tickled out the start of a melody, one her father loved. And though the tears didn't flow, her fingers trembled from the aching in her heart. She grabbed the lid to the piano and slammed it down over the keys.

"Damn you, Pop! Damn you!"

The horses were secure, not an easy feat. There was a full moon, and something in the air. Even he was unsettled. Jarrod ran the back of his hand over his sweaty brow. Plucking his work gloves off by the fingers, he walked out of the stable, worn thin from a day's work. His faded Wranglers were dusty and grass-stained, his boots caked with the muck he'd just shoveled out of several stalls. He grimaced, knowing he'd have to give Wes another talking-to. The job was only going to stay his if he showed up for work. Jarrod pulled on the brim of his baseball cap and completed the motion out of habit, pushing his brown hair behind his ears.

His mind did an inventory of the things he'd need to tend to before sunrise, until the rumbling sounds of a pick-up truck traveling fast over his land drew his eyes up. It was Antonio's old white Ford. He marveled at the sight: Antonio had somehow kept that ancient thing running since they were sophomores in high school. The truck kicked up dirt and grass in its wake. As it turned, Jarrod saw the driver was Becca, Antonio's wife.

Sticking his work gloves in his back pocket, he walked over to the truck. Becca rolled down the window and tossed her light-brown hair with a bright smile.

"Hey, you done for the night?" she asked, looking back to the stable.

"What's up?" He peeked out at her from under the brim of his cap.

"She's here."

"Who's here?" he stalled.

"Jarrod... she's *here*!"

"She's here for her father's funeral. That's got nothing to do with me."

"Aren't you going to go see her?"

"What for? It's been fourteen years. What's done is done."

He turned toward his farmhouse. He heard the truck shut off and the door creak open, then slam. Sighing, he stopped and looked back.

"The hell it is and you know it! I kept your secret. I never betrayed your trust. But old man Abraham is dead! It's time for her to know the truth! It's time you two healed."

Healed? He scoffed at the idea. The time for healing was long past. They were both different people now.

"Let it go, Bec."

"I will not! She's over there in that house right now, alone. After all this time, she's come back home to us. Don'tcha wanna see her?"

Jarrod exhaled. "You think you know everything, Becca, but you don't. I promised Abraham that I would honor his wishes. That's what I did, and that's what's going to happen now." He looked toward his house. The pause between them lasted another long minute before his eyes cut back over to her. "The truth doesn't always free you. Not our truth anyway."

"It wasn't the truth that broke you. You let that old man guilt you into that sick promise all those years ago. Now she's home and you plan to just let her go, all over again? This is your chance, Jarrod. Don't pretend you don't want it!"

He shook his head, saying nothing. He couldn't lay eyes on her. He didn't trust himself if he did. He'd been the one to find Abraham. He'd sat in the Robinsons' living room, surrounded by pictures of her, with her father upstairs dead. He wanted to phone, to tell her all of it. He wanted to apologize for failing her, but he didn't even know where she lived in New York City. Besides, what would he say? Too much had happened and too much time had passed since he'd hurt her.

"You're a fool, Jarrod Pennington! A fool!" He heard Becca call out to him as he kept on toward his empty home. He threw his hand up to her. So he was a fool. He'd been a fool then, too. Why should that change now?

Aaren climbed the stairs. She walked along the aged runner she used to push the carpet sweeper on every Saturday. When she arrived at her bedroom door, she called upon her courage to push it inward.

Her room was just as she remembered it. Time had passed it by. The white, blue, and green quilted comforter was tucked around the mattress of the twin bed with the pillows fluffed underneath. The top of the bed was littered with a colorful assortment of Beanie Babies. She hadn't seen Beanie Babies in so long she couldn't help but smile wider. It must have taken her forever to collect so many different kinds.

MC Hammer, Digital Underground, Paula Abdul and New Kids on the Block posters were tacked to the walls. The shelves her Pop built housed her trophies from cheerleading competitions and track. On the dresser, a small pink-and-yellow music box drew her attention. Her Pop had given it to her on her twelfth birthday. She picked it up and studied it, before opening the cover to release the soft tune of *Somewhere Over the Rainbow*. A fairy princess spun around on one leg with her arms raised. The up-and-down of her tiny tutu kept time with the chimes.

The inside of the music box was lined with a pink satin cushion. Aaren lifted it and uncovered a picture she'd forgotten she'd tucked away. Since her father was so strict, she hid anything that told of her love affair with Jarrod Pennington. The picture was of the two of them, arms looped around each other, after a football game back at Pennington High. She wore her hair up in one ponytail with blue and yellow ribbons that matched her cheerleading uniform. Draped around her shoulders was his letterman jacket. He'd scored two touchdowns that game, and later that night, another one with her. It had been their first time together.

It had been the first time for both of them.

It all seemed like it happened to someone else. She didn't know that girl anymore.

Aaren stepped back and sat on the bed. She dropped against the mattress, causing some of the Beanie Babies to bounce off. She stared at the photo. Excited, youthful faces stared back at her. They looked so in love.

"It was all a lie. Everything about us was nothing but a lie," she mumbled. Closing her eyes, she sighed and went back to the first time Jarrod told her he liked her. It was right before summer, the beginning of the few happy memories she would have of her time in Penns Point.

SPRING 1989

Aaren, fresh out of the shower, padded into her room in her robe as she ran the comb through her wet locks. Pop was downstairs in his office going over his books. She would go and clean up the kitchen after she finished her roller-setting. She was digging through her bag for the biggest rollers when a smack sounded against her window pane. Twice, birds from the oak tree outside had flown directly into the glass. Each time, Pops had to replace the pane. He wouldn't be happy if this made it the third. She put down the rollers and moved the curtain back.

The window wasn't broken, but movement pulled her focus. Jarrod Pennington stood in the ankle-high grass below, just outside the slice of light cast by her window. He shrugged back into his blue-and-yellow varsity letterman's jacket, a smart grin on his face.

The light night breeze tossed his hair over his brow but she could still see the dazzling sparkle of blue eyes glistening up at her.

Becca had told her he was going to ask her to the dance. Aaren had been flirting and hanging out with him at school, and sometimes even met up with him to swim at the creek on the Jackson farm, but he never made it anything more than usual teasing and jokes most of the boys played. She was beginning to think she was making a fool of herself. He not only lived on the north side of Salt River but was from the wealthiest family in the county.

That, and he was white.

In Miss Griffin's class, she kept catching him staring at her when he thought she wasn't looking. She just knew he would approach her today, but when the bell rang, he got up with Antonio and walked out. Now he was standing below her window. If he got caught, her father would skin him alive for sure.

Unlocking the latch, she grabbed the bottom rail and pushed it upward. The curtains blew inward from the rush of the night wind. She leaned out, knowing her long locks would thicken and frizz into tangles thanks to the breeze.

"Jarrod, what are you doing here? My Pop catches you and he'll tan your hide!"

"Then grant a dying man his one true wish. Come down here and talk to me."

Aaren laughed. "Are you crazy? I said my Pop is downstairs."

"You want me to go to the door and ask then?" he said, pretending he was going to turn and head to the front of the house.

"Wait!!" she exclaimed in a loud whisper. "Give me a sec!"

Coming in from the window, she raced around the room to find her baby blue gym shirt and the matching shorts to put on. Forgetting her bra, she went to the dresser and got one of her banana hair clips. She twisted her hair into a thick strand before clipping it to the back of her head. She grabbed her Keds and slipped them on her feet, trying to be quick about it. She couldn't believe that Judge Pennington's son was outside of her window. Was he finally going to ask her? She got all nervous just thinking about it. Going to her bedroom door she peeked into the hallway. She then stepped cautiously out, stopping at the top of the stairs.

"Pop!"

"Yes?" His voice was deep and powerful, commanding authority even when he wasn't enforcing it. He sounded to her to be in the kitchen, which was at the back of the house.

"I'ma go to bed. I'll clean the kitchen first thing in the morning."

"Night."

"Night, Pop!"

She raced back to her room then closed and locked her door. She'd never blatantly lied to her father. Never. Definitely not a lie that would have her sneaking out in the middle of the night to talk with a boy. But she'd known Jarrod since kindergarten, and of course so had her Pops. What harm could really be done? Aaren leaned out of the window. There was only one way down. She'd climbed up and down that tree hundreds of times when she was ten, but now she was seventeen and it seemed a lot riskier. Throwing one of her legs out, she looked down to see Jarrod back up with alarm in his eyes.

"Hey, what are you doing?" he called up.

"Shut up before he hears you!" she hushed him. Tossing her other leg out of the window she reached with both hands above her to the largest branch, testing her weight on it. Feeling safe in her maneuver, she grabbed it like a gymnast, swinging her long, powerful legs back and forth until she reached the other branch beneath her. She was able to balance herself, then let go of her hold, to scale down the rest of the way.

She dropped down in front of him, grinning, and he shook his head. "Aaren Robinson, you're a tomboy, aren't ya?" he chuckled.

She pushed him playfully. "Jealous much?"

The light to the back porch flipped on and they both jumped. Aaren grabbed his hand, giggling, and ran with him in the opposite direction around the house. They kept running across the tall grass to the stables. Aaren dropped his hand as it turned into a chase, one she was winning. Jarrod kept after her. He was soon panting, faking fatigue to give her the lead. She sprinted the rest of the way and got there first, moving so quickly her clip broke. Her hair fell wet around her shoulders.

She tossed the latch upward and pulled the large wooden door open. The horses snorted at the disturbance. Aaren kept running, now into the semi-darkness. She didn't dare turn on a light. Besides, the large windows above allowed enough moonlight to illuminate the stable. Jarrod ran in after her, then stopped in his tracks, looking around. Aaren smiled, making kisses at her favorite gelding, Bishop, to settle him down. She heard Jarrod approaching from behind her.

"Nice race. Do you want your prize?"

"I know you let me win, Jarrod Pennington. Seen you run a ball clear across the green. Don't try it."

"You're just faster than any running back I know."

Her eyes slipped over to him. "Mmmhmmm."

"You're good with him." He nodded to the horse. "What's his name?"

"Bishop. He's my baby. Born right here, weren't you sweetie?"

She looked over at him. Jarrod was staring, and not at the horse. "What are you doing here, Jay?"

She stroked Bishop's nose and tried to pretend he had no effect on her. He wasn't just any boy: he was Jarrod Mitchell Pennington. He put his hand against the stall and moved in close.

"I came to ask you to the dance," he said in one breath.

"You came all the way across Rachette to the south side of town to ask me to a dance? You could have asked me in class." She cut her eyes over to him once more.

His cheeks burned scarlet. Now that was cute. Dropping her hands to her hips she faced him. She couldn't wait to tell Becca about this night visit. Her friend was going to flip.

"I was out riding my bike…" he started, then realized how silly it sounded. He shook his head. "Yeah, I came out to see you."

"You're crazy, Jay-bird!"

"Okay, cut the Jay-bird stuff."

"Yes, sir," she smiled.

She was so pretty. He wondered at times if she knew that. She wasn't like most girls in school. She was different. He felt like a grinning idiot, staring at her the way he did. In the dark they could make each other out from the moonlight pouring in through the windows. He'd put every one of her features to memory. Her large almond-shaped brown eyes, her button nose and high cheekbones; the dimple in her left cheek and her full, thick lips were a perfect pair on her heart shaped face. Often he found himself staring at her in Biology class. And tonight when she moved, it was hard not to notice the bounce of her breasts under her tee shirt. He found himself cataloguing every curve, admiring her flat tummy and long brown legs. She stood there smiling sweetly at him, her wet hair drawing up as she tried to tuck it behind her ears.

"I like you, Aaren. I figured I'd do it up right and all," he stammered.

"What would your folks think? I mean asking *me* to the dance?"

"My mom is cool. She's not like the rest of them, but my father? Screw him. He don't tell me what to do."

Aaren eyed him for a moment. Pops would bust a vein if he knew she was keeping time with a boy, no matter what color. But Jay was different. She couldn't help but feel a surge of flattery and excitement over the offer.

"Sure, Jay… I'll go to the dance with ya."

His head lifted. "You will?"

"Yeah. Why you seem so surprised?"

"I… well… I thought you were going with Scott," he stumbled over his words. "Truth be told, I was kinda expecting you to reject me. So I had this whole thing worked out on how I'd convince you."

She laughed, girlish giggles that did something remarkable to her eyes. "I wouldn't go to a carwash with Scott."

Jarrod felt relieved. "Good. So should we ask your dad?"

Aaren's smile faded. "No."

Jarrod brushed her arm, wanting to see her eyes.

"He said I can go only if he takes me and brings me home. So we will just meet there, if that's okay," she said, walking out of the stable. Jarrod followed her back into the moonlight.

"That's cool."

Aaren stopped and looked at him. "I can't believe you came all the way out here to ask me to the dance."

Jarrod stuck his hands in his pockets. "We've known each other since we was kids, Aaren. Why is that so shocking?"

"Just is, that's all."

She smiled, he smiled back, and for a moment, Aaren thought he was going to kiss her.

"Well, I better be going."

"Yeah, it's getting late… I guess I'll see you tomorrow?"

"Yeah, tomorrow," he said, rushing off.

She watched him from her position at the stable door. His father was the law, the only Judge in eighty miles. No one dared cross James Mitchell Pennington. His ancestors had built the mill, the town and everything in it, and the subsequent generations had run it. The Pennington house was the biggest in the county. Even from the outside, she could tell it was as big as the Robinson house and the stable, combined. All the little white debutantes in Bullitt County wanted to catch Jarrod Pennington's eye. And why not? He was rich, athletic, and the handsomest boy around. He was also the kindest, keeping friends on both sides of the bridge. And here he was, having ridden his bike across town to her bedroom window to ask her to the dance. Life couldn't be better than that.

What a fool I was! Aaren crumpled the picture in her hand. She hated him for hurting her the way he did, making her believe that life wasn't defined by class or skin color. She hated everything about this place, and who she was in it. Sighing, she buried her face in the stuffed animals and willed herself to go to sleep. She was home again, and miserable as ever.

Chapter Two

THE PRODIGAL DAUGHTER RETURNS

The persistent rap-tap downstairs caused her eyes to flutter. Aaren rolled over, snuggling the sea of stuffed animals. Then the sound came again with more force. She squinted at the light from the morning sun. Her head lifted and the fog cleared. The tapping was actually knocking. Someone must be at the front door.

"Alright! I'm coming," she mumbled. She wiped at the corners of her eyes. Sleep had never come easy for Aaren. If anything, falling asleep had gotten harder as she'd gotten older. So it was surprising that a night in her old room had given her some rest. Sitting up, she scratched her head and waited for her vision to focus. Sleeping in her clothes? Nice. And now she had company. She hurried. Aaren worked her hands back through her tangles, trying to smooth them out. Her mouth, dry and cottony, made her crave the toothbrush buried down in her cosmetic bag. The only problem with that was all of her luggage remained in the trunk of her car.

Coming down the stairs, she saw Reverend Morris, and who she thought was Miz Marie from the Murphy Brothers Funeral home, at the front door. They peeked in through the thick paned windows. Aaren cursed silently to herself for falling asleep the way she had. Her watch said it was after nine in the morning, and for country-folk that meant she'd overslept.

She opened the door and offered a small welcoming smile.

"Good Morning."

"Aaren? My Lawd, look at you, sugah!"

Miz Marie, who had to be the same age as her father, nearly deafened her with her greeting. Hands reaching, she threw open the screen and overwhelmed Aaren with a tight hug. A little surprised by the affection, Aaren stepped them back into the foyer. Their arrival confirmed it. Pops was really dead. She tried hard to mask the hurt. They were sure to look for any sign of it. Instead, she focused on her visitors. Neither had changed much. Aaren towered over Miz Marie, who stood maybe four foot ten and was quite plump. She had short, chubby legs and a rounded face with large cheeks that transformed her eyes into little slits when she smiled. Each smile sparked a twinkle from her gold front tooth, gleaming amongst her pearly whites.

Aaren looked up to the Reverend, who'd always stood as a giant amongst them. His head was crowned with gray hair knotted like sheep's wool. He rubbed the neatly trimmed beard that outlined his jaw, stretching into his sideburns, and returned her smile.

"Hello, Aaren," he said. She closed her eyes to the memories in his soothing voice. He'd led the flock of black southern Baptists in this town since before she was born.

Miz Marie let go of her, but brought her fingers to rest on Aaren's cheeks. She studied Aaren as if it had been a lifetime, instead of a decade and a half, since she'd seen her last.

"Please come in," said Aaren, leading them into the living room.

"I hope we haven't come too early, Aaren," Reverend Morris asked.

"No, it's okay, really—I needed to get up." She smoothed her hair again while running her tongue across her teeth to clean them. The truth was she would have appreciated it if they'd called first. She waved her hand at her guests to sit. As they did, she realized that the chair left for her had been her father's. She'd have chosen another seat. It hurt too much to sit in his place.

Aaren faced them, waiting patiently for what was to come next: pleasantries, small talk, and then the business of burying the last member of her family. The Reverend smiled and Miz Marie looked on with closely-held tears.

"I'm so sorry for your loss, Aaren." She placed her briefcase on the coffee table. The edges pushed aside her mom's figurines. Aaren flinched at them being disturbed.

"Yes, Pop was a good man," she replied softly.

"Amen. Your father was a great man and everyone south or north of Salt River respected him," the Reverend chimed in.

Aaren gave a thin but polite smile, not knowing what else to say. She had no idea what Pop had been doing for the past fourteen years, and she knew they knew that. There was no need for pretense with them.

Miz Marie opened her briefcase.

"Let's see here. Abraham left detailed instructions on how he'd like to be laid to rest," she said, her tone proper and businesslike. But when their eyes met as she handed over the contract, Aaren took note of the glint that slightly altered her professional smile. A pregnant pause extended between them as Aaren hesitated. She swallowed the lump in her throat and accepted the stapled paper.

Contract in hand, she scanned fine print then stopped. She hadn't really thought of the next step, but Pop had planned out her life so it should be no surprise that he planned out his death. Thumbing through the documents, she saw he was to be eulogized at First Macedonia, and then buried next to her mother. The figures for the service stated paid in full. He didn't want her money.

It stung that he might have thought she wouldn't have come, or been willing to cover the expense.

"Aaren, he's also left with the church the hymns he would like for the service. He made a special request."

Aaren looked to the Reverend.

"Special request?"

"He wanted a solo by you. He asked that you sing *Thank You Lord*," the Reverend said.

Aaren blinked. She hadn't sung in public since she'd left home, since she left the Reverend's choir.

"He what?"

"Baby-girl, everyone in this parish loves that angelic voice of yours," cooed Miz Marie, evoking the name Pops would use. The forced kindness caused the hairs to prick and stand at the nape of Aaren's neck. "Your father would brag on you all the time!"

"I…" Her voice choked at the mention of her father's praise. She sucked in her bottom lip and tried to digest his request. Pop wanted her to sing?

"We have him resting down at Murphy's, sweetie." Miz Marie cleared her throat and straightened her back. Aaren's eyes dropped to the way she fiddled with her hanky's frilled edge and the persistent tapping of her left foot. The action caused her wide lap to shake. Abraham Robinson's passing took a toll on Miz Marie too. "We needed to know what you wanted to dress him in. He was a stickler for details, but everyone forgets that one."

Aaren looked between them. She slowly closed her eyes. The gravity of her mounting sorrow anchored her heart. *He died alone in this house, alone and in this house.* It hit hard. Closing her eyes, she tried to regain control as waves of grief kept moving through her. Miz Marie's brows drew together in concern. Her eyes turned to the Reverend, who also wore a look of worry.

"Aaren?"

Aaren blinked away the tears and opened her eyes. She wanted this over and done with.

"Can we do the service tomorrow?"

Their brows rose jointly in shock. "Well, uh…." stammered Miz Marie.

The Reverend chimed in. "We thought you might want to prepare, maybe decide on—"

"No, Pop left no room for preparation. There's nothing left to decide. I can come over to the church and take care of things, but I'd like to have the service tomorrow if that's okay. I need to get back to New York."

"I don't think—"

"Of course, Aaren. We can have the repast at the church as well." The Reverend smiled.

Aaren nodded. "Miz Marie, let me get you some clothes for him."

She rose and walked out of the living room. She could feel their eyes on her and ignored it. She couldn't stay there much longer, in Pop's chair, having that conversation. It was too much. Racing up the stairs, she felt a sense of relief to be alone again.

She paused at her father's door. The old tobacco-and-leather smell that he carried with him greeted her. She stood there with her heart in her throat. His cowboy boots sat side by side, neatly next to the bed. They always did when he'd stepped out of them for the day. She looked over to his straw hat hanging off the post of the headboard and his pipe laying on the nightstand. Her chest went tight. His presence was so strong, she could barely fill her lungs with air. She wanted it all to stop. Aaren dismissed sentiment for common sense. He was gone, and people waited. She had to do what was expected of her.

She went to the closet. Inside were two suits, a black one and a gray one. She pulled them both out and threw them across the bed. The shirts were underneath, and the belt to the pants hung from the hanger. Tears dropped down her cheeks despite her resolve. Abraham Robinson was a striking man when dressed in his Sunday best. She retrieved his Stacy Adams. They were still polished to a perfect leather shine.

"I can do this," she mumbled.

Their last conversations echoed in her mind. Neither of them had ever had much to say. And the one time he'd visited her, she'd told him to leave. The last night she'd spent under this roof with him, she'd told him she hated him. She never retracted that statement. Now, she wished she could at least understand why he hated her. Wiping at her face, she looked over to the bed. An empty impression left by her Pop was all that remained. She gathered the rest of his things, including undergarments to wear. His suit bag was in the corner of the closet; she put everything in it neatly, then zipped it up. She desperately wanted out of the room and away from the flood of memories this place brought.

She could hear their quiet voices as she made her way downstairs.

"She looks pretty," said Miz Marie. "Her life must be good, wherever she is."

"Yes, she looks well, praise God. Aaren was always a very beautiful girl, just like Noelle."

"So sad how things turned out for Abraham and Noelle. After all that man done. He should have told her of his sacrifice."

Aaren stopped cold.

"Please respect the dead, Sister Marie. Wagging tongues are an instrument for the devil. We aren't here to pass judgment on this family."

"Of course. Abraham was a good man. I'm glad she came home to show some respect. Didn't think she would." There was a pause, "What? Forgive me, Reverend, but you have to admit, this family caused this town a great deal of pain."

Aaren held the bag tight. She and Jarrod—what they'd done before she left had nothing to do with the town! What was Miz Marie yapping about? She cleared her throat and continued down the stairs.

"I think you'll find what you need inside," said Aaren, her tone dry.

Miz Marie stood. "Thank you, baby-girl." She took the suit bag with a smile and upward toss of her chin.

"Reverend, how about two this afternoon? To go over the service?" Aaren asked.

"That will be fine, Aaren."

It was evident he would like to say more. She just wanted them to leave. The uncomfortable silence hung between them for several seconds. Finally, the Reverend stepped over and kissed her cheek.

"It's good to have you home, Aaren." He grasped her hand. "I was the one to baptize you. I watched you grow into a beautiful young woman. Your mother and father would be very proud to see who you've become. Very proud."

"Thank you, Reverend," she said weakly.

Miz Marie came up behind him holding the suit bag folded over her arm. "We'll take care of him Aaren. Don't you worry. How about a viewing tonight at six? I'll swing by the radio station on the north side to have it announced. There are a lot of people that loved your father, who'd like to pay their respects."

"That will be fine," replied Aaren. "I mean, of course. Yes."

She nodded and walked out with the Reverend. He stopped halfway out the door and looked back. "God bless, Aaren. God bless." He then turned and left.

Aaren stood in the living room, watching the front door close. She'd spent all that time alone in New York, but she had to come home in order to feel truly lonely.

Jarrod crossed the kitchen to his pot of coffee. The rich aroma opened him up as he poured a cup. He'd gotten little sleep last night. How could he? Staring at the dark swirl in his mug, his thoughts drifted to her. Again.

"Aaren," he said softly, shaking his head.

Becca told him she was back, but she didn't say whether she was alone. What did it matter? Fourteen years later and married to boot, she probably didn't give him a second thought. Still, he couldn't help but wonder.

Up early, he'd already been out to greet his hands, who were at it before sunrise. He gave them their instructions for the day, making sure the right things were prioritized. He had a team of four that helped groom and train the show horses that he bred, along with some of his race horses. The horses weren't the only thing to tend to on his farm. He also had a smaller herd of cows that he had to let out for grazing during the day, and a cornfield to manage.

He picked up the paper and thumbed the pages for the obituary section. He wondered about Abraham's service. Then the phone rang, drawing his eyes upward.

"Hello," he said, sipping his coffee.

"Jarrod, its Sam Spence." The voice of the oldest attorney in Penns Point came through the line.

"Morning, Sam. What can I do for ya?" He tucked the phone into the crook of his neck as he turned the page.

"I was going to call out to the Robinson place to ask that Aaren come to my office this week." He coughed and hacked through the last of his words. He'd been diagnosed with lung cancer two months ago and refused any treatment. The cough that plagued him was becoming increasingly worse. Anyone who clucked over him got the same response: 'When it's your time to go, it's your time to go.'

"Okay?"

"It's Abraham's will."

"And?"

"I'll need you present as well. He's requested you." Sam's voice was still scratchy from the coughs.

"He what?" Jarrod dropped the mug down on the counter. Hot liquid licked over the rim and spilled down the side, splattering his hand. "Shit!" He flinched at the burn, putting the side of his finger to his mouth. "Say again, Sam?"

"I can explain it better in person. Going to schedule it with her and then I'll let you know."

"I can't, I mean I don't want—"

"Hey. Don't give me a rough time on this one, Jarrod. It's what Abraham wants, okay?"

Jarrod said nothing. He couldn't process it further. Why would Abraham do this? They'd been close the last couple of years, mostly because he'd made an effort to forge a relationship with the man. She was gone and it was Abraham and his father's fault, yet he couldn't let Abraham live his days out in isolation. So he did what he knew Aaren would have wanted. He made sure that her father was all right; in the process, he'd learned a lot about Abraham Robinson. He'd learned a lot about himself.

"Sure. Fine."

"Good, then. I'll be talking with ya later," Sam said before hanging up.

Jarrod hung up the phone. His eyes went to the window over the sink and he gazed out across his land. Being in Abraham's will could mean anything. What more could the man want from him, even in death? Shaking his head, he reached across the counter to grab his sun-worn baseball cap. He pulled it down on his head and turned to head back out to his fields, cursing under his breath.

Her senses seemed to sharpen on the land. Everything was bright and green, smelling of earth, pine, clean air and fallen leaves. The sun warmed her face. She slipped her hands in her front pockets, looking up at the clear blue sky. Had she missed this? Yes. She could easily recall the reasons why her father worked himself to the bone to preserve this place for them. Her eyes lowered and swept her father's land. She wondered what he'd done all this time she'd been gone.

Her eyes eventually fell upon the stables. It was both the first and last place she wanted to go. She was walking toward it before her brain even registered the movement of her legs. That shabby building held some of her most treasured and most heartbreaking memories. Halfway there, Aaren stopped when she heard a truck coming around the forested bend of the property. Her head turned and her hand went up to shield her eyes, wondering who else the day could bring.

Becca stopped the truck and jumped out. The sight of her girlhood friend brought a smile to Aaren's face. She opened her arms to welcome the loving hug. Becca was exactly what she needed.

"Oh my goodness, look at you! You sure do look good!" cried Becca, stepping out of the embrace and giving Aaren a once-over. She always spoke with her heart and she always gave it to you straight. Becca hadn't changed at all. Her long hair was pulled back into a low ponytail, revealing her girlish charm. Half Irish-American and half Italian, she had deep brown eyes and a natural tan. Even now, years later, she'd give a 20-year-old a run for her money.

"You look pretty good yourself, Becca!"

"I called you last night, but you didn't answer."

Aaren frowned. "Oh, I must have slept right through. I was tired from the drive."

"I can imagine! Where you headed?" she asked, looking over Aaren's shoulder.

"Just to the stables," she said quietly. "Wanted to see if Pop did anything more with it after he sold the horses."

Becca's eyes went from Aaren's to the stables. She looked to question Aaren's decision, but thought better of it. "Well, the word is the service will be tomorrow and the viewing tonight?"

Aaren looked away. "I forgot. News sure does travel fast in these parts."

"And your husband? He must be arriving separate, then?"

Aaren paused. This detail, she'd overlooked. She'd exchanged Christmas cards with Becca: it was the one small indulgence of home she'd allowed herself all this time. For the last six years, it had been a photo of the two of them, elegantly dressed and posed smilingly in front of their tree, just above their gold foil-imprinted names. She grimaced, remembering how he'd insisted on having the *Esqs.* stamped at the end of the line. To Aaren, it was more than just a social faux pas. To her, it was putting on airs.

"He's not really in the picture anymore." She swallowed, shifting her eyes left to catch Becca's response.

"Well, I'm here for you. You know, anything you need to do. I want to help."

Aaren exhaled, glad there would be no further questions.

"No need. As usual, Pop took care of it. He'd rather we just wrap it up and get on with living," she said bitterly.

"A lot has changed since you left. Your father really did miss you."

"What would you know about that?"

"Only what Jarrod told me."

"Yeah, you mentioned him having some kind of friendship with Pop—what on earth was that about? Pop hated Jarrod. When did they become so chummy?" Aaren tried to make the question sound casual, uninterested, even.

"Can we go talk?" asked Becca, looking back at the porch.

Aaren shook her head and walked away. She didn't want to talk. Just thinking about Jarrod Pennington was hard enough.

The sun remained a relentless, blazing fireball in the sky, despite the hour creeping past two. Moisture gathered on Jarrod's upper lip and under his arms. Beads of sweat trickled down his temples. It was too hot for more planting and too early to abandon his chores.

He settled on helping out in the stables with the horses, getting their feed together on the far side of the adjoining barn. Hard work wasn't just an escape: it was a cleansing. Even in the desert sands of the Middle East, with blood on his hands, he put in work wherever needed to keep his mind clear. Digging trenches, setting up posts, hauling equipment, breaking down equipment, you name it and Pennington was your man. His reward? Mind-numbing silence where he could shelve away those dirty little secrets he didn't want to live with. File them away neatly and endure for just a little longer without regret. Possible? Not really, but damn. The work was all he had. Jarrod grunted and shoveled more, minimizing the pauses between his movements.

Out on the land was the only place his life had purpose. He worked silently, oblivious to his surroundings, as was his habit.

Carrie Benson watched him from the shadows, her hands concealed behind her back. She knew exactly what was under that sweat-stained shirt. Those hard angles defined the chiseled perfection of a tight abdomen. Each time his biceps flexed with the tossing of hay, she was reminded that Jarrod Pennington was one of the few boys from high school who just got finer with age.

The raspy voice of an old Springsteen tune played out of the little transistor radio, and he moved with the rhythm, unknowingly. Tossing her golden locks around her shoulders, Carrie strode through the stable, confident in her own self-worth and determined to make him recognize it. Jarrod finally looked up. The brim of his baseball cap prevented her from seeing the look of irritation burning in his eyes.

"What are you doing here?" He leaned on his pitchfork, letting his breathing slow.

Carrie stepped closer. "Hello to you, too."

"No time for jokes, Carrie. Whatcha want?"

"I came to see if you had lunch," she said, revealing the picnic basket. Jarrod looked at it, then at her. Pushing his cap up, he wiped the sweat from his forehead with the back of his hand. "I know how you are. You won't eat unless someone reminds you."

They'd been sleeping together off and on for the past four years. She'd known since high school that he couldn't be pushed, but she wasn't above trying to make him jealous from time to time. For Jarrod's part, he'd been clear from the outset about his intentions: whenever she began making plans for their future, he made himself scarce for a while. Abraham had teased him, not long ago, that she was his penance. Well, so were several other women, the kind that offered little and wanted less. Carrie just never let go easy.

"Look, I was an ass. I came in Rory's all in your face 'cause I saw you with Sheila. I know it was innocent, Jarrod. Just you two having a beer. I swear, sometimes I don't think. C'mon, let's just forget about it, 'kay?"

"I told you, Carrie. I don't have time for your games. Take your lunch and head out."

Carrie sighed. "It's been a week. How long you gonna pretend to be mad at me?" Her voice dropped in pitch as she drew in her bottom lip and made her eyes wide.

"I'm not mad. I'm just… done." He bent to pick up a large bale of hay and dropped it on top of a stack near the stable wall.

"Jarrod. Baby—"

"Can you just… leave?" He turned away from her to continue his chores.

"I hear Aaren's back." Her voice went high again with mock innocence. "Abraham's death finally bought her home. The whole town is talking about it. Miz Marie done told everybody."

Jarrod continued his work. He knew Carrie hated Aaren, all the way back since high school, and he had no interest in reliving that time. Especially not with her.

"Whatcha gonna do now she's home? Light up that torch you been carrying for years? Don't deny it, Jarrod. I know you itching to see her."

Is he hearing me? she wondered. Of course he was. Same old Jarrod, no talk, plenty of 'tude. Why he had to make it so hard was beyond her. Not that he couldn't be sweet, when away from this farm. And that's what it was: this place she was never truly allowed to venture to. His sanctuary. Here he could be miserable, until he found it insufferable and needed the escape of her arms. Fine. She accepted his terms because she'd always known he was the one, but she was not going to stand by and watch Aaren Robinson come in and take him away. Not again. Carrie chewed on her bottom lip.

"Maggie at the diner said she's burying old man Robinson tomorrow. Said she just came into town in the middle of the night. Told Miz Marie to just get it done and over with, like she was bored by the whole thing."

Jarrod kept at his work, not missing a beat. She watched for some type of response and saw none. He was an expert at hiding his emotions. Even when he was angry, he looked bored. It was getting harder and harder for her to get a reaction from him.

"You know she hates you, right? I mean the whole town knows she hates you and her father. I hope you don't think—"

"Are you done?" he shouted over his shoulder, the blue of his eyes cold and exact.

Carrie jumped. "Looks like you do have your limit. I just meant—"

"Don't matter! You're speaking on things you know nothing about. Now get out of here before you use up the little bit of patience I have left!"

"I know you, Jarrod. You can pretend not to need anyone. Push your family away and mope out here on this land all isolated and alone, away from the world and whatever haunts you. But inside you're a dying man, Jarrod Pennington. Sooner or later you're gonna need a lifeline and I'll be there waiting when you do." She turned with her picnic basket and flounced out.

Jarrod watched her go. She spoke part of the truth. The heart of him had been dead for fourteen years, but she was wrong about that lifeline. He'd given up hope when the one person he loved most in this world stood before him, swearing to hate him even after death. That sealed his fate. He cared for little else after that.

Reaching over, he turned up Bono's voice until it blared out of his radio and went back to work, trying to forget the fact that Aaren was closer than she'd been to him in fourteen years. He wouldn't let his heart even acknowledge it.

"Do you want anything to drink, Becca?" asked Aaren, heading toward the door.

"No, Aaren. Sit with me." Becca walked over to the porch swing.

Aaren gave in to the request, dreading a conversation about Jarrod. She really didn't want to go there.

"I think you should know something—"

"If this is your attempt to tell me that Jarrod never meant to hurt me, well save it. Jarrod made it clear he did, and I believe him." Aaren averted her eyes. "Besides, that was eons ago. Neither of us cares."

"He had no choice. You know how things were then! He did what he could to protect you."

"See, I don't get that! How do you protect someone by telling them that their love for you was a lie? You saw how that boy humiliated me in front of this town. You were there when he said it to my face!"

"That's the way it happened but—"

"Becca, my Pop's dead. What does Jarrod Pennington possibly have to say that won't just compound upon that?"

Becca rocked the swing. Except for its squeaking, they moved in silence for several minutes. Aaren hoped the subject was dead.

"After you left he joined the Army."

Aaren laughed. Surely she'd heard wrong. She cut her eyes over to her friend, who simply stared back. "The Army? No he didn't." Becca met her stare, and Aaren's smirk dissolved. It made no sense. "Jarrod Pennington joined the Army?"

"Yes. Right after you left."

"Why didn't you ever tell me this?"

"I'm sorry. He swore me to secrecy. And back then you wouldn't even come home. We barely spoke those first few years. I just got the feeling you didn't want to know."

"Jarrod was supposed to go to the University of Louisville and then Ole Miss for law school. That was always… that was very clear."

His family had been adamant about that: four generations of Pennington men had done the same. Jarrod would have been the fifth. Aaren frowned, digesting the news. The Pennington history was something everybody knew and Jarrod was their all-American golden boy.

"He used to say his father wanted him to become the youngest judge in Bullitt County history. Had to happen before he was 33. That was the plan."

"Yeah, I remember, what he called it—"

"The Pennington curse," mumbled Aaren.

Becca nodded. They rocked in silence on the porch swing.

"The Judge must have flipped when Jarrod joined the Army."

Becca sighed. "The very next day after your father put you on that train to school, Jarrod hitchhiked over to Fort Knox and met with a recruiter. Enlisted and *left* Aaren, with just the clothes on his back, not ten days later. He didn't even tell me and Tony till the night before. Now does a boy that says you weren't good enough go run off to the Army 'cause he felt like he done the right thing?"

"Whatever reason he did that it had nothing to do with me, trust me. Jarrod—"

"Jarrod loves you! That's not even the end of it. He came back and bought the Jackson property. He built a house near that creek you two loved so much. Turned that sour land into a goldmine. Raising the horses you guys wanted, and farming. Did it all with nothing."

Aaren's head hurt. She didn't want to hear any more. "That's enough."

"I'm not trying to upset you, hun, but you have to listen. Really listen to me. Remember how it was before it got crazy. There are things—"

"I said *enough*, okay?"

Becca bit down on her bottom lip and nodded.

The porch swing rocked, carrying them back and forth. Yes, Aaren remembered. She hated remembering. Though even in her own bitter resolve, she admitted buying the Jackson farm was odd. She recalled driving past that property last night on her way to the house. She and Jarrod had plenty of dreams back then. Dreams of bulldozing Clancy Jackson's ratty old shack to build their perfect home near her creek. Jarrod always called it *her* creek after their skinny dipping adventure. He'd said he would never look at that creek the same again.

"He bought the Jackson property?" mumbled Aaren.

"Sure did. He raises horses on it. Grows corn… I think soy, too. Your Pop was a big help with him getting his business off the ground."

Aaren was impressed despite herself. Most people who worked the land around Penns Point either farmed or raised horses. She searched her memory, trying to remember if there had ever been anyone besides her Pops who'd been hardworking enough to do both.

"I don't care about any of this, Becca. I just don't care." She sighed and made to rise. Becca touched her arm.

"Hey. He's been here. He won't even speak to his people, but he came here every day to see about your father. It's weird, Aaren.

Like he and your father had some *thing* going on. I think you need to find out what. Think about it for a second. Your Pop and Jarrod Pennington being friends?"

Aaren stared at her.

"Why would my father and the boy I… why would they be…?"

"Exactly. Why would they?" nodded Becca.

Aaren sat back in the swing, looking out to her front yard and considering all the new pieces of information she'd collected in the course of the day. She'd overheard Miz Marie say that her family had almost ripped Penns Point apart. She'd always felt there was something odd with the way the Robinson name was whispered about in town. She'd even had a classmate call her mother a tramp once, saying he heard his mother say it. At the time, she hadn't known what the word meant, but she was smart enough to know that she shouldn't go asking her father for a definition.

And once she'd left town, the two people that hurt her the most had joined forces? Been *buddies*? Becca was right. She needed answers.

Shirtless, sweating and irritable, Jarrod headed across his land trying to decide if he was going to go to the viewing. Reggie, one of his stable hands, had told him that it was at six. His service watch on a wide brown leather band that covered most of his wrist read a quarter to five. He wanted to pay his respects, but he wasn't sure if he was ready to see her.

No, he was positive. He didn't want to see her.

Then he heard the spinning wheels of a fast-approaching car.

"What now?" he grumbled.

Out in the distance a golden dust cloud bloomed behind a silver sports car blazing a trail over his freshly-cut lawn. Jared stopped and squinted at the approaching vehicle. It didn't take long for him to guess who it was. It was Aaren Robinson, and she was headed right for him. He clenched his teeth and shrugged himself back into his shirt.

The car swung around, coming to a full stop with the passenger side of the vehicle closest to him. He could barely see her through the dark tint but he felt her eyes watching him. Why had she come? A cynical inner voice cut through his thoughts. *Just get it over with, Jay. She's not here to run into your arms. More like to run you over.*

The engine turned off and the door opened slowly. Jarrod braced for the reunion that, until now, had only happened in his dreams. She climbed out with her sunglasses on. First she looked at his land, then her head turned and she looked over the roof of the car at him. Stepping all the way out, she slammed the door and pushed her sunglasses up into her hair.

"Hello, Jarrod."

He stood before her with his hat pulled down on his forehead, looking as if time had stood still since the last time she saw him. Under the brim of that cap, his blue eyes took her in calmly. He didn't look surprised to see her. His stillness annoyed her. If she was going to be the only one bothered by this reunion, then she'd definitely miscalculated. She heard his years-ago voice yelling.

"No, I don't love you! It's over! I don't want to see your face again! You're not anything I want. I could never want anything with someone like you!"

Aaren shook off the raw flash of hurt and came around the car, holding his gaze. She gave a confident upward toss of her chin. Gone was the girl he knew: more than once, she'd taken down a roomful of men who could buy and sell this pathetic country hick fifty times over. Even so, when she looked back into his face, she was thrown by the way he stared. Part of her wanted to know what he thought of the woman now standing before him. Part of her hoped he still desired her some, so he would know what he'd tossed away so foolishly years ago. Then she gave herself a mental shake. It didn't matter. Men constantly gave her the same look he wore now. Why should he be any different?

"We need to talk," she began in an icy, hardened tone.

"Yes, Aaren, I reckon we do."

At that, Aaren leaned back into the side of the car. She waited for him to show his hand first. She'd learned a lot in fourteen years. And not for a moment would she allow herself to forget how she despised him.

Jarrod's silence was of another kind. He wondered about the woman she was now. Was she happy in the marriage Abraham had told him about? Did she ever think of them and that summer they had so long ago? Did she remember even a little?

Why does he look sad? she wondered. Then she scoffed. Some lawyer he'd have made. His emotions showed all over his face. Tilting her head, she decided there was nothing there she couldn't already see. She narrowed her eyes, ready to finish with him.

"*You* found my father?"

"Yeah, I did," he said dryly.

"Becca said he died in his sleep?"

"He went peacefully."

"Well, out with it, Jarrod. What's this thing between you and him?"

"Thing?" he asked.

"Don't play with me. You know what I'm talking about!" she said, crossing her arms.

She wanted to smack him, scream in his face, scratch his eyes out for pushing her away. She'd thought she could do this but as each second passed between them, the pain from years ago bloomed in the center of her chest. *Run*. She should run, just get away from him and his lies, or whatever it was that defined him now. She should keep running and never look back at this town.

"There was no 'thing' between us. We just became friends in the past couple of years."

Aaren laughed a cold, empty laugh. She dropped one hand to her hip.

"Friends? You and my Pop became friends? Wow, I have been gone a long time."

"Let me explain."

"No." She held up her hand, commanding him to stop.

Jarrod shook his head slowly, absorbing the venom in her voice. He saw hate in her eyes and it broke his heart again. His Aaren never hated anyone; she wasn't capable of the emotion. This woman standing in her place was bitter, which was not at all how she was supposed to be. What he did, what Abraham did, what they'd done together, was supposed to give her a chance at happiness. She wasn't supposed to turn into some kind of ice queen.

"I know you're hurting because of your father's death—"

"You don't know a damn thing about me."

"Look! If you aren't going to let me talk to you then why the hell did you come here?" Jarrod shot back.

"I came here to tell you that I hate you! I wanted to say it to your face! I wanted to look you in the eyes and tell you I've hated you for years. And *him*! I hate you both!!" she shouted, determined to stay angry, and stem the tears that threatened to fall.

Jarrod flinched. She had hit her target, but in the process gave him something she hadn't intended. She'd given him a clear view into the pain she carried, how scarred she remained. When he stepped forward, she stepped back, bumping the car.

"Don't! Stay away from me!"

"Aaren..." his voice was as gentle as a caress and his hand tempting, once he extended it to her.

"Don't touch me!" she said, moving away, trying to collect herself.

How could she be so foolish to come out there and behave like a heartbroken teenager? She hated herself for the outburst. She didn't want his pity. She'd stopped wanting anything from Jarrod Mitchell Pennington a very long time ago.

"I didn't come here for your sympathy. I came here for answers. Becca said you two kept something from me! What is it?"

Jarrod stopped his approach. "Becca said *what*?"

"She said you and Pop shared some kind of secret. That you conspired against me. Is it true? Did you? Did you purposefully set out to use me?"

"No, I never purposely set out to hurt you. I never meant to hurt you back then. There's so much you don't understand."

"But you did. Don't you remember, Jarrod? Everyone in Penns Point sure as hell does. Hey, tongues flapped in the wind around here for months, maybe even long after I left. It was a grand performance, your best ever. Though that crap you fed me to get me to give you my cherry was pretty priceless too."

"Okay, stop!" he said, having reached his limit. "I think this is… I mean… you should go," he said, his voice low and unnaturally even. "I'm sure you have more important things to do than waste your time on me."

Aaren gave a bitter chuckle. "Well, I'm not here about what you want. I want answers. Why would a Pennington befriend a Robinson? I mean I know why you went after me, but after I left, what, you needed someone else to scrape off your boot?"

"Aaren, stop."

"The truth, damn it!!!"

"I befriended him because he had no one else! He was out there alone on that farm, and he needed someone to see about him. I did it for you."

"For me?" she drew back, hand to her chest. "Me? This is a joke."

"It's the truth."

"Yeah, right," she glared.

Angry, happy, it didn't matter. She was still beautiful to him. Her eyes were sharp and unforgiving but the same soulful brown he'd see in his sleep. How could it have been fourteen years since he saw them last?

"Look around! Open your eyes, and look around!"

And her head turned. Her eyes swept the farm as if seeing it for the first time. There were stables with men leading horses in and out, a huge, covered work ring, cows in the pasture, and a cornfield to the east. Further up, she saw his house, built where Clancy Jackson's old shed once stood.

She looked back at him as he pulled his cap up off his head. She could see his face clearly. His skin was a deep olive tan, and blue eyes clearer than she remembered bore into hers. His hair, still longer than fashionable, was slicked back from sweat after a day's work, and it made him more ruggedly handsome, which annoyed her. Why couldn't he have gotten fat? Or gone bald? Or both?

She looked back into his eyes and caught a glimpse of the love she knew when they'd talked of a home just like this.

"Nice *farm*," she snipped.

Shaking his head, Jarrod pushed his cap down in his back pocket.

"Are you happy?"

"Do I look happy? My father's dead! Why would that make me happy?" she snapped.

"I mean in New York. Abraham said you married some big-shot lawyer up there."

"What's it to you?" She dismissed the question with a flip of her wrist.

Jarrod's brows rose. "You're not?"

"What business is that of yours?" she snapped.

He blushed and bit his tongue.

She sneered at him. "I didn't come here to play catch-up-on-old-times with you. I came here for answers and once again you're either a liar, or a hypocrite. Either way you're a waste of energy, like you always were."

Aaren turned on her heels and walked back around the car. She looked up at him over the roof as she opened the door.

"Don't come to the funeral. I don't want to see your face again. Remember those words? I got them from you."

He watched her fire up her fancy car and spin out, spitting grass, rocks, and dirt across his land as she sped off. Uncharacteristic tears stung the corners of his eyes and he blinked them away. The part of him that was more rational and less clouded by his love for her had feared this moment. Aaren had returned, but she was changed. The innocence and optimism that once made her so special were gone. And it was because of him.

"Hey, was that Aaren Robinson?" Gene, one of the stable hands, was heading to his beat-up truck.

"Yeah, it was," mumbled Jarrod, staring after the trail of tire marks burned through the grass.

"Wow. She looked different."

Jarrod exhaled. "She is different."

Chapter Three

A DAUGHTER'S PAIN

Aren swerved on the two-lane road, reaching for tissues from her purse while steering. "You're so stupid! Stupid!" she cursed herself.

She actually thought she could talk to him. At least be civil, but one look at him and it was if they were teenagers at the fair again and he was standing with his arm around Carrie Benson, laughing at her pain and embarrassment. In that memory, the eyes she'd once compared to summer rain were cold and void of love. He disposed of her and her heart that day without pause. She would never forget how bad it hurt.

She reached up and pulled down her shades to cover the tears in her eyes. Within minutes, she was in front of the funeral home. She felt relieved to put the car in park. She couldn't handle driving another second. How she wished to escape this town. Again!

Then she laughed. From nowhere she broke into a hysterical fit of laughter. Here she was, trying to collect herself before getting out of the car in tears, at the one place where she was expected to cry. Was it Pop's death that had her unraveling, or was it seeing the only boy, now a man, she'd ever loved in her entire life? Whatever it was, she laughed and cried all at the same time.

Aaren removed the keys from the ignition. She wiped underneath her shades and steeled her nerves. She had to tend to the burial of her father. The sooner she did, the sooner she could get back to her life, back to the one place she was in complete control.

As she got out, the wind caught her hair and blew it in her face. The hem of her dress billowed around her knees. It was her favorite and it had cost her a small fortune. It was the perfect New York dress: you could wear it at the office, in court, to dinner, all with just a change of shoes or jewelry. Now, though, she wished she had dressed a little more conservatively. Something with sleeves, or a less-open neckline. The whole town would have their eyes on her.

"Aaren? Is that you?"

She would know that syrupy voice anywhere. Sucking in her breath through clenched teeth, she turned. Carrie and her mother were getting out of their car.

"Hello, Mrs. Benson. Carrie."

"Hello, Aaren!"

The heavyset woman came slowly over to hug her. The offering of sympathy was sincere. Aaren hugged her back. Her eyes lifted over Mrs. Benson's shoulder and locked with Carrie's. Even as girls they'd never liked each other. Her thick, blonde hair was longer now, falling around her face. Carrie still wore her jeans too tight, and her makeup like face paint. Some things never changed.

"I'm so sorry about your father," said Mrs. Benson, resting her palm to Aaren's cheek.

"Thank you, ma'am."

Carrie stepped up. "Have you been inside? Would you like us to escort you, or did you bring your husband?"

Aaren smiled at Carrie. Apparently the news of her marriage had spread through town. "Actually I didn't, but I'll join you two in a moment. Don't let me keep you," she said sweetly, glaring from under her designer shades.

Carrie rolled her eyes, but after a moment, pulled at her mother's elbow. "C'mon, mama."

Mrs. Benson allowed her daughter to lead her up the sidewalk. Aaren glanced over her shoulder at Carrie, who glanced back as well. The smiles on their faces, Carrie's secretive and Aaren's appropriately sad, effectively masked the longstanding hostility they held for one another.

"Aaren?"

Turning again, she saw a friend of her father's walking up. She couldn't remember the man's name. Soon she was approached by several others, all arriving at once. Maybe Gavin was right and she should have let him come. Standing in front of the funeral home at that moment, she'd never felt more alone in her life. Putting on a brave face was possible because her shades concealed the pain in her eyes, and she accepted their condolences with the appropriate words and gestures. She allowed the gentlemen to escort her inside.

Aaren was shocked by the number of people gathered to sign the register. A black board with white stick-on letters gave her father's name and viewing time. She felt queasy.

"Hey, you okay?" asked Becca, coming up behind her and touching her bare back. Aaren moved half a step away, then saw the genuine concern in Becca's face.

"I don't know if I can do it," she said in a voice just above a whisper. It was never like this for her. She was never nervous. But her legs were threatening to go out from underneath her.

Becca looked back over her shoulder at others gawking. They all wanted to see the moment the prodigal daughter atoned at the coffin of her abandoned, shut-in father.

"Of course you can, sweetie. I'm right here with you."

Miz Marie waddled over, her eyes gentle. She spoke loudly, for all to hear, in her funeral director's voice.

"Aaren, baby-girl, I'm glad you finally got here."

Aaren tired of the phony sweetness. The room went quiet around them prompting Becca to act, her eyes locked on Miz Marie when she spoke. "It's a private moment. I'ma need you to clear these folks out so she can see him alone."

Miz Marie frowned. "*What?*"

"You heard me. Clear the room."

Aaren shook her head. "Becca…"

"Hush. *Now*, Miz Marie, if you don't mind," she said with enough force behind her words to let the woman know she meant business.

Miz Marie rolled her eyes and stepped inside.

"Attention everyone, I apologize but the family wants some alone time with Abraham."

"What the hell does she mean she apologizes?" mumbled Becca. "I'ma kill that busybody bitch."

"Stop." Aaren gave Becca's hand a squeeze. She didn't feel like a battle. She was still reeling from her confrontation with Jarrod. Mourners and friends filed out. Aaren was surprised at how many had come. She wondered selfishly how many were here for Abraham, and how many were here for a front-row show of her grief. But she was pleased when Antonio, Becca's husband and once, Jarrod's best friend, walked out with them.

"Aaren!" He came to her immediately and pulled her into a hug.

"You look good."

"Thanks."

"I'll need you to keep everyone out, Tony, while me and Aaren go in." Becca eyed those who clearly weren't Abraham's friends crowded around them in the foyer.

Antonio nodded. "Sure thing, no problem at all. We all respected Abraham greatly, Aaren. He'll be missed."

Miz Marie came out with the last viewer.

"Its all clear," she said sharply, putting both hands on her wide hips.

Aaren sucked in a deep breath for courage, and Becca squared herself alongside. They walked through the crowd, which parted to accommodate them. Aaren kept her head bowed, not daring to look up. She heard the doors close behind them, and with that, her heart finally broke. Feeling Becca release her, she pulled off her shades and looked forward. He laid in the casket stiff, foreign to her. His face was an ashy dark brown puffed out with more wrinkles than she knew he had. His hair, knotted into tight gray locks, was cut low behind his receding hairline. It wasn't Pop, the man that wore overalls everyday of his life, the man that was never seen in public without his pipe. This was not the man she loved in spite of it all, and wished he could love her back.

"Pop," she said softly.

Aaren stopped in front of the casket. She gazed down at him. He looked peaceful in his gray suit. Had his final days been one of peace? Her eyes were drawn to his Masonic pin on his lapel. Immediately she felt a pang of guilt for not remembering to ask that it be included. She wondered if Miz Marie had found it and put it on him. She hoped it was one of his lodge brothers, instead.

Aaren placed her hand against his chest. She found it hard, rigid, unnatural to the touch and empty of the life-force that was so strong in him. Silent tears slid down her cheeks. She dropped her head, crying. It hurt to remember the last time she saw him.

MAY 1999

"Pop! What are you doing here?" Aaren asked stiffly. He'd been standing quietly at her office door, apparently for some time.

"Hello, babygirl."

He smiled, but his smile was uncertain. He stood before her dressed in a dark suit, holding his fedora in his hand. She didn't look him in the eye, but focused instead on a shiny gold and black Masonic pin that rested on his lapel. She hadn't seen him since he'd come to her college graduation. That day he'd taken her to lunch. They barely spoke the entire time. They'd said an awkward goodbye and he'd left so quickly. For the remainder of the evening, she'd ended up celebrating her accomplishments with her roommate's family.

Over the years she'd spoken to him on the correct occasions, always calling him on his birthday and Father's Day. They'd never say more than a few words and she always felt as if he wanted nothing more than to get off the phone with her.

"What are you doing here?" she asked, not happy to see him at all. The risk of a confrontation, here at her office, threatened all she'd been working so hard for.

"Well, I thought I'd take my babygirl to dinner." His smile was fading now.

Aaren's eyes narrowed on him. First, she hadn't heard him call her his babygirl since she left home. Next, an impromptu visit from Kentucky in the middle of the week was unprecedented. She couldn't trust its sincerity. She rose slowly from her chair to face the man she still loved more than she thought possible. It amazed her, that even now, with all the pain between them, with all she'd suffered after he cast her out, she loved him still.

"You flew to New York to take me to dinner?" Her voice sounded almost childlike.

He held his tense smile and dropped his eyes from hers. "Well, actually I'm here for a Masonic convention. Today, it's my last day, so I thought—"

"Wait. You've been here for how long?"

"A week."

"A week! You've been here for a week and you didn't call me? I haven't seen you in five years and you didn't call me?" she asked, hating that he could still wound her.

Once again she was an afterthought for a man who was supposed to love her. He'd made her promise never to come home and she'd kept that promise. She hadn't understood that it meant he would never come to her either. She couldn't fathom how he could hate her that much.

"Aaren, I—"

"Look, Pop, I've got work to do." She turned and went back around her desk.

Abraham looked into his daughter's pained eyes, ashamed. "Of course, I figured you'd be busy. I just wanted to stop by," he said, backing up.

She sat back down, not bothering to look up at him, returning her attention to the brief she was reviewing.

"I'll call you, you know. Sometime, just to check in. You take care, babygirl."

Aaren continued to ignore him.

"Bye, Aaren," he said quietly as he walked out.

Aaren's eyes flipped up from the ledger pages after the door closed. She fought the urge to run after him and throw her arms around his neck. Shaking her head, she gave in to the coldness around her heart. What did she need with his love? She'd survived this long without it.

Aaren opened her eyes. Her vision, blurred by tears, soon focused on him again. She gripped the edge of the casket. "Pop, I should have told you sooner. I should have told you that I loved you with all my heart, even if you didn't love me in return. I should've found a way."

Becca rose to join her weeping friend. She rubbed her arm as Aaren leaned forward, seized by unbearable grief.

"Sweetie, he loved you."

"No, Becca. He didn't. He couldn't wait to get rid of me. He was burdened with me after my mother died and he…." She pressed her lips together.

"Did you talk to Jarrod?"

Aaren pushed away the question. *Jarrod. Always Jarrod with her.* She put her hand to her mouth, feeling as though she'd choke on her grief. And then, it was too much. Trapped, heartbroken, confused, Aaren let go until she couldn't hear anything over her own sobs. Becca just held her friend, wanting her to get it all out.

The crowd had thinned considerably since the show everyone was hoping to see was evidently not going to happen. Antonio leaned against the door to the viewing room, waiting patiently for the girls to come out. He and Miz Marie, along with the remaining mourners, looked up at once when the door opened and Jarrod Pennington stepped in.

"Hey," said Jarrod, sticking his hands in his pockets. "What's up?"

Antonio looked him up and down. Jarrod wore chinos and a white collared shirt with a blue blazer over it. With his hair freshly washed and his beard trimmed, he knew he looked miles different from the appearance he normally sported.

"What's up with you, man? Look atcha. Took a bath?"

"Funny," said Jarrod.

Antonio smirked. The others whispered.

"Why you guarding the door?"

"Aaren's in there now. All the gossip-hounds were here earlier and Becca cleared them out to give her time alone."

"Was she all right?"

"Why? Thought she was no concern of yours."

"I know what I said."

Jarrod understood the curiosity. He'd spoken to Antonio after he found Abraham. He'd asked Antonio to make sure Becca took care of Aaren. He vowed to his friends that he'd make himself scarce when she returned to town.

"I'm here to pay my respects. That's all." He ran his hand nervously through his hair.

"Do you want to go in?" Antonio stood away from the door.

"No. I'll just hang back. Wait, right?"

"Right."

"Right."

Before Jarrod could turn away, the door opened. Once again, they faced each other. Aaren's eyes flashed confusion, then something else that was so fleeting he barely registered it. He did see she was in terrible pain, even if she hid it from the others. He felt it, because he shared it too. Abraham Robinson's friendship had come to be the one thing Jarrod could count on in Penns Point.

He looked her in the eye.

"I just wanted to pay my respects."

"Of course, Jarrod, come in," said Becca. She was quick to bridge the gap between her friends, even though none could miss the disapproving, heated stare on Antonio's face.

Aaren looked away, arms folded and lips tight, as he walked past. He felt her eyes on him as he approached her father. His posture was stiff, forced. It was strange to be in a room with Abraham and Jarrod again, no matter the circumstance.

Aaren cut her eyes from the scene, her stomach cramping with age-old bitterness. She needed air. Walking out the door, she ran bodily into Travis Pennington.

"Excuse me," she blushed.

"Aaren, how you doing?" he asked, reaching for her. She allowed the embrace.

"Hello, Travis."

The younger Pennington wasn't quite as handsome as his older brother. Travis favored his mother's fair looks, but the family resemblance was strong enough. She wished it weren't.

"Do you remember my sister Macy?"

Jarrod's brother and sister came too? she thought. *Who next? The Judge himself?* Travis stepped aside to reveal a twenty-year old girl that had been six the last time Aaren saw her. Aaren smiled at her blue eyes. They sparkled exactly like her oldest brother's.

"Wow. Macy, you're all grown up."

Macy nodded and smiled back. From anyone else, that observation would have been irritating.

"I'm so sorry about your father. We all came to pay our respects."

"Thank you. Thank you both. It was nice seeing you," stammered Aaren.

Unable to manage anything more, she strode away. Their eyes followed as she hurried out to her car.

Becca stepped to his side. Her gaze fixed on Abraham, then shifted over to Jarrod, who stared down in silence.

"Why didn't you go after her?"

Jarrod's eyes slid over, full of barely-suppressed rage. "Why didn't you??"

"I wanted *you* to, you idiot."

"Why'd you send her to the farm?" he asked through his teeth. "Why would you pour salt on those wounds? Hasn't she been through enough?"

"Actually, she has, and its time you stop hurting her and start helping her. She's all alone now, Jarrod."

"Alone? Where's her husband?"

"He ain't here, is he? I think they divorced. She's alone out there… and she's changed. Can't you see it?"

"I see a lot of things," he replied, looking back at Abraham.

Becca glared at him, then moved to place her face in his line of vision.

"You're a fool, Jarrod. I'm tired of trying to get you to see that! We aren't in high school anymore. Whatever makes you think she's too weak to handle the truth is the lie you tell yourself. That's the lie you use to keep from admitting that you're just a damn coward!"

She thumped her palm against the casket and stormed out.

Jarrod closed his eyes. Two minutes ago, Aaren Robinson, his Aaren, had stood next to him, close enough to touch. And despite everything, he still wanted to touch her. Opening his eyes, he looked back into Abraham's serene face.

"So what is it, old man? Looks like we failed her and we did so miserably. She deserves the truth, you know. It's not my place to keep it from her any longer. I'm sorry for my family ruining yours. I'm sorry for all of it. Can't we just let it go? Can I try again, Abraham? Haven't I paid enough?"

His teary eyes scanned the flowers on either side of the casket.

"She's not happy. You and I agreed that her happiness was what was important. What was it all for if we've both lost her?"

He smiled down at the man that had become his friend, almost the father he wished he'd had. It was ironic that all roads ended here. No one knew Abraham Robinson like he did.

"Hey, Jay."

Jarrod turned. His younger brother and sister stood behind him. "What are you two doing here?"

"We came to pay our respects, Jay," reproved Macy. She missed her brother, who never came by or called, but lived only ten miles away.

"Well, I was leaving."

Travis stepped in his way. "Mom and dad are coming to the funeral."

"Why?"

"Abraham's dead. C'mon Jay, we've suffered enough as a family. Can't this be a new start for us?"

Jarrod smirked. "So that's why you came? Dad sent you?"

"No, Mama did. She misses you so much, Jarrod, and she hasn't been feeling well lately." Macy's eyes glistened with sadness. "She was in the hospital again the other week."

Jarrod rubbed his jaw. "Her sugar again?"

Travis nodded. "Dad wants to see you too."

"I get it. I'm sorry for not being there for you guys and I'm sorry that mom is sick but I won't be coming back over there until that man is either gone or dead!"

Jarrod turned to leave.

Macy covered her mouth. Tears sprang to her eyes and Travis grabbed his arm.

"You wait a minute. He's been a good father to you. He loves you, and he deserves your forgiveness—if not that, then at least your respect, damn it!"

Jarrod snatched away. "Funny, those are the same words mom said to me. You know who hasn't? Ask yourself why Judge Pennington won't travel south of the bridge to see his oldest son. You don't know everything, Travis. *Neither one of you does*!"

Home. The sun had set. Aaren was glad to see the day go. She moved through the rooms of her house, restless. She hadn't eaten, but that didn't really matter because her stomach was so twisted into dreadful knots she couldn't hold anything down anyway.

Venturing upstairs, she closed every other door before returning to her room. She tried to shut out the emptiness. She just wanted her bed and a long, dreamless sleep. Peace. Tomorrow she'd have to do it all over again. How do you say goodbye to the last of your family?

She tossed her purse to the bed, and then reached behind her neck to release the clasp at the back of her dress before pulling it down over her hips.

Tomorrow was the funeral and she would have to stand and sing for him. It was the only thing he wanted from her. This was the only thing she could do for him now. She needed to practice, be ready to sing her heart out. Reaching for her robe, she slipped it over her nakedness, then pulled her thick hair out of the collar. She sat on the bed with a thump and bit down on her thumbnail.

The image of Pop formed strong in her mind. She laid back, remembering, and curled into a ball atop the quilt. This robe had been a Christmas gift, one he'd chosen himself, and she remembered how he'd watched her as she opened it, to see if she really liked it. *There were moments*, she thought, *little moments where it was normal.* The memory made her tears flow anew.

Sighing, she wiped them away and closed her eyes, trying to get the image of her father from her head. Hearing a tapping noise at her window, she opened her eyes warily. It was after nine. Her head lifted from the pillow, eyes on the window. The tap came again. There was only one person who threw rocks at the glass. She jumped from the bed and stepped to the window. When she moved the curtain, she saw Jarrod standing below with his hands in his pockets. His eyes searched hers and she stared back at him, wondering why he'd come.

"What the hell are you doing here?" she mumbled. She undid the latch and pulled it up.

Jarrod stepped back to watch her lean out from above. He swallowed his nervousness and tried to muster courage that ebbed away when locked in her cool stare. There she was, in the dusty-pink robe from her youth. Her hair, loose and untamed, fell over one eye. Beautiful.

"You can't come to the door like a normal person?"

"I need you to know something," he yelled up at her.

She leaned further out the window to hear, and made sure to let her irritation show.

"What do you need me to know?"

"That I'm sorry, sorry for every tear you shed because… because I messed up. I need… I wanted to say that I lied back then when I said I didn't love you. I should never have let you think otherwise."

Aaren rolled her eyes upward and gave her head a slow shake, then looked back down at him. Jarrod's heart lurched when she gave a half-smile. Even the small gesture returned the light to her face. He smiled, nodding at her, that what he said was true.

"I'm sorry too, Jarrod. I'm sorry that it took you fourteen damn years to say that."

She backed out of the window and slammed it down shut.

Jarrod watched in stunned silence as the curtain fell over and the light in her room went out.

Abraham was right, thought Jarrod. *You can never go back.*

"Good night," he said softly before turning to leave.

Aaren remained at the edge of the window, watching. She had turned off the lights so he couldn't see her. She saw him mumble a few words, then turn away. Jarrod Pennington was the last person she wanted to hear from. Hopefully he'd stay away.

Chapter Four

THE FIRST TIME

FALL 1989

"So your dad's not coming back until Sunday?" asked Jarrod, inching closer to her on the bench seat of the bus. The game was over. They were on their way back to the high school, having beaten Madison County with a score of 24 to 22. It was Jarrod who'd run in the final touchdown, under the watchful eyes of recruiters from Notre Dame. Aaren wondered if his amorous mood was just the after-effects of his post-victory high.

She looked over into his eyes as his hand crept under her cheerleading skirt. He was getting bolder, and she was growing weaker. It was a dangerous combination for them both. Out of pure reflex, she slammed her knees shut. However, she made no move to dislodge his hand, threaded tightly between her thighs. Jarrod's touch was something any sane girl in the Point would want. She was no different.

Their relationship was still a secret. They'd been going out since the night of the spring dance. Aaren had spent the summer days sneaking off to meet him on the Jackson farm near their special creek. It was there the friendship had turned to kissing, and bit by bit, more. Now that school was back in session, she found herself fantasizing about a future with him during Biology or wondering, as he scored a touchdown, if their children would have his athletic prowess.

"C'mon baby, one feel." He spoke directly into her ear, so soft and low that her eyelids fluttered. His hand crept higher along the inside of her thigh. She drew in a nervous breath just thinking about where this would lead. *Tonight.* First base wasn't that big a deal, but this? If what he was doing now was second base, she had no idea what third base could be. And doing *it*? They'd never crossed the line. Aaren clenched her hands, not sure what to do with them. *Shove him away? Keep them still? Touch him?*

Penns Point was a small town, and though all the kids were brought up understanding their differences, it mattered little during their youth. Fooling around was one thing: even the adults in town understood. What was there to do in the Point but drink, smoke, and screw? But going out openly with a white or black from across Rachette was something totally different. They had to be careful.

If her Pop discovered she was secretly keeping time with a boy, he'd kill them both. And according to Jarrod, his father would do even worse, them being Penningtons and all. Aaren always found the Judge pleasant enough. She didn't understand why Jarrod thought so little of him.

"That's enough, Jay. Move your hand." She heaved a passionate sigh, her eyes darting around the seats to see if anyone was paying attention. Antonio and Becca sat across from them with their tongues down each other's throats. She envied their freedom to be openly in love.

"Why? You're my girl, right? I want to touch you."

She forcefully removed his hand. Sitting up, she readjusted her skirt, embarrassed she'd let it get this far. Sure, she loved him, but she wasn't the kind of girl to get fingered in the back of a smelly school bus. Not even for Jarrod Pennington. The heat of his stare warmed the side of her face. He constantly needed her reassurance that she was his. Her eyes roved over him and she gave him a smile that promised more.

"You touch me all the time," she said softly. "I thought you wanted more?"

Jarrod's left brow winged upward. Aaren relaxed. She'd let him nibble on that bait until they were somewhere more private and she would have to deliver.

"Yah, well… yeah."

"Okay. Then behave."

He did, in his own way. She watched from the corner of her eyes as his gaze travelled over her cheerleading dress. The boy was a walking, talking, sexual lightning rod. Lately, it ruled his every action.

"I love the way you look in this." He touched the blue-and-yellow trim of her skirt. "Always have." His voice grew thick again with desire.

The top, sleeveless, was form-fitting, revealing her thin waistline and lifting her perfectly rounded bosom. Centered on the front were the letters PH for Pennington High. She smiled to wear those letters: it was just another way she was his.

"You do? Why is that?" she asked, wanting to be seduced.

"The way it looks on your skin. I dunno, when I see you do those leaps in that little skirt and your—"

"I got it." She smiled and moved his hand from her knee with a nervous chuckle. "You're into cheerleaders."

"Nope, just into you."

Aaren blushed. He was so sweet. She let him run his hand over her lap. The pleats fanned out across her upper thigh, showing off her long legs. His hand once again brushed her thigh. Giving him a taste of his own medicine, she boldly touched him, only to find him covered by his cup. Still, her hand there made his eyes lower, then spring open when she began to rub.

"Are you going to stop?" she smirked.

He moistened his lips and shook his head, wanting her to continue. Aaren sighed and pulled her hand back. He leaned in to sniff the inside of her neck. "How do you manage to smell so good? You've been doing flips and jumps all night!"

"I dunno...."

He brought his mouth to the curve of her ear. "So, you didn't answer my question. Are you sure he won't be back early? Is he really gone?"

Aaren cast her eyes downward. "Who leaves the Races early?"

"True," he said, smiling. "My dad's there too. Mom won't even miss me tonight. She thinks I'm staying with Tonio. So um... tonight, right, tonight is it?"

"Is that all you think about, Jay?"

"Huh? No."

She swallowed the smile and gave him a serious look. Didn't work. He knew it was all she thought about lately, too. She'd written him two poems and put them in his locker just this week. He wrote her one, and it was pitiful, but at least he tried.

She nudged his side. "I asked Pop if Becca could spend the night and he said yes. We are good, so yes." Aaren lowered her voice shyly. "Tonight is the night."

"We don't have to do it. I don't want to pressure you."

"Yeah, right!" Her laughter released them both from the mounting tension. Jarrod tickled her side then sneaked a kiss to her cheek. The moment was interrupted when Vincent jumped up, yelling at Matt that Vanilla Ice couldn't out-rap or out-dance MC Hammer. Others were jeering or cheering on the confrontation, oblivious to the seduction both of the girls were undergoing at the back of the bus.

"I think we should skip hanging with everyone and just go to my house. What do you think?"

"You're so sexy." He wedged his hand back between her thighs.

"Jay! What do you think?"

"Huh? Oh yah. Sounds like a plan."

Leaning over, Jarrod inhaled deeply. Even her sweat smelled sweet. She was making him crazy, being this close. He ran his hand further between her legs, teasing her.

"Jay, I'm not kidding! You need to cool it. Just wait!" She knocked his hand away for the final time.

Jarrod sulked against the back of the bench seat. Her hot-and-cold was getting old. All he had was the touch-and-feels. What if she changed her mind again? It's not like she hadn't in the past. He told himself to chill, though the pain in his groin told him he better seal the deal. If he didn't, she'd make him suffer through the agonies of wanting her through another long night. He chose to cool it. Besides, he wasn't exactly on top of his game. He could barely stand himself. He reeked of sweat and grass. It wasn't exactly a turn-on.

When those Bambi eyes of hers cut over to him again, he gave her his most pathetic pout. She responded with another eye roll.

"I'll cool it."

"You're a sweet boyfriend Jay. I love you, okay?"

"But?"

"You want to rush things. Your hormones got me wrestling with you all the time. Sometimes it's just easier to let you get a quick feel."

"My hormones?" he snapped. Several kids looked back and Aaren blushed. He checked himself once more. "So it's my hormones now? Is *that* hormones?" He nodded toward the hot-and-heavy session going on across the aisle.

She looked straight ahead, tight-lipped. It was clear that he was pushing her too hard, so maybe she had a point. How did he explain it, though? It wasn't hormones. It was her. She looked over and smiled. Softened. Confused by the signal she was giving, he hesitated, remaining locked in her gaze. She leaned back into the corner of the seat, up against the window, while the bus jostled them around as they drove over Old Rachette Bridge.

"Look at you, girl. How could I not want you?" He moved in on her, capturing the soft pad of her earlobe. The feel of that soft spot caused his breathing to grow labored. A shiver went through his body when he touched her again. "Don't you know I love you? Mmm… if you let me, I'll show you," he whispered.

He tongued her earring as her legs parted a little more for him. He'd pushed her so low on the seat her submission went unnoticed by those yelling and laughing around them. He lifted the center overlay of her panties and rubbed her before dipping his finger in.

"Okay, that's enough. We're almost there." She pushed back so abruptly he felt it like a punch to his gut. But he didn't object. Now he knew she was ready. And so was he. It was going to happen, *tonight*.

The bus turned into the parking lot and the triumphant school call broke out in a loud chorus among the players and cheerleaders. Jarrod leaned out into the aisle to his best friend.

"Hey, change in plans, man. We're going straight to Aaren's."

He knocked Antonio in the shoulder to get him to come up for air. Becca giggled, fixing her top behind the protective cover of her boyfriend.

"Cool, that works for me," said Antonio, squeezing Becca's thigh. "How about you, babe? You cool?"

Becca peeled her gum off the back of her hand, popped it in her mouth, then winked. She leaned forward to look over at Aaren. Her friend nodded that it was her idea. To this Becca shrugged. Jarrod figured she would agree. Antonio told him just the other day that she'd given in to him after the fireworks on Labor Day. Aaren didn't know. Jarrod understood, though. He could imagine them sitting on Aaren's porch, making a pact to save themselves for the right moment, the right night, the right time. Antonio was less patient than him. And Becca hadn't told Aaren, probably because she didn't want to disappoint her best friend any more than she'd wanted to disappoint her boyfriend.

"Okay, let's go."

Jarrod watched as Aaren slid out of the seat. He dropped his varsity jacket over her shoulders, and though her eyes smiled up at him, she acted like it was no big deal to the rest of them. Her ponytail, decorated with yellow and blue ribbons, swayed across her shoulders, but Jarrod's eyes remained trained on her backside and the slight flip of her pleated skirt. Her perfectly rounded ass flashed at him several times as he navigated the narrow aisle of the bus.

Tonight was going to be a big night for them and he was very nervous. Finally, he'd make her his.

For Jarrod, Aaren Robinson was the hottest girl in Penns Point. Many of the guys on his team had made moves on her, but she always shied away. They knew her dad was extremely strict, so no one, black, white or Hispanic, dared pursue her. His crush went all the way back to the second grade, when the kids had picked on him for his new clothes and rich family.

He'd fought the boys around him to get their respect, and Aaren, a tree-climbing tomboy, joined the fray. He'd never seen a girl fight back the way she did. Even then, her strength and courage impressed him. After that, whenever he could, he'd sneak away and return to the south side to play. But gone were the days of scraped knees and snowball fights. Now, she was all girl and she loved him. That meant anything—everything—was possible.

Coming off the bus, Jarrod saw Aaren with a couple of the girls on her squad, laughing and talking. She looked up at him to smile and he winked.

"Aaren, let me get a picture of you!" Carrie called out to her from the crowd of cheerleaders.

"What's that about?" asked Aaren, under her breath.

Becca popped her gum, eyeing their nemesis and captain. "She been taking instant pictures all night. She took mine and Tonio's. Sumthin' up with that."

"Watch this," smirked Aaren. She turned, flouncing over to Jarrod. His eyes dropped to her shapely legs and hips at her approach, then flipped up to meet hers with a mischievous smile. "I want a picture." She took his hand and led him over past the staring girls, noting the way Carrie's eyes narrowed. Aaren pulled him close and Jarrod's arms went around her. She just wanted to be sure that Carrie got it. Jarrod had no problem helping her send the message.

"Go ahead."

With no other choice, Carrie snapped the picture.

"Let's go," he said, giving Aaren a squeeze and walking away. Aaren grabbed the picture and winked at Carrie, then waved goodbye to her friends. Becca looked back to see the scowl and flushed anger on Carrie's face. She caught up with Aaren and kept in step.

"Now why you go and do that? You know that bitch will ride us at practice!"

"Yeah, but she won't be riding Jarrod, that's for sure."

Becca laughed. "Girl, you a mess."

Carrie had been Jarrod's girlfriend last year, briefly. She could tell that something was up with the two of them. Everyone fooled around but Aaren. And now, she was paired off with Jarrod more and more. She turned back to the rest of the squad, pretending it didn't matter how Jarrod opened the car door for Aaren. But both she and Aaren knew it did.

"Man, you got the sweetest car in Penns," Antonio said, getting in. It was true. He'd gotten it just three weeks ago and everyone was still talking. It was a restored bumblebee-yellow Camaro with a T-top roof and black racing stripe. What made him the envy of every boy on the team was the souped-up engine his father had installed.

Aaren thought it was great, on the one hand, to have a boyfriend with wheels, let alone wheels as cool as these. But on the other hand, if you saw the Camaro, there was only one person who could be behind the wheel. Late night rides with Jarrod were few and far between. She had to sneak out her bedroom window and meet him out past the abandoned grist mill to keep the busybody neighbors from telling her Pops.

Becca and Antonio piled in to the back seat while Aaren scooted closer to Jarrod. He started it up. The car's engine raced, then turned over with a powerful purr. He'd only had his license for about a year, but he'd been driving tractors and farm equipment since he was 12. They all had. She sat next to him and listened to her friend's giggles in the back seat as she and her boyfriend kept at it.

"Do they ever stop?" she asked, rolling her eyes.

Jarrod looked over at her, grinning. "Do we?"

She leaned up and kissed his cheek while he drove. "Guess you got a point."

Passing the Jackson farm on their way to the house, Aaren's attention turned to the condensation on the passenger window and the shadowy land beyond. She searched the forested terrain that surrounded their special creek, her eyes familiar with every tree, every blade of grass.

"I really can't wait until we can move out on our own, Jarrod." Her voice came in a wistful murmur.

"To build our house by the creek?" Jarrod knew what her heart desired. She didn't have to remind him. How many times had she stolen away to their creek and shared those dreams with him?

Aaren closed her eyes and smiled. Pops told her she could have anything, be anyone she chose: a doctor, lawyer, scientist. If only he knew. Her heart's desire was a simple one. She wanted only to be Mrs. Jarrod Mitchell Pennington.

"You think I'm being silly, huh? Clancy Jackson would never let go of his land."

THE FIRST TIME

"Why does it have to be the Jackson property?"

"Jay-bird, I fell in love with you at that creek. The day we stripped to our undies and went for a swim. Remember?"

Jarrod flashed her a sly smile. "Oh yah, I remember."

She laughed. "It was in that creek swimming with you that I realized the truth. I'm talking about destiny, Jay. Yours and mine. You're my destiny. I want our babies to grow up there. I want us to have our own horses, maybe cows. Oh, look. We could plant corn and hay over there!"

Jarrod groaned. "I can't believe you want to stay in Penns effing Point," he said, rolling his eyes. "Everybody's going to college or the Army. But Aaren Robinson, the smartest senior in the county, wants to stay, and have me out there sweating, planting corn. I'm no farmer, babe."

She flinched and looked away to hide the hurt. "That's not what I mean. Of course I want to go to school. I just thought... I love Penns Point. Call me crazy, or whatever, but I'd never leave here. It's my home. It's your home too, Jay. Shoot, your family *is* this town."

She looked back over and saw his lips press together in a thin line. He was so sensitive about his lineage, wanting to just fit in. She was proud of who he was. She wished he'd feel the same.

"Anyways, no place on this earth could be as beautiful as Penns," she said, resting her head on his shoulder as he drove.

They turned into the lane that led up to her house. It was completely dark except for the light on the porch. Aaren lifted her head and looked over Jarrod's arm to the back seat. Becca was still, of course, tangled up in Antonio's arms.

"If you guys can come up for air, we're here."

Becca pushed Antonio off her. "Stop," she said, trying to fix her cheerleading skirt. Aaren lifted a brow to her friend's appearance. Several loose strands hung out of her ponytail and her lipstick was smeared all over her face. Aaren turned back around and shook her head. *Becca still a virgin? Yeah, right.*

Aaren got out, fishing her key from her bag as she hurried up the front steps. The others followed. She opened the place for them, turning on lights as she went. Becca was the only one that had been inside before. Antonio and Jarrod weren't as eager. Both knew they were stepping into forbidden territory.

Jarrod grabbed hold of his friend's arm, stopping him from going forward. His eyes followed the girls, making sure they were out of earshot.

"Dude! What's up?" frowned Antonio.

"The rubbers, you got them?"

Antonio reached in his pocket and gave him three.

Jarrod palmed the silver wrappers, trying to be discreet. "Okay, so I should just… you know, put it on when I know we're going to do it? Timing, right?"

Antonio cut his eyes to his boy's nervousness. "Chill, dude. It's real simple. Wait until you two are both naked and you want to stick it in, and then just roll the rubber on your dick. What don't you get? Be smooth about it so you won't stop the mood. You do, man, and you give her a chance to chicken out."

Jarrod had asked him over and over about this detail. He could tell Antonio was tired of him. Still, he had to be sure. Aaren was a brain, so giving her time to analyze this would be a bad move. Jarrod released a slow, deep breath. He wanted Aaren to be comfortable with him. He walked inside behind Antonio, keeping the hand with the rubbers behind him and trying to remain cool. Cool was easier said than done, though. His stomach was twisted like a pretzel. Aaren and Becca were in the living room to the right, giggling. They both looked up with cute smiles on their faces when their guys appeared. One look into Aaren's brown eyes and he relaxed.

"Okay guys, time for the tour," said Aaren, rising. "Over here is the bonus room. You two can use the Chesterfield, but there's no TV in there. As if you need it!"

"Shut up, girl!" Becca hit her arm and Aaren laughed, but cut Jarrod a sly look.

"Blankets are in the hall closet and you can help yourself to anything in the fridge. Oh, the shower is upstairs, plus you have a half-bathroom down here. Becca-girl, you know the drill."

Jarrod leaned against the door panel, watching her. Antonio patted him on the back before going over to scoop up Becca, throwing her over his shoulder. Aaren watched her friend squeal in delight as he carried her into the bonus room.

"Looks like they're all set." Aaren shrugged. She stared at Jarrod as the laughter and giggles faded into the other room. Neither of them spoke. This was it. They were really going through with it. Walking over, still wearing his jacket, she put on a brave smile.

"I have to call my dad at the motel and tell him I'm in for the night. You can go shower. I'll meet you in my room."

Jarrod's eyes went to the ceiling. Then he grinned at her. He already knew where her room was, at least from the outside.

"Right across from the bathroom," said Aaren.

"Come here," he said, pulling her close and kissing her.

She gave into the kiss, feeling his hand slide down her back, lifting her cheerleading skirt to squeeze her gently, while pressing his cup into her.

"Hurry," he said. "This is our first all-nighter. I don't want to waste a minute."

He kissed her awkwardly on the cheek then let her go. Trying again to be smooth, he pulled her back once more and kissed her on the mouth, then turned and headed for the stairs.

Aaren watched his cute backside in his football knickers as he climbed. She rushed to the kitchen, the excitement of the night adding to her nerves. She flew to the refrigerator to get the number for her dad's hotel, then snatched up the pea-green receiver and dialed the number.

"Thank you for calling the Holiday Inn," a woman answered.

"Yes, ma'am. Can I have room 312 please?"

"One moment."

The phone rang twice before her father picked up.

"Hello?"

His deep, authoritative voice replaced her sense of adventure with fear.

"Pop?"

"Aaren, you home?"

"Yes, sir."

"Good. I want those horses fed first thing in the morning."

"Pop, we won our game!"

"Oh. Good," he mumbled.

"Were you sleeping?"

"No, but you girls should go to bed. Don't stay up too late and you know not to have anyone over."

"Yes, Pop. When will you be coming back?"

"Sunday afternoon, but I want you in church Sunday morning. Mrs. Landry will come and pick you up for Sunday School."

"Yes, sir," she said, rolling her eyes.

"Goodnight, Aaren," he mumbled. "And—um, that's good about the game."

"G'night, Pop." She waited until she heard the click on his end, then hung up. At least he'd acknowledged her excitement. She placed the phone on its receiver, staring blankly. He was always making sure she adhered to the rules of their lives as he saw them. All his rules were for her own good, she was sure. Still, she wished she could talk to him about things. Things were changing so fast for her. She wished she could talk to him, period.

Turning, she shook off the mood. It was Friday night, which meant they had all day Saturday, *and* Saturday night, to hang out before Mrs. Landry's nosey butt showed up. Racing out of the kitchen, she grabbed her purse, then climbed the stairs two at a time. That's when she saw him.

THE FIRST TIME

He strolled out of the bathroom with a towel wrapped around his waist. Running the ball instead of throwing it had paid off. His body was tight with muscular definition that made her catch her breath. His shoulders and chest were hard as bricks, glistening with the remnants of his shower. His skin, fired by the summer sun to a deep tan, was still golden.

Aaren couldn't move at the sight of him. She'd seen him at the creek, tried hard not to look, but tonight was different. Tonight those angles whispered a promise of desires she was just beginning to realize. What hid under that towel had her throat closing and her pulse racing. It was as if all the blood siphoned from her heart and rushed to her face. Aaren blinked under the weight of the moment. Then he stopped. Right before her door. Those eyes, blue as the ocean neither of them had ever seen, slipped over to her. Her smile wavered and she cleared her throat.

"That was fast."

"I'm just going to get dirty again," he smirked.

Aaren walked toward him, feeling like she was floating on her legs. Before she realized it, she was standing close enough for him to reach. When he touched her, her skin sizzled at the contact. His hand ran cool down the length of her arm.

"You should have joined me."

She stepped past him and headed into her bedroom. When the door closed behind her, she cast him a look. He met her gaze with a challenging one of his own. There was no backing out now. Aaren fished through her purse for the picture Carrie had taken.

"Look," she said, holding it out to him like a stop sign. She needed to buy some time. He accepted it, so it worked. Aaren pointed at her smiling face. "I'm surprised she went ahead and took it. Everybody knows she has a thing for you."

"Carrie? Please. That was over last year."

"Mmhmmm."

She caught his frown as he eyed the picture.

"You look cute. I look stupid." He passed it back to her.

"No, you don't." She kissed his jaw, then retreated. Eyeing her music box, she opened it, and lifted the pink cushion under the lid to tuck it inside. She would keep it well-hidden to look at when she was away from him.

Jarrod pulled her back, running his hands over her hips. She liked the feel of them on her skin and pushed back into him. He was tight all over. It sent a nervous flutter through her stomach.

"Let me go shower."

"No, enough stalling Aaren. Come here."

"Jay…"

"Come here."

He reached around her to unzip her shirt. She smiled into his face as he helped her pull her top up over her head. As soon as her white sports bra came into view his eyes grew heavy with desire. She reached up and alleviated the pressure that the tightly wound ribbons gave as they held her ponytail in place. Her hair came down, stiff, still in one long, dark curve behind her shoulder.

He leaned in and kissed her. It was such a different kiss. Less hurried. Aaren closed her eyes, tilting her head in reception. Her hands, shaky from nerves, lifted slowly and landed gently on his shoulders. She didn't understand why her body was trembling, why her heart was surging. She loved him so: she thought that should make this easier. Her hands went up the curve of his shoulders over his neck, into the hair he'd slicked back from the shower. For his part, he fiddled clumsily with the tab of her zipper. Aaren smiled to herself as he became more desperate to ease it down. Reaching behind, she went directly to it, moving it down so that the skirt could drop off her hips and fall past her knees to the floor.

Jarrod slid his hands into her uniform's bloomer panties, feeling her cotton ones underneath. He stopped the kiss and looked down at her shapely curves. He then whispered against her neck.

"Get naked for me."

He stepped back, his feet a little awkward as he went to her bed. He found it hard not to stare at her. When he cut his eyes away, he frowned. She had the bed covered with a million stuffed animals. He pushed them to the floor, ridding her of one of the last vestiges of her childhood innocence.

"Hey! Don't do that!" she snapped angrily, going over to the side of the bed to get them.

"Sorry, babe, but why do you have those stupid things?" he asked. "Macy's six and she collects them out of her Happy Meals."

She looked up angrily. "I like them!" she huffed, taking them to her chest under the window sill.

Jarrod laughed, dropping back on his elbow to watch her. She flashed him an unforgiving glare for the smug smirk on his face. He checked himself quick. But not quick enough, considering the tone she used with him.

"It's no different than your baseball cards, Jay, which are just as stupid to me!"

"Babe, I'm sorry. Come back here," he said quickly. He didn't want to piss her off. Not tonight of all nights.

When she softened, his anxiety eased. He actually blew out a breath of relief. She did as he asked. Climbing on the bed, she crawled over to him on hands and knees. He kissed her nose and pulled her closer.

"Well, now since I know you like them so much, I'm going to McDonald's tomorrow to get you ten more!" he announced.

"You're too good to me, Jarrod Pennington."

He kissed her, running his hand against her taut tummy. Breaking the kiss, he looked back down at her. Really looked at her. She was perfect. Her full lips, breasts, hips, all of which had him crazy with need. And when he looked into her eyes he was lost. How was he going to get through the night without losing his cool? Aaren Robinson was every boy's dream.

"I really want this to be special. Maybe I should put on some music," she said, trying to rise, popping the bubble of naughty thoughts.

He actually blushed, considering. She was a good girl, his girl, and this was her first time. His too for that matter. He needed to slow down and make it special. She shouldn't be the one searching for ways to do that for them.

"No, no, don't get up, it's cool. Here, let me help you get out of this."

He lifted himself up on his elbow and pulled at her sports bra. Raising it over her head, he looked down at the breasts that bounced out to greet him. They were round, with dark, ripe nipples he'd only sucked once. Jarrod moistened his lips; his throat went dry. Reaching to her hips, he pulled off her bloomers, then panties, revealing her fully.

Aaren hadn't been shy when they'd been together at the creek. He'd had several peeks at her before, in the back seat of his car, but now, with the way he stared at her, she was more nervous than she'd ever been. That was unexpected, but in a way, good. It made his mistakes less awkward.

Jarrod told himself to relax, willing himself to control his urges. She was ready to be his: she'd told him so. He just had to take his time.

"Gosh, you're beautiful," he said under his breath, taking her in with all the passion his eyes could get. He'd asked Antonio what to do first and had gotten his instructions. Looking back up at Aaren, he saw she was covering her breasts with her arms. He smiled at her shyness. Usually, she was bolder than he was.

Rising from the bed, he went to the door and locked it, then turned off the wall light.

THE FIRST TIME

Aaren watched him, curious. She saw him bend, then retrieve something silver and square from underneath his clothes. It had to be the rubber. She was so glad he had it. She didn't want to ruin the mood and ask for it, but she wasn't going to go forward without it. He came back to the bed and dropped his towel.

And then she saw it, erect, saluting her. She looked away to keep from laughing at the way it curved. Jarrod touched himself as if he would explode.

"You ready, babe?"

She nodded, holding back nervous giggles. She was no idiot. Laughing now would certainly kill the mood.

Jarrod's knee dropped on the mattress. She moved back as the springs creaked with the addition of his weight. He slid in over her. Stopping, hovering, he stuck his hand under the pillow. Antonio said never let them see the rubber or they'd get scared and back out. It was all about timing. That, and making the girl think she was in control. He just had to be smooth about it. It was a hard task, considering what opportunity awaited him. He'd caught many a hand cramp at night dreaming about this moment.

He inhaled her, allowing the strange, erotic mix of womanly smells to thread their way up his nose. He pressed a kiss into her neck and ran his hands all over her. She was so soft. Her skin was the softest thing he'd ever touched, warm and smooth. He could find not a single flaw. Jarrod felt the muscles in his hips tighten as the pulse in his groin beat like a mad drummer; he ached in ways he hadn't before.

She must have sensed his battle because she kept her thighs tightly shut. Jarrod smiled.

"You okay?"

"Mmhmm," she whispered, nodding.

He rubbed her hip. Aaren released the pressure between her legs, letting them part slightly. He moved over her, covering her. The feel of her thighs pressed against him had his heart hammering in his ears. He dropped lower to suck at her taut nipples. This part, they'd practiced before. This part he could handle.

Aaren squeezed her eyes shut. He was always rough with her nipples, stroking and pinching too hard under her clothes. She held back from telling him so. Instead, she rubbed the tension out of his back. His mouth covered one nipple, and she sighed at the roll of his tongue. Then he clamped down, sucking hard. She winced and felt his eyes look to hers. She tried to give him an encouraging smile, tried to relax and enjoy it. Soon his love bites were reduced to soft licks, as if she'd communicated the need for ease telepathically. A warm flood of desire pooled in her center as her nipple became a sensor rod. With each flick of his tongue a current shot through her pelvis putting a slow move to her hips. It felt so good. Sensations took over causing her to gasp for air. There was a swooping pull at her innards as the passion he drove through her coiled into a tight ball in her core. Something was happening to her under his touch, and she liked it.

Jarrod's hand moved further down her body to rub the thick folds of her sex. He did not hesitate, because he'd always wanted to touch her there. Pushing the swollen lips apart, his finger went along the inside of the silky ridge. A collective gasp escaped them both. His touch was sparking off such heat and need that neither wanted to stop. Liking the response, he pulled her tongue into his mouth to suck and taste her. She squeezed her thighs in reaction to his tunneling finger, fusing her lips and tongue with his. The way he devoured her made it easy to let her body and mind go.

Jarrod eased his finger out of her and came up for air. His groin ached so desperately he felt it near impossible to keep from a release. And he'd be damned if he'd ruin it before they even started. Reaching under the pillow, he kept his eyes locked with hers, until they closed and a sweet smile rested on her lips. Antonio said that she would be too caught up to know what was about to come next. Quickly, he tore at the wrapper. Sitting back on his bended legs, he pulled out the yellow-colored rubber. It was slippery wet in his nervous hands.

"Shit," he mumbled to himself, wishing he had just practiced putting it on like the other guys did. But he'd thought practicing for this deducted cool points, so he hadn't.

Aaren opened her eyes to hear him curse and saw him fumbling and dropping the condom.

"Everything okay?"

He looked at her, mad at being caught.

"It's cool, I got it," he said, turning red in the face.

He pulled at the reservoir in the middle. It unraveled some. He bit back a smile, finally understanding why he was told to roll it downward. Going to the head of his penis, he put the tight band around the tip of it and the rubber popped off, bouncing across the bed.

"Shit!" he said frustrated.

Aaren giggled, reaching for it. "Let me try," she offered, sitting up. He looked at her, shocked.

"You don't know what you're doing," he snapped.

"Neither do you," she shot back. They'd seen a movie in health class and she knew the intent. It just wasn't that difficult.

Her comment stung, but he had to smile that she was right. She reached and touched his penis lightly and he shivered. It was the first time she'd touched it outside of his pants. He'd tried to stick her hand in several times and she would freak.

Slowly slipping the condom over his erection, she gripped the rolled edge and pulled. The rubber snapped and broke. She looked up at him, confused.

"Sorry."

"It's okay. I've got another one," he said, leaning over and getting the other two. He handed them to her. She inspected the silver wrappers.

"You sure are prepared," she giggled. "Wonder why they always package them in this foil like candy?"

"Bet it don't taste like candy!" He gave her a slick smirk.

"Why don't you try it and tell me?" she laughed.

"Very funny."

"Open it and I'll put it on." She passed it back to him.

Jarrod took the condom. He bit at the edge, freeing the new one from its wrapper and gave it to her.

She looked down at the part of him that remained erect, with veins bulging through the skin. She couldn't believe how long and thick it was. And more than that, she couldn't wrap her mind around the idea of it being inside her. Jarrod laid back. She rose and put the rim of the condom on the head of his penis again. Instead of pulling it down she rolled it slowly and smiled as it slipped over his length with ease. He sat up to look at how she did it. His erection jerked in her hand and he tightened his muscles against the urge to explode just from her touch. This was greater torture than the bump and grind sessions in the back of the car.

"How did you know?" he breathed out hard, trying to refocus his mind and therefore, his need.

"It just made sense," she said. "Is it too tight?"

He shook his head, though his face was beet red with restraint. "No, just feels weird." He spoke through his teeth.

She gave him a puzzled look. He reached up and kissed her, silencing the question he knew she'd ask next. She came back down and laid next to him. Drawing away, he smiled. Crisis averted.

"You know they aren't a hundred percent safe, so if it comes loose or you think it's ripped then—"

"Enough talking," he said, rolling on top of her.

She bit her lip as he parted her legs.

"Wait!" she said, pushing him back.

He looked at her, confused. "What now?"

"When you... you know. I might bleed."

Jarrod looked at her shocked and a little disgusted. "What are you talking about?!"

"I read it, and—"

"Do you want to do this or not, Aaren?" he asked, not able to hide his irritation.

"No, Jay, I want to. I'm just saying we can't do it on this comforter." She pulled the covers back.

Jarrod rolled his eyes. He saw what Antonio meant. If he had got the damn rubber on he would be sticking it in her by now. Now he had to get her in the mood all over again.

Aaren climbed into bed and he joined her, easing on top of her body. He kissed her and rubbed her breasts. She closed her eyes, trying to relax. Jarrod pushed her legs further apart then aimed his erection at her opening, fumbling, searching. Finding what he sought, he thrust into her and a searing pain ripped through her. She grunted, putting her hand up to his chest.

"It hurts," she said, stopping him.

He looked down at her and pulled back out.

"I'll go slow. Okay? I just need you so much."

She nodded.

"Just let me get it in, okay? It won't hurt long. I promise."

He pushed in, his hips stiff with tension and his jaw rigid. She was so tight. That was the best part.

For Aaren it was different. She didn't like the feeling at all. She knew it would hurt at first, but this? Why would anyone do this a second time?

Jarrod saw the cord in her neck strain as her body locked up underneath him. He wondered if he should kiss her or something to make her relax.

"Do you want to stop?"

She looked over at him, her eyes glistening with tears.

"No, I can do this," she said with a weak smile, feeling him inside of her.

It was different than she'd imagined, but then how could she have known what to expect? She just wanted it over. He kissed her again, sliding his tongue in her mouth as he broke through her tightness. He almost exploded, feeling the warmth of her inner walls through the condom. It was so different than anything his hand had applied. Aaren's discomfort increased and she almost verbalized it. But opening her eyes, she saw the pleasure in his and allowed him to continue. She felt envious that he was enjoying it and she wasn't.

He pushed further into her. It did feel a little better: she relaxed some as her body adjusted to his width. She put her arms around his neck and looked up at him. His thrusts became increasingly bearable. She had barely begun counting his strokes before he groaned loudly.

"Oh… shit!"

Jarrod's body convulsed. He buried his face in her neck.

She frowned to hear him grunting in her ear. Aaren blinked, confused, her eyes trained on the ceiling fan. It wasn't like that in the movies. He laid on top of her, simultaneously embarrassed that he had no control, but obviously wanting to do it again.

"Take it out," she whispered, tense under the weight of him.

He lifted up.

"Sorry, baby," he said, pulling out of her. "Does it still hurt?"

Tears of disappointment in her eyes, she nodded then pushed the blanket back. There in plain view were small specks of blood on his rubber and her sheets. Jarrod looked down and frowned.

"Let's shower and change the sheets," she said masking her disappointment. She knew her voice was too loud, forced, but it was their first time and it went off like a science project. No fireworks, no loud proclamations of undying love, just a few grunts and it was done.

THE FIRST TIME

"Aaren, you okay?"

"Mmhmm, yeah. I'm fine," she said, keeping her head down.

Boys never understood, and she wasn't surprised that Jarrod didn't either. He helped her pull off the sheets, and waited patiently while she put the new ones on, then followed her to the shower. Once under the spray he tried to play and joke with her but she just couldn't hide it anymore.

"Hey, what is it?"

She turned off the shower, turning to escape him, but he took her by the waist and drew her back. "Aaren, what is wrong?"

"Nothing. Everything. It wasn't like I thought Jay. I mean, it just wasn't."

"Okay, then what did you think it would be?"

"Huh?"

"What wasn't it like?"

"It was supposed to be about love. *Our love.* Somehow it just felt—" She couldn't bring herself to say the word *mechanical*, so she just heaved a burdened sigh. "It was like something we did, not felt. Does that make sense?"

He frowned. "Yes, it makes sense."

Reaching for her robe, he covered her, then walked her back to her bedroom. "I'm sorry babe. It's my fault. I wanted you so much, I couldn't think straight."

"It's okay. Everyone says your first time is no big deal. Guess they were right," she said, getting back in bed.

He slid in beside her, the comment stinging. Truth be told, it was great to him. He was now even more concerned that she didn't feel the same way. He looked over and she gave him the smile that had made him fall in love with her in the second grade.

"It's not okay," he said, arm around her waist. He nuzzled his nose into her neck and spoke just below her ear, against her beating pulse. "Everything about us is special. Tonight is special to me."

Jarrod lifted his head to take her in, first with his eyes and then with his heart. Seeing her again, wanting her to look at him the way she had before, it became clear. She was as close to perfect as he would get. Even in his limited experience with girls, he knew Aaren was the one. His eyes searched her face, then went lower. There was a mole at the center of her neck, in the hollow made by her collarbone. He leaned in and pressed a kiss there. It was a tiny imperfection he'd missed so many times before when they'd been close. He made a silent vow to know all of her, learn everything about her. Jarrod kissed the spot again, softly this time, barely brushing his lips across her skin.

"Jay…."

He looked up to see confusion in her eyes. *Just kiss on her till she's relaxed, then stick it in*, he heard Antonio's voice. Jarrod had strategized for his first time with Aaren like there had been a playbook to follow. Now, it came to him that Antonio had no clue how to love his Aaren. Only he could do that.

"Let me show you…"

"Show me *what*?"

"How much I *do* love you"

He touched the top of the sheet and pulled it slowly down, uncovering her. Firm nipples pointed north on perfectly-shaped breasts. They sat up, full and pert. He brushed his lips over them, inhaling the clean soapiness of her skin. His eyes went up. Her eyelids lowered in response to that simple brush. He rested the side of his face in his hand, elbow propped on her pillow. With his index finger he circled her areola. He looked to her face and watched her closely. That's when he caught it. A slight flutter of her thick lashes, and the eye roll beneath her lids. He twisted the dark nub then gave it a light pinch. It stood up in greeting. Her lips parted a fraction; a soft breath of pleasure escaped her. That's what he wanted. Lowering his head, he used his tongue to graze her nipple then coaxed it into his mouth. It was delicate yet firm. The contrast sent a ripple of pleasure through his veins.

"Aaah…" was all he heard.

That was what he wanted. Smiling, he lifted and sampled the other nipple, then returned to lick and suck the first tender morsel. Underneath him, he felt her rubbing her thighs together. Her attempt to extinguish the small flame of desire encouraged him to go further. She was enjoying it, and then it struck him. Remarkably, her pleasure had become his. Jarrod understood her, in a way he hadn't before.

"You are so beautiful," he said with wonder, pulling the sheet all the way down. He was so aroused he could feel his erection pulsing and strengthening, but he spoke with restraint. He didn't want his own arousal to eclipse hers. "I mean it, there will never be another girl as beautiful to me as you are."

Aaren closed her eyes as he touched her face. The same hand made a slow descent over her curves. Aaren, without being asked, parted her thighs. When his hand returned to her throbbing center she was surprised at the slow, sweet burn of his touch. Her eyes opened and met his. She licked her lips to the tasty way his fingers gently played against her folds, teasing her clitoris to the point she moved her hips. He wasn't just inserting a finger to do it, scratching her and being rough. She again parted her lips for a desperate intake of air, and was rewarded with his tongue. It slipped across the bow of her mouth and then inside eagerly.

Jarrod felt an arousal he'd never gotten from a simple touch. What had started as an experiment to make her happy had become something more. Somehow she felt different, tasted different under his kisses. It was like she was there with him. Not like before.

She blushed, now thrusting her hips upward in response. "So gooood…" she managed.

"I love you, Aaren."

For the first time, these weren't just words. Aaren felt them in a way that would stay with her always. His body moved up and down hers, stroking her while brushing his lips against her skin and whispering of the sweet, sinful things he wanted to do to her. The feel of him against her bare skin heated her senses. When he brought his face back up and looked into her eyes, she welcomed him to her. Jarrod slid between her legs; this time it just happened. He entered her slow, unsheathed.

"I love you, Aaren Noelle Robinson." He kissed her tender and sweet. "I'll never love anybody as much as I love you."

She heard portions of his words, but her every thought centered on where they were joined and the deliberate rotation of his hips. She arched her back from the pleasure it drove through her.

"I- I- I love you so much, Jay."

"Promise me we'll be like this forever," he whispered, kissing her eyelids, nose, cheek and then mouth.

"I promise to love you always. Always." She received him in her heart, whispering in the spaces between his burning kisses. His arms went under her and drew her tight to his chest. He rocked in and out of her and she matched his rhythm.

This time, their souls were speaking.

This is what love feels like, she thought. Kissing the side of his face, she felt his hands grab her bottom and squeeze as his body tensed. She locked her legs around his and slid her hands down his back, gripping him the same way.

"Oh Aaren…." he moaned, shaking. "I'm… I'm…"

Aaren pulled him deep, wanting something she couldn't articulate, and then Jarrod lifted his head. Their eyes met, her lips parted, as he released within her; this time, she could feel the strong, uncontrolled pulses. It was the most aroused she'd ever been. But more than that, what took her breath away was the way he stared down at her through it all. She'd never felt she belonged to anyone, not until that moment.

For Aaren Robinson, things would never be the same.

Chapter Five

THE FUNERAL

They waited for her, offering support and care without being asked. After years of going it alone, Aaren bristled as she descended the steps. She placed her feet carefully on the unevenly worn treads. Her hand slid along the aging banister. Her eyes, weary, barely lifted to acknowledge them. She managed a small, hollow smile of thanks.

"Morning, sweetie," said Becca.

"Morning," Aaren answered softly.

When she passed them, Becca followed. Aaren sought her purse in the family room. Her reflection came into view in the mirror above the fireplace. She'd chosen a simple, short-sleeved black dress that was fitted, stopping well above the knee. The neckline had tasteful beading, which probably made it too dressy for a country funeral. Her hair was pulled back into a braided bun and she wore her two-carat diamond studs. They'd been a first-anniversary gift from Gavin. Aaren had second thoughts about wearing them. But despite the reminder of him, her life waiting for her in New York gave her something to hold on to as she said goodbye to her past.

THE FUNERAL

Unwilling to face herself any longer, she pulled her eyes away from her image.

"I'm ready," she said in a stilted voice. She plucked up her purse and walked out.

Antonio helped them into the back of a black Lincoln Towncar. Aaren was surprised to see him come around and take the wheel. Becca held her chin at an angle and stared straight ahead, saying not a word. She must have arranged to borrow the car from Murphy's, Aaren realized. A wave of gratitude swept over her: Becca had saved her from Miz Marie's phony concern, at least for the moment. And she needed the time to prepare.

From behind the cover of her shades, she stared out blankly at the trees as they flashed by. The journey was short and her burden heavy. Becca's hand eased into hers. When the car slowed, so did her wildly beating heart. Pops was dead, and this would be their only and final goodbye.

Parked cars lined both sides of the road, spilling over to the open grass on either side of the small church. Aaren surmised that behind the weathered walls, everyone north and south of Old Rachette Bridge was in attendance. Pop was respected by many.

"I don't think I can do this," she mumbled to herself.

"Sweetie, I will be right besides you," said Becca, squeezing her hand.

"No, you don't understand. If I go in it's over. He's gone. Gone."

Becca moved over to put her arm around Aaren, and kissed her cheek.

"We can stay right heah as long as you need," she said softly.

Aaren dropped her head. "Did you talk to him in the past years, Becca? Did he… did he mention me, say anything?"

"Yes, I saw Abraham often, and he would ask me if I spoke sometimes. But Aaren? To really understand him, to know about these last years, you need to talk to Jarrod, hun."

Aaren's head lifted slowly, tears dropping from her lashes. The insides of her sunglasses misted over. *Jarrod*. Again Becca pushed her toward the one person she knew to stay away from. Why? Antonio looked up in the rearview mirror, waiting for the signal. Everyone waited. They all wanted to see Aaren Robinson, the faithless daughter, give her pound of flesh.

"Let's go," she said, opening her own door.

Becca hurried to catch up; she locked her arm through Aaren's. Antonio went ahead of them up the church steps to the double white doors. They were greeted by ushers holding programs. One of the ushers closed the door to the sanctuary so she could go through when they were ready. Sister Penny came up and smiled at her sweetly. Time had been kind to the soft-spoken woman whose eyes always carried a smile. Aside from graying roots and crow's feet, she looked exactly as Aaren remembered.

"Hey, dahlin," she said in a low whisper. "Wait right here."

Aaren removed her shades, taking her arm from Becca's in order to slip them inside her purse. She stepped out of Becca's reach, craving some space. It was short-lived. The organist played *What A Friend We Have In Jesus* and the doors opened again. Every head inside turned to look at her.

"Right here with you, girl," said Becca firmly, from her side.

Aaren barely heard the words. She felt herself go numb all over. Her eyes were riveted to the closed casket. A neat arrangement of white lilies rested on top. Reverend Morris stood at the podium smiling at her, beckoning her to come forth, but she couldn't move. People were everywhere, filling each row, watching, waiting, holding her to her charge. It was her responsibility to send her father to the Lord, but no one even cared if she was ready. The choir began to sing, each stroke of the organ like a hammer to her heart. She closed her eyes and swallowed, waiting for the tension in her muscles to subside. She could do this. She would do it. It wasn't just the memory of her father, she owed this to her mother, too. She opened her eyes, trained them on the flowers and not the casket, straightened her back and walked in.

It was the longest walk of her life. Becca offered support as they solemnly took their seats in the front row. The pew was completely empty, minus uncles, aunts, cousins or siblings to accompany her and share her grief. The last of her family stopped with her. Her Pop never knew his real parents: he had run away from an abusive foster home at the age of 13. He'd educated and fended for himself, working as a farm hand all over Kentucky, until meeting her mother in Penns Point.

Her mother's mother had an affair with a married man. It had ended badly. She'd left Louisville pregnant, and alone. Then, with a brand new baby and no family support, she'd ended up in Penns Point struggling to take care of the daughter she'd named Noelle. Her mother had been an only child. Now everyone was gone.

Deacon Beaufort rose to read a scripture and the program proceeded. The choir sang two of her father's favorite hymns. Soon she heard the Reverend asking for her to come up to the pulpit, a request she couldn't possibly deny. Becca squeezed her hand to see if she was okay. Aaren grimaced. Her friend meant well. She knew that. Still, she couldn't handle a moment more of the constant hovering. She rose from her seat with her head held high and walked forward in a haze, on jellied legs.

The Reverend leaned over and kissed her on the cheek when she neared, whispering in her ear. "God is with you, Aaren."

"Thank you, Reverend," she whispered back as the choir director gave her the microphone. She heard the music cue up but her throat went dry. The last time she'd sung had been in this room, with many of these same people watching. But she wasn't that girl anymore. Looking out into the faces, many with unsympathetic eyes, Aaren began to lose her nerve. She couldn't deliver a note. She swallowed, preparing to apologize before exiting the stage.

Then her eyes locked with his.

Jarrod Pennington leaned against the wall at the back of the church. He nodded at her, watching her carefully, not with the pity or curiosity she'd endured from the others, but with a look of encouragement. It was the way he looked at her when he'd taught her how to drive a stick shift, though she nearly ground the gears in Antonio's truck to dust. It was just as the day she'd almost tossed her application to NYU, fearing rejection. It was the look of patience, of devotion, that look that said he would always be there for her, no matter what. It should make her furious that he'd ignored her wishes, but instead, it helped. As much as she hated being in a room where her father lay stuffed in a walnut box, she hated being in a room with Jarrod Pennington even more. And rather than focus on him, she lifted her eyes to the carved motif above the double doors and began to sing.

Jarrod was mesmerized by her voice. How long had it been since he heard Aaren sing? Too long. He watched with such longing he had to look away. The tears streaming down her cheeks cut him to the bone. And from the mournful silence of the others, he knew they felt the same. Aaren's voice was filled with so much pain, no one could deny or enjoy her suffering. Did Abraham know? Jarrod wondered. Was he here in that moment to see her as Jarrod did? If the old man was, he'd have his answer. She was still his baby-girl, as Abraham had always called her.

Jarrod's eyes dropped to the floor. Aaren's voice opened wounds he couldn't bear. When he dared to look up once more, he captured her tearful eyes before her lids fell shut and she closed him out for good. She was beyond him now, and he needed to accept it.

Aaren finished the song to praises and hand-waving from the parishioners. She couldn't stop her tears, though she desperately wanted to. She dropped the microphone, hands flying to her face. Her body shivered, weak with a cold, lonely grief that threatened

THE FUNERAL

to take her under. Becca was on her feet, rushing to the pulpit to help her. Two deacons held her up, crying uncontrollably, as Becca took her from them and guided her back to her seat. Aaren kept her eyes closed. It had been years since she'd cried in public, years since she'd cried at all, and she wished she could get herself under control. Someone else reached for her. She felt strong hands, powerfully set arms. Confused, she opened her eyes and stiffened with anger to find it was Jarrod.

"Let me be here for you," he said softly.

She could barely see him through her tears. She had no energy to fight him. He pulled her closer, so that her arm slid around his waist. Aaren relaxed into him. She didn't care that she'd vowed to carry her stone of hate for him forever. She didn't care that most watched; she ignored the flurry of heightened whispers. Years ago, the two of them had almost caused Abraham's death. Now that it was here, Jarrod was the only one who could understand her guilt. She needed him so desperately, she just didn't care who stared.

And people did watch, leaning forward in the pews to get a good look at the two.

No one watched more closely than Judge James Mitchell Pennington.

The Reverend called the pallbearers forward, marking the end of the service. Jarrod didn't want to let go of her, but this was his final chance to behave honorably in the presence of Abraham Robinson. He rose with the others to carry the casket out.

Aaren, a prisoner to her pain, trapped by feelings of regret and profound sorrow, felt the tears begin to pool again when Jarrod shifted her back to Becca. When they finally rose to walk out behind Abraham, she saw the way Jarrod stood tall behind her father's casket, and began to feel a sense of control. She shrugged off Becca's tight grip and walked straight, on her own. Antonio got ahead of them, bringing the car around so they could leave for the cemetery. Soon after the Reverend spoke his final words, she found herself standing in front of the hole that held her father, gently tossing a rose on his casket.

"Pop, I never… I'm sorry, for… for everything. I wish… I pray you and mama…"

Her voice failed. The words didn't come. The pain did, though, in such continuous waves she felt dizzy with grief. She had already mourned the loss of their relationship as a girl. How could she be here again? This time she stood before him, before what was left of him, with no hope of reconciliation. All she had was the stark finality of goodbye.

"Rest in peace," she mumbled.

The crowd began to thin as everyone left to head back to the repast. Several people came to her to pay their respects. Aaren remained composed through it all. She even managed a small smile for Jarrod's father and mother as they approached her. She looked around, her eyes searching for him. Jarrod had kept a respectable distance, well off to the side. He was still there—alone, watching. Strangely, his face darkened with anger as he observed his parents approach.

The Judge stared at her, stone-faced, with blue eyes that so resembled Jarrod's. There was sadness there, and something else. So intense was his gaze that Aaren's cheeks grew warm and she shifted a little uncomfortably. Why was he looking at her like that? The sound of Mrs. Pennington's high voice broke through.

"Aaren, your father was such a good man. I'm so sorry for your loss."

To her surprise, Laura Lee Pennington hugged her.

"Thank you, Mrs. Pennington. Thank you for coming. Thank you, Judge Pennington."

"Aaren, forgive me. You look so much like… like your mother. It's… um, it's really remarkable," he said, in nearly a whisper. Laura Lee looked at her husband and Aaren saw her pale. An uncomfortable silence settled between them. Aaren met the Judge's eyes once more.

"Thank you. I have pictures of her, but I can barely recall her face."

"Just look in the mirror," he offered. He looked away from her, shaking his head.

Becca came up to Aaren's side, saving her from the awkwardness.

"Hey, Judge, Miz Laura Lee," she said and they nodded, returning the greeting. She touched Aaren's back gently. "Everyone is heading to the repast. You ready?"

Aaren's eyes slipped over to Jarrod. He continued to watch them from his self-imposed distance, and then returned her gaze to his folks.

"Sure, Bec. Thank you, again, for coming." She nodded to the Penningtons, then stepped away.

Jarrod turned away as well and made a beeline for his truck. Their paths crossed just as Laura Lee called out his name.

"Jarrod!"

Aaren's head lifted. He was so close she could touch him. She looked back, as did several others, responding to the desperation in which Laura Lee spoke her son's name. When her eyes met Jarrod's, she saw how torn he was.

"Yes?" he answered.

"I need to speak to you, son?" Laura Lee took a step around the grave markers with the Judge following reluctantly.

There was definitely something wrong between him and his folks, Aaren saw. Jarrod's jaw twitched with tension and his eyes narrowed on them both. Becca tugged gently at her arm, but Aaren remained rooted to the spot. It wasn't nearly her problem or any of her business. Still, she couldn't turn away. She sensed his turmoil, because she felt the same way. He didn't want to be left alone. Not with them. She nearly made a step toward him out of pure instinct, but Becca solved the problem for her.

"Jarrod, we'll see you at the church. Don't be long, okay?"

Their eyes met just before she was pulled away, and that invisible thread of memory between them could be felt. He opened his mouth to speak, but she dropped her eyes away and moved from his space. He watched her leave, resisting the urge to follow, resenting his father's presence. He wasn't crazy. He'd seen it in Aaren's eyes, her concern for him. The moment was fleeting and gone. He feared Aaren would put her walls back up at any moment, destroying the small bit of progress he'd made. He glared at his mother, not bothering to hide his irritation.

"What is it?"

Laura Lee, assisted discreetly by her husband, moved stiffly toward him. Even going downhill, she was exhausting fast. She shouldn't be out; she should be taking it easy so she could get better. Why did his father bring her to Abraham's funeral of all places?

"I know you've been hurt. We all have," she began sadly.

"Not him!" Jarrod said, pointing at his father.

The Judge shook his head. "You can't hate me more than I hate myself."

"Oh, I think I can."

"That's enough!" Laura Lee snapped, wavering.

Jarrod reached for her but his father held her steady, so he withdrew. "Mom, what are you doing here? Haven't the doctors—"

"Never mind that. *This* is a time for a healing. That's why I came. Abraham Robinson is dead. He will not keep my family hostage a moment longer. What's past is past. I need peace, I need for you to love each other. I can't go on like this, Jarrod, please!" Tears welled at the corners of her eyes.

Jarrod stepped close to his mom and touched her shoulder tenderly. She came into his arms. She had grown small and too thin in the past months.

"You're not well. You should be home. Rest."

"Please, Jarrod. Please."

THE FUNERAL

He looked directly into his father's eyes, for the first time, as he spoke.

"How you could stay with him all these years? He's the reason our family fell apart, not Abraham."

Laura Lee pushed back from his hold, then pressed both her hands over his.

"He's your father, Jarrod, and he and I love you more than life. You can't keep punishing us for something that had nothing to do with you."

"Nothing to do with me? He destroyed me and Aaren. He ruined my chance for happiness."

The Judge cleared his throat. "You're a man now, not some punk kid that got his heart broke. Your mother isn't well. Show some respect. Stop this war for her sake, if not your own."

"Don't you tell me what to do."

"You think you can punish me, make me feel any worse than I already do? You have no clue. It fixes nothing to cut me off, shut your mother out, ignore your family. These matters just linger between us son, and for *what*? I never meant to destroy anything. I fell in love just like you did."

"What?!" Jarrod glared at him, disgusted. He stepped close in to his father. "How the hell can you stand in front of my mother and speak of loving another woman?"

"Stop it, both of you!" Laura Lee pleaded.

"Your mother knew about my affair with Noelle. Who do you think told Abraham?" the Judge smirked.

Jarrod looked at his mother in shock. "You did *what*?"

"I didn't mean for things to get so out of hand! Jarrod, please. Can we just get past this?"

"You two are sick. Sick! Stay away from me! And stay away from Aaren!" He turned and stalked away.

"Jarrod!" Laura Lee shouted through her tears. The Judge grabbed his wife and pulled her into his chest. Laura Lee clutched to her husband and let the tears flow.

Chapter Six

BURYING THE PAIN

"Can I get you guys something to drink?"

It was so surreal. Aaren walked inside, followed closely by Antonio, Becca, and of all people, Jarrod Pennington. Becca had pointed out that with the towncar back to Murphy Brothers, they'd need another driver. Before Aaren could argue, Becca had her settled in Tony's truck, and flounced off without another word to ride with Jarrod in his. Now, it was the four of them back in her house again. It was just like the night she surrendered to the love they shared, the love she'd fought so hard to forget. She looked back at Jarrod, wondering if he felt it too. He avoided her eyes. She knew he did.

"Got any beer?" asked Antonio, going into the living room.

Becca squeezed his hand to stop him.

"Aaren, we're going to head back out."

Aaren couldn't hide her disappointment at their leaving.

"Why? We can have some drinks, and we got plenty of food left over."

She looked steadfastly away from Jarrod as he passed her, carrying two trays prepared for her by the church.

"Yeah, Bec. We can hang back for a few," Antonio pouted.

Becca flashed him a look that silenced him, then turned to Aaren.

"You're leaving tomorrow, right? Come to the house to have lunch with us before you get on the road."

Jarrod put the trays down on the breakfast table. Becca's words rang hollow in his ear. She was leaving? Tomorrow? How was he supposed to just let her go, without any time to make it right again? He stood in the kitchen, watching the two women embrace. He closed his lips over the question. He'd nearly asked it aloud.

"Thank you for today. The both of you being there for me meant a lot."

Antonio rubbed her back and kissed her cheek. "We love you, Aaren, and we loved him too. Come by tomorrow before you leave. Okay?"

She nodded quietly, understanding the need for a little space. And, she admitted to herself, understanding why Becca and Tony were giving it to her. She needed to talk to Jarrod and clear the air. It would be her last bit of business before she left Penns Point and all the painful memories behind.

"I have a meeting with Mr. Spence tomorrow, for Pop's will. I may need you two to check in on the house and land for me, until I hire someone to tend to it. If that's not too much trouble?"

"No problem, sweetie."

Becca gave her another quick hug, then walked out with Antonio close on her heels. Aaren watched them go to their truck, and waved goodbye before closing the door. Turning, she saw Jarrod standing at the end of the hall. He was leaning against the entryway to the kitchen. He looked her up and down and she felt as if she were seventeen again, with her Pop gone to the races.

But she wasn't seventeen any more. And Pop—she bit her lip.

"I'll just go upstairs and change, then you and I can talk," she said. Jarrod just nodded.

She nodded too, then headed up the stairs.

Jarrod watched as she climbed the stairs, admiring the long legs that seemed to stretch forever. Shaking his head to get the erotic thought out of it, he stepped into to the living room. The last time he'd been here with her, those feelings destroyed her life.

SUMMER 1990

"Boo!"

Aaren jumped, dropping the bucket of feed she'd carried out of the stall. He grabbed her from behind, spinning her around to face him. Laughing softly, she fought to get free, pushing him away as his hands did their usual groping.

"Jay, are you crazy!! My pop's here!" she grinned, looking around the barn. She was afraid he would appear at any moment. It had been a year, and Pop still had no idea they were a couple.

Jarrod looked her over and grinned back.

"I like this skirt." He tugged at it.

"Stop!" she said, knocking away his hand.

"Your dad's gone. Saw him leave with Mr. Clifford." He ran his fingertip along her shoulder.

Aaren's brow dented in confusion. If Pops was to be gone for a spell, he would come tell her. It wasn't like him. "You did? When?"

"Everyone is going to town for the auctions, remember? He's gone for at least two hours, Aaren. You know how those things are."

He moved into her space, captivated by her brown, almond-shaped eyes. She caught the desire and smiled back at him, feeling warm inside. Lately he wanted her all the time, causing her to find creative ways to escape from under her father's watchful eye. She bent to pick up the spilled bucket of feed.

"No, we can't do it here. It's too risky. I'll try to meet you at the creek later today after my chores."

"Please, pretty please, pleeease don't send me away," he begged, reaching and pulling her back to him. Leaning into her, he kissed the inside of her neck, allowing his hands to roam her curves. Closing her eyes to the teasing kisses he applied to her skin, she enjoyed the shockwaves of passion racing through her veins. Weakened by her own urges, she gave in.

"Did you bring one?"

"You know I did," he said. He stepped back from her, sticking his hands in his pockets and revealing several condoms. Aaren grabbed his hand and pulled him to the back of the stables, yanking a blanket from a hook on the wall as they went. She led him to the last stall, knowing that it was kept empty to store Pop's farm tools. Straw was scattered over the floor, and bales of hay were stacked along the back wall. It wasn't perfect, but they had to be quick, and besides, in a few seconds she wouldn't be feeling anything but him. She spread the blanket neatly over the straw and looked up to see Jarrod reach behind him and pull his shirt over his head.

"Wait a second," she laughed.

"Can't!"

He unbuckled his belt hurriedly, kicking off his shoes and working the button to his jeans. She laid down on the blanket. Resting on her elbow, she amused herself by watching his fumbling. When he looked down, the sight of her thick unruly hair swaying behind her tilted head only heightened his desire.

"Don't get all naked."

"You worry too much," he snorted.

Aaren giggled. "Guess what. I decided I'm not leaving next month."

Jarrod got down on the blanket. He moved over to kiss her bare shoulder. "What are you talking about?"

"I don't want to go NYU. I can go to U of L with you," she said, smiling as he eased himself on top of her.

He kissed her lips, slowly sliding his hand between her legs to touch her warm, wet center.

"Your dad won't let you go to U of L," he said, dismissing her news and pushing the fabric of her panty aside so he could slip a finger into her.

She gasped from the penetration, and then recovered to put her hand up to his chest, stopping him. "I'm working on it now. I told him that I can come home and help out more often. He's warming up to the idea. I can tell."

Jarrod stopped massaging her breasts through her tube top. "But you've already paid your housing deposit. Everything's set for you to go, Aaren. You said you wanted to go to NYU."

"I changed my mind." She smiled sweetly at him. "I don't want to leave you. Isn't that great?"

Jarrod cut his eyes away, trying to hide the irritation on his face.

"What is it with you? Are you trying to get me to go away? Do you want me to be stuck in New York all far away from you?"

"No, I didn't mean—"

"Jay, I'll be eighteen in a few days. Once we go off to school we can get married and everything. My dad or yours can't stop us. We can have our farm and our business and…"

Jarrod sat up, releasing her from the touch that earlier had sent waves of passion through her body. The mood was lost with her talk of marriage. He loved her, but they hadn't done anything yet. Living in Penns Point was the pits. They were supposed to see more of the world. He just wanted a chance to enjoy college and how could he do that with her clinging to him? Being on the football team meant he would be traveling and doing all kinds of cool stuff. He wanted her, of that much he was certain. But he was equally sure he didn't want a wife this soon.

Aaren, confused, sat up, and touched his back that was now turned to her. "What is it?"

"I just don't know. When you talk about marriage and stuff it gets weird for me. I'm just barely eighteen for Christ sake!"

The comment stung. "Don't you love me?" she asked weakly. "I know I come on strong with my dreams and stuff, but I thought you wanted it too. When you get mad, it… well, it kind of scares me, Jarrod."

He cast his eyes over and she nodded, blinking back tears. "What if we go off to school and things change? You find someone else?"

"That'll never happen, Aaren. I love you too much." He moved his face closer and rubbed his nose against hers. She smiled into his eyes.

"I don't mean to scare you. We don't have to get married right away. I just don't want to go to New York. It's too far."

Jarrod kissed her softly. "It is too far, and you're right, babe. We should go to U of L together. It's the only way to make sure we have each other. Besides, I can't stand the idea of you being that far from me either."

"You mean it?"

His eyes had been staring down at the nipples he'd hardened with his touches, but he lifted his face to look deliberately into her soft brown eyes.

"I could never be apart from you," he said, pulling her top down. "Never."

Moving slowly toward her, he took one of her pointed nipples into his mouth and she sighed from the delicious feeling his tongue gave her. She groaned as she felt his hands on her hips, pushing her jean skirt up to her waist and pulling at her panties. She desperately wanted to feel him too. They rarely had opportunities to do this at her place and something about the forbidden deed intensified the pleasure they gave each other.

Jarrod caressed her other breast with kisses. Finally, he freed her from her panties while pushing his own jeans and boxers down to his knees. He was an expert at slipping on a condom now and while she moaned from him grinding into her, he ripped open the wrapper.

Gone were the days of their clumsy lovemaking. They constantly found new ways to please each other and now, Jarrod's movements were purposeful. Parting her legs wider, he rubbed his covered manhood against her, feeling the warmth that made him ache. She sighed as he ran his tongue slowly and delicately across her lips. She opened them and gave in with the sounds of passion she'd been holding back since he first touched her.

"I love you, Aaren, so much," he said, gently pushing his way inside of her.

Her chest rose and fell from the pressure of his entry and she grabbed him, bringing his lips back to hers. Darting her tongue in and out of his mouth, she lifted her heavy lids to see his eyes roll into his head. The kiss became greater than either of them. Their moans and the delicious friction of their bodies sparked that familiar heat between them, until they were both panting and writhing in ecstasy. Jarrod ran his tongue over her throat as she tilted her head further, arching her back.

"Ahhh! I love you," she cried out and before another passionate outburst escaped her, his tongue slid past her lips, again stealing her breath.

"Love… you too," he whispered.

He pressed his face to her throat, letting go a deep moan against the beat of her pulse, before running his tongue over her skin and sucking hard. Aaren pushed at him, worrying his passion would overwhelm him and he'd be stupid enough to leave a hickey. Then they'd really be in trouble. How was she going to explain a turtleneck in July? But he would not be denied. Deliberate slow thrusts took her to the edge and pulled her back.

He could do things to her that she never imagined possible. Every cell in her body felt as if it were on fire. She heard him whisper how good she was. There was little she could do to hold on. So instead, she ran her hands across his back, riding that wave of pleasure with him. Jarrod grasped her hips with both hands, tilting her pelvis so he could bring himself deeper each time. His tongue, now in her ear, made her buck against him with delight.

"Oh, Aaren," he whimpered, keeping time with the rhythm they both set.

Aaren looked up at him. She found his eyes tightly shut, his face contorted with lust. Moving underneath him, she touched his cheek.

"Open your eyes, baby."

He was too caught up in her to respond.

"Jay, look at me," she smiled.

Her voice came through to him and charged every nerve-ending in his body. She held his stare, wanting to see their love. It was their love that made this special and she could spend the rest of her life trapped under him, pleasing him the way he pleased her, because of that love. Their movements were so synchronized now that she could anticipate with each thrust what current would rip through her. They'd learned each other so well that they didn't need to talk, but she liked the way his eyelids fluttered in response when she did. She could feel how close he was, waiting for her.

"Baby, are you ready?" Aaren said the words quietly, concentrating. When he nodded, she tipped her head up close to his and tightened herself against him. His thrusts became frantic and desperate, but what once had been painful now brought her exquisitely over the edge. Her cries eclipsed his for a moment, until he drove deep to his own release. Aaren exhaled the long-held breath from her lungs to the feel of him pulsating through her. She kissed the curve of his neck and stroked his shoulder, wishing he could stay with her, inside her, forever. Jarrod's breathing slowed, and when he spoke, she thought he was reading her mind.

"Aaren, I don't ever want to lose you." He brought his face to hers and looked down at her. "I do want to get married."

"But you said—"

"We belong together," and with that said he gave her another demanding kiss to seal their fate.

There came a violent jerk and she felt him roughly pulled off of her. She opened her eyes to see Pop throwing him across the stall.

Aaren screamed when she saw Jarrod hit the wall, then fall over like a rag doll to the straw-covered floor, with his pants at his knees.

"Pop, no!!" she yanked down her skirt and tried to cover her exposed breasts.

Abraham grabbed Jarrod by the throat, lifting him off the ground. He began to choke the boy as he kicked and clawed at the bigger man's hands. Aaren's screams had the horses neighing and snorting with agitation. She got to her feet and rushed to her father, trying to get him to release Jarrod before he killed him.

"Stop it!! Stop it!"

Abraham was blinded by his rage. Jarrod's blood diffused beneath his skin, turning him several ugly shades of red. Aaren feared he couldn't hold on much longer. She hit at her father with her balled fists, bringing his focus to her. Abraham swung with his backhand, slapping her across the face. The blow shattered her senses and sent her flying to the packed dirt of the floor. He dropped Jarrod and turned on his daughter.

"How could you do this!" he roared over her. "You whore!"

She looked up at him, dazed.

Jarrod began to retch. He threw up a little. Still struggling to get air, he rolled away coughing, then pulled up his jeans to cover his nakedness.

Abraham had gone insane with anger. He snatched Aaren up to her feet. She was crying loudly, holding her bruised face. Her lip was split; there was blood in her mouth. She backed away from him in fear, trying to escape his grasp.

"I raised you better than this! You lower yourself for him! You whore!! You whore!!" he yelled, charging at her.

"Daddy, noooo!" He grabbed her and swung her around to slap her again.

Jarrod managed to stand and went after him. "Let her go!"

"Daddy I'm sorry, please… nooooo…." she whimpered, weakened by the attack. She was only standing because she was held, painfully, in his grip.

Abraham was out of control. He shook her violently. "You're just like her! A whore!!" he shouted.

Panicked, Jarrod looked around. All he saw was a shovel. There was no time to think. Swinging it like a bat, he smacked it to the back of Abraham's head. The sound itself was awful, and then the man dropped in a heap, releasing Aaren. Both teens were shocked to silence; then Aaren let go a wild, pained scream. She dropped on all fours and scrambled over to him. Blood pooled rapidly over the dirt and straw. It was coming from the back of his head.

"Oh God, oh God, oh God," she said over and over again. "Daddy… Daddy noooo, wake up, please Daddy."

"I… I didn't mean… he was beating on you. I didn't mean…"

"Jay, he's hurt! Help him! Please!"

Jarrod dropped the shovel, his eyes stretched wide.

"JAY!!!"

Snapping out of it, he nodded that he understood. He grabbed his shirt and yanked it over his head, pushing his arms through.

"Stay here. I'm gonna call an ambulance," he shouted, forgetting his sneakers and bolting from the stall.

Leaving the desperate sounds of Aaren's sobs behind him, Jarrod Pennington said a silent prayer that Mr. Robinson would be okay.

PRESENT

She worked hard to make little noise, but Jarrod could hear her. The Robinson house was small. He stuffed his hands in his pockets and paced near the foot of the stairs. Minutes passed, ebbing by so torturously slow. *Any normal person would have gone up there by now*, he thought, *just to check.* Jarrod climbed the stairs quietly, knowing it wasn't what she wanted him to do.

"Don't cry."

She heard him behind her. Wiping at her tears, she tried to cover. "What are you doing up here?"

"It has to be so hard, coming back. On top of him passing, I mean. The memories."

"He almost died because of me," she said, staring at the track ribbons on her dresser mirror and making sure to avoid his eyes.

"I was more to blame than you were," said Jarrod.

"When they took him to the hospital, I stayed right by his side until Miz Marie had me removed from his room. She had to get Chet Jones to carry me out. Did you know that? She took me home and I cried the whole way. I was so scared."

"Of course you were, Aaren. You didn't mean for him to be hurt. Neither of us did."

"Jay, he barely spoke to me for days. The Sheriff came."

"Sheriff Maddox?" Jarrod asked.

Aaren nodded. "He had a skull fracture." She turned and looked at him. "He came, but Pop refused to tell him what happened. He protected me even then. Told him to stay away from me. I suppose a black man beat across the head with a shovel wasn't worth investigating any further than that."

"Maddox was an idiot." Jarrod wondered if it would help or hurt to tell Aaren that Maddox had been in his father's pocket back then, right up until he died. He decided against it.

"True, but Pops wasn't. He knew what he was doing. He was protecting me. I was too young and in love to see it then. And then, when I was allowed to see him—"

"Aaren, there are things I want to say to you, explain to you."

"Save it. I mean, seriously. What's the point now?" She moved further away from him, determined to continue her side of the story, on her terms. "When I was allowed to see him again, I cried constantly at his bedside, begging for forgiveness and begging him to understand. And you know, when he finally did speak, what he said to me?"

"What?" asked Jarrod with dread.

"'*You are not to see that boy again.*' Just like that, Jarrod. He dismissed us, everything about us. And God help me, as much as I wanted his love and forgiveness, I couldn't let you go. I refused to. No wonder he never forgave me."

"Aaren—" he stepped toward her but she stepped back. Wiping her eyes, she turned away from him once more.

"We could have killed him that day. He had a skull fracture. A skull fracture." She repeated it aloud to remind herself of her guilt, to remind him why they were never meant to be. "I can remember working so hard to prepare for him to come home, thinking he'd be all right once he got back around his horses. He wasn't. He was never the same, Jarrod. Never."

"I remember," he replied, eyeing her carefully as she picked up a tiny Beanie Baby and pulled on its fluffy ears. "I remember feeling just as guilty. I remember sneaking back over here at night just to hold you. Afraid of Abraham, afraid of my parents, and most of all afraid of losing you. That's when I came up with the plan."

Aaren nodded. "Right, to tell Pop that we'd get married. You were going to do the right thing. What a fucking joke!" she threw the toy back on the bed.

"Aaren, you don't understand."

"Get out! Just go downstairs. I... I just... need to be alone for a minute."

"Let me tell you the rest."

"Jay, please! Just go!"

"Okay, okay. I'll wait downstairs."

Aaren sat down on her bed and put her face in her hands. Oh, she remembered it well. The day he went to see Pop to talk to him before he was released from the hospital was the end of it all. He'd never returned after that visit and when Miz Marie took her to pick up her Pop, she'd expected him to mention Jarrod.

He didn't.

After that, Jarrod wouldn't accept her phone calls and when she finally cornered him in the hallway at school, he wouldn't meet her eyes. He told her it was over, calmly and directly. He told her to stay away from him. Aaren wasn't fooled. She knew it was Pop. He'd gotten to the boy she loved and made their devotion into something ugly, something obscene. Her Pop must have forced as much guilt down Jarrod's throat as he could swallow. She knew it well, because Pop's silent retreat from her had delivered the same suffocating dose. She'd fought with her father, telling him she wouldn't go to school. She'd threatened to run off with Jarrod. To this day, even the memory of Abraham's words ripped her apart.

"That boy doesn't love you, babygirl. He admitted it to me. Ask him yourself!"

Aaren knew no matter what guilt they shared over hurting Pop, Jarrod would never denounce his love for her. Her faith in Jarrod was solid, permanent, unshakable. She told him so. Smiled and flat out told her Pop he was a mean, spiteful man for saying hurtful things like that. Abraham Robinson looked calmly at his daughter and stated, simply, that if he was proven correct, she would agree to leave Penns and never return. That bargain, to send her permanently from the only home she'd ever known, was his idea of atonement. How he'd hurt her in that moment. How it hurt still. She sucked in a deep breath, remembering it all.

Back then, she didn't understand why he would want to send her away. She'd asked him haltingly if he didn't love her anymore, and flinched when her own father couldn't look at her. Even then it didn't break her. She was his daughter, after all. If her own father didn't love her, she knew for certain one person who did. She told her Pop she'd fix it all and prove to him that Jarrod loved her, even if he couldn't.

She'd believed Jarrod just needed some time, and then he would come for her. And then, they'd leave this place together, forever.

Jarrod sat in the Robinson living room, waiting, reflecting on how much time had passed. But Aaren was home again and that was enough to give him the hope he'd lost those years ago. Scanning the room, his eyes fell on the family portraits that lined the shelves. The pictures of her family that he'd seen hundreds of times surrounded him, but his eyes clung to the single portrait of Noelle Robinson. Today, his father had watched Aaren too closely.

Jarrod rose from the chair and walked over to look into the eyes of a woman he'd never known. He touched the silver of the frame, then picked it up. The fashions were different, but Aaren was nearly identical to her mother.

Noelle wore her hair pulled to the back of her head like a dark crown. The photo, now faded, had an overall pink cast, but her beauty was not diminished. She wore large hoop earrings that hung to her shoulders, and a paisley-print shirt. Her frosted copper lips and her eyes, outlined in black with long lashes, tipped upward. There was no mistaking her seductive appeal.

Yep, she was Aaren and Aaren was her. Staring at the beautiful woman that was a mystery to him, he thought about his father. He'd had no shame in claiming to love this woman in front of his wife today. What really went on between her and his father? Was it an unrequited love affair? Was it any different than the one he shared with his Aaren? He shook his head.

"You always hurt the ones you love," he mumbled softly to himself.

"You do?"

Aaren stood, barefoot, on the bottom step. She'd taken down her braided bun, causing the lower half of her hair to hang in waves past her shoulders.

"Yeah. You do," he said, putting the picture back. "At least that's been my experience." He stuck his hands back in his pockets and looked directly into her eyes.

Aaren moved through the living room, smiling tensely at him.

"I owe you an apology for my behavior. I know you were just trying to be nice. The way I attacked you the other day—that was uncalled for. What happened between us was a long time ago."

"You were right. I hurt you, and I still have a hard time living with it. I need to be the one apologizing. I handled everything wrong. Everything, Aaren."

"I *know*, Jarrod."

Jarrod went completely still. "You know what?"

"The secret. The one you and my dad shared."

His heart started to pound. He looked on warily. "Secret?"

"Yeah," she said, giving him a small smile. "I was hurt back then, and pretty naïve. I didn't put it together until I came back here. It's forced me to face my past a little bit. I've been walking these empty halls and seeing everything from the perspective of a woman, not a seventeen-year-old lovesick girl."

"Aaren, I can explain."

She held up her hand to stop him. "I want to thank you."

"You do?"

"Yes. You did me a favor." She shook her head, realizing how that must sound. "And Pop was wrong to make you feel guilty."

"He was hurt, Aaren, after everything—"

"Hey, it's done—"

"I don't think you understand—"

Her hand went up again. "—but I can barely talk about this stuff."

Jarrod closed his mouth at her admission. Aaren focused on his cheekbone as she spoke, not his eyes. Never his eyes.

"I'm not sure I want to hear your take on it." She shifted forward, ready to rise.

Jarrod stared at her. He understood. She thought it was the event in the stables that caused him to push her away. Although that was the catalyst, Abraham's revelation about their parents' past was what came between them. Abraham had asked him not to do to him what his father had done, and Jarrod had sworn he wouldn't. He'd kept that promise. Maybe they should leave it at that. Aaren didn't have her parents anymore. All she had was memories. He would rob her of the good ones she carried for her mother if he told her the truth. Jarrod couldn't bear hurting her again. But he'd thought about this moment for years; he'd made this decision long ago. The truth might not set them free, but it had to be told.

"Aaren, please. Stop for a minute and listen. Really listen. Can you do that?"

Embarrassed at the way she wanted to run from room to room whenever he scratched at her emotions, she sat back against the sofa.

"Fine. How did the two of you become friends? Tell me that."

Jarrod smiled. "Actually, it's an interesting story."

She just stared. He saw the familiar distrust in her eyes. He'd earned that distrust by breaking her heart. And now, he was going to have to explain why he sought any excuse or opportunity to be close to her, even one as calculating as befriending her father.

"A few years ago, I got a wild horse at auction, for a pretty good price. An Arabian, gorgeous, but I couldn't handle him." Jarrod cleared his throat. "Breaking him was a challenge from the very beginning. He injured Gene while we were trying to get him in the trailer. We get him home, and couldn't do a thing with him. He even kept the other horses agitated. Word spread through town that I'd either have to sell him off or put him down. This was during the time when I had just started my business and my reputation was on the line. People around here couldn't wait for me to fail. It was all over that I didn't know what I was doing and, Aaren, to be honest, I really didn't."

"I remember you weren't that big on farming," she said dryly.

Jarrod nodded. "By nature, everyone in Penns is a farmer but I guess you're right. I had to work at it harder than others."

"So what did you do with the horse? Did you sell him?"

"No, I decided to show this town I was man enough to manage things myself. I even tried to gentle him on my own. Damn crazy horse almost kicked me to death."

Aaren frowned. "That doesn't sound smart."

"Yeah, I knew better. It took me weeks to recover and I must admit I wanted to quit. I mean, he was just one damn horse and none of it was worth my trouble. I'd pretty much convinced myself it was okay to give up. And then I had a visitor."

"A visitor?"

"Abraham. I walked in the stables to find him feeding that horse out of his hand. It was an amazing sight, Aaren. I couldn't believe it."

A smile tipped the corners of her mouth. "Pop was an amazing man, especially when it came to horses. He loved them so."

"Yeah, he was. He told me he'd just got back from New York. From visiting you."

Aaren's smile faded. "He told you that?"

"He said he'd heard of my troubles and wanted to offer some help. See, prior to his visit with you, I'd gone over to his place a couple times just to check up on him, to offer any help, cause people talked about—" He stopped.

"Go on?"

"He shut people out. They kept saying he was up here on the farm alone. That his mind was gone. I knew that wasn't so, but still, I wanted to check on him. See if he needed anything. Most only saw him during harvest when it was time to sell. Then he'd disappear again. The first time I showed up he got his Remington after me," Jarrod said, smiling at the image of Abraham with his shotgun, shouting at Jarrod to get the hell off his land. "It took some courage on my part to try again," he chuckled.

Why did you? she wondered. Aaren sat up. "Then he just came to you out of the blue?"

"I didn't question it at the time, but now I think his trip to New York changed him, or at least changed his mind about me."

Aaren didn't understand. Her Pops didn't even call her when he got to New York and they definitely didn't bond, at least not the way she would have wanted.

"Did he say anything about me?" she asked, looking over to the bookcase at a picture of her parents. It was the only one she had of them together.

"He told me that we did the right thing and that you were successful and happy. He apologized for blaming me all those years ago and he offered his hand in friendship."

"So, that's how you two became friends?"

"That's how we became friends. You see, no matter what, we both had one thing in common."

"What's that?"

"You."

She felt tears well in her eyes and suppressed the urge to let them fall. Looking around the living room, she began to understand that maybe she was wrong. Her Pops did love her, in the best way he knew how.

"Thank you, Jarrod. Thank you so much for telling me that."

"Thank you for giving me a chance."

She looked down. "What happened with you and your folks?"

"What do you mean?" He swallowed.

"You joined the Army? Was it because of us? Because we—because you wanted to come after me or something?" she asked, surprised and more than a little ashamed at the hopeful tone in her voice.

He smiled at her. "Yeah, it was because of us. Me and my parents just don't mix. I'm sure you can understand that."

"I can."

They sat in silence for several minutes and Jarrod worked up the courage to turn the conversation to Aaren again. "You leaving tomorrow?"

"Yeah, I've got to tend to Pop's will. But after that…" She rubbed her hands over her thighs.

He'd been nervous about tomorrow's meeting ever since he'd gotten the call from Sam Spence. Seeing as how the conversation between him and Aaren was finally pleasant, he didn't want to discuss that with her now. He decided to put the reading of Abraham's will aside for the moment.

"Maybe you could stay for a couple of days," he ventured.

Aaren shook her head. "I got to get back. Cases and stuff."

"I see," he said, his voice trailing off.

She smiled at him. "Are you hungry? There's plenty of food and I won't be taking it with me."

"If you'll join me," he smiled back.

"C'mon," she said, getting up.

Jarrod followed. For a few moments there, they'd shared a familiarity that had him remembering, and even worse, thinking about a future with her in it. He set that wish alongside all the others of her return. They stood around the table, heaping food onto two plates she got from the open cupboard. His eyes trained on her. He found it impossible not to really look at her as she moved gracefully around the chairs. He tried not to even think of what it would be like to hold her, and then, he had to look away.

She went to the refrigerator and pulled two bottles of Budweiser out of her father's six-pack. "I'm sure Pop wasn't supposed to be drinking these," she said, shaking her head.

"He marched to the beat of his own drummer. He never really listened to any of the doctors."

Aaren popped the cap off the beer and passed it to him.

"So how's your business? Your farm?"

He turned the cold liquid up, gulping it down. Placing the bottle on the table, he pulled off his suit jacket, then sat in the chair across from her to eat the cold chicken, macaroni and cheese, and string beans kind neighbors had brought to the family.

"It's good. I actually love what I do."

Aaren nodded. "What about the Army? Did you love that too?"

"Well, not exactly. I, uh… I was deployed to a forward unit, right after boot," he said, his voice trailing off. "Mechanized Infantry."

"Wait. That was 1990." Aaren stopped mid-chew, her eyes widening with shock. "You fought in the Iraq War??"

Jarrod's face darkened and he sighed. "Yeah, I did. Desert Storm."

He didn't have to say much for her to understand what he must have gone through. They were from a small town and he was a pacifist. To have lost each other and left his family, then fight in a war, was too much. She'd always thought of him as being in college at frat parties and screwing sorority girls. She'd made some crucial decisions based on that assumption, and if that wasn't what he'd been doing—

Aaren reached across the table and grabbed his hand. Jarrod looked up at her, then down at her hand over his. Turning his hand over, he held hers, running his fingers over her soft skin.

"I was such a fool, for a lot of things," he said looking into her eyes.

"It was a long time ago."

"Not for me. I dreamed of you every night over in that desert. I wrote you letters, you know."

"You wrote me?"

"Every night. I'd burn them afterwards but it helped, thinking of you. You helped me survive over there."

"How?" Her eyes went wide.

Jarrod shrugged. "Just knowing you were out there... I mean, we weren't together anymore, but knowing that, it kept me from taking too many risks. From doing anything too crazy, no matter how much I wanted to."

Aaren clenched her teeth together, thinking of her own behavior, and how self-destructive she'd been. He had found a way to survive, done something positive. She'd done the opposite, finding ways to punish herself. Over and over.

"Well, we all went through things. But I'm sorry you were thrown into a war because of it." She mumbled, avoiding his eyes, for fear he'd see on her face who she'd been during that same period.

Jarrod squeezed her hand.

"I don't want you to apologize."

"Good!" She laughed appreciatively. She'd never liked apologizing, and he knew it. "So what *do* you want, then?"

"Good question. I just want the same thing I've always wanted."

"What's that?"

"You."

Jarrod clamped his mouth shut, because he'd done it. He'd gotten it out. Aaren stared at him for a long moment, not believing he'd actually said it out loud. Then she yanked her hand from his. She'd been enjoying his touch, which was wrong even before he'd made his admission.

"Me," she breathed. She stared at him in disbelief. He was waiting for a response. "Don't. I can't."

"Why? You said you're not married and it's obvious you're not happy."

"I *never* said—" she stopped herself. Her marriage was barely a fact any more, and besides, it was her business, not anyone else's. "And who said I wasn't happy?"

"I can tell. Look at you. You're different, cold."

"*What?* Cold? Did you just call me *cold?*"

"Don't you sit there and pretend to know about my life!" She hit the table with her fist, then shot up and strode out of the kitchen.

Jarrod immediately went after her. He had to hurry to catch her. Before she escaped, he grabbed her arm, turning her to face him.

"Let me go!" she shouted while shoving back at him. She was furious. It was too painful. She should never have let him in this far. All she wanted to do was escape.

"Stop it, Aaren! Tell me what's got you so scared."

"Don't. Don't! Let me go!"

"Not until you… Wait. Just listen. What did I say? What's wrong?"

"I don't want you! I don't need you *or* Pop!"

She drew back, swinging her free hand up to slap him, hard, across the face. Jarrod responded from instinct. He jerked back so she missed, then went in close, pinning her arms between them. When she struggled to free herself and strike him again, he looked at her, stunned. For a split second, he considered shaking some sense into her, but that moment passed.

"Listen!" He yelled in her face, breaking the silence standing between them. "I am *done* lying to you! I'm telling you the *truth*!"

Aaren glared at him. Her lips pressed into an angry line; her fists balled tight. She twisted her wrists, but Jarrod continued to hold them tight to the front of her. Her eyes burned with the kind of fury that worried him. He took a very deep breath and tried to speak. He couldn't do it. The pain pooled in those soft brown eyes stalled Jarrod's words. She was so broken, so lost, and anything he said might hurt her more. If he had more time, maybe—

"Well?" she snapped. "Say it! I've taken worse, trust me!"

"I took care of that farm for us. I built that house for you. I had our dream to tend to. I never gave up hope that one day you'd come back to me."

"Come *back* to you? I never asked you to build a damn monument for me. I don't owe you anything!"

"Aaren—"

"No! I'll have you know that I'm very happy! I haven't been sitting around waiting to join you on that farm. As a matter of fact I didn't think of you at all! Why would I? You sure as hell didn't give me a reason to!"

"Talk to me, Aaren. It's me. Tell me what just happened!"

He released her wrists and she stumbled back from him, hand to her forehead. The day she walked out on her husband, he'd told her she was no longer capable of letting anyone in. She'd agreed, and taken it a step further. She'd told Gavin she was no longer capable of love. But now, standing across from Jarrod, her first and only love, only to find they'd held the same dream, separately, for years? Only to learn that it had all been real? She was close to believing again. Dangerously close. She spoke slowly, not just so there would be no argument, but to keep control.

"I'm not that girl any more. And today, with everything… this is not me."

"What do you mean, not you?"

"All that, today, with the service," she said, gesturing to the food on the table and the funeral they'd come from. Then she pointed back and forth, between them. "And this. I don't do *feelings*."

At first, Jarrod didn't follow. Then, a light came in his eyes and he nodded.

"I'm sorry. I just—"

"It's fine," she dismissed him, still breathing hard. "You can do feelings. I just don't."

"Then *don't*."

He leaned in gently, brushing his lips across her cheek, and moved her hair away from her face. She smiled despite herself, understanding his challenge, and liking how it felt to be the object of his desires once more. Looking into his eyes, she remembered the way he'd held her today when she'd felt her loneliest. It was so unfair she'd been separated from him years ago. The injustice of losing him, of how different her life could have been, washed over her again.

"What do you want from me?" she asked, needing to hear him say it.

"Stay. Give me a week."

"A week?" she laughed, but stopped herself when she saw the look in his eyes. He was completely serious. But why? "What the hell for?"

Jarrod didn't have a ready reply. "To... to prove to you that you can feel again."

"I don't see how one week could erase fourteen years."

"Sleep on it. We'll talk tomorrow," he said reluctantly, pulling away from her.

She looked at him and smiled. She never backed away from a challenge. "Oh, we will?"

He nodded to confirm their future meeting. "Thanks for listening, for hearing me out."

Aaren gave a shrug of her shoulders, forcing her hands down in the front of her jeans and rocking on her heels. Realizing how awkward she must look, she removed her hands and rubbed them at her sides.

She watched him go to the table, finish the beer she'd given him, and then put on his suit jacket.

"Look, you don't have to go," she said quickly. She stepped to the table. "I mean, we could—"

Jarrod looked up sharply. Neither one of them moved a muscle; neither one of them gave an inch. Aaren realized with shame that her entire body was afire with need. Even as she resented the idea that Jarrod's presence could still arouse her, it had been a terrifyingly long time since her body had responded to anyone. That excited her even more. She hoped to hell it didn't show on the outside.

She smiled again, praying for a distraction. "A week, huh? So what now?"

Jarrod took her hand. He led her quickly through the house. He said goodnight, then let the screen door slap closed behind him. Her mind raced with memories of the way they'd been together, both before and just a few moments ago, as she watched him walk to his truck. But that was then. He could be no match for the woman she'd become. Aaren squared her shoulders. She felt herself return to normal. Closing the door and turning for the kitchen, she bet herself she could have the dishes done before his stupid grey pickup turned out onto the main road.

Chapter Seven

THE WILL

In a town like Penns Point, there were two people that knew the heart and soul of each resident: their minister and their lawyer.

The lawyer to most of them, Samuel Spence, was too young to die. Sixty-six and the last of the Spence men, he'd been told that his lung cancer was terminal. Even chemotherapy wouldn't extend his life. True to form, Sam, as everyone called him, fired up a stogie and thanked the doctor for the news before breezing out. It wasn't denial. He was a Spence. He had always lived, and would soon die, on his terms.

Sam was prone to hacking fits that brought up blood and mucus. That's what brought him to the doctor in the first place. In the last few days, however, the coughs had become more frequent. To Sam, it mattered little. Even with the shadow of death hovering, he remained at his desk, absorbed in the messy details and secrecies of the residents of Penns Point. For the most part, land disputes and wills were what came across his desk, and that was what kept him going, even now.

Yes, Sam was relatively satisfied with the life he led here.

That was true except for the year 1978, when his faith in his town imploded.

THE WILL

The death of Dr. Martin Luther King ten years before hadn't really done much for small-minded, simple country folks. Segregation was a staple in Penns Point, one that everyone adhered to. The blacks and the few Hispanics lived south of Salt River and the whites lived north. The removal of segregated signage from public places didn't make it to Penns until 1976. America celebrated its Bicentennial and some nosey reporter out of Louisville decided to spotlight their town and its enforced color divide. At the time, Judge James Pennington, who had more influence than the mayor he'd endorsed, made a big deal about moving the town forward. Everyone obliged, to a point. After that, the color boundaries were implied rather than expressed.

Apparently James Pennington took his own speech to heart. Shortly afterward, his obsession with Noelle Robinson ripped the heart out of the town and rocked it to its core.

Sam loved his small town for its sense of community and family. That was the good thing about a small town. The bad thing was its ability to keep a secret, and every town had one. Noelle Robinson's death was the secret hidden beneath the warm smiles of the townsfolk in Penns Point. Now Abraham, the gatekeeper of that secret, was gone, and Sam feared that his beloved home would implode once again. Today, he would read his will to Abraham's only daughter and she would have plenty of questions. It would be interesting to see if Jarrod Pennington would answer them.

Aaren knocked, then opened the door.

She hadn't seen Mr. Spence since she'd left. He looked remarkably different. Becca had mentioned his battle with lung cancer, but nothing prepared her for the gaunt, frail-looking man before her. Samuel Spence used to be an extremely portly man, weighing a solid 300 pounds and standing only five foot ten. Now, he looked to weigh no more than Aaren did. His hair, grayed and thinning, was combed over the center to cover his baldness. She would think him to be in his nineties as opposed to his sixties.

"Aaren," he said. "Come in."

His smile was warm. His eyes were full of the life missing from his pasty skin as he rose to greet her. He pulled her into a hug which she returned carefully. He was so thin.

"Please have a seat," he said, helping her to the plush chair facing the desk.

From behind her, Aaren heard the door open once more. She barely turned before she heard Jarrod's voice. He stood just over the threshold, his voice failing in his greeting when their eyes met. Her brows knitted and her eyes sharpened on the guilty look in his.

"Jarrod, glad you made it."

Sam waved him in as a hacking coughing fit gripped him. Aaren's eyes returned to the aging man with concern. She stood to rub his back, and took the opportunity to shoot Jarrod a questioning look. Sam pulled out a hanky to stop any blood from escaping and quickly excused himself.

Aaren watched him go, then wheeled on Jarrod.

"What are you doing here?"

"I was invited."

"What? By who?"

"Abraham included me in the will. Apparently."

"Why didn't you mention this last night?"

"Subject didn't come up."

"Jarrod ! I—"

"I know. I figured it would bother you," he replied, forcing the strain from his voice.

Aaren kept her eyes trained on him, noticing the way he found it hard to maintain her stare.

"Why would Pop put you in his will?"

Jarrod shook his head. "No idea. We'll just have to wait and see."

She sat with a thump as Sam rushed back in. "I'm so sorry for this. Let's get on with it. Shall we?"

Aaren's eyes slipped over to Jarrod. He looked off. His posture was stiff, his jaw clenched. He didn't appear to want to be included, which meant this was all Pop. But again, why? How deep did the relationship between her father and Jarrod run?

"First, Aaren, let me share what I know you already know. Abraham Robinson was a fine man and a good man, and I'm honored to serve him today."

Aaren nodded tightly. Sam looked over to Jarrod before continuing.

"Now before I read the will, I have a letter that Abraham wanted read aloud to you both. He brought this to me two months prior to his death and he was adamant that you be together when it was read."

He pulled a clean, folded handkerchief out of his top desk drawer and dabbed at the sweat on his forehead. Then he slid the letter out of the brown envelope and unfolded it. He looked it over, then looked up at them before speaking.

Babygirl,

If Sam is reading this to you then I'm gone and you're left with the task of disposing of your old man. I'm sure it's been painful for you having to come back and deal with this all. I tried to make it easy for you with making arrangements and I hope I succeeded at least at that.

I have so much to say to you. I just don't know where to begin. Let me say first that I'm sorry. I want to apologize for failing to be the father you needed. When I came to your office years ago, I was a lost man. I'd spent years in my own bitterness, blind to it. Then I reached the breaking point. I was going to tell you what I've written in this letter today. But I failed you again and I can never get back what we lost. I am and was a foolish old man, a bitter one, and I allowed that bitterness to grow between me and you. I will forever regret that, my sweet girl. Pop is so very very sorry. You see I wanted to protect you from the world, and mostly from ever experiencing the pain I've had to live with in my life. But instead I pushed you out into that world, without love or family. I just sent you away with no guide. I am so proud of you for your achievements in spite of it all. I won't dare take any credit for that. I just wanted you to know that you are the best part of me and Noelle.

If Sam has followed my instructions, Jarrod Pennington should be seated next to you. I'm sure when you arrived to learn that we became friends it was a shock to you. Well it shouldn't be. You were right about that boy. I'm sorry for learning that too late. He's a good man, and he loves you even now. I know you have moved on with your life, but I believe that your future can only be complete if you deal with the past.

So I brought you both here today to give you that chance. I owe you two such a deep apology for hurting you the way I did. I've gotten to know Jarrod. I see why you loved him. Here is my confession. He came to me years ago to ask for your hand in marriage. He was so scared, Babygirl. I remember how his hands shook as he stood at the foot of my hospital bed crying and apologizing for disrespecting you and me. He told me he loved you. He told me that he wanted you to be his wife. I had the power to give you happiness in that moment. Instead I let my hatred toward his father cloud my judgment. I said some mean and ugly things, I destroyed his spirit. May the good Lord have mercy on my soul for what I did to him that day. I can't apologize to you enough Jarrod for coming between you and your family. I robbed you because I thought you guilty. The burden of guilt was never yours or Aaren's. Who am I to tamper with a father's love?

Because of my actions that day, I set into motion the painful events that followed. When Jarrod told you that he didn't love you, it was my voice you heard, not his. What he did to you that day broke your heart, but I want you to know that he only did it to protect your heart. He made a promise to me in hopes of securing happiness for you. He kept that promise all these years.

So, Jarrod, you have been released from the burden I placed on your shoulders all those years ago. My daughter deserves to know the truth. I'm going to you let you tell it to her. I just wanted to say that I'm ashamed for what I did to you both. I hope one day you two can truly forgive me, so I can rest in peace.

THE WILL

My sweet beautiful Babygirl, you've had your mother's free spirit from the moment you came into this world. It frightened me. I tried to break it. I know now how wrong that was. Aaren Noelle, Pop loves you and always has. Be well and be happy, and just know that everything I did, whether right or wrong, was because of my love for you. There's nothing stronger than a father's love.
With all my heart,
Pop

Aaren gripped the edge of her chair. She tried to process, to breathe through the processing, to understand, all the while replaying the words in her mind and heart. Pop said he loved her. He had all along. It was something she never thought she'd have, his love. Not only his love though, there was more. She looked to Jarrod. Years of pain and regret laid silently between them. Pop had a change of heart, while hers remained of stone. How ironic that was. Aaren shook her head roughly, not having any place to put the emotions she felt.

Jarrod pushed his chair closer. His hand went to hers, resting on her knee. She dropped her head at his touch and their fingers intertwined. Aaren tensed and cut her eyes away, unable to share the hurt, but still grateful he was there. She eyed the window pane and the blowing leaves of the sycamore branches that scraped it as the questions began to line up in her mind. Who was her father? What was the story between him and the Judge? Letting go of Jarrod's hand, she looked at him through her tears, utterly confused.

Jarrod took in a deep breath, releasing it slowly. It was easy to read the questions in her eyes. What could he say? Nothing could give them all that was lost between them. She looked away and so did he, both feeling and understanding. His eyes lifted to Sam, a witness to it all. He saw the attorney shake his head in pity. Pity? Samuel closed the envelope and opened the folder.

"Abraham owns the six acres where his house stands. All the taxes are paid up on the property. He also has a portfolio worth over thirty-five thousand dollars of investments that you can liquidate. There's an insurance policy of ten thousand. Miz Marie has already submitted a claim in your behalf."

Aaren wasn't completely listening. Jarrod took her hand in his again, lacing his fingers through hers while avoiding her eyes. It would only be a matter of time before Aaren's sharp instincts focused her questions on his family.

"Abraham asked that the money be given to you, Aaren, but he stipulated that the land and everything on it be held jointly between the two of you."

"What?" Aaren snatched her hand free once more and sat up straight. She wiped at her tears.

"He what?" asked Jarrod, equally stunned.

Sam erupted into a coughing fit that had Jarrod standing. He waved him away as he was forced to turn away to expel mucus into a tissue before tossing it in the can under his desk.

"He wanted me and Jarrod to share the land?" she repeated slowly to herself.

"That's right. It was his hope that after you heard his confession and returned home, he could bring you two together. His attempt to fix from the grave what he ruined in life. I spoke with him about this. He was clear, young lady. You two are to handle the property jointly."

"Was Pop sick? Did he know he was dying?" Aaren asked.

Sam looked away. "I don't know."

Aaren suspected that he did. She looked over to Jarrod. It made sense but it didn't. Her father wanting to set things right with Jarrod could be explained, but Jarrod's duplicity irked and confused her. "What did he mean about his hate for your father? Is there something more I should know?"

Jarrod wiped hard at his jaw. His eyes darted between her and Sam.

"Jarrod, answer me!"

He finally looked over to her. "Yeah, there's something you should know."

"Well? What is it?"

Sam cleared his throat. "Aaren, would you excuse us for a moment?"

"I beg your pardon?" she asked, shooting him a challenging glare.

"You're an attorney, right?" Sam closed the folder and passed it across his desk to her. "Please give us a minute. You can wait outside and review these documents. Then the two of you can talk afterwards."

Jarrod looked at Sam, confused as well, then gave Aaren the best smile he could muster. "I'll explain it to you. I can explain. I swear it. Let me talk to Sam?"

"Why, so you two can get your stories straight?" she snapped angrily. "You were with me last night. If there was more to their history, you should have said something, damn it. I won't let you—" She stopped herself, now shaking with anger.

Jarrod stared at her with concern. He didn't dare touch her, but he spoke with as much care as he could, pleading with his eyes. "I need you to trust me," Jarrod said. "Trust me to do what's right. There's no conspiracy, I'll prove it. Will you give me that chance?"

Her analytical mind worked to weigh it all. Jarrod had lied before… that made him a liar. There was no disputing that. Yet, that lie hadn't been his idea. He'd been a scared boy. She'd been an equally naïve girl. Neither of them had made fully-informed choices back then.

And now? There was no malice in his eyes. All she saw was the boy she'd fallen in love with those many years ago. She'd trust that boy once more. Not because he'd earned it, but because she so desperately wanted it. She wanted to believe he was in there somewhere. Because if he was, then the girl of long past, lost to her the day she left Penns Point, could still be somewhere within her, too. Aaren stood, taking the folder and her purse.

"I'll be right outside. When I come back, you and I will have that talk," she said with conviction. "I'm telling you Jay, the time for secrets has passed. I want to know the truth."

Sam cleared his throat after the door closed behind her. Jarrod finally looked back to the attorney. "What is it, Sam? You know, don't you?"

"I've watched you grow up from a little boy. My sister's boy works on your farm. I have a lot of respect for you."

"As I do for you."

"Then listen to me. You don't know everything about your father and her mother. If you open that can of worms it could be explosive to this town. And more importantly, to your family."

Jarrod frowned. "This town pretty much knows that Noelle and James had an affair."

"What this town knows would shock you."

"Then enlighten me."

"If I tell you, it'll prevent you from ever having her. I see how you look at her. Just like the Judge looked at Noelle." Sam shook his head again with what Jarrod thought resembled pity. The sickly attorney hacked up half his lung into another tissue. He swallowed then steadied his breathing before speaking again. "Trust me, son. It's a dead end. I suggest you find a way to explain this without dragging Noelle Robinson through it. You don't want to take Aaren down that road."

"She's not stupid, Sam. It *is* her mother."

"You don't understand."

"I don't have to. I have no choice here. I lost her once because of lies. I won't do that again."

"Jarrod, it's not that your father slept with her mother. That's just the beginning. The ending gets much worse. There's a reason why her mother's name is never spoken in this town. Ever wonder why the gossip-hounds skip over any reference to that affair? Heed my warning. Find a way to give Aaren closure, but leave the secrets of Noelle Robinson buried with her." He began to wheeze, fighting off another coughing attack. "You stand to lose a lot as well."

"What the hell does that mean?"

"Tell you what. Ask that question of your folks. But until then, if you love Aaren and want to protect her, you need to get her away from the past and focused on the future. Abraham left the decision up to you. He decided long ago to protect her from the truth of her mother. Old fool withered and died with guilt in his heart because he thought he failed her. Truth is, he's just as much a victim as Aaren is." Sam gave Jarrod a pointed look. "He's hoping that you will do a better job. I told him it wouldn't work. He wouldn't listen. He actually thought his death would be the end of it." Sam coughed again, shaking his head. Jarrod realized he was laughing, a bitter cold laugh. "He believed that the truth would set this town free. I have to disagree. I was here in seventy-eight when all hell broke loose. I saw the ugliness in this town and its people, and I don't want my dying days spent around it."

Aaren came back into the office, refusing them the courtesy of knocking. "Time's up."

Sam nodded. "Yes, it is. I have another appointment, so you two talk and work out the details. Just contact my office with what you've decided."

Aaren stared at Sam, who refused to look back up at her. Jarrod rose and walked to the desk, extending his hand. "Thank you, Sam. Thanks for everything."

Sam looked at Jarrod, then accepted his handshake. "Good luck to you both."

Jarrod approached her, his lips shifting with tension. "Let's go to my place. I want to tell you at my place."

She looked at him sideways. *Not there*, she thought. *I can't.* "No."

"The creek, then. Can we… will you do that for me?"

He spoke so quietly, so carefully. Aaren was touched by the way he made his plea.

"I can do that."

Aaren allowed him to lead her out into the hallway. Looking back over her shoulder, she saw Sam watching them as they headed out the door. She could swear his face held a look of fear.

Chapter Eight

TRUTH AND LIES

Aren waded through the knee-tall grass with her sandals in her hand. Her feet sank into the moist earth, blades of grass pricking her calves. Jarrod walked on the other side of her with his hands in his pockets, deep in thought. He'd been that way since they'd left Sam Spence's office. He'd asked quietly if they could ride together, and seeing the darkness in his face, she had not wanted to argue. That had been the extent of their conversation. They'd each looked out their own side of the pickup truck all the way back to his farm.

Jarrod was wound tight with tension. She desperately wanted to know why. She'd been patient, but he didn't explain his mood. A pessimist of long standing, she was surprised to find herself calm in the wake of what she'd learned that morning. In so many ways, as he'd wanted, her father's will freed her. So many of the things that happened to her had been simply beyond her control; given what she'd known and when she'd known it, she'd made the only choices she thought she could.

The only thing that worried her now was Jarrod's continued silence. There were secrets hovering around them: that much was obvious. But whatever those secrets were, they would handle them together. It calmed her to know that she was exactly where her Pops wanted her to be.

"Jarrod?"

He gestured ahead. "Look."

Aaren's thick, even lashes lifted as her eyes followed his hand. They'd arrived at a clearing that was totally different from what she remembered. He'd removed sections of the forested area that concealed their creek, revealing blue liquid beauty. This place seemed calmer somehow, even more inviting.

"You did this?"

"It was always beautiful here. I just helped it along."

She could barely hear him over the sound of the water rushing east-to-west out of the Salt River.

"I've forgotten what this place was like," she sighed.

"I never could." There was a pause, then he expelled a weighted breath. "Aaren, let's talk." He extended his hand and led her to their tree. It sat at the side of the stream with a large branch that stretched over the water.

They had sat there often with their feet swinging, watching the water as it rolled beneath them in bubbling waves. Jarrod watched her climb over and smiled at her agility. She sat next to him and exhaled, relaxing. It was an unspoken invitation she hoped he wouldn't ignore. He didn't. Jarrod slid closer, positioning himself so their hands were almost touching on the bark. He took a deep breath.

"I love you, Aaren. I always have. You can believe in it. Do you?"

He loves me. Aaren looked away over the water, her chest suddenly tight again. Jarrod remained frozen next to her. Out of the corner of her eye, she could see how much he needed her to trust him. And except for that one time, that one awful night, he'd never given her a reason not to.

"I can."

"Good. Good." His voice was hollow. Sadness wrapped thickly around both words. It caused her to look over at him and soften more. He was in just as much pain as she. She stared at his profile.

"I'm a big girl, Jarrod. Grown. Whatever it is, it's not your secret to keep any more. Please. Just tell me the truth."

"I told you I would go see your father. That I'd ask for your hand in marriage."

"I remember."

He looked across the water. "I did. I stood outside of that door just terrified. Even in the war, I wasn't that scared. When I saw Miz Marie and the Reverend leaving his room, I hid. She was crying. The Reverend helped her down the hall. My stomach was so twisted I kept thinking I was gonna puke."

Aaren put her hand on his knee. "Go on."

"I took off my cap, straightened my back and walked right in."

"That must have been hard."

"Yeah. Hard. He was in bed, with all kinds of tubes coming out of him. His head was turned facing the window. He looked over at me with pure hate, Aaren. I've never had anyone in my life hate me as much as your father did in that moment."

Aaren withdrew her hand. *That's only because you never knew how much I hated you*, she thought. She cleared her throat quietly.

"I'm sorry."

"Don't be," said Jarrod, struggling to form the words. "I asked him if we could talk but he just laid there angry. Cold. He just stared through me." Jarrod sucked in a deep breath to continue. "I said: Sir, I'd like to apologize for my behavior the other day. I was wrong and it was my advances that led to you discovering us that way. I'm sorry."

Aaren smiled tensely. "I can imagine Pop didn't take that apology well."

"He told me to get out. I told him that I came to ask for his daughter's hand in marriage. That I'd do right by her and…"

"And what, Jarrod?"

"He laughed."

Jarrod looked over to her, his eyes liquid. "It was a very mean laughter. It hurt like hell, but I deserved it. So I didn't run. I stood firm like my father taught me. I wanted to be a man, but Abraham knew I wasn't. I was just some punk kid banging his daughter."

"You were more than that," she corrected.

"He said I was just like my bed-hopping daddy."

"What??"

"He asked what it was with Pennington men and black women?"

Aaren took in a deep breath and it was Jarrod's turn to watch her.

"Abraham wasn't a racist. So I didn't understand why he was behaving like one. I tried to ignore it, just keep going. I told him I wanted to do the right thing."

"And?" she asked, looking straight ahead, her back stiff.

"Abraham said: Oh, so you want to do right by my Aaren? By screwing her in a stable? Just like your daddy wanted to do right by my wife, by screwing her in my bed!"

Aaren sucked in a deep breath but no air got in. Her lungs tight and her nails cutting into the bark of the tree, she discovered she still had enough heart left inside to break. And the pain was intense.

"I told him it was a lie! He said the hell it was. I told him my father wouldn't do that. He would never do a thing like that. He just laughed again. He said I was just like him. He wanted to know if my father told me to give you a whirl, if we compared notes."

"I don't want to hear any more," she stammered, keeping her face turned so he wouldn't see her tears. Jarrod touched her hand and she moved it away.

"I told Abraham that I loved you. I loved you with all my heart. But he was so angry, and justifiably so. I nearly killed him. My father had taken his wife. He said my people knew nothing of love. He said he'd might not been able to save Noelle, but he'd never let me take you from him. There was no reasoning with him. No way for me to explain myself. Then he made a request. A demand, actually. He told me it was the only way to… fix things." Jarrod took her hand, and this time, though she still couldn't look at him, she allowed it. "He asked that I not destroy you like my father did your mother. And when I tried again to deny it, he told me to ask my father. To learn the truth, then be a man and let you go."

"Let me go?" she echoed, her voice cracking with suppressed sobs.

"End things with you. Give you a chance for a life away from… me, from who I am. From the arrogance that made me think I was entitled to disgrace you the way I did."

Aaren's head shot up. Jarrod tensed visibly at the tracks of tears on her cheeks as the wind blew strands of long hair into her face.

"You were a child! He had no right to lay that on you."

"He said if I did it, Aaren, he'd never tell you what your mother and my father did. He'd protect you. He warned me. He said if you learned the truth, you'd hate me forever, and I was so scared… just totally afraid of you hating me."

"I cannot believe Pop did this. That he kept this from me," she cried bitterly.

"I almost killed him. He said I owed him in return. He told me he would protect you with his dying breath. That I owed him his daughter's life and future, since my family had already robbed you of so much."

"What did you say?"

"What *could* I say? He was right. I got the hell out of there. Ran to my car and sat in the front seat bawling like a damn baby. I'd lost a lot that day, a lot."

"We all did," she mumbled.

"Aaren, I—"

Aaren broke down. She couldn't hold it a moment longer. "That's why you did what you did? That's what brought it on?"

"I'm sorry, Aaren. I'm so sorry."

SUMMER 1990

"Have you spoken to him?" asked Aaren, twisting the curly phone cord tight around her finger.

"No, but Antonio said everybody's going to the fair. He'll have to be there," answered Becca reassuringly. Aaren had done little besides call her up and cry into the phone, trying to find ways to get Jarrod to talk to her. Becca could do little besides listen to her friend.

"I have to talk to him. He's avoiding me at school. He doesn't understand, Bec! Pop is making me go. He says I have to go to NYU."

"Calm down, Aaren. We'll figure this out. Meet me at the five and dime off Claire Street with your bike and we'll ride over there."

"Okay, I'm leaving right now!" she said, hanging up.

"Where do you think you're going?" asked Abraham quietly. He'd been on the other side of the kitchen wall, leaning on his cane.

Aaren's eyes slipped over timidly. He'd been home for two days and said barely two words to her the entire time. She was doing her best to take care of him, but it hurt the way he looked through her instead of at her. It was as though the bond she thought they'd shared, however small, had been permanently severed.

"To the fair."

"No. You're still grounded. You aren't leaving this house!"

"Pop—"

"NO!"

"I'm going!!!" Aaren stood and shouted back. Abraham looked at her, surprised. Up until a few weeks ago, he'd thought she was a very obedient child: she'd never before been openly defiant.

"What did you say to me?" He took a step toward her.

"Pop, what did you do to Jarrod? I know he went to see you. He hasn't spoken to me since. What did you say to him?"

"I did nothing to that boy!" Abraham scoffed, moving around her to the refrigerator. He retrieved a beer he wasn't supposed to have.

"You did too! Please, Pop. We love each other. Why is that so horrible to you?"

"That boy don't love you, only what he can get from you. He just wanted what you were giving away. He all but admitted that to me."

"That's a lie!"

"Is it?" Abraham mocked. "Well, he's eighteen…. an *adult*. Where is he? Why isn't he here asking for my forgiveness and begging to have you as his wife?"

"You scared him away," she said, her voice lacking confidence.

"No, Aaren, but you go on off to the fair and you ask that Pennington boy point blank if he loves you. If he says yes, you have my blessings."

"We will?"

Abraham, twisting the cap from his beer, avoided the hopeful eyes of his daughter. He had seen Jarrod's defeated stance and hoped the boy could be man enough to see it through. If the boy let her go, she might be able to be happy again, away from this town and especially, away from him. She needed to be away from the both of them.

"Yes, I'll let you get married. But if that boy says otherwise, then you will have to promise me you'll go to school."

"I don't want to go to New York! You need me!" she shouted, hurt that he still wanted to send her away.

"I need you to do what you know is right and that's college. I want you out of this town!"

"Well it won't matter, because Jarrod loves me and I will marry him. Whether you like it or not!"

She stomped through the kitchen, out the back door to her bike, and raced off, sure she would prove him wrong.

"Hey! What's wrong with you?" asked Vincent, pulling Charlotte under his arm.

Jarrod walked alongside, disinterested in their chatter about leaving for college soon. He had lost Aaren and nothing made sense to him anymore. Vincent had come to his house and all but dragged him to this fair.

"Hey man, I'm talking to you!" Vincent snapped.

"What?" Jarrod frowned.

Charlotte smiled and popped her gum. "Got a surprise for you, Jay!"

Jarrod looked at Charlotte. She was a redhead with freckles and green eyes. She had big breasts for her size, bigger than all the other girls in school, and most of the varsity team had buried their faces in them at one time or another. Lately it had been Vincent's turn.

"What kind of surprise?" Jarrod asked, irritated.

"Surprise!" sang Carrie, pushing at his elbow. She'd been standing behind him.

Jarrod looked over his shoulder and saw her. He clamped his teeth together and turned around. "What's up?"

"You, that's what's up!" she said, smiling wide. "Where you been, Jay? No one's seen you for weeks."

"Around, I guess."

"He's pussy-whipped," said Vincent, snickering.

Jarrod stuffed his hands in his pockets and ignored the comment. Everyone knew how he felt about Aaren even if they'd never announced they were an item. Three more guys from the varsity team strolled over to where they were standing, pairing up automatically with the girls. Jarrod was surrounded by giddy couples. It made him feel sick.

Antonio parted the crowd, heading straight for him. "Damn, man. Where you been? Aaren's flipping out. She's got Becca all over my ass."

Before Jarrod could speak he saw Aaren and Becca riding up and his heart lodged in his throat. Aaren, smiling, met Jarrod's eyes as she climbed off her bike. Jarrod reached to pull Carrie next to him. Antonio, and everyone else, went silent at the move, knowing something was about to go down.

Becca got off her bike as well, waking quickly to catch up with Aaren. Their crowd was hanging by the Tilt-a-Whirl. Kids, screaming and spinning, filled the ride just behind them. The air smelled of buttery popcorn, caramel apples and cotton candy. Families raced by, heading to the Ferris wheel or bumper car rides, their excitement a stark contrast to the tension of that small group of teens. Aaren came through the crowd to stand in front of Jarrod. She set her jaw in disbelief at what stood before her.

Jarrod hugging on Carrie?

"Jay, can we talk?" asked Aaren. She looked at Carrie, who had a triumphant smirk on her face. She saw the scene before her eyes, but refused to make herself understand.

"Talk about what?" Jarrod said dismissively. He wouldn't look at her.

Aaren looked nowhere else, wounded by his response, which evoked laughter from the other teens. Becca tried to move closer, but Antonio pulled her back.

Aaren saw the set of Jarrod's face and took a cautious step forward.

"What's wrong?" she asked weakly.

"Look. I told you already. We're done. Why don't you just go away and stop harassing me!"

"Harassing you? What's wrong with you?" She reached for his face. He quickly slapped her hand away.

"You heard me. I'm about to go to college. I don't have time for this any more! It's too hard with you. It's over. Don't you get that? Just step off!"

"You don't mean that. What did my Pop say to you? Jarrod... why? Why are you acting like this?"

"Hey! You heard him cry-baby, step off!" Carrie let go of Jarrod and moved into Aaren's line of sight. She'd been itching for this fight. Aaren, stunned, barely registered the challenge. She looked on at Jarrod with horror. He reached across and snatched Carrie back. He didn't want to hurt Aaren further. What he was doing already was killing her, but he thought she'd see Carrie and just leave. Now, he couldn't think of any other way to make her go. Looking back into her face, he saw tears rolling down her cheeks and he lost his nerve. People were stopping to look at the crowd, thinking there was about to be a fight.

"Do you love me?" Somehow her father's words were humming in her ears.

"Just go already!" He spat the words at her, avoiding the question.

Aaren shoved him. The crowd of teens all hummed a synchronous *Ooooo!*

"Answer me, damnit! Do you love me?!" she screamed in his face.

Jarrod turned and glared at her, furious that she was making this harder than it had to be.

"No!! Are you happy now? No, I don't love you!"

Aaren stood frozen, stunned. His words hit her so hard she could not speak.

"Why are you making me do this? What do I have to say to get through to you?" shouted Jarrod. "It's true. You were nothing but an easy lay!"

The teens gave another collective gasp and Carrie chuckled with her friends.

Jarrod and Aaren saw and heard none of them. It was as if they were in a bubble where time and space were suspended. Both shook with rage and pain Jarrod couldn't stop. He wanted to hate her. He wanted to, desperately, because if he thought even for one second how much he loved her, he'd break.

"We had some good times, now it's over! Over!" He yelled in her face, clenching his fist and holding his breath. He felt tears pricking the corners of his eyes and used sheer will to keep them from cascading all over his face. "Just get out of here!"

Aaren saw anger in the blue eyes she loved so much and her world came crashing down around her. She began to back away slowly. A look of horror and raw hurt clouded her usually pretty features. That look would haunt Jarrod for many years to come.

"You fucking bastard!" screamed Becca, bringing Jarrod out of his daze. She charged at him, ready to claw his eyes out with her bare hands. Antonio grabbed her and dragged her away. Carrie's friends laughed and whooped it up as Aaren, still reeling from his words, continued to back out of the crowd. Humiliated, she finally turned, and ran to her bike.

Jarrod, still holding his breath, waited until the last possible moment. Then something in him snapped.

"Aaren, wait!" he shouted, but she didn't hear him through her loud sobs.

She jumped on her ten-speed and raced away, the wind drowning out the sound of name-calling as she fled.

Vincent looked at Jarrod, shaking his head in disgust. "Damn, man. That was totally cold. You didn't have to do her like that."

"Bitch deserved it," Charlotte snickered to Carrie behind Jarrod's back. Carrie laughed, turning away so Jarrod wouldn't see.

But he didn't hear or see any of them. He watched Aaren until there was no sight of her. He then smashed away his tears with the heel of his hand and stormed off in the opposite direction so no one could see him cry.

PRESENT

Aaren's eyes lost focus. She blinked and tears fell into her lap; then she blinked again to clear her vision. She stared down at the stream rolling under her feet. Jarrod watched her closely, waiting for her to speak. As the silence between them lengthened, he moved his hand over hers.

"My dad confessed it. He didn't even try to deny it. It was all true, Aaren. So I went back to the hospital and told your father that I'd break up with you. I swore it to him. Told him it would be my fault, my choice. That I didn't want you to know what… what my dad did with your mom. But I couldn't, Aaren. I'd see you in school and it *hurt*. I'd get your notes in my locker, or my mom would tell me you called… and then… then you came to the fair, and I… I'm sorry. I really am."

Aaren shook her head. "All of these years, all of these lies."

"You had a right to know. We were wrong to keep it from you."

"Yes. Yes, Jarrod, you were." She shot him a look, then quickly looked away. She decided to put her past with Jarrod aside. Her mother's past was, for the moment, hurting her more.

"My mother slept with your father. Judge Pennington. The most revered man in this county and my mother was his dirty little secret?" she asked, still bouncing between believing and disbelieving.

Jarrod blanched. He'd anticipated her hurt, but wasn't sure how best to deal with her anger.

"And my Pop just blurted this out to you?" Aaren's strained voice choked on the words.

"He was in a lot of pain. Imagine what it looked like to him, finding us the way he did—"

"I feel sick. I have no idea who she was. How could my mother be capable of this? What type of woman was she?" Aaren wiped away the tears that slid down her cheeks.

"I don't know. My father never made a secret of his feelings for her after I confronted him. It's like he was proud of it, or something. For weeks we argued. He flat-out told me he wouldn't apologize for being with your mom. And him and me, we kept fighting." Aaren looked over at Jarrod, curious. "When I told him I wasn't going to school, he slapped me and took away my car keys. That's when I decided to leave. You were already gone. There was nothing left for me in this town."

Aaren hugged herself. "I don't know what to say to all of this. My dad must have seen my mom in me, more times than he liked. It explains a lot."

Jarrod moved closer and put his arm around her. "That letter said you were the best part of both your parents. You know this, Aaren. Your mother was human. I don't know why or how she got involved with my father. And I have to believe that it had nothing to do with how she felt about you."

Aaren leaned her head against his shoulder. "It hurts, Jarrod, to think that she would do that to my Pop. To our family."

Jarrod understood that pain. He couldn't look at his own father because of it. His parents' being together was a lie, especially when his father so evidently wanted someone else. Listening to Aaren's sniffles made Jarrod think about what Sam had said.

"Can I ask you a question?"

She lifted her head and looked at him. "Sure."

"How did your mom die? Do you remember anything about it?"

Aaren sighed and looked back into the rushing water. "I was so young then. Five, maybe? Four? I remember being with our neighbors when Pop came in saying my mom went to heaven. The only strong memory I have is that he was soaking wet. I mean, for years I thought heaven was full of water and that's why he was so wet. He and Mr. Clifford were both drenched. You know... it was the only time I ever saw my father cry."

Wet? What does that mean? Jarrod frowned, looking deeper into the water. "What did he say happened to her?"

"Pop always got upset when I asked how she died. The most he ever said was she got sick and was gone."

"You never tried to find out more?"

Aaren looked over at him, speaking slowly to keep the tears at bay. "No, I never really gave it much more thought. She was dead for so long that she kind of just became this… figure I created in my head. Someone pure and good, like an angel or something. I had no idea she was your father's whore."

"Aaren. Don't call her that."

"Why not?! It's true, isn't it? It's what my dad called me when he found me with you. I mean no wonder Pop flipped when he caught us. He had to see in us what he saw in your dad and my mom. How sick is that, Jay… how sick am I?"

Tears flowed and he pulled her into his chest, comforting her.

"It's an ugly situation, but it has nothing to do with us. I spent a lifetime blaming myself for what our folks did. I won't let you do the same thing."

"How can you say that? Look at what our families did to each other. No wonder your dad stared at me the way he did. It's disgusting!"

Jarrod shook his head. "We handled this badly before. This is our chance to make it right. Your father wanted his death to bring some closure, for both of us. Abraham wanted to set us free. Don't you want to be free?"

She looked over to him. Panic welled in her chest. What was he asking? He wanted her to go through it all again, trust him, trust herself? Flashes like some ghostly picture show played in the back of her mind. She remembered how badly his rejection scarred her so long ago. Now to learn it was all orchestrated by her Pop was hard to accept. She spent so many years hating Jarrod for how he hurt her. Even now she clung to the bitterness. It made sense of the loneliness. Without it she'd have to face herself and what she'd done over the years, in the name of that bitterness. How could she ever do that?

Aaren looked away, off to the furthest reach of the river. It was too much to process. Everything she'd been, everything she'd done, everything she'd become, was because of events set in motion fourteen years ago by her Pop and enacted by Jarrod Pennington. Now, it turned out neither man was who she thought he'd been. And the mother she'd always idealized, the woman she pretended was looking down upon her from heaven, the woman she'd tried so hard to make proud? Aaren could barely think about that part of the truth.

She thought about her mother and the secrets that had just been revealed to her. Could her mother have loved James Pennington the way she once loved Jarrod? Did her father drive her mother into another man's arms? Desperate for a way to believe in her mother despite the truths, she let all the questions roll through her head. Then she thought about Jarrod's question.

"Why did you ask how my mother died?"

"It's something Sam said."

"When he asked me to leave the room?"

"Yeah. He said that the affair was the beginning and that the end was much worse."

Aaren frowned. "Was he talking about my mother?"

"I think so. He told me point blank to let the secrets stay buried with Noelle. I think something happened in this town because of that affair. Something Sam wouldn't talk about."

Aaren stared ahead, trying to wrap her head around the ominous message. "You mean like a race riot or something?"

"I don't know." It was obvious he wanted to comfort her. She was glad he resisted. "What do you want to do?"

Aaren stared straight ahead, silent for an overlong moment, until the pressure of Jarrod's gaze pushed her to speak.

"I wanna go for a swim."

"What? Now?"

"Yeah. You just told me that my mother was an adulteress and that my Pop forced you to keep it from me. I feel…" She stopped and smirked at herself. *I feel*. Those were words she never used. "Water's supposed to be healing, right? I think a swim in *our* creek is something I need right now."

Aaren maneuvered over him to the base of the tree and swung down, then walked toward the sparkling water. She got nearer to the edge. Her bare feet stepped over stones worn smooth by the rise and fall of the water. Jarrod, left behind, was speechless.

Drawn to the memory of times spent in this water with him and carefully refusing to think about the future, Aaren stepped in. The hem of her dress puffed up with air as she moved further into the creek. She turned and looked at him.

Jarrod watched, disbelieving, as she stood there, boldly removing her wet sundress. Her beauty was still breathtaking to him. Immediately, he wished he hadn't cut away the cover of overgrown trees that lined their creek. Looking back across his land, he didn't see any of the others. It was late in the afternoon, late enough that they should all have gone by now. With little inhibition, she tossed her dress up next to her sandals and dove, almost naked, into the water. Jarrod pulled his shirt over his head, then scrambled hurriedly down the tree. He undressed as he watched her swim against the mild current and then float back toward him. She dipped under the ripples and came back up, dancing in the water like the mermaid she'd always been. Looking at her, it was easy to feel the past falling away behind them. Aaren was right: it was time for a healing. And Jarrod felt he was right, too. It was time for them to have their shot.

He waded through the shallow end of the calm waters, which was still warm from the heat of the spring sun, then swam out after her. As he got close, close enough to touch, she grinned lightning-quick and disappeared under the water, urging him to follow. He caught her and wrapped his arms firmly around her.

They pushed to the surface and let the current carry them the way it did when they were younger. He wiped his hair from his face, smiling for the first time since he'd known she was coming back to Penns Point.

She smiled back defiantly. "Guess what? You're right. It's not our fault, and we paid for their sin. I don't want to pay any more."

"Here's to no more secrets," he said.

"No more secrets," she agreed.

Chapter Nine

THE HEALING

Jarrod carried Aaren's sandals for her on the walk back, listening intently to her as she told him why she chose law. Through it all, through everything she'd endured, she'd still wanted to help people.

She walked at his side with her wet dress clinging to her body. They reached the shade of the house, and the cool evening air made Aaren shiver. Until then, she'd been too focused on Jarrod and the day's events to notice the chill.

Now, stepping over the threshold, Aaren took a first look at the house that Jarrod had built with his own hands. He closed the door, noticing how she now stood very still, her head moving from one side to the other, taking the entire place in. The memory of the way she always talked about living happily ever after was present with them now, in the room.

When she spoke of their dream home, certain things were key. First, there would be large rooms with plenty of windows. She imagined an entrance that would open up to a sunken foyer that panned out beyond the front walls into a large living area to the left and an open, spacious kitchen to the right. The floors would be hardwood, and there would be a stairwell to the upper level in the far left side of the house, toward the back, to give an airy appeal to lower level.

The teenaged Jarrod had teased her mercilessly, saying she was a little young to be giving him architectural advice, but he'd taken in every word.

Her chill forgotten, Aaren quietly observed every feature. Jarrod's living room had a piano and one long leather sectional sofa that wrapped around the stone fireplace. French-paned windows were spaced two feet apart, bordered by wide, carved casings. The walls were painted sage and bordered in a soft lavender trim. The effect was decidedly feminine, and doubly unexpected. They were her favorite colors. It appeared her fairy tale dreams had come true.

Aaren stepped down to the living area, turning around to see windows that cast long rays of natural light through the house.

"You put in the windows?" she asked softly.

"You like them?"

She looked at him with joy in her eyes. "You remembered?"

Jarrod walked in behind her. "I remember every detail of our time together. I heard you even when you thought I wasn't listening. When I was out in that desert, I sketched every room of this place and put it to memory."

She gave him a warm smile. "I don't know what to say. It—it looks just like I envisioned it. I mean, it's as if you pulled it right out of me," she said. Then she laughed. "Look at the stairwell smack in the back corner! You said no house would have it there!"

"Yeah, well it took some work, but I was wrong. It belongs right there."

Aaren remembered the bedroom she'd dreamed of. She turned and looked at him. "You didn't!"

Jarrod folded his arms and looked at her smugly. "Why don't you go see?"

She crossed to the stairs, her steps hesitant, then bolder. At the first step, she cast him an unsure glance, but he nodded for her to continue. He had waited and waited for this day. It was surreal; he never really thought this moment would come. She'd gotten married, she lived thousands of miles away, and she hated him. And that, all of that, had changed. It just didn't seem possible. But it was.

Aaren tried to calm the nervous flutters in her stomach. There was no need for the increasing levels of panic rioting in her chest. Her rational mind realized this. Still, this place unnerved her. Not just its existence, but stepping into these rooms was like being through the looking-glass. It made her question her concept of reality.

Made to order, the bedroom was situated at the back of the house so they could look out at their creek from the deck he'd built. The double maplewood doors that stood closed in front of her looked to be hand-carved. She ran her hands across the planes in awe. She then pushed the doors open, anticipating what lay behind them. Was it as she said it would be? Her hand closed on the cool steel of the handle, then pushed the door open.

She crossed the room holding her breath. The room was open and welcoming, with a bed in the middle, facing heaven. That's what she'd told Jarrod they would call it, because it was to face the most precious part of the Jackson land. Two large, square-paned doors led out to an upper-level deck. She'd wanted shutters, so they wouldn't be disturbed by the sunrise, but she'd teased him wickedly that if they wanted, they could open them and make love with sunlight beaming in through the surrounding windows.

He'd done it. He'd done everything she'd ever asked of him.

The scents of spring washed over her. The landscaping from this view, by his hand, gave a perfect view of the flowing creek where they'd fallen in love. That familiar bitterness of time lost swelled again. She had to force herself to release it.

Jarrod stepped into the room. He found her on the redwood deck. The sky behind her was a deep purple as the sun dipped toward the horizon. She looked exactly as she did in his dreams, all those times he'd laid in bed with the doors open, willing her to come back to him. She was here, within reach. He wanted to touch her, to hold her, and his desires chipped away at the sense of duty that had kept him at bay, away from her, for years. He wanted his Aaren back.

Only one thing stopped him. She'd given no indication she wanted the same.

Jarrod touched her and she didn't move. His hand went smoothly down her arm. He leaned in and kissed her shoulder. She tensed. He withdrew.

"Let me get you a towel. You're soaked."

"No. I can't stay."

"Just a minute longer, till the sun's down. It's um… it gets chilly out here in the evening. One minute."

He stepped quickly into the bathroom. Instead of a towel, he reached for his robe and shook it out, then hustled back to the deck. Aaren remained where he'd left her. He draped the robe carefully over her shoulders.

"Much better," he whispered close to her ear.

"This is… this place, what you've done… Jarrod, it's beautiful," she said, turning her head, returning her eyes to his from over her shoulder.

"Not as beautiful as you," he answered, and it was true.

She glowed in the light of the sinking sun. Again Jarrod had to fight the urge to keep his hands from her. When she turned on him, he actually took a step back to keep from stepping forward.

"Why would you do this?" she asked.

He breathed slowly, staring at her lips, full, two-toned, voluptuous. He licked his own and swallowed.

"This place," she said, forcing his eyes to lift to hers. "I don't understand, Jay. You *planned* for me to come back?"

"I never stopped—" he sucked in a deep breath. "I had to." He looked away.

She wanted to scream at him to let her go. To make it harder so she could go. But she saw it in his eyes. She felt it in the creek. He had no idea what it was doing to her. What *he* was doing to her. Nothing in her life was perfect. She'd just learned that her mother and father weren't. She hadn't shared that she wasn't quite divorced yet. But this house, this place? It was perfect.

"I need to go," she said, trying to step around him.

He blocked her move. "Aaren, listen to me. I know I put you through hell. I lied to you. It'll take time for you to forgive it. You'd be crazy not to question my motives now."

She chuckled bitterly. "Question your motives? That's not even the half! I question my existence, Jay. I can't go there. Not where you want to take it."

"You don't know where I want to take it. You're too busy running from me to let me explain."

She crossed her arms and gave him her best attorney's stance. "Answer me this: how long has this house stood here?"

"Six years."

"Pretty long time before this little reunion, don't you think?"

"What are you asking?"

"The ladies, Jay. You're a handsome man. A *Pennington*. I had to beat them away from you in high school. They must really love this! The view, swims in the creek, the whole rich- country-boy-who-isn't-afraid-to-get-his-hands-dirty act."

She figured he'd be insulted, but he smiled.

"Wrong," he said flatly.

"So what, you're a monk now? Please! Move."

He gripped her arm, staying her retreat. "I've been with women. A few. But I've never brought one of them here. This is our place, whether you knew it existed or not. That bed in there has never…"

Jarrod lost his voice. Aaren looked up at him, disbelieving, her eyes begging him to continue. "I... saved it..."

"For what?"

"For this moment."

Jarrod released his grip on her arm but moved closer to her.

She backed up. He captured her hand and held it tight. He used his other to touch the front of the robe. "Let me in, Aaren."

"Oh, Jay, don't ask that. I can't—"

"You can," he said, grabbing the collar of the robe and pulling her to him. Their faces close, his breathing matched the rhythm of hers. "You can." He slid one sleeve down, off her shoulder. Aaren shivered in the wet dress. But his touch warmed her, made her want to draw in closer. She stared deep into his eyes, and knew his desire mirrored her own.

Aaren closed her eyes and put both hands up between them. "You're not listening to me. This can't happen. It just can't."

Jarrod stared at her, his eyes conveying his only wish. One look at his face and Aaren felt her will dissolve. Back then he'd been a teenager, all barely-controlled need, but now he observed her with slow-burning want. Desire like she'd never seen turned her to stammering.

"I just don't know what we're doing here, especially now. What happens next? Jay, be serious, you act like this would just erase the last fourteen years!"

Jarrod closed in so her hands dropped to his waist. "This doesn't change any of that."

"I'm serious. What about my mom and your dad? I don't think either of us can ignore that. And then, on top of that, I don't know if I can go back there with you."

"Her... situation, and their lies, is not what's important. Forget about what our parents did. Forget about back there, back then. This is just me and you, Aaren." He touched her chest just to feel the beat of her heart. "You, and me. Tell me what you want, what you truly want."

She sucked in her quivering bottom lip and exhaled a pained sigh, fighting the impulse to run. Aaren closed her eyes and tuned in to her surroundings. The light evening breeze stirred up the scent of pine, dried leaves, grass, the far-off smells of the cow pastures were faintly covered by the new blooms and below her she could hear the low drone of the generator that ran electricity out to the stables. She picked up Jarrod's breathing. His face was so close her cheeks were warmed by it. She felt the pounding of her heart as every part of her took on the unseen current of feelings she'd thought were long ago destroyed.

"Aaren? Talk to me. What do you want?"

If she ran now, she'd be running from the only thing she'd ever dreamed about having. Finally, she opened her eyes.

"I want to just be her again."

"Be who?"

"Be her. Be that girl, be who I was when I was with you."

"I can help you with that."

He scooped her up in his arms, pressing her into his chest, holding her close. Her body stiffened and she pushed back out of reflex, wanting to evade his touch. Then his lips brushed her cheek, then lower. The instant jolt of heat and lust was to be expected, but the tenderness she found in his arms was not. Aaren closed her eyes and tried to summon the will to leave.

Jarrod understood her struggle. He welcomed it. He'd learned that the things you wanted most were the things you fought the hardest for. That was what he'd show her, teach her, and prove to her to win her back. He folded her into his arms and kissed her face, starting with her eyes, nose, the dimple between her furrowed brows, and ending with her lips. And she responded. To his relief, she lifted her arms and circled his neck, molding herself to him.

The scent of her was subtle, cool, and alluring. It bloomed in his nostrils, mixing with the warm, wet smell of feminine skin. Jarrod took another hit, running his nose over her cheek once more. This was a part of her he hadn't even known he'd missed.

The kiss he longed for was the beginning; his tongue sought hers, tunneling deep, then stroking her lips and drawing her essence into him. She tasted exactly the way he remembered. Past and present began to melt against the swirl of their kiss.

Together, their awkward steps led them off the deck into the room. The robe was the first to go. He peeled it from her shoulders, over her arms, letting it drop to the floor as they went. He fumbled with the zipper at the side of her dress. He was so nervous his fingers kept losing their grip on the tiny tab.

Their feet stopped when they neared the canopy. Jarrod managed to ease the zipper open, allowing the dress to fall away. With effort, he pulled back. Aaren thumped down to the bed in her bra and panties, her eyes never leaving his. He couldn't move. He couldn't speak. He stood before her, struggling for the words.

"You... afraid?" she asked, breaking the silent stand-off.

Jarrod wiped his hand down his face. She had no idea what her rejection would do to him at this point.

"Yes."

"Of?"

"Us. You."

"Of me? Why?"

"I think if I touch you, you'll disappear."

Aaren reached for his hand and brought it to her breast. She gave him a small smile.

"Still here."

He nodded, lowering himself to the mattress as she scooted back over the quilt. Jarrod's eyes roamed over a body he'd seen only in his dreams. Here was the woman he thought he'd never know.

"Aaren—" He started to speak, to explain, but the rest of the words failed to come.

She reached and touched his face. Her eyes, wide and aware, locked with his. He needed her to go first. She understood.

"I'm sorry my Pop hurt you back then."

"If you are, then don't ever apologize for it again," he said, turning his face into her palm and kissing the inside deeply. "I don't need your apologies. I just want you." His eyes dropped to her lying beneath him. "All of you."

Aaren smiled. "I can help you with that."

"You'll stay?"

She looked away, then directly into his eyes. "Better. You trust me and I'll trust you."

Her message was clear. That was all he was going to get for now. Jarrod nodded solemnly. It was enough. He lowered his face to Aaren's neck and tasted her. She closed her eyes slowly as her fears melted away under his now ever-so-soft kisses. His lips explored the curve under her chin, while his hands traveled over her lower body, retracing each curve burned into his memory.

Aaren tried to relax as he lowered himself on her. He drew her further beneath him, the stare they shared never breaking. Her legs parted until the heel of her left foot rested on his lower back. Blazing heat pumped through her veins, shocking her down to the soles of her feet. His tongue flicked, licked, sucked her nipple to erectness. Her body remembered, and her heart remembered, too.

The years had passed, but somehow, he still loved her with the passion of their youth, unchanged. And then it occurred to her, as he rained kisses over her belly, that her unfeeling existence hadn't been a choice she'd made. Real love was something she'd been *denied* for the past fourteen years. Tears of painful regret bled silently from the corners of her eyes. Feeling him now just showed her what she'd needed all along.

Jarrod slid down her body. Aaren couldn't help but tense. She hadn't made love to anyone in over a year. She and Gavin had stopped long before she'd left him. Aaren wondered if Jarrod saw, if he could sense, how changed she was. His kisses slowed, then stopped altogether.

Aaren opened her eyes to see him studying her through the hair tousled in his face. His cheeks were flushed, and from the deliberate movements of his shoulders, she knew he was covering himself.

He can tell about me, she thought, awash with shame. She let her eyes drift away to focus on the ripples in the sheer curtains.

Jarrod pulled her underneath him, taking one leg up against his chest and hooking the other around his waist.

"Aaren."

His deep voice brought her back. He wanted to see her face, watch her watching him. He'd always delayed, held that moment of entry until she was looking directly into his eyes. What she saw there now was still enough to send her over the edge, just the way it had been back then.

Aaren lifted her hips to receive him; she gasped as he obliged. A powerful thrust had him deep within. She held him tight and worked her hips desperately for more. Her body, shocked into remembrance of his girth, welcomed the invasion. Soon they found a shared rhythm that had them rocking the bed on its posts.

Jarrod's loving was slow and methodical, every stroke in harmony with her own. Aaren clung to him for fear of him letting go, of it ending too soon, desperate to be one with him. She grasped his hair and returned his passion, matching the depth of his thrusts. She felt him everywhere, felt him radiate through her. And she could hear him, too. His excitement had him forgetting how to breathe. He spoke in short, barely coherent sentences: how she felt and how he needed her. She shook with satisfaction as the only thing she'd ever longed for was returned to her.

Jarrod snaked his hand between them to her chin, making sure she met his gaze. She wasn't nearly ready for what she saw in his eyes, much less what she felt as he touched her. Aaren could barely get her head around the fact that she was with Jarrod Pennington, again, a lifetime later.

"So good," he moaned, drawing a deep breath.

He began to move feverishly, his hands everywhere, as he pulled her tight against him. Aaren, feeling the rush of pleasure, wanted to escape him. She was too close. She needed a break, but he was having none of that, and it was making her crazy. When she felt him pull out, which he did at times to prevent a climax, she used the opportunity to shift out from under him. He looked at her tensely as she sat up, panting.

"My turn," she said with a voice hoarse from the passionate cries he'd stolen. She pushed him to the mattress and straddled him.

Aaren gave a wicked smile, running the tip of her tongue over the bow of her lip while moving over him. His eyelids drooped as she became filled with him once more. She ran her hands over his tanned, tattooed muscles and immediately felt a rush she could not conceal. Sliding down on him, she focused on the blue heat under heavy lids. The intensity of his love for her was evident, even as his eyes rolled into his head from her maneuvers.

Jarrod put both hands to her hips. "I can't stop touching you. Damn baby, I can't let you go."

She smiled, satisfied—more than satisfied. It had never been this way with anyone else but him. Aaren quickened her pace. He groaned loudly when she tightened herself around him, squeezing him through her thrusts.

Jarrod held tight to her hips, trying to slow the motion of her rocking. She settled momentarily, just until she saw him relax, then rose and fell, bouncing on him with relentless intensity. Jarrod's eyes flipped open, then glazed over. He squeezed her waist and grunted through a mounting release.

"Wait… baby… not now," he pleaded.

"Now," she whispered, letting her head fall back.

She drove them both to the pinnacle, listening with delight as he groaned loudly through his orgasm.

"Oh, God… yes, God…." he panted, well afterward, as he reached up to hold her tight in his lap. She felt him shaking, his heart beating so fast against her breast. Aaren thought it might explode in his chest.

She knew the desperation he felt. It meant they both remained a little fearful. It made their experience more real, since everything now was like a dream.

He fell backwards as everything spiraled down to a puddle of sensation and pleasure. Aaren lifted herself from him. It had to be 65 degrees inside the room with the night air blowing through, but they both lay drenched in sweat. Jarrod, unable to speak, just focused on steadying his breath.

Aaren leaned on her elbow, watching him. She ran the long tip of her fingernail across his chest.

"What's with all the tattoos?" she asked, tracing one of them in the dim light.

He opened his eyes and looked at her. "Why? Don't like them?"

"'Course not. I'm just not used to them."

She loved everything about his body: the truth was she couldn't get enough of him. Already she wanted more. But she held on to that confession. This man had wielded too much power over her heart, once. Love or no, she wouldn't allow that much control now.

"What do they mean?"

He touched her hair, now almost dry, but tangled and wild like a lion's mane.

"I got the first one two months after I enlisted."

She examined the colors. She'd missed it during their swim, and she'd been focused on other things during their lovemaking. It was a crown with a heart coming out of the top. A ribbon ran across it and she saw lettering. She leaned into his chest. Her eyes popped with recognition.

It was her name.

"You…" she gasped, not able to comprehend what she saw. "Why??"

"I missed you so… and I wanted you with me. So I had your name put in as the queen of my heart."

Her eyes brimmed with tears. She ran her hand across the ink, amazed. She'd thought all this time she wasn't loved and here he was, loving her more and more from thousands of miles away. Looking back to him, she saw how deep his hurt was, but also how Jarrod had protected their love from the moment they'd been discovered in that stable. No one and no thing had ever made him abandon her, not in his heart.

She wished she could say the same.

Jarrod descended the stairs slowly. He'd planned to rise first and make her breakfast, but he'd overslept by more than an hour, which never, ever happened. He'd been almost frantic to wake up in their big bed alone. Then he'd heard movement downstairs, and realized she hadn't left him. So he leapt out of bed, brushed his teeth and splashed water on his face, then grabbed a pair of jeans and made his way to the kitchen, not quite believing.

Aaren was twenty feet away, wearing one of his tee shirts. The hem barely covered the curves of her shapely hips. She was singing along with the radio he kept in the greenhouse window installed over the sink. He tried to breathe quietly as he moved closer, so he could keep watching her.

He didn't want to break the spell.

"You can't sneak up on me, Jarrod Pennington."

"Never could," he chuckled. "You got eyes in the back of your head."

"You know it." She waved him toward the kitchen table, which was already set. She poured steaming coffee into his mug. "You still like eggs?"

"Yeah, but those are yesterday's. Let me get you some fresh from the—"

"Sit."

"Yes, ma'am."

Aaren moved through the kitchen with a familiarity borne of routine. She was seven when her Pops taught her how to make them breakfast: that had been her job because by the time the whistle from the mill woke her up, Pops had already been at work two hours. The toaster popped up and she coaxed the eggs out of the pan, over easy just like Jarrod liked them, arranged the home-fried potatoes she'd made opposite the eggs, then sliced the toast into triangles, tapped them on the cutting board to knock away the extra crumbs, and fanned the points just so around the edge of the plate. She hadn't made breakfast for herself or anyone else in fourteen years, and she grinned because she hadn't lost her touch. She wiped her fingertips on a towel and set the meal in front of him. Jarrod looked up at her, amazed.

"Close your mouth, Jarrod Pennington."

He did, and picked up his fork.

"Wait, wait—" She raced to the fridge and pulled out the ketchup and the Tabasco. "I didn't forget."

She put them on the table and crossed her arms.

"You didn't forget," he grinned.

"Well, go ahead. Mess up my beautiful eggs." She shook her head, laughing.

He laughed too, and poured a big plop of ketchup over the yolks, then dashed Tabasco over the top, before looking up at her again.

"Disgusting," she smiled.

"I can't help it."

"I know. It's the way Miz Leonora always made 'em for you." Her face tightened for a moment. "Is she, uh… still with us?"

Jarrod pressed his lips together. "No. She passed in '97. Her son's over in Louisville though. Dwayne? Assistant coaching the Cardinals. Basketball."

Aaren nodded, then turned to make a slice of toast for herself. She sipped from her mug of coffee. Her eyes remained on him as he ate. Last night and this morning didn't feel like a one-night thing: she should know. But she had no idea what came next.

The telephone rang, extra loud, from its perch on the wall. Aaren jumped. It was one of the things she'd forgotten about farm life. The ringer was turned all the way up so you could hear it even if you were outside. Jarrod made no move to answer.

"Aren't you going to get that?" she asked over the top of her coffee.

He looked straight into her eyes.

"Everyone I want to talk to is right here."

Aaren bit her lip, pleased with his answer. Then she put down her coffee and reached across him for the phone.

"Pennington Farms," she cooed sweetly.

Jarrod dropped his fork and watched her, shocked. She raised her eyebrows and touched his hair. It made her girlishly happy that he'd kept it long.

"Well this is Aaren Robinson. And who am I talking to?"

Aaren smiled with a devilish wink for Jarrod.

"Oh, hi, Carrie!"

No one had to tell her what this call was about: even through her grief, she'd seen how Carrie Benson had watched Jarrod yesterday. She knew right away they'd been together, probably even recently. Now she wondered how it had made her feel to touch this gorgeous man, knowing all along whose name was tattooed on his chest. She made her voice extra cheerful.

"How are you this morning? Oh, I'm doing fine. As well as can be expected, I guess. We had a very long night last night."

She met Jarrod's eyes and raised her eyebrows to him again, this time a question. He looked like he wanted to bolt out the door. Aaren stifled a laugh. She was probably laying it on a little thick.

"Uh huh. So, Carrie, what can we do for you?" Aaren nodded. "Well, I'm happy to leave him a message."

Aaren went back to the counter, trailing the long yellow cord of the phone behind her. Jarrod's eyes never left her; he stared at her wide-eyed as she returned with the coffee pot.

"Gosh, Carrie, I'm not really sure. He slept in this morning, and then he said something about getting me fresh eggs for breakfast, and after that I lost track of him. But one thing I know about my Jay—he'll be back."

She freshened up Jarrod's coffee, then reached over to rest the pot on the wooden trivet in the center of the table.

"What kind of question is that? Of course I'm in the house. You called the number, I answered the phone…"

It was Jarrod's turn to bite his lip. He could guess what this part of the conversation was about. He'd never once brought Carrie into his home. The front porch was the closest she'd ever come. Aaren's face registered surprise, and when she spoke, she spoke honestly.

"Really? Never? Well, that doesn't sound like the Jarrod I know at all. What can I say? I suppose he had his reasons."

Aaren's eyes flashed with hostility for a split second. Then she straddled Jarrod's lap, snaking her free arm around his neck so their noses were almost touching. Her eyes locked with his as she ran her finger up and down his spine and curled her full lips into an evil smile.

"Oh, you know I absolutely plan to do that, Carrie Benson. Bye now."

She reached over him to hang up the phone, enjoying that she had to push her breasts right into his face to do it. Then she rearranged herself over him; his hands went automatically to her hips and she felt him stir, rising, beneath her. Aaren gazed at him solemnly, breathing through her nose and daring him to look away first.

"What did she say?"

"She told me to enjoy you while you last." Aaren clasped her hands at the back of his neck and brushed her lips over his. "How long can you last, Jarrod Pennington?"

Chapter Ten

IN LOVE AGAIN

It was bliss.

There was no other way for her to explain it. She stared up at the crown molding in the ceiling, her eyes roving over the curves and corners. The toilet flushed and the tap turned over. She could hear him going through his routine. The soft swish of his toothbrush, then the low gargle as he spit out the minty suds. The clippers working to smooth off the growing beard he got from spending the past two days locked away with her. She listened to the sounds, seeing without seeing. Knowing him.

"Should we ride today? After I'm done in the fields. When was the last time you were on a horse?" he called out to her.

"Sounds nice. It's been awhile."

"Good. Let's do it."

Aaren drew the sheet up over her nudity. Her body ached in places she wouldn't name. The bed smelled of him, her, sex… and love. She closed her eyes, remembering a time when doubt and bitterness didn't rule her emotions. She focused on channeling that girl he believed had returned. She had to, to keep from ruining it.

"Hey, you going to stay in bed all day?" He looked her over wishfully, as if he might join her.

"Think I'll clean up some, since I am a guest. Don't want to take advantage of your hospitality."

He gave a deep chuckle from the back of his throat. His eyes became clear as crystals. He walked over with that boyish smile, his hair wet from the shower, his chest bare, and smelling of soap and sunblock.

"Past couple of days, Aaren," He took a seat at the very edge of the bed. "It's been nice."

"Nice." She nodded.

He looked like he wanted to say more. Same old Jay. Words were never his strong suit. She watched him, saying nothing, until his eyes flipped away.

"I'm thinking that maybe…"

Aaren turned to her side and stretched to run her hand down his back. "No, Jay. You said no pressure."

"Right. I meant it, too."

"Let's not overthink it."

"Right."

"Take our time, get to know each other."

"Right. Right. I was thinking that we needed time. More time."

"Jay…"

He turned and what she saw in his eyes filled her with hope. Aaren sat upright, allowing the sheet to drift to her lap. She reached for him and he turned into her arms.

"I really did miss this. You."

"Me too, Aaren, me too," he said, seeking her mouth. His kiss brought in the mint freshness of his breath. She actually licked the remnants of toothpaste from his bottom lip. Slowly she eased back, bringing him with.

"Aaren, I wasn't right. Wasn't right at all until you came home. I don't know if I can be if you leave. I don't know."

Her hand went to his cheek, capturing the curve of it and stroking softly to hush him.

"Shhh."

He nodded, accepting her kiss again as reassurance. He finally broke away, only because the farm called.

"I'll be back for lunch. Then we ride, okay?"

She nodded. He walked over, plucked his shirt from the dresser, then cast her a parting wink before leaving. Aaren exhaled as he did, hugging herself as the door clicked shut. Alone again with her thoughts, she considered her situation. Truths he knew and truths he didn't. He was right. The clock was ticking and soon they'd have to label their reunion. Define it. Part of her hoped for that moment. Part of her dreaded it. She closed her eyes, saving that analysis for another day.

"Working hard?" Aaren asked, walking around the wide-open gate of the barn.

Jarrod turned. He dropped the heavy sack of feed. Again shirtless, muscles tight, his skin was blessed by the sun to a golden tan. He wiped the back of his head with his hand and grinned.

"I was just about to come up for lunch."

"Too late, brought it." She revealed a picnic basket. "I'm getting quite handy in your kitchen. Not going to ask why you have a basket and such, being that you never really entertain here." She eyed him.

Hands to his waist, Jarrod shook his head and caught his breath.

"Never said I didn't entertain. Said I never entertained in our house."

"Our house, huh?"

"That's right. Ours." He smiled.

She liked the sound of that but refrained from saying so, choosing to say only what she knew was safe. It was a habit she was mastering with him. He hadn't yet caught on to her evasive maneuvers. At least, she thought he hadn't.

"Blanket?"

"Let's take it up top," he said, pointing upward. "Smells less like a barn when you open the window. Besides, you don't want to eat on the land right now. Sun's a bitch and the noonday gnats will fly away with our food."

"Good point," agreed Aaren, laughing as she went to the ladder. She looked back once more to see him washing his hands as best he could from the running hose. She hooked the basket on her arm and climbed, thinking the entire time of the day they'd stolen away to her father's stables, and how the events that afternoon had tarnished her life.

Aaren let the memory go. She accepted the part of it she could stand and released the rest. That was something else she was learning to do. She'd been learning a lot. Jarrod bounded up as she cleared away some bits of straw with her foot. Jarrod spread out a thin blanket and she dropped to her knees. Suddenly, she was famished. She pulled out the plastic containers as he opened up the windows, ushering in the fresh spring breeze. He was right. She could smell the sun, the cornfields, even the mist-blue scent of Salt River that flowed through the town.

"What-cha make?" He dropped down beside her and grabbed a container. Aaren popped his hand.

"Slow down. I will do it."

"Aaren Robinson, you were never big on fixing my plate."

"I was a little girl then. I'm a woman now, in case you haven't noticed. I know how to treat a—my man." She peeked over at him, not believing she'd just said those words.

"Oh, I've noticed," he grinned, clearly liking the idea of being her man.

She shook her head, dishing him up some of the macaroni salad she'd made, and a sandwich. She gave him the plate, then fixed her own. They settled into the meal, into their new routine of talking over each other and laughing at nothing, of being together again, and never, ever talking about their past.

When lunch was over, she rested between his legs and drank from her water bottle. She stared out the open window.

"Do you think if our parents hadn't done what they did, we would have made it, Jay?"

"I do."

"Odds are against first loves, you know?"

"Says the people that never known our kind of love."

"We were good once."

"We're good now, Aaren. You feel that, don't you, baby?"

"Yeah, I do. But we're different."

"Different isn't necessarily a bad thing."

"Right. I know."

Her voice trailed off. She wanted to say more but didn't know where to begin. So again she withdrew, keeping her secrets. His arms folded around her and she relaxed. He kissed the top of her head.

"Happy?" he asked.

"Yeah," she replied quietly. "I am."

Jarrod opened the iron gate to the pen inside his barn, blocking the early-morning sun with his arm. He needed to guide his livestock out the back into the field. He was so caught up in his thoughts of Aaren that he didn't hear someone come in behind him. The cows moved lazily out into the pasture and Jarrod thumped the stragglers on their backsides to quicken their pace. Letting the last one out, he turned and closed the gate to see Wesley standing behind him, staring.

"Something wrong?" Jarrod wondered why Wesley was in the barn and not at the stables with Gene and the others.

"Could be," replied Wesley, coolly.

Jarrod's eyes narrowed into blue slits, focusing on the nervous, freckle-faced kid. Barely twenty, Wesley stood before him, jittery and ready to flee. He stuck his hands nervously in his pockets. Jarrod latched the gate, then went to the double barn doors and pulled them shut one by one, so the cows couldn't return inside.

Wesley wiped his forehead with the back of his hand, struggling to hold on to his courage. Jarrod was a pretty cool boss and peaceful dude, but if pushed he'd fight like any of them would. He'd seen it happen: he remembered how Stan, who was on meth, came to work strung out one day, and when questioned about it, pulled a knife on Jarrod in the stables. Wesley had watched as whatever Army training Jarrod had kicked into gear. He'd delivered a swift uppercut to Stan's jaw with the point of his bended elbow. The bigger man had been knocked out cold within seconds. Now, Wesley was to make his move and he had to be very careful how he played it.

"Can we talk?"

Jarrod wiped his hands against his jeans and walked over. It was obvious the kid was after something, but Jarrod didn't know exactly what.

"Sure, what's on your mind?"

"Went to the funeral," said Wesley, leaning against the slats.

Jarrod nodded. "Yeah, thanks. Saw you at the burial."

"Uh huh. Well, I heard you."

"Heard me?"

"You and your folks."

Jarrod stared at him. "So what?"

"Everything been whispered 'round this town, for years—it's true. Heard the Judge say so."

Jarrod stood mute. He put his hands in his pockets and stared down the other man, his nostrils flaring. Wesley swallowed. He clearly had his boss' full attention. He decided there was no going back. Pushing from the gate, he stepped toward Jarrod.

"You know Samuel is my uncle. Yeah. Um, after hearing what-all the Judge said graveside, I done a little digging on my own. Come to find out, you and that Aaren girl got some land."

Jarrod itched to flatten him for the nonchalant way he referred to Aaren, but he held in as best he could. He took a measured step toward Wesley. Wesley took a step to the side.

"What does any of that have to do with you, boy?"

Wesley ground his teeth at the dig. He sucked in a deep breath and poked out his chest.

"I was thinking you could convince her to give me that land. At a reasonable price, a course." He spoke with caution, aware that Jarrod was now directly in his face, his eyes darkening and beginning to ignite with rage.

Jarrod let go a soft, amused laugh. "Were you, now?"

"Yeah. 'Cause if you do, I won't be forced to tell her how your folks and this town killed her mama."

Jarrod swung, connecting his blow to Wesley's lower jaw, so swiftly it knocked him to the ground. Rage like he hadn't felt in years caused him to drop on the young man. Wesley spit up blood as Jarrod's hands went around his throat.

"Hey, man! You're fucking crazy!! Get the fuck off me!!" Wesley threw his hands up to ward off the incoming blows, his lips crimson with his own blood.

Jarrod stayed the punch but spoke through clenched teeth. "What do you mean my folks killed her mother? What the hell are you talking about?"

"I cain't breathe!! Can't. Breathe!!"

Wesley kicked underneath him. Jarrod tightened his hold on his neck, tempted to snap it.

"Answer me."

Wesley, turning blue, clawed at the backs of Jarrod's hands.

"ANSWER ME!!" Jarrod saw the young man's eyes roll back into his head and released him.

Wesley coughed, grabbing his throat. Jarrod kept him pinned to the ground, struggling against the urge to beat him senseless. He'd taken care of Wesley since he was 16 years old, old enough and foolish enough to quit school. He'd paid good wages and treated the kid like family. To be hustled in return angered him deeply.

Wesley looked up, his face flushed and streaked with tears. "You're crazy!"

"Answer me right now, or I'll snap your neck and make it look like Dynamo did it." Jarrod cocked his head to the horse in the adjacent ring, then glared down at Wesley.

"Get off me!" Wesley pleaded, flailing for an escape. His plan had backfired. He just wanted to get out from under Jarrod's wrath. Jarrod rose and dragged Wesley to his feet. Wesley stumbled back, spitting out blood.

"I think my tooth is loose," he whined.

"NOW!"

"I don't know the details, man! All I know is there was a meeting at my mom's house the other day, after the reading of the will."

Jarrod blinked at the news. His brows connected and his eyes hardened. "Who was at this meeting?"

Wesley shook his head. "What about the land? Man, y'all don't need two farms!"

"Damn it, Wesley. Stop stalling and talk!" Jarrod grabbed him by the shoulders and pushed him toward the wall.

"Okay, okay! It was Miz Marie, Reverend Morris, Uncle Samuel, your father—"

Jarrod let go of him and stepped back. "And what happened?"

"They were scared. My uncle said he told you not to talk about Miz Robinson, but he thought you planned to. He said they needed to find a way to keep you from the truth. I mean, Miz Marie was crying through the whole thing and your dad was, like, pacing around. I couldn't hear the rest because my mom busted me. But what I did hear said a lot."

"Which is?"

"Your dad, man. He said Noelle Robinson's death was his fault and he would stand alone in taking the blame. He wouldn't drag anyone else into it. And he weren't gonna let no one drag anyone else into it, neither."

Jarrod sighed. "Shit."

Aaren loaded the dishwasher as Becca wiped down the counters, then helped put up the food. They'd come over to a mini-feast of pot roast, macaroni and cheese, turnip greens, and homemade biscuits. Aaren took great pleasure in cooking for her friends, and for that man she'd never stopped loving.

"So you two seem to be back on track," smiled Becca.

Aaren beamed as she closed the dishwasher and turned the dial, sending it into its eternal spin.

"Better than okay. These past few days. Girl, I can't explain it,"

"Tony said that you were staying. Is that true?"

"That's Jarrod talking." Aaren shook her head.

"Is it true?" Becca pressed.

"For now," Aaren evaded.

Becca went to hug her. "Finally, there is peace in the valley!"

Aaren laughed. "Not exactly. We do have some problems."

She let go of her. "I noticed something between you guys, but I couldn't put my finger on it."

"Sit down."

Aaren pointed at the kitchen chairs and took a seat as well. She clasped her hands tight in front of her, not knowing how to talk about everything she'd found out. But she needed to unload. Becca looked at her and recognized the old pain. Her friend reached across the table to touch her hand.

"It's okay, sweetie. You can tell me."

It was true. If there was anyone she could talk to, it was Becca. "It's my mom, Becca. I've learned some things that have me torn up. Confused."

"Things?"

"Apparently her marriage to Pop wasn't a happy one."

"Okay."

"She had an affair."

Becca sat up and looked at her, shocked. "Who told you that?"

Aaren lifted her face to the ceiling to keep the tears from rolling down her cheeks.

"Jarrod," she said sadly.

Jarrod sat on the front porch drinking a beer with Antonio. They talked about the latest goings on at the plant and some of the local politics with the last auction of horses. But all of that was a cover. Jarrod dropped his head under the weight of his thoughts. More secrets were coming at them and he was powerless to prevent it.

"You got her back. I had to admit I thought you were crazy when you built this shrine and held onto her the way you did. But damn! You made a believer out of me," Antonio chuckled, gesturing with his bottle.

Jarrod drank his beer, hearing his friend and not hearing. He knew he could share his torment; Antonio had listened to him many times over the years. But there was so much to cover. At this point, he didn't know how to start. It wasn't just Wesley Bellingham and his threats. His own father's overheard admissions bothered him more.

Jarrod had run from his family. He'd chosen that route, considering it to be just punishment for what he and his father had done. He'd hurt his mother, his brother and sister, all because he couldn't live a lie. All this time, he'd thought the lies were behind him, but now based on what Wesley reported, Jarrod didn't know how far the lies of the Penningtons and Robinsons reached.

It was crazy to him: he'd finally reached the woman he loved and convinced her to be with him, but he would still have to fight for her.

"You there, man?" Antonio's voice cut through his thoughts.

He nodded. "I love her even more, if that's possible."

"I don't think that's possible."

Jarrod looked over at him. "What do you know about her mother?"

"Mrs. Robinson?"

"Yeah. What have you heard?"

Antonio shrugged. "This town's full of wagging tongues. I never pay it no mind."

"Ever hear how she died?"

Antonio tilted his head to the side and thought about it. "Actually, no. I never heard how she died. Not a real story, just talk. You heard the crazies saying that she jumped from Old Rachette Bridge, that she ran off with some man who killed her. All that jazz."

Jarrod nodded. "Don't you find that strange? I mean we know everything about everyone in this town but no one ever talks about Noelle Robinson."

"Well, you know where to go for answers on anyone in this town."

Jarrod grimaced. "Miz Marie."

Antonio chuckled. "That woman is a walking, talking encyclopedia of gossip. If anyone knows about Noelle Robinson in detail, it's her."

Jarrod drank more of his beer, hoping it would help displace some of the panic he was feeling.

"You got a point, Tony. Miz Marie is definitely the place to start."

"Jeez," said Becca, putting her hand to her mouth.

Aaren swiped at her tears, a reflex action now. "It's all true, and I can't get my head around any of it."

"Wait. Jarrod carried this burden all these years? I mean I knew he held a secret, but not this."

"Pop destroyed his life in retaliation. He wanted revenge against the Judge, for… for destroying my mom."

"Damn, you two were innocent. How could Abraham do that?"

"Jarrod says it doesn't stop there."

"What does that mean?"

"It means he thinks something bad happened to my mother. We haven't discussed it further, but I can tell you neither of us can stop thinking about it."

"What on earth makes him think that?"

"A conversation he had with Sam Spence, the day of the will."

Becca sat back, suddenly remembering the inexplicable actions of her own mother. She remembered how her mom's voice would drop to a whisper during conversations about Aaren's mom. She always thought it was because she and Aaren were playmates.

"Something *bad*? Like what?" Then Becca waved the question away. "If something happened, we'd know! This town can barely hold the water that runs through it."

"You're probably right."

"No wonder you were acting strange at dinner. This has to be killing you."

Aaren ran her fingers through her hair, pushing the few stray strands back over her shoulder. "Actually, that's not what's got me wound so tight."

"Okay, then what does?"

"I haven't told Jarrod everything about me. About my life in New York, and what happened to me after I left."

"Why not, Aaren?"

"I don't know. I don't want to screw things up, and…" her voice trailed off. "And it's not good. If I don't explain it right, or if he doesn't take it well…. well, that could be it."

"It?"

"Bec, I'm afraid it could destroy us."

Becca frowned, then leaned over and grabbed Aaren's hand again. "There is nothing that can destroy the bond you two share. You two are soulmates, just like me and Tony. You know this."

"You don't understand."

"I understand that secrets are what kept you apart. If you have any intention of having the life you wanted with him, you both need to let go of all those damn secrets. Starting with the ones you're keeping."

Aaren smiled, glad to have Becca as a friend.

"How did you become so wise?"

"Comes natural," she grinned.

Aaren lay back amongst her pillows, facing the night. They'd left the doors to the deck open so the breeze could blow through and cool off their bedroom. The moon was her spotlight. Its rays cast a bluish white glow that illuminated their bed.

In the country, there were so many stars at night. She could see millions. They twinkled like diamonds on top of a velvet cloth. She found such serenity lying there, and wondered to herself if it was their beauty, or Jarrod's. Her head dropped over to see him sleeping next to her, his hair partly in his face. He was so handsome, so caring, and genuine in his love for her. She believed that now. And if she believed it, she couldn't carry the burdens of her past alone. He deserved the truth.

Scooting nearer under the covers, she brushed the stray strands from his face and kissed his lips softly. Instinctively, he reached for her, pulling her close. He refused to let her sleep in one of his tee shirts, much less one of the nightgowns she'd brought over. He wanted her beauty open to him, and through the night when he stirred she could feel his hands touching her everywhere.

"I need to talk to you," she said against his lips, mid-kiss. He ignored her request and deepened the kiss. She felt his hands roaming, pulling her into him. She lifted her leg, rubbing her inner thigh across his hip. Already erect, the tip of him brushed between her legs. She moaned through their kiss, wanting to have him again, but first she needed to tell him. Before she could say more, he rolled her to her back and his kisses went to her neck. The moment her eyes closed, he reached for the drawer in the nightstand.

"Jarrod, let's talk, first," she whispered, trying to do the right thing as his body began to dominate hers.

"No, Aaren, I need to feel you," he said, his voice hoarse from sleep.

Pushing his way into her, he let go a deep sigh. His body craved her. He lifted up on his hands to stare down into her face as he thrust deeply and then pulled out with long, slow strokes. Her eyes remained closed, but she moved with him in perfect harmony. The moon gave her brown skin a satin glow, causing him to smile at her beauty and quicken his thrusts. She moaned louder. He couldn't resist tasting her again. Not when she was like this, supple and ready. Running his tongue across her lips, she parted them and he kissed her, teasing her, trying to please her.

"Look at me." He whispered into her ear and she looked up at him. He wanted to see his love reflected in her deep brown eyes. It made him feel whole in ways he didn't think were possible, twice in a lifetime.

Aaren rotated her hips, matching his rhythm, and her mind flashed to the night he proposed. It was the one hopeful moment of that summer, after her father discovered them, before Jarrod broke her heart at the fair, before everything changed for them. Looking away, she forced the memory away from her head and gave into their passion. She would concentrate on that instead.

Chapter Eleven

END OF LIES

Today would be their first day back to reality. Aaren tried to prepare herself for a full dose of it: in a few minutes, they'd drive into town. They were going to find out the mysteries of her mom's life and they were going to do it together.

She chose a backless yellow sundress, a little number she'd bought on her last vacation in Paris, and over it, her favorite Armani jacket. Maybe it was flashy, but it felt right: she might be back in Penns Point, but much about her had changed. She intended to make that clear.

Looking at herself in the mirror, she saw her mother, and wondered again about her life. She had so few memories of her Mama.

Actually she had only one: biscuits.

Every morning, her Pop would come and wake her with tickles and kisses. He would carry her from the bed like an airplane. He'd sail her through the air then down the stairs to her mom's biscuits. Thick and buttery with golden brown tops, mama would cut them in squares and serve them up with cane syrup or jelly.

They'd sit, her mother and father with Aaren in between. Her parents would wait for her to say if the biscuits were good or not, before anyone could eat. That was their breakfast ritual, the way they all started their day. It was her strongest memory of her mother's love.

She smiled, dipping into the wish bucket she carried as a girl for a mother of her own. Someone to braid her hair, or tell her what to do when her first cycle came on at the age of thirteen. Aaren had been riding her favorite horse, and though she knew what it was, she'd still been scared. She'd needed someone to make her hot tea, like Becca's mom did for her daughter when she suffered cramps. She'd needed someone to talk her through that first unrequited crush. She'd needed someone when Jarrod—

Aaren closed her eyes, grimacing. It hurt still. Maybe it would hurt always. She'd been robbed of her mother and if this town had done something to facilitate that, she would make them pay.

"You look beautiful."

Looking back up to the mirror, she saw Jarrod standing behind her. His jeans, worn and faded, were pulled on over pointed boots. He worked at the buttons of his shirt.

"Let me get ready. Ten minutes, okay?" He headed to the bathroom.

She continued staring after him as he walked into the next room. He'd been so sweet with her last night, but she knew there was pain as well. Things changed so fast with them. Always did. Years of friendship as kids and then, bam, they were an item. Sex, love, pain, heartache, separation, loneliness, all of it had brought them here, to this moment. And they still weren't home free. The past would continue to come between them until they confronted it, head-on.

The ringing of her cell phone drew her from her thoughts. It was the call she'd been dreading. *Who else?* she sighed. Aaren opened the flip phone and headed out of the bedroom.

"Hello."

"Hey, are you back?"

"Gavin, I'm glad you called. And no, I'm not back."

"What's going on?? It's been days now, and you haven't called or anything. I've been waiting for you to get home so we can talk."

"I need you to send me the divorce papers," she said in a hushed voice as she hurried down the stairs.

"What?"

"Send them to me overnight so we can finish things."

"Wait. When are you coming back?"

"I don't know."

"How can you not know?"

"Hey, stop with all the questions and just send them!"

"No, not until you tell me what's going on. You said we'd talk after you buried your father. Why aren't you back?"

Aaren paced the foyer, her eyes fixed on the ceiling as though she could see Jarrod through the plaster.

"What difference does it make when I come back? It's over between us. We agreed!"

"You agreed to hear me out."

"I did not."

"You did! I deserve that, damn it! It's my marriage too."

"Oh, Jesus," she said, her heart racing. "Please don't start this again. We agreed, Gavin!"

He got quiet on the phone. She knew Gavin well, could read so much in his silence. He had plans to win her back. He probably had it all worked out. He'd take her back, broken and all.

"I just can't take it anymore, your running, the way you pushed away my love for you. I actually thought the separation would make you realize... hell, forget what I thought." He sighed sadly.

Aaren felt horrible. She understood his reluctance. She knew he loved her. She should have never married him if she couldn't love him the way he deserved. She'd waited to sign the divorce papers this long, and he'd convinced himself it was her way of holding on.

"I still love you." He spoke in a strained voice.

"Please don't do this."

"If you want your divorce, then you face me. You come home and deal with us. Then we'll decide if our marriage is over—"

"Don't try to renegotiate it now, we're done and you know it!"

Jarrod descended the stairs. His brow furrowed at her outburst. She averted her eyes quickly. "I'm sorry, I have to go," she said, hanging up.

"Something wrong?" asked Jarrod. He had changed his shirt to a blue one, with the sleeves rolled up above his elbow. He had on his favorite cap. She found him ruggedly handsome as ever. "Got a client trying to snatch you from me?"

She smiled calmly. "Just unfinished business in New York. Nothing I can't handle."

He went to her smiling, pulling her into his embrace. "I forget you're some cut-throat legal eagle. Mmm... c'mere."

She wrapped her arms around his neck and looked up into his eyes.

"You sure you want to do this today, Jay? We can always go back upstairs and... you know."

"If it was up to me, I'd keep you in that room naked for the rest of our days. Unfortunately, we do have a world to tend to."

She agreed. "That we do."

"Come on."

Jarrod made sure to open the truck door for her. Even when they were kids, he always opened doors for her. It was one of the many things that separated him from the other boys. Aaren always made a point to tell him how different he was. He thought on his behavior with girls outside of her and realized it wasn't him that was different. It was her, and how he felt when he was with her. She inspired him to be the better man.

He slid in on the driver's side. The foreboding feeling was still there, unnerving him. It clawed at his gut and made his throat dry as sandpaper. Tightening his grip on the steering wheel, he fought against it. Having her close helped. Jarrod eyed her attire. On his farm she dressed comfortably, more like he remembered her. Now, she looked like the world that had a hold on her, with a sophistication that he certainly didn't hold up to. He feared that world, that other half of her that she had yet to truly reveal. Carrie said they wouldn't last. He refused to believe that.

She rolled her window down and flashed him those sexy whites. "Smell that Jay? Smells like springtime. That's the smell of Penns Point to me. I really feel like I'm home."

And for the first time since she'd come back, she thought maybe she was.

"Where do we go first? The courthouse?" As a teenager, she'd imagined she'd grow up to practice law inside that building, but she'd never been inside.

"Marie Landry," he replied.

"Why?"

"I spoke to Antonio last night, and—"

"You told him about our parents?"

Jarrod looked over at her, smiling. "No, baby, I didn't tell him."

She felt relieved. Of course she'd told Becca, but she didn't want everyone to know. Not yet anyway, though she figured half the town must know it already.

"I asked him about your mom, and of course he knows about as much as we do. He suggested Miz Marie."

"I thought the Clifford's would be a better place. I was with them the night she died."

Jarrod looked over at her solemnly. "Cyrus Clifford is dead, Aaren."

"When?"

"Couple years ago."

"And Mrs. Clifford? Where is she?"

"She moved to Chicago to live with her sister after he died. They never had kids of their own and she couldn't tend to their land herself."

"Wow, I had no idea."

Jarrod reached over and grabbed her hand. A bluesy country tune filled the silence between them. Her eyes remained trained out her passenger window at the farms they passed, remembering her childhood again. As a child, she'd just known not to ask about her mom, and she didn't remember why. Was it something Pop said? Or did she know, deep down inside, that something was wrong in the way her mom was taken from her?

Driving back up to Murphy Brothers Funeral Home, Jarrod pulled his truck right behind the hearse parked on the circular drive. He turned off the engine and looked over at Aaren.

"Are you ready for this?"

"Definitely," she said, putting on her best game face. She was in her element. She'd prepared for this moment her entire adult life. She would put Miz Marie's ass on the stand and that woman damn well better tell the truth.

Jarrod got out with her and waited for her to come around the front of the truck to hold her hand. He walked her up the steps to the double white doors and pushed one open. They walked into the cool, serene funeral parlor, their feet sinking into the thick, dark magenta carpet. Before they could go further, Miz Marie came out of her back office, flipping through a folder. She glanced up to see them. The portly woman stopped in her tracks. Aaren recognized that look. It was the look of the guilty: she'd seen it many times before. Miz Marie covered with the fake smile she reserved for the customers. *Well*, thought Aaren, *it won't work this time.*

"What brings you two here?" Miz Marie tried to smooth her hair back into its neat bun. "We've taken care of everything, right?"

"We came to see you," said Jarrod, putting his arm protectively around Aaren.

Miz Marie looked at him and then Aaren before waving her folder.

"Okay. Of course. Come with me."

She turned to go back to her office and they followed. Aaren's heart raced. She tried to steady herself, tell herself this was like every other cross she'd ever done. Still her palm sweated within Jarrod's hand.

They entered the back office. Miz Marie moved around her small desk. It was covered in papers, folders, and contracts. Aaren could never find anything if she worked that way. She sat down before being invited to do so. Jarrod waited politely for Miz Marie's nod.

"Well, looks like you two are back together," Miz Marie said with an unmistakable chill.

"That surprises you?" asked Aaren.

"I only meant—"

"Oh, I know what you meant."

Jarrod touched her hand to silence her. He didn't want to alienate the woman too soon. "We came here because we need your help."

The older woman sat back, staring at them. She twitched at the edges of her grey polyester jacket, trying to get it to close properly over her large bosom. "What kind of help?"

"How long did you know my mother?" Aaren's eyes never left Marie's face.

Miz Marie looked at her, amused. "I've known you all your life dear."

"That's not what I asked you."

"I knew Noelle for many years. We grew up in this town together."

"So you knew her and my father pretty well, would you say?"

Jarrod looked at Aaren, noticing her change in tone. She ignored the worry in his eyes. He would just have to trust her.

"Yes, we were all friends."

"Did you attend their wedding?"

"I was her maid of honor," replied Marie, narrowing her eyes on Aaren.

"Why aren't there photographs?"

"There was a fire before you were born that destroyed almost everything. Their furniture, those pictures, everything."

There weren't any photos of her parents when they were young and in love. As a child, she'd assumed it was because they didn't have the money. The fire was news to her.

"Your father built that house more than once to provide for his family," lectured Marie. "Noelle was lucky to have a man so committed to her."

Aaren didn't take well to hearing her history roll off Miz Marie's tongue. So they had a fire before, and Pops rebuilt their home. It was just like him to do something so loving, and never seek attention or credit. A slow smile began to form. Aaren caught the gleam of smugness in Miz Marie's eye and composed herself.

"How about her funeral?"

Miz Marie looked away. "What is this about? I'm a busy woman—"

"It's about doing what you do best," glared Aaren. "Telling everyone's business. Instead of talking about the Robinsons behind their backs, how about we have an honest discussion about my parents? Right now."

"What was the question? You come in here all sass and I can barely speak—"

"Did you attend her funeral?"

Miz Marie sighed. "Yes."

"How did she die?"

"What??"

"How did she die?"

"Is that why you came here? To question me about Noelle? This makes no—"

"HOW DID SHE DIE?"

Jarrod looked to Aaren, then back at Miz Marie, who was beginning to perspire. The wall-mounted air-conditioner blew cool air into her tiny office, to no avail.

"She drowned," said Miz Marie flatly.

Jarrod and Aaren frowned. They looked at each other then back at the woman who told them something neither could have imagined. Aaren put her hand to her mouth, shocked.

Jarrod leaned forward. "She drowned?"

"Yes, in an accident. It's public record, no big mystery there. So why don't you leave!"

"Not so fast. Where did she drown?" demanded Aaren.

Miz Marie glared at Aaren. "I knew your father very well. He was a good man and you had very little respect for him. You broke his heart by taking up with *him*!" she snapped, pointing at Jarrod.

"How would you know anything about me and my father? All you did was hang around and…"

Aaren noticed the way the old woman's eyes brimmed with tears. The wrinkles around the corners of her mouth tightened. She remembered Miz Marie always being there to cook them holiday meals and take her shopping for women's things. She was always around, fussing.

"Why didn't I see this before? You were in love with him, weren't you?"

Marie cheeks burned red.

"Will you two leave now?" she croaked.

"Where did my mother drown?" Aaren snapped. She was done playing games with this woman.

"In Salt River!" Marie shouted at her.

Jarrod shook his head. "How on earth did she drown in Salt River?"

Marie shot him an angry glare. "You did this! Samuel warned you to leave it all alone, but you couldn't. Even now, your daddy's carnal desires burn within you! You chasing after her is perverse and neither of you knows—"

Aaren sat forward, seething. "You watch your mouth! What I have with Jarrod is not perverse! I know my mother had an affair with James Pennington, and it makes no difference!"

Marie shook her head. "You're a stupid girl. All that fancy learnin' up in New York City taught you nothing. You're just like your impulsive mama—like your grandmama!"

"Is no one safe from your venom? Your jealousy? Are you so hateful that you can't respect the dead?" Aaren leaned back in her uncomfortable chair and arranged an icy cold smile on her face. She tipped her chin at Marie. "Fastest way to get me out of here is to tell me what I want to know."

Jarrod reached to touch her wrist. Aaren yanked her hand away from his and crossed her arms over her chest. The little contretemps was not lost on Marie, who smiled at Aaren.

"You want the truth about your mother? I'll gladly tell you. Penns Point was a good town, full of good people. We had our problems, sure the racial lines were drawn here like the rest of the world, but everyone knew their place."

"Their *place*?" asked Jarrod.

"That's right. Coloreds south of the Salt River and whites north. No one crossed those lines. That was until Noelle wanted to start a sewing club."

"What does that have to do with anything?" Aaren demanded.

"Oh, it's everything, dear. It's time you knew the truth, since you in such a hurry to run off into the sunset with a Pennington."

"Jarrod has nothing to do with this."

Marie sneered. "Penningtons always get what they want, and from the looks of you two that hasn't changed."

"I'll tell you what's changed, *Miz* Marie. I'm no longer that naïve girl that looked to you for guidance. I see you for who you are: a bitter old woman who spent a lifetime chasing after a man who never loved her. All these taunts are based on your jealousy, because even dead and gone, my mother had my father's love. You must have baked a thousand cakes and pies, and for what? He was never going to love you."

Marie's nostrils flared and her eyes bulged. She looked as if steam were about to explode from her ears.

"You don't know your father any better than you knew your mama. It wasn't just that Noelle had to have the handsomest man in Bullitt County. Or that she had to have him build her house with his own bare hands as some kind of monument to her. She had to have it all. Abraham farmed, worked at the plant *and* trained your daddy's horses, putting more money in the Judge's pockets!" she sneered at Jarrod. "All for the love of his sweet Noelle—"

"And none of that was your business!" snapped Aaren.

Marie clucked her tongue and smirked. "Noelle always bored easy. Sitting in that house and tending to her little girl wasn't enough. She constantly wanted your father to take her on trips, or run off to Louisville for the weekend. Then one day, she picked up Abraham, from your house." Marie raised her eyebrows at Jarrod. "Noelle was allowed to come inside and there was Miss Laura Lee and her sewing circle of friends. Noelle discovered what bored, rich white women did. She was fascinated. I think that little trip was the first time the Judge ever laid his eyes on her."

Aaren swallowed, shifting in her seat. Jarrod pulled his chair closer to hers. He sensed that the story had taken a turn and they were going to learn some ugly truths. Turning her eyes away from Jarrod, Marie gave Aaren a triumphant stare.

"Your mama was mixed. Did you even know that? That married man whose family chased your grandma out of town and sent her pregnant to Bullitt County was a white man."

"Just stick to the facts," said Aaren, glaring back.

"But that is a fact, dear. His name was Aaron Fitzgerald, and even after he didn't want your mama she still thought herself white. She named you after him."

Marie might as well have struck her. She'd had no idea. No one had ever told her. The news took all the fight from Aaren. She blinked and swallowed the bitterness of the truth.

Satisfied that she was in control, Marie continued.

"Your mama thought she belonged over there with those white women sewing while their husbands gave them the run of the house. She was always making excuses to go over and pick up Abraham and greet those prissy ladies. And for all her airs, Miss Laura Lee is a sweet enough woman. She let Noelle sit in on one of their sewing sessions. She came back home that day and called us all together. We were going to start our own sewing club. When most of us told her she was crazy, since none of us owned sewing machines, she had your poor daddy break his savings to buy her one. As if the man wasn't trying to please her enough."

Aaren cut her eyes. She knew Marie was jealous, definitely putting her own spin on the story, but it didn't matter. Every syllable at this point was another dagger into her heart. She felt like she was losing her mother all over again. How could she not? The crystal ball she kept Noelle's memory in was chipping away.

"When did the affair start?" Aaren managed.

Marie shook her head. "Hmmm, good question. I suppose it began the day Noelle drove over to Poke County where we could get cheaper fabrics from a store there. It was seventy-eight, but you'd never know segregation was supposed to be over." She cut her eyes over to Jarrod for the rest of the tale. "You know how white folks are? They find other ways to remind you of your place, subtle ways. Like a store closing when you entered or just being outright ignored when you tried to purchase something."

Marie smiled. "But of course Noelle found it all to be foolishness. She wouldn't let anyone turn her away. She wasn't in the store for a good five minutes before she got into it with a white woman, and the store manager was about to have her arrested. That was until your mother intervened." She pointed at Jarrod, then turned her eyes back to Aaren.

"Your mama, she was lucky Mrs. Pennington was shopping there. The people accused Noelle of shoplifting. It wounded her haughty little pride. Laura Lee made the store manager apologize to her in front of everyone. Then she stayed with Noelle, shopping like they was sorority sisters. Laura Lee got us a discount on our fabric."

Jarrod smiled. His mom was a kind woman, always putting others first, which is why he hated his dad's betrayal even more.

"So Laura Lee and my mom were friends?"

"Friends, how strange you chose that word. I suppose Laura Lee thought of Noelle as a friend. But Noelle, well—"

"What happened between them?" asked Aaren.

"The sewing circle became what you might call 'integrated' because of that *friendship*. We all met at the Penningtons' on Wednesdays to share our latest creations and swap patterns. Laura Lee even bought a couple of sewing machines for the ladies whose husbands wouldn't."

Aaren smiled. It helped to hear that her mother was a pioneer of that sort, something to prepare her for the part of Noelle she dreaded hearing about.

"My mom brought the town together," she said proudly.

Marie snickered. "Oh, she did more than that. There were some whites that weren't as financially fortunate as the women in the sewing circle. They was offended that we were included, and they made a pretty big stink about it."

Aaren sighed. "So what happened? A riot or something? Is that what this town can't get over?"

Marie stared her in the eye. "The sewing circle was just reasons for ignorant folks to hurl nasty names at each other. What Noelle and James Pennington did was what ripped out the heart of this town."

"Why? Because they fell in love! You ignorant hicks couldn't deal with it so you destroyed her!" Aaren shouted.

"Don't sit in judgment of us. Your mama didn't befriend Laura Lee to start that sewing circle for us ladies to come together. She was already sleeping with the Judge by then. Stealing away to run errands or not even attending the sewing meetings so she could sneak him into your father's bed."

"You're twisting things! You're just—"

"No, you wanted the truth so here it is."

"How did Noelle drown?" asked Jarrod.

"Her car went over Old Rachette Bridge. Abraham and Cyrus Clifford got there too late. They tried, liked to drown themselves, to get her out. It was terrible."

"Then what is with all the secrecy? Why couldn't Aaren have been told this?"

Marie glared at them. "Talk to your folks for the gory details. I'm done protecting your family. Abraham is the one that asked that we let it go as an accident to spare our town an ugly scandal. No one wanted to bring outsiders here. We take care of our own."

"Spare them from what? If it was an accident why would my Pop lie to me about her death?" Aaren asked.

"Ask his folks!" She pointed an accusing finger at Jarrod. "The rest of the story is theirs!"

"Wait. How did their affair get all over town?" Jarrod asked. He knew there were other women in his father's life, not just Noelle, but after her, too. His father would disappear for a few days, from time to time; he was twelve when he figured it out. But there was never a whisper about who he was with. The Judge had always been discreet.

Marie clucked her tongue once more. The smacking sound made Aaren want to strike her.

"Jennifer Benson was in the sewing circle. Noelle had slipped away to get more fabrics from out of the attic. She was actually in the sun porch rubbing up on James... just a kiss-and-feel session that they indulged in whenever they could. Well, Jen saw it and before long everyone knew it."

"And my mom told Abraham. Didn't she? That's how he found out?"

"Yes, she did," said Marie, nodding. "When confronted, Noelle just admitted to it. Abraham lost it. He struck her so hard, he had to call the doctor to make sure she came to."

"My father hit her?" Flashes of Abraham slapping her and calling her a whore like her mother returned. She'd never questioned why he made the comparison, but finding her half-naked with a Pennington explained a lot.

"Then his jealous rage caused him to raise a mob. He and Cyrus Clifford and even Reverend Morris rode over to the north side and got in a standoff with the Judge and his friends. He wanted to defend his wife's honor. The fight got escalated and the hatred was everywhere. People that had been friendly regardless of color became mortal enemies. A church was burned down here, right off Clancy Street. And the old Salt Mine monument on the north side was desecrated. It was the coloreds versus the whites and those of us that didn't want any part of it were forced to choose sides."

"This makes me sick," said Aaren, clutching at Jarrod's hand.

"You want to know anything more about any of this, you need to ask your folks. I wasn't there that night. But Judge James and Miss Laura Lee definitely were."

Aaren looked at her with disgust. "What are you saying? It wasn't an accident?"

"Are you saying my father did something to Noelle?" Jarrod asked stunned.

"I'm saying since you want to know it all, let them be the ones to tell you the ugly truth. This happened years ago. Contrary to what Sam and the Reverend think, we'll survive it. All of us. So you will please take your questions elsewhere. I've said all I plan to on this."

"Let's go," said Aaren, escaping the room.

Jarrod rose to go after her but stopped. He looked back at Miz Marie. "How would Abraham feel about the way you handled things today?"

"Abraham is dead, and she asked for the truth. I helped that man all these years because I loved him. He never let go of Noelle. He never let anybody in. I feel no guilt because what I said is true, but you, Jarrod, you are the one who stands to lose it all. So go ahead and dig up those skeletons. It's your funeral," said Marie, enjoying the irony.

Jarrod cut his eyes and walked out. Aaren was sitting inside of the truck. He found her crying.

"Let me take you home," he said quietly, reaching for her.

"No! Take me to your parents' place!"

Jarrod's stomach clenched. He refused to believe his dad had killed her mom. There had to be some other explanation. "Please. Let's just go home and talk this thing through."

Aaren glared at him. "You take me or I'll go myself!! I want to see them both! I want to know what they did to my mother! I want the truth."

Jarrod feared he truth. What they'd heard about her mother was hard enough, but Miz Marie's implication was clear: James had killed Noelle and then he and Abraham covered it up. That was unbelievable madness.

They rode in silence all the way to his folks' place. Crossing Old Rachette Bridge, they both looked into the Salt River in shared shock.

They drove through the exclusive subdivision that surrounded his parents' home. Aaren hadn't been on this side of town since returning; she'd forgotten how beautiful this part of Penns Point was. But the storybook homes hid a seamy tale. Miz Marie told her that her mother had carried on like some brazen slut. It couldn't be true. There had to be more to it and Aaren wanted to know. She wanted to know the truth about her mother and James Pennington.

Jarrod's pickup turned up the circular drive to his family home. White, with Colonial-style architecture and dark shutters, it stood formidable with large trees on both sides. She'd never been inside. But she'd heard it was one of the prettiest in the county.

Jarrod turned off the engine and pulled the key out of the ignition before summoning the courage to look at her once more. His father's sin, however long ago, had become his own. The irony of thinking he and Aaren could begin again only to run up against the biggest lie of their lives had his faith slipping. He could lose her. Worse, he'd never really had her again.

"Listen to me. We don't have to do this, Aaren. You've been through too much."

"I appreciate that you want to protect me, but this isn't just about me, you know. These are your folks. If you don't want to face them, I understand. I want you at my side but I understand, Jay. So, which is it?" she asked, staring at him.

He looked back at the house. "Together."

She nodded. "Let's go."

They both got out of the car and walked up the winding path. The door opened before they reached it and his brother looked at them, shocked.

"Jay!"

"Hey, Travis."

He looked at her and smiled. "Aaren, how are you?"

Aaren smiled weakly. "I'm okay. Are your parents home?"

"Yeah, I suppose that's why you came?"

Jarrod frowned. "Huh?"

"Mom, she had another attack. We called out to the farm and they said they would try to reach you—"

Jarrod pushed past his brother, racing inside. Aaren followed quietly behind, keeping her head down. Travis closed the door.

"Thank you for bringing him home."

"It's, um, no problem."

"How are you really? I mean with your dad and everything."

"I'm fine," she said, swallowing a ball of guilt. They weren't there just to visit with his mother. They'd come for answers.

Looking up, she saw James Pennington coming down the hall. He was the spitting image of Jarrod, just an older, more distinguished version, minus the tan. He looked her up and down. Aaren saw it in his face. His feelings for her mother were obvious. She stared back at him with hatred and hoped he'd discern the reason for her visit.

"Hello, Aaren," he said pleasantly.

"Judge Pennington. I'm sorry your wife isn't feeling well."

He nodded then looked at his younger son, confused. Travis pointed upstairs. "Jay's here. He's upstairs with mom."

"Oh," he said, returning his gaze to Aaren.

She cleared her throat. "Can we talk?"

He stared at her for a moment before speaking.

"Of course. Travis, tell your brother to join us in the parlor when he comes downstairs."

Travis nodded, curious about the tension he saw between them.

Aaren walked into the parlor and went over to the bookshelf that was covered in family photos. Her eyes traveled over Jarrod's football trophies and pictures from high school. It helped seeing him during a time when they were happy and secrets weren't lurking in the shadows. Or at least that's what they'd thought.

"Would you like a drink?" he asked.

Feeling the Judge's eyes on her, she turned around. "I look that much like her to you?"

James sighed and went to his bar. "Yes, you do. It hurts to look upon your face even now, after she's been gone so many years."

"Did you love her?"

Pouring his drink, he looked up at Noelle's daughter. "I did."

"But you made her your whore?"

"What?" he snapped. "Don't you ever call her that!"

"Why not? It's what she was, wasn't she? Screwing you here in between sewing sessions and then taking you to my Pop's bed. I think that meets the definition. Maybe not whore of the century, but close enough."

The Judge slammed his glass down. "Your mother was a good woman. I know people in this town think she set up that sewing club to get at me, but it's not true. She resisted my advances from the start. It was I who wouldn't quit, who had to have her. She consumed my nights. She was on my mind constantly—"

"Well, that's you," said Aaren with a dismissive wave. "Why did she betray my Pop? Why would she destroy our family?"

He shook his head. "She loved Abraham, she just wasn't in love with him. Or at least that's what she told me. She married him with you in her belly and vowed to stick with him for you. You meant everything to her. She wanted you…"

"Me?"

"When the town went nuts over our affair, it scared us both. Fights breaking out on both sides of the river. I faced your father in the middle of the town square. Both of our boys had shotguns pointed at the other. I tried to barter peace but he wanted no part of it. He wanted blood and it was killing everyone. So we decided to end it by leaving Bullitt County. I told Laura Lee I was leaving her and the kids. But your mother wanted you. She was convinced your father would let her take you with us. She wouldn't leave without you."

"So how did she die? What did you do to her?" Aaren asked.

"Sit down, Aaren. It's time you knew the whole truth," he said sadly, gulping down his whiskey. "I've lived with the pain of failing Noelle all these years. Let's end the lies and secrets, once and for all."

"Mom. How are you?" It hadn't been a week since the funeral, but she seemed smaller now, and even frailer.

"Jay, that you? I'm glad you came, son."

Laura Lee's skin was pale and pasty. Her eyes were dark, with circles underneath. Macy stepped closer, offering a glass of water.

"My pills, Jay. In the top drawer. The red ones. Please?" Laura Lee pointed to the antique dresser nearest to Jarrod.

He reached into the drawer and found her prescription, then opened the bottle for her automatically, knowing she would be too weak to manage the child-proofed lid by herself. She shook out the shiny capsules. Jarrod helped his mother up to drink, watching her carefully. She had trouble getting the pills down. He wondered why the doctors prescribed so many, then immediately felt guilty. His mother was trying so hard to get better, and he knew the reason was so she could be there for her children—even the one who'd separated himself from her years ago.

"She's been asking for you nonstop, Jay." Macy looked at her brother with tears in her eyes.

"What's going on?"

"The doctors don't know why she's not getting better."

"Then why was she at Abraham's funeral?"

Macy looked at her mother, whose eyes remained closed. "She wasn't supposed to be. She came for you. To try to get you to come back to us, and—"

Laura Lee cut her off. "Macy, sweetheart. You're my baby and I love you, so much. You know that, right?" Macy nodded, her eyes round and worried. Laura Lee smiled to reassure her. "Now let me speak to your brother alone."

"Okay, Mama," she said, coming over and kissing her forehead before leaving and closing the door quietly behind her.

"Jay, I need to tell you something."

Jarrod picked up her hand and kissed it. "Mom, I'm sorry. I didn't know it was this bad."

She smiled weakly at him. "We need to talk, son. A talk we should have had so long ago. So long, Jay."

"You don't have to—"

"Hush now, let me speak. First you need to understand who your father is."

"I have a pretty good idea who he is," smirked Jarrod.

"No, Jay, no." Laura Lee coughed. "You have no idea. James was born a Pennington. At one time that meant something in this state. It meant responsibility and obligations that you can't understand. Our fathers, they…" Laura Lee's eyes rolled. She fell back on her pillow and sucked in breaths. Her wheeze had her chest seizing. It was frightening. But she soon relaxed.

"Don't talk, Mom. Just rest."

"No Jay, listen. Our fathers went to law school together. They made a deal on how their families would join, way before me and James were ever born. James was so handsome, Jay. I loved him so. I loved him from afar as a little girl, always. He never paid me any mind. We were kids. And by the time I joined him at college, he was a boy like any other. Wanting to be free."

"I don't understand why you're telling me this."

"Because your father never meant to hurt me. He never meant to marry me. He wanted to marry someone else, a girl from school. He even threatened Boss Pennington he'd walk away from the family. But Boss ran all of Penns, all of this county and the next, clear on up to Louisville. He ruled his son with an iron fist. He got that girl taken out of school and sent off, out west somewhere. Your father didn't find out what happened until years later: she just disappeared. James was to be a judge and I was to be his wife, whether he liked it or not."

"You're saying your marriage was arranged?"

"That's right, Jay, it was. James was pleasant enough, sweet about it, but secretly he resented it. Just like you, when your father tried to get you to go Ole Miss. How you wanted to go to the University of Texas. Play in the Southwest Conference, remember that fight?"

Laura Lee started coughing. Jay got her water and put the straw to her chapped lips.

"Yes, I remember."

"I loved him so much. I believed that in time he could love me. And I think that part of him did. But most of him, the heart of him, belonged to another woman."

"The one from Ole Miss?"

"No, Jay. Noelle Robinson. She's the woman that had your father's heart."

"Mom, please. This can wait."

"I need to tell you about Noelle and what happened the day she died."

"That's not your job," Jarrod said angrily. Here she was, covering for him again. It should be his father that owned up to the story, and faced what he'd done to his mother, not to mention what he'd done to the entire town.

Laura Lee smiled at her first-born son.

"You're in love with her daughter, aren't you? You never told me, Jay. It wasn't until after you left that I learned how much you cared for her. I wish you had come to me. I could have spared you so much pain."

"Mom, there's nothing you could have said to change my mind about her. There is nothing wrong with me loving Aaren."

Laura Lee shook her head wryly. "Both my boys loved those Robinson women. I think Noelle is up in heaven now having a big laugh at my expense. I lost your father, and then I lost you too, just the same as if the truth had come out back then."

"No. You never lost me." Jarrod said, starting to cry. "I don't want to know."

"Yes, you do, and I'm going to tell you. What I really need for you to do is listen. Now, son. It's time."

Chapter Twelve

NOELLE

"Abraham, please!!" Noelle screamed until her throat burned. She barely saw him through her tears. Since he'd discovered her affair and thrown her out, she'd been sleeping on Marie's couch. Today, he told her she could come over and get Aaren. When she arrived, she found he'd already sent her baby away.

"Please, what? Help you steal my daughter so you can run off with that man you've betrayed me and your family with!" he growled at her, pushing her against the wall. "I thought you wanted to spend the day with Aaren, but Marie tells me you running off with the Judge. Is it true? Is it?"

"Stop it, Abraham, please!"

"It is true?" he asked, stepping back.

In that moment, Noelle saw another truth in his eyes. He'd made sure Aaren was hidden, someplace out of her reach.

"Do you really think I would let you take her from me?" he snarled.

"You don't understand—"

"I understand that you have completely lost your mind!!!"

Abraham glared as Noelle brushed away her tears. She shivered in her light dress despite the afternoon heat, and he took notice. The dress was too tight, her hair was flipped stylishly away from her face. Her make-up was expertly applied despite the run of mascara from her tears.

"You've changed so much for this man," he said in disgust. "I had hoped you'd stop this madness and help me save our family. But it's too late for that, isn't it, Noelle? Isn't it!"

"I just want my baby."

"I know what you planning. What you planned! It's not gonna happen!"

She looked up at him, shocked. *He knew?* Then Marie did betray her. She'd called over in hysterics, asking for a place to sleep the night Abraham threw her out. And that night, she'd unburdened herself, thinking how lucky she was to have a friend like Marie. Marie had nodded soothingly as Noelle shared how she planned to meet James on Old Rachette Bridge. They were going to leave the insanity of this town. And Marie had obviously turned right around and told Abraham.

"I need my baby," she said, crying again. "Give me my baby."

Abraham grabbed her by both arms and pinned her to the wall. He squeezed tightly at first, the urge to strike her so strong, he squeezed even tighter. Then he shook her hard, until her brain rattled in her skull.

"Noelle, look at me. Look at me!!"

She looked up into his face, trying to see him through her tears. He was in such pain. It was all her fault. She knew he loved her more than she loved him. He had always been a good, loyal husband. To hurt him like this was killing her. Yet, to stay with him would only hurt him more. James was the man in her heart.

He hesitated, losing the words he'd planned to say. His heart took over and he began to beg her. "I can forgive you, Noelle. I can find a way to forgive you. I need you to let this go and come home to us."

"I love him," she said weakly.

"No you don't!! You love me, damn it!!"

Hearing her say she loved the Judge was a cut to his heart with a sharp knife. He grabbed her and shoved her back against the wall, causing her to bump her head. This brought a scream, and more tears. Abraham was insane with grief over the loss of her love. It made him manic, a man he didn't know, a man he never wanted to be. He'd become a man capable of hurting the only woman he'd ever loved.

Abraham had never seen fear in her eyes before, but he needed her to understand. There was no way he would let her go with that white man. He'd rather see her dead before he let her damn herself that way.

"You love me!" he cried, his voice and spirit breaking.

"Oh, Abraham, I'm sorry. I never meant to…"

He broke. The last of his resistance snapped and tears, hot and angry, slid down his cheeks. Dropping his head in shame, he wished to understand his failure. What had he done to drive her away? How could he fix it? She was his entire world. His family was his entire world, his only world. He'd never had family of his own, this was it. She and Aaren were all he had. He'd be damned if he would let Judge Pennington take them away from him.

"Tell me what I can do. Tell me, Noelle, and I will do it."

Before she could speak, he kissed her softly, so much pain and pleading in his kiss. In return he received her coldness, her resolve to leave him broken and alone. He tried harder, kissed her with all he had.

"Noelle, please. Just…" He clung to her and kissed her hard and long as she pushed at his chest.

She cried, still allowing the kiss, because she did love him. She would always love him. She just hadn't understood how deep love could flow until James came into her life. She felt Abraham's kisses go to the inside of her neck as he pressed his body into hers. She knew he was desperate and all she could think about was Aaren. She had to find her.

"Tell me, baby. What should I do?" he whispered, pinning himself closer to her and continued to press kisses to her neck.

"Give me my daughter, Abraham. I need her. I can't live without her."

Stopping his attempt at seduction, Abraham looked her in the face. He was so close he could feel the breath from her nostrils tickling the hairs of his mustache.

"You can't take her from me, Noelle. Do you really think I would let you do that? Take my babygirl and leave town? Do you? You need to make a choice. It's either your life with us, or with that man who's made you his whore!"

Noelle shook her head wildly. "Abraham, everybody gone crazy. This is crazy right now. Listen to me. Just give me Aaren, tell me where she is. I'm her mother! She needs me now!"

"We can fix this, Noelle. I'll sell the farm and we'll leave."

"And go where?"

"I don't know, damn it!!"

He released her to begin pacing, clenching and unclenching his fists. He would sell the farm, then get his family away from here. It would be a new beginning for them. But when his eyes returned to hers, he had to face the truth. It was etched over her face, a coldness in the liquid brown eyes that used to gaze at him with such love. She wanted out. It tore at what was left of his battered heart.

"What does he give you that I can't? Is it because he's rich? White? What is it?"

Noelle wiped her tears. "We didn't mean for it to happen. We fell in love—"

"What do you mean you *fell in love*? How could you abandon your husband and child, for... *sex*? You were supposed to love me!" He hit his chest.

"I do. It's just not the same."

"Get out! Get the hell out!" he snarled, his anger at a dangerous level. He hated her for loving another, for rejecting him this way. And most of all, he hated her for not seeing how desperately he loved her.

"Where's Aaren?" she asked pitifully. She took a step toward him, pleading once more.

Abraham charged at her, grabbing her by the arm. He dragged her to the front door, flung it open, and threw her out like a rag doll. Noelle fell on the wooden porch, knees first. She turned to look back at him, shocked.

"Abraham, where is my baby?" she shouted.

"Don't you ever show your face here again!! I'll tell our daughter you took ill and died. It's better than telling her of the whore you've become!"

Then he stepped back, glaring, before he kicked the door shut. Noelle raced to the door. Slamming both fists against it, she cried out desperately.

"Abraham, don't do this!! Tell me where she is!! For God's sake, where is Aaren?"

"Where do you think you're going?" cried Laura Lee, following James outside as he put his suitcase in the trunk of his car.

"I'm leaving, Laura," sighed James. "We've been through this."

"I have two babies inside! And you're going to run off with that... that... *slut?*"

She seethed with emotion, veering between fear and rage. Her mind was still reeling. He'd sat her down and told her calmly he wanted out. *Out?* What did that mean? He'd said he'd tried, but he couldn't stay in this town and their marriage was over. She couldn't even speak for the first few minutes, just watched mutely as he'd packed a single, small case. In her wildest nightmares, she'd never imagined his philandering would bring them to this.

She thought of the first time she'd caught him stepping out on their marriage. It was with her childhood best friend. He'd begged for forgiveness once discovered. She'd welcomed him home and in that passionate moment, their first-born was conceived. That was how they'd created Jay. Over the years she'd put up with his indiscretions and suffered silently the many women her husband had taken to bed. He'd never done it to hurt her: he'd been kind to her, sweet even. Laura Lee had understood from the outset that theirs was a relationship based on duty and obligation, not love. It wasn't really his fault.

But even in his wanderings, he'd never gone this far.

A black woman from the south side? One that she'd befriended! Laura Lee had never imagined he would leave. He wasn't supposed to leave, damn it!

James couldn't look her in the eye. He'd hurt her badly. It tore him up inside. She was a good wife, an excellent mother, and his selfishness had her constantly fighting to keep her family together. But it wasn't fair she had to put up with his... his nature. She couldn't possibly be happy, he reasoned. She needed to be free as well. They'd barely touched each other since Travis was conceived.

He was tired of pretending. He was tired of trying to be what she and this town thought he should be. He'd never signed up to be the town's patriarch. But he hadn't complained. He'd marked his time until, in the midst of a life he'd found mind-numbingly monotonous, something remarkable had happened to him. He'd fallen in love and he finally understood why Laura Lee wasn't enough.

He'd discovered passion, the kind that keeps you awake at night. The kind that makes your heart skip a beat when the object of your desires casts you a look. That's what he had with Noelle. It was the kind that made his pulse race when he heard Noelle's sweet voice, or when he felt her soft hands on his body. He'd also come to know kindness and sharing that he'd never thought possible between a man and a woman. He loved Noelle and for the first time, he knew what that meant. He would never let her go.

"You can't leave! I won't let you!!" cried Laura Lee, running over to him. She flung herself at him, throwing her arms around his neck and clinging. "I love you. We're a family. We can't live without you. Oh James, please! Please!"

"Laura Lee, I'll do my best. I swear it. I'll take care of them; I'll take care of you. Your cousins can have the business. They can run it with you." He looked at her ashen face. "Or for you. It'll be taken care of. I won't let our children suffer because of me."

She let go and stepped back. "What kind of life will they have in this town with their father who ran off with a married woman? A *colored* woman?"

"Stop—"

"No! You made vows to me! You swore you would honor them, James! You can't just walk away…" She touched his face, then smiled weakly through her tears. "I forgive you. We've been here before, remember? I can handle it. With a little work, we can get past it. Now come back inside."

"You're strong, and… this." He shook his head. "This is not your fault. Laura, I do care. But this has never been love."

"How could you say that?"

"I can't give you what I don't feel. Don't you understand? Don't you want to be in love, feel passion? Feel desire in your life?"

"I have that, James. When I'm with you, I feel passion and love beyond my wildest dreams. You are my life, my soulmate," she said, grabbing his cheeks and kissing him.

James pulled her hands from the sides of his face and forced her away, breaking the kiss.

"I can't do this any longer. I'm sorry."

He walked past her to go back in the house, fetching the last of his things. He wanted to hug his sons and say goodbye. He didn't know when he'd see them again.

Laura Lee was on his heels, desperate to make him stop. She saw him heading upstairs to the boys' room and panicked. He was really going to do it. He was going to walk out on her.

"Oh God, no… please God, what should I do?" she panted, pacing around in the grand foyer at the bottom of the stairs.

Her heart was racing. The tears kept flowing. She wheezed as if an age-old asthma affliction had flared up. She clutched her chest, squeezing her fist against it. Her father was two years with the Lord, but Laura Lee knew he still watched over her. What would he think? Her mother and her cousins and her friends in church, how could she ever face them?

She rushed into the parlor, headed straight for the gun rack. She didn't have the key. James always kept it hidden. But she had to stop him. Looking around, she picked up a snow globe. He had bought it for her on their honeymoon at Niagara Falls years ago. She gripped it with both hands, then threw it into the glass of the case, which shattered immediately.

Everything was falling apart.

She reached in and grabbed the .38, figuring it was small enough to handle. She wasn't completely aware of all she was doing, yet she felt her desperation to do it. Going to his desk, she pulled the different drawers open until she saw his bullet case. Laura Lee popped it open and flicked open the chamber of the gun. She dropped the bullets inside, one by one, the way Papa showed her, then closed the cylinder and used both thumbs to draw the hammer back.

James heard the crash of glass from third floor and came racing back downstairs.

"Laura Lee, are you all right?" He turned the corner to see her pointing the gun at him, still crying hysterically.

"I won't let you destroy our family! I'll kill you before she can have you!"

Noelle drove to several of their neighbors' homes looking for Aaren. Either they slammed their doors in her face or refused to open them. She didn't know who had her baby. It was as if the whole town had turned against her. She was crying so hard, she could barely see the road. Finally giving up, she headed to the bridge. James, her Jamie, would know what to do. He would help her get her daughter back. Aaren needed her mother. Surely Jamie could make them see that.

Noelle steered to the north side of the bridge, then her heart dropped. His car wasn't at the designated spot. Where could he be?. She pulled over to the side of the road to wait for him. Her tears were consuming her. She forced herself to think of him. Think of James.

The first time James approached her was when she'd waited for Laura Lee in the parlor of their elegant home, to ask her about starting her own sewing circle. He offered her a drink and she accepted nicely. The way he looked at her made her feel flushed. The deep smoky sound of his voice left her faint. Laura Lee came down the stairs all aflutter and excused herself, saying that she had to get to the hospital to see about her cousin, who'd just delivered a baby. Noelle offered her congratulations and James walked his wife out to her car. Abraham was working at the plant that day so when James returned, Noelle thanked him, saying her goodbyes. She had to go pick up Aaren from the church pre-K program and then head home to start supper.

James had smiled lazily and told her not to run off just yet. Noelle was flustered by his interest. Judge James Pennington was the most powerful man in Bullitt County. Her husband and his friends respected him greatly. And he was fair, not just to the whites but to the Negroes too. He paid Abraham equally for the horses he trained and gave him an extra bonus if any of them brought a big return at the Derby.

James refreshed the drink he'd offered with something both bitter and sour. Not predisposed to alcohol, she smiled through it, feeling it would be impolite not to accept. Then, as though she were a frequent visitor to this man's opulent, tasteful parlor, they sat and talked about the town and the people they had in common. Soon the conversation drifted to her life. The year before, her mother had died of a stroke. James told her he'd met her mother before, and extended his condolences. Noelle carried a lot of pain over the circumstances of her birth and the poverty she'd lived through when she was a child. But she had only good memories of her father. Though he couldn't acknowledge her publicly, he had visited her three times in her life and each time he treated her like she was special. She cherished those memories and even named Aaren after him. James Pennington had her father's same blue eyes.

She shared that story with James that day, shyly, because she'd never told it to anyone else, not even Abraham. James was sympathetic, going over to sit next to her and comfort her. He placed his hand on her knee. The contact made her frown and she looked into his eyes, both leery of and attracted to the beauty she saw there. Noelle pushed his hand away. He furthered his advances, leaning in to plant a delicate kiss on her.

To her surprise and horror she liked it. It was unexpected, spontaneous and plain wrong, but she liked it still. Abraham never talked to her. He just grunted and spoke of his day and his needs. When she tried to tell him of her fears and desires, he would either want to have sex or turn the conversation toward what he needed in return.

She didn't feel desired at all in life, but in that kiss she did. James was different.

Pushing him away, she fled the Pennington house, vowing never to come back. No matter how much she needed to feel something in life, she was no fool. James Pennington wanted an easy feel and she wasn't about to submit to his advances and destroy her life in the process.

The next day, when Abraham was at work, James appeared at her home. He said he'd come to apologize. Aaren was at school and there was something warning her that her home was too isolated, too far from prying eyes, but she let him in. They talked and she relaxed again around him. He told her she was beautiful, that his advances were just a reaction to her beauty. She couldn't believe that she was listening to him, alone at her home: racial taboos were still very much a part of Penns Point. But she couldn't help but be drawn to the way he phrased things to her and the way his penetrating eyes warmed as they traveled over her body. She felt compelled to answer, to respond to him.

James asked her what she really wanted out of her life. She revealed that she'd always dreamed of being a designer, which is why she was so fascinated with his wife's sewing circle.

James was a perfect gentleman. He didn't sit too close that time and he didn't stay long. When he stood at her door and shook her hand goodbye, she fought the impulse to rise on tiptoe to kiss him.

Later that week, when Abraham was at the Pennington stables tending to his horses, James paid him an unexpected visit. He soon told Abraham about his wife's visit to the sewing circle. He said he thought it would be good if their wives could be friends. He said that if Abraham would work an early shift and get his horse, Major, ready for delivery ahead of schedule he'd give him a bonus, enough to acquire a sewing machine for the missus.

Abraham loved the idea. It was the kind of man and husband he was. He would do anything to make her happy. He shook hands with James, setting into motion the beginning of their ending. When Noelle learned of James' generosity she went to his office in the courthouse in downtown Penns, just to thank him. She wasn't there for five minutes before he had her pinned against the wall, kissing her passionately with his hand moving slowly up her skirt. It was one of those fashionable, shiny tea-skirt dresses that lifted with ease. She was not inclined to stop him. Her guilt over that office tryst haunted her for weeks, yet it made her want more. The betrayal of her husband was well underway.

Placing her head against the steering wheel, Noelle cried harder. The beginning and the end all came crashing down on her.

"Oh, Lawd. What am I going to do?"

She couldn't think of what to do next. She needed James. He knew how to deal with all the madness in their life. She knew herself. With him she was much stronger. Starting the car again, she pulled back onto the road and drove across the bridge. She was going to Jamie for help.

Cyrus Clifford got out of his truck, worried about his friend. He didn't see Noelle's station wagon, so he figured that she'd either run off or hadn't arrived yet. Either way, he'd left little Aaren with Emma.

Cyrus went up the porch and knocked on the door. It was strange that no one answered.

"Abraham! It's me, Cyrus! You in there?"

A few moments later Abraham opened the door. Cyrus was surprised by his appearance. His eyes were red and puffy from crying. The man looked pale. What shocked him most was the gun in his hand. Cyrus couldn't take his eyes off it. He'd ridden out with him once on a mission for revenge, and they'd just come up against more guns. It couldn't continue. Somebody was going to get killed.

"What's going on, buddy?"

"He's taken my wife, now he wants my daughter. I'll kill him first!" He spoke through clenched teeth, spittle coating his lips. He looked mad with pain and grief, and Cyrus understood. Abraham didn't deserve this.

"So Noelle been here?" he asked calmly, his eyes trained on the gun.

"Yeah, begging for a life with that bastard. She actually expected me to hand Aaren over, our child, so she could run away with him!"

"She what?"

"They planning on leaving now."

"Then we have to stop them."

"Oh, I plan to, Cyrus. He's not going anywhere with her!"

"Look, Abraham. Things are really bad right now. We can do this without that pistol. Please?"

Abraham glared at his friend but held tight to his gun. He wasn't a violent man, but since he discovered his wife's betrayal, he'd been bitter, prone to fights. He'd already broken a man's nose over at Red's. He was coming undone, because no matter what he said or did, she was leaving him. Trying to clear his head, Abraham walked back into the house and laid the gun down on the end table in the den.

"What am I doing? What is happening to my life?"

Cyrus felt his friend's pain. Abraham was the kindest man in this county. Noelle was killing him and it made Cyrus so angry.

"Its not you, Abraham. It's her."

"I want her back! How can I get her back?" he asked, looking to Cyrus for answers.

"She's your wife! We'll go collect her. No one can keep you from your wife. Just leave that gun here."

Abraham nodded. "Let's go."

Noelle got out of her car. James' Jaguar was in the driveway with the trunk open. His suitcase was inside. She smiled and wiped her tears away. He was really going to take her from this town, and they would have their second chance. Her eyes took in the house. The front door stood open. The wind blew her hair from her shoulders and dried her cheeks while she stared at that open door. She could imagine the pain that Laura Lee must be going through. If it was anything like what had happened when she told Abraham, it was not a pleasant scene.

Noelle had already endured one confrontation with Laura Lee. She regretted that heated exchange between them. Noelle had lost her temper. She told Laura Lee she'd driven James straight into her arms. She told her that no matter what, he'd never love Laura Lee like he loved her.

Now she was standing on the woman's property, ripping her family apart. An unexpected sense of remorse hit her. Maybe she and James were wrong. Maybe they shouldn't do this. In his arms, locked in passion and lost in dreams, all she wanted was James Pennington. She loved him completely. But that dream, those desires, couldn't come at the price of her daughter. Aaren was never to be left behind.

Noelle closed her eyes as a shudder of regret and grief forced the small breakfast she'd had up into her throat. She was going to be sick, she *was* sick with all she'd put them through by recklessly abandoning her senses and following her heart. She'd go inside and tell James not to leave his family. She couldn't leave Aaren, so there was no hope for them. In the end, it was family that mattered. Aaren needed her mother. Noelle would sacrifice her heart to make sure her baby was safe.

Walking across the lawn, she smoothed her dress and climbed the steps. She knocked on the open door, sticking her head inside.

"Hello?"

She waited a long moment but there was no response. Then she heard shouting from the left. That was the parlor, the place she'd first talked to James. She turned and headed down the hall.

"Put the damn gun down. Are you crazy? The boys are upstairs for Christ's sake!"

"What do you care about our children? You only care about what's between your legs!" she shouted. Lowering the gun, she aimed it at his manhood. "I bet if I level the playing field, you'll appreciate your family more!"

James put his hands out, shaking his head at his wife's hysteria. She was breaking his heart. Laura Lee was a gentle woman and he'd reduced her to this.

"Laura Lee, please. You don't want to hurt anyone."

"The hell I don't!! How could you, James? How could you even think of leaving us for her?"

James froze. "We can talk about it. Let's talk about it."

Noelle came around the corner and Laura Lee's eyes grew wide.

"You brought her to my damn house!!" she screamed. Aiming the gun at Noelle, Laura Lee's hands began to shake violently. "Are you going to move her in now? Is that what you plan to do? Toss me out and then move her in??"

Noelle looked at her, paralyzed by the sight of the gun. James whirled around to see Noelle behind him and for several seconds, he too couldn't move. He didn't understand what she was doing there. They'd agreed to meet at the bridge. Why was she here? He turned his focus back to his wife.

"Laura Lee. Give me the gun, damn it!"

"No! No, that's not what you—" her voice caught and her eyes went wide. "Wait. I know. You want to keep me upstairs in bed and her downstairs in the back room like the old days? Is that how your Daddy did it?" she shrieked.

Before he could respond, Laura Lee fired. Noelle screamed and fell backward, clutching at the collar of her dress. James wheeled to see his wife with her eyes closed, her finger still on the trigger.

He raced to her as she fired again, the bullet barely missing his face. Reaching her before the next blast, he forced the gun to the left as it exploded like a cannon, shattering a very expensive crystal vase they had received as a wedding gift. Laura Lee howled and fought against him, holding the gun tight, but he was able to wrestle it from her hands. Turning to look back, he saw blood pooled in the entranceway of the parlor, but no Noelle.

"No!!" he yelled.

He could hear Laura Lee's screams behind him, begging him not to leave. He ran out of the room, sidestepping the blood, and charging directly into their children's nanny.

"Mr. Pennington?? Are you—" Her voice stopped short when she saw the blood on the floor and wall.

"Take care of her. Don't let her out of your sight!" James shouted, shoving the woman toward Laura Lee and racing out of the house. Noelle must be terrified. He had to find her, quick.

Noelle drove frantically, feeling herself go weak. The front of her dress was soaked with blood. She could barely see the bridge as she approached it. God help her, she'd never been so terrified. She needed to get to help. Find someone to help her. She didn't want to die, she didn't want to lose her little girl. At the blast of a horn behind her, she looked up in the rearview mirror. The loss of blood coupled with her terror had her confused. She thought it was Laura Lee coming after her to kill her.

James blew his horn to try to get her to pull over. She was swerving on the road and he was desperate to stop her. But she didn't pull over. He watched in horror as she picked up speed, racing straight for the bridge.

Abraham gunned his truck straight for Old Rachette with Cyrus riding at his side. As he drove onto the bridge, he immediately recognized a green-and-brown station wagon swerving, driving dangerously fast. Cyrus leaned forward in his seat, focusing on the car.

"Is that—?"

"What the hell?" Abraham's voice pitched with alarm.

The road became a blur of haze and tears. She felt more than saw the bridge approaching. She blinked rapidly but more tears came, and soon she could see nothing more than shapes. She tried to steer, but her fingers had gone numb around the steering wheel. *I don't want to die. I don't want to lose my little girl.*

"Please, God help me. Please!" Noelle pressed the gas instead of the brake. The station wagon's engine roared and the acceleration made the steering hard to control. "Please God!"

She strained to see the road. Her vision cleared momentarily. She saw Abraham's truck headed toward her. He swerved; she cut the wheel hard to return to her lane. Her station wagon burst through the railing on the side of the bridge and Noelle screamed as her car lifted over, gliding through the air into the Salt River far below.

Abraham slammed on his brakes, as did James, just a few feet away. All three men jumped out of their cars, looking at the bubbled water where the station wagon had already disappeared.

"Is she in there??" Abraham screamed at James, his voice strained with fright.

The Judge, not wanting to believe what he had just seen, looked over the broken railing of the bridge in shock. He was unable to speak. Abraham couldn't wait any longer and jumped from Old Rachette. Cyrus jumped after him. The Judge, pale, gripped the torn railing as the gravity of what he'd witnessed hit him. He could see the men go under, then come back up in the muddy waves of the river. Each time they submerged themselves he prayed she would come up with them. He prayed that God would give him one more chance and spare her life.

Several minutes passed before James' instinct kicked in. Blinded by tears he barely felt drop, he raced to his car and drove straight to the Sheriff's office.

They spent half the night with a rescue team and divers in Salt River. The Judge called in favors all the way to Louisville. He used every crumb of influence he had to launch the rescue. He believed in his heart it would be a rescue, because to believe otherwise wasn't an option. He remained nearby, pacing and running his hands back through his hair. No one dared approach him, but they all knew his pain. He made no attempt to cover it. He was a wreck.

After five hours the divers came back up with her body.

Abraham and Cyrus waited with the majority of the town, watching in shock as Noelle's lifeless form was carried over to a waiting gurney. The Judge was nearby, protected by the law and friends who knew better than to hammer him for answers. He leapt to his feet when she was brought to the surface.

The sight of her destroyed Abraham, broke the Judge, and rocked the people of Penns Point to their core. Cyrus had to work to keep Abraham on his feet. The Judge, on the other end of the bridge, vomited violently. The color division and tensions evaporated as whites, blacks and Hispanics all comforted each other.

The Sheriff was the first to move from the cluster of men near the gurney. His scowling eyes were set on one person only: Abraham Robinson. Out of respect for the Judge, he kept his voice low.

"Did you kill her? Answer me, boy!"

Abraham didn't respond at first. His grief was that profound.

"Answer me!"

"What?"

Sherriff Maddox cut his eyes over to the Judge, who had been weeping like a baby at the sight of the dead woman. Maddox hooked his thumb into his belt so his fingers curled over his holstered gun.

"Did you kill your wife?"

"No." Abraham glared in disgust, not at the Sheriff, but at the ground. He pulled in deep, ragged breaths.

"Don't you move." The Sheriff spat a dark stream from the dip tucked under his lip. He adjusted the belt under his protruding potbelly and walked over to his poker buddy and benefactor. "Judge?"

The Judge dropped his face into his hands. His shoulders shook with sobs. Maddox shot his deputies a look and they all backed away. "Pull yourself together." Maddox hissed. "Walk with me! Now!"

The Judge managed to stand, stumbled, then straightened and stepped away with the Sherriff. The townsfolk to their backs, they faced the flowing waters of Salt River.

"She was shot," said Maddox, giving him the eye.

The Judge didn't speak.

"Talk to me, dammit. What am I dealing with here?"

He tried to push down his grief. He tried hard but the tears kept flowing. He kept seeing her, smiling in bed with him when he tickled her awake from a stolen tryst, when he'd tasted the pie she'd baked and brought to his office, when he'd smelled the apricot lotion on her skin. His Noelle.

"Judge? You know anything about this? Cyrus over there says you were chasing her on the bridge?"

James looked over and then beyond the Sheriff. He saw Cyrus and Abraham staring back. "Laura Lee did it. We can't... I can't..."

Sheriff Maddox looked him over. Miss Laura Lee was a fine white woman. And Pennington had turned the town upside-down for that nigger. For what? Pussy? He snorted in disgust, but held his tongue. This was the Judge, after all. "I'll take care of it."

"Abraham," the Sheriff called back.

Abraham rose shakily, wiped a hand down his face, then approached in step with Cyrus.

"Not you, boy." Sherriff Maddox gestured to Cyrus, his gun-hand never leaving the holster.

Cyrus stopped. He and Abraham exchanged looks. The Sheriff patted the Judge on his shoulder. "Go on home. Take care of Laura Lee."

"No. I'll tell him."

"Not a good idea."

"I'll tell him."

Abraham approached. He stopped in front of Maddox, unable to look at the Judge. He feared what his rage might make him do. The Sheriff sized him up and stepped in close.

"Listen, boy. You two are going to end this here. I suggest you hear the man out and decide on how to do that. I won't have this town ripped apart any further. We clear?"

Abraham narrowed his eyes. He finally looked over to the Judge.

"Clear."

The Sheriff stepped aside, mumbling to himself about cleaning up Pennington shit, and headed straight for the Coroner to explain how this one would go down. Abraham frowned, sensing there was more to the horror. More to his wife's destruction.

"I loved her—" began the Judge.

"Don't!" snapped Abraham through clenched teeth.

"It was an accident."

"Why was she driving that fast? Why were you chasing her?"

James Pennington's eyes went back to the river that had stolen her away.

"She was shot, Abraham."

Abraham doubled back. A few looked over but they were too far away to hear the words. The deputies started moving everyone back up the incline, until there was a crowd on the bridge looking down.

"Sha-shot?"

"Laura Lee. An accident… she didn't…"

"Shot?"

"It's my fault. Mine alone. I can't let Laura Lee suffer because of what I've done."

Abraham looked to his wife's body, now covered by a sheet.

"Shot," he stammered. "Shot?"

He stumbled away and the Judge followed. Abraham went directly to the gurney and crowded the Coroner aside. He drew back the sheet, and both men nearly lost it again at the sight of her. Abraham broke. He scooped her up in his arms and held her to his chest. The Judge, shaking, wiped his hand down his face again and spoke quietly, so that only Abraham would hear.

"We can't let anyone know what happened here today. Do you understand? For the sake of Aaren, for Laura Lee, for all of them. We can't."

Abraham groaned. He let go a deep, mournful wail that started from the bottom of his soul and passed his lips in a painful howl. The Judge backed away, leaving Noelle, at last, to her husband.

Chapter Thirteen

AFTERMATH

"Laura Lee killed my mother," repeated Aaren. "Laura Lee."

The Judge's eyes lifted from his glass. "Noelle's death was my fault. I drove Laura to it."

Remorse in the face of his lies meant nothing to her. She refused even to look at him. He cleared his throat and spoke in a low, defeated voice.

"Laura never meant anyone any harm. She was young and innocent when I took her as a wife. When I…" his voice trailed off to a whisper. His eyelids sagged with sadness. "I made vows that I didn't believe. She never had a say in her life, or our marriage. And this, it was her only act of rebellion. The blame can't be laid at her feet. Not when I was the one to give her nothing but years of pain."

"And you expect me to what—agree? You're both to blame! I know you run the law here. Only a Pennington could get away with murder in this town! That's right, Your Honor. MURDER." Aaren choked down the sob in her throat.

"Abraham and I agreed that night that we would bury it all with Noelle. Neither of us wanted Laura Lee to go to jail. Neither of us wanted you growing up with the shame of your mother's death. So yes, I chose the path, and used my influence to sway the town from what little they knew. It wasn't hard, Aaren. We all wept for Noelle, we all wanted to let go of the hate. Your mother didn't die in vain. You see, we found a way to heal."

"Heal?? Bullshit!! You and your *wife* did this to save your asses!!!" Aaren's voice crackled with bitterness, each word spoken through clenched teeth. Her eyes were hard and unforgiving as she glared at the man who'd destroyed her family.

Judge Pennington closed his eyes to the sight of her. "It was a horrible accident. But it was an accident."

"MURDER! She was murdered! Just say it!" Aaren sat up. "You killed her and this entire town ignored it because her life wasn't worth trouble. What kind of people are you?" her words echoed back to her again. That accusation would have to be leveled at her father as well. He'd signed on for the lie, too. She closed her eyes and her heart to that ugly truth. She'd made peace with him. Now this?

"You covered it up! And my father let you! Sweet merciful God, how could he do that?"

Judge Pennington rose. "You have to listen to me—"

"Why? So you can convince me to ignore the fact that she was murdered?"

Aaren looked around. She stiffened, panic rioting in her, her hands gripped tight into fists. She nearly leapt from the chair, recoiling from the Judge. Her eyes darted everywhere as the entirety of the truth dawned on her.

Her mother was murdered. Her mother had been shot in this house.

"Was it in here? Was it right here?"

"No, no, sweetie. It wasn't." He went to her, his arms wide. She knew he was lying. She could see it. She was standing in the spot where her mother had been shot. Aaren felt her knees weaken at the realization. James reached for her, trying to steer her away from the painful acknowledgement.

"Don't touch me!" she screamed, reeling back.

Travis and Macy came running from separate directions. They stopped at the sight of Aaren's hysteria. Their eyes, wide with shock, tracked from Aaren to their father, then back again, unable to comprehend the scene. Aaren whirled away from them, imagining blood that wasn't there. Her lungs were heavy with the burden of truths long hidden. She held her breath to ward off a panic attack. Finally, the sights real and imagined were more than she could bear. She closed her eyes and prayed for a return to blissful ignorance.

"Mom, you shot her?" Jarrod sat up abruptly, yanking his hand out of his mother's.

Laura Lee let her tears flow. "That woman, Jay, I swear, you don't understand. When I first found out about the affair she was unapologetic for it. She was supposed to be my friend, and—"

"And you killed her?" Jarrod stood and backed away.

"It was an accident. I swear. The gun just went off, and I was in such pain. So much pain, never in my life have I experienced that kind of pain." Laura Lee's voice broke as she struggled for breath. Her hands, trembling, lifted from the bed sheet, her fingers stretching toward him. "Jay, I want you to know something. Have to tell you something…"

He shook his head, refusing her plea for understanding.

"It wasn't your father. He didn't mean to hurt us. Stop blaming him. If you love Aaren then you have to forgive him. It is the only way you two can be free of us, of what we've done. Don't hold on to hate, Jay. It gets you *nothing*. Look at it what it made me do."

Jarrod couldn't speak. In the last few days, he'd discovered Abraham's lifeless body, learned of Aaren's unhappiness because of his thoughtless plan to protect her, and now this. His mother had killed the woman who should have been his mother-in-law. He backed away from the bed, his mind reeling. He turned away from the mother he adored, unable to look upon her, even in her current state.

"This is not happening," he stammered.

"Jay, come back. We don't have much time."

He turned on her, furious. "No more. We're done!"

Laura Lee struggled for breath. "Jay," she sighed sadly, her eyes weepy. "We *are* done. There is no more. He—" she laughed, a hollow victory. "Abraham showed me the way. I've only been waiting for you."

Her words didn't make sense at first. Then, when her meaning registered, Jarrod was frozen absolutely still. Now, he could see how pale his mother was, why she could barely breathe, why her lips were almost white, why her hands had been burning hot under his, for the short time she'd let him touch her. Now he could see why she'd been so determined to swallow all those pills.

"Christ! Jesus! I'm calling Dr. Swanson!" He went for the phone, but his mother's weakening voice stilled him.

"It's already too late, Jay."

Jarrod looked at her in abject horror.

"My heart breaks for you son," she said, between sharp gasps of breath. Tears of regret spilled. "My baby, you feel so much, you lost so much, and it's my fault. My fault you lost your way. If I had only known how much you loved her, Jay. I'm so sorry."

She tried to sit upright but didn't have the strength. Instead, she leaned toward him, grasping. Jarrod leapt to her side, afraid she'd roll from the bed.

"Mom, we have to call the doctor."

"I love you so much. I've told you the truth. Too late, but I've told you, and now I can let go. Promise me you will forgive your father, forgive us both. Promise me you will try so you can be happy," she pleaded.

Jarrod's eyes cut to the phone for a split second before he reached. Laura Lee stayed the action, wheezing, but managing to grab his sleeve.

"Promise me. No more lies. Truth, Jay, then love."

"Mom..."

Laura Lee gasped in a deep breath and let go of it slowly. As she slipped away, the fire that blazed behind her hazel eyes extinguished. Jarrod, realizing his loss, grabbed her to him. He pulled her up into his chest and held her, his face buried into her mass of curls, the familiar smells of mom assailing him. He could feel her warmth ebbing away as her life-force drained.

"Mom... no... mom, please! Don't leave it like this!"

"Stay away from me!!" shouted Aaren at Travis' approach. Her shrill plea stopped him. Her body shook; her eyes darted between the two men, then settled on the Judge. "You did this! Why? I would have had her if you had just left my family alone!"

Aaren wanted nothing more than to run from this house. She wished she'd thought to drive her own car, and railed silently at Jarrod for taking so long upstairs with... with a woman she no longer had civil words for.

The Judge rubbed his face. Arguing with Noelle's daughter over the mistakes he'd made decades ago was too much. He itched to refill his glass with Bourbon.

"I'm so sorry, Aaren." His voice was barely a whisper: it was all he could manage,.

"No you aren't! But you will be, damn it! I'll make you pay. I'll make you all pay!" she shouted through her tears. To hell with restraint! She wanted blood for the blood her family shed.

Macy peeked out around Travis to look at her father, alarmed. "Dad, what's going on? Why is she screaming?"

Travis turned to his sister. "Go get Jay!"

Jarrod came from behind them, his face pale, void of emotion or tears. "I'm right here."

Aaren finally tore her eyes from the Judge. They fell upon a stoic Jarrod. His face clearly registered some new truths of his own.

"Jarrod. Oh, Jarrod," she said, stepping back from him.

Part of her still wanted to seek his arms, but seeing him truly the same as his father, she felt herself pushing him again from her heart. That familiar hurt, the pain she'd almost let go of tore through her. The loss was so deep it began to drain her of any lasting hope. She closed her eyes to it and tried to focus.

Jarrod looked away as well. His father, sister and brother stood in a semi-circle around them. His eyes went past their questioning faces and looked back once more up the stairs, to the room where the only other woman he'd ever loved besides Aaren lay in undeserved repose.

"Mom's gone."

Aaren looked back at him, shocked.

Macy screamed and took off, with Travis trying to catch her. Aaren watched as the Judge stumbled back into the parlor. Still clutching that drained glass of whiskey, he seemed to age years before them. Aaren wanted more than ever to flee. She didn't belong there. But something in the way Jarrod said *gone* reached her. He looked so lost. Then he stepped inside the parlor and despite her own inner voice warning her to let him go, she followed.

"You were a selfish asshole," Jarrod said, a finger pointed at his father. "You've destroyed everything. Everyone who ever came near you. I hope you spend the rest of your days in hell for what you've done!"

The Judge set the glass aside with a shaky hand. His eyes focused away, seeing something none of the rest of them could. Tears ran down his gently-lined cheeks. Then he lifted his eyes, sunken with grief, to his son.

"I died when Noelle went over that bridge. There's nothing you can say to me that I don't say to myself, every damned day."

Jarrod didn't care. He and Aaren had so much pain between them it didn't matter what his father's penance was. Aaren came in behind him. He felt her before she spoke. Her hand went to his arm gently. "Your mother's dead?"

"Just like yours," he mumbled. "Justice."

He avoided her touch and eyes as he headed toward the door. He stopped at the sounds of his sister's screams from upstairs. He nearly went for her, but remembered that Travis was with her. So he kept going.

Aaren looked at the Judge with pity and disgust. He just sat there staring at his hands.

"I will always blame you for not protecting her."

"She loved you most of all. I want you to know that. Think what you want of me, but know that she wouldn't have left you if she'd had a choice—"

"She did have a choice. She chose you."

She strode out of the room without another word. It was over for Aaren, the worst of it had come and she was still standing. She pushed her pain to the place she shelved all the things she'd rather not deal with and left the Pennington home. Outside she saw Jarrod sitting in his truck, waiting for her, staring straight ahead. The engine was running at a high idle. She went to the truck and got inside. Jarrod sped out of the driveway so fast she gripped the dash.

"Are you okay?"

"No."

Sinking into her seat, she held her tongue. The truck jerked into more speed as they raced out of the subdivision. They rode in complete silence, with only the noise of the gears shifting between them, as they rushed toward the bridge. The dark waters ran below in a never-ending current of their parents' tears, secrets, and lies. All her life she'd wanted answers to her father's indifference and her mother's absence, and this is where they'd been all along. Salt River. The truck's engine groaned and Aaren's eyes dropped to the needle on the speedometer. For a two-lane crossing, they were going too fast.

"Jarrod?" He didn't respond. Aaren looked from his pained expression to the road. "Jarrod, slow down."

Instead, he went faster.

"Stop it, Jarrod! Slow down!"

He shifted again, faster, then let his hands grip the steering wheel tight. Pain etched his face. His jaw twitched. Aaren could see his nostrils flaring. She'd never seen him look like this, crazed with grief and something else she couldn't read. She looked away to the bridge and then back at him. He must be in shock, she realized. How could he not be, if he was there when Laura Lee passed away. If she'd told him what she'd done. Aaren steeled her nerves and spoke to him softly.

"Slow down," she whispered, slipping her fingertips just inside the opening of his shirt. She stroked his collarbone, then lower, until the palm of her hand lay flat and she could feel the pounding of his heart.

Jarrod let up on the gas. The truck pulled over to the gravel patch at the foot of the bridge and fishtailed sharply to a stop. He dropped his head, tucking his chin down, away from her. Aaren saw his chest rising and falling and knew he was trying to keep from crying.

"Jarrod... Jay."

"She did it, Aaren. My mother killed her. What type of person does that?" He pleaded for an answer, eyes glued to the river.

"It was an accident," she mumbled, partly disbelieving, partly wanting to give him some sense of comfort. *Maybe it was an accident*, she reasoned with herself. *Maybe.*

"An accident?" He looked over at her in shock. "Are you *defending* her?"

"No, but I'm not going to blame her. Look out there, Jay. What's the point? She's dead. They're all dead but the Judge. What does blaming anyone do?" Her voice broke off and she shook her head, tears dropping from her lashes. "Pop blamed you, you blamed your father, Laura Lee blamed Mama, and she probably blamed herself. For what? For *what?*" Aaren choked back her tears, and put her hands to her eyes to stop the flood. "Jarrod, it was over twenty years ago. The river washed it away."

When he didn't reply, she lowered her hands and looked at him. He continued to stare at the murky, rushing waters of the river. "It didn't wash anything away, Aaren. Look at what this did to you, to me. What those secrets continue to do to us, both."

Aaren looked down as well. She imagined her mother's fear as her car went over the railing. Watching the waves roll the water along, she prayed again silently that she didn't suffer. She hoped her mother had died on impact. She closed her eyes.

"Let me drive," she offered.

He gave in. There were no words. Nothing either of them could say. So he got out and gave her the wheel. Aaren started up the car and they rode onto the bridge slowly, both looking straight ahead, not at the railing or what ran beneath, neither of them speaking a word about what happened that night in Penns Point.

Aaren poured. Boiling water sloshed into the mug. She tried to steady her shaky hand. The steam curled up, carrying the strong, sweet aroma from the dissolving tea through the kitchen. She set the kettle back on the eye of the stove, then reached for the razor-sharp kitchen knife. It sliced the lemon with ease, which she then squeezed into the darkening liquid. Going through the motions, taking time and care to do everything just right, that was her peace.

AFTERMATH

A pinch of ginger was added with a scoop of honey, then she stirred over and over, tears drying upon her cheeks.

Tea was always a source of calm and strength for her. Becca's mom had taught her how to make this brew and after all these years she still made it the exact same way. She looked up at the ceiling and sighed.

He was upstairs. She could see him lying there on the bed, staring out the doors to his terrace, looking beyond the trees back through the memories of his mother and all the lies. He'd gone from being minimally verbal with his anger and pain to retreating somewhere far inside himself that she couldn't reach. He hadn't cried. Not a single tear. She'd never seen him like that before. But she understood that darkness. She'd been forced into retreat, too.

Aaren blew the tea to cool it, a familiar bitterness swelling inside her. She tried to ignore it, tried to set aside blame and hurt. She wanted desperately to undo all the heartache of their shared past, or at least make sense of it. So much had happened and it was too much for her to process: there was too much to unravel. There were still secrets, hers, left to reveal. And telling him wouldn't change a thing about what they'd learned today.

She headed out of the kitchen returning to him. She took each stair slowly carefully holding the mug with both hands. She found him and the room as she'd imagined she would. The double French doors opposite the foot of the bed were flung open. The cool evening wind blew in the Kentucky scents: soil and wildflowers. The sunset cast a soft orange glow, putting his face in shadows. She closed the door gently, but Jarrod didn't move. He didn't acknowledge her, just stared ahead, with both hands behind his head. His cap was tossed aside and his legs were crossed at the ankle. If it weren't for the hard set of his jaw, she could believe he was relaxing, accepting, but it was not so.

"I made you some tea," she said softly. He gave her no response. "Jay."

Aaren stepped to the bed, set the mug on the nightstand, and rubbed her hands at her sides.

"Jay, look... I... um... drink the tea, okay?"

She failed miserably at this. It was too raw for them both. She chewed on her bottom lip. She stepped out of her sandals, then scooped her yellow dress under her as she sat on the edge of the bed. Placing her hand to his chest, she smiled sweetly before speaking.

"So much happened today. A lot of painful truths. And I know... I know you loved her. It's okay to grieve her, no matter what she's done. It's, um... it's the lesson I learned from all of this. I think we need to find a way to separate who we are from what they did."

Slowly, his head turned. His eyes, glassy pools of repudiation, locked with hers. There in the bluest depths she found ageless hurt, and a familiar sense of loss she knew too well. Jarrod always felt so much, but always held back. Even when they were young, he'd held in. Aaren's hand went over his arm soothingly. She forced a smile for his benefit, and her own. She wished that looking into his eyes would make the horrors of the day evaporate. He tried to speak, but the words never came. They didn't have to. Aaren went to him. His arms welcomed her automatically. She let the motion pull them over, settling herself beside him. She looked up at him with a wry smile.

"It's okay. I know how it feels. I know what you need."

He frowned. Her fingers spread over his tensed jaw and dug in, drawing his lips to hers. She kissed him softly, silencing the makings of protest in his throat. But she felt him tense and pull away.

"Aaren, no, I can't."

"Sure you can. We need it, we both need it," she breathed.

Passion pooled at her center, throbbing in time with her beating pulse. No doubt he wanted to forget as much as she wanted to forget. She forced the kiss again with a seductive tease of her tongue; he weakened, as all men do. His capitulation was a shot of adrenaline through her. For the first time since the day began, a renewed sense of control overtook her. She moved over him, causing him to roll back with a deep sigh. Her thighs locked him beneath her, and she ground her desire for him into the bulge hardening beneath his zipper.

"Aaren—" Jarrod gripped her arms to stop her, turning away from the fever he felt in her kiss. They'd just learned the unspeakable and she wanted to make love? He shook his head at her, trying to understand her. His resolve weakened as his body temperature rose.

"It's okay, Jay. I feel it too." She shook off his hold and intertwined her fingers in his, driving his hands back to the stacks of pillows behind his head. Her lips went to his neck, applying kisses where she could feel the warmth of his skin, then down past the collar of his shirt, where she couldn't. "I know what you need. Trust me."

"You do?"

Aaren lifted her head once more. There was something in her eyes, something he didn't like. It excited him as much as it worried him. She was out of his reach, in a place he couldn't touch. With a flash, it was gone. She gave him a knowing smile and ran the tip of her tongue over her lips.

"You feel empty now, Jay. That hollow feeling? It's like there's a hole in you." She whispered the words seductively into his mouth.

"Aaren—"

"Stop talking. Stop."

She sat upright, releasing his hands. Riding his lap, she undid the snaps to the halter behind her neck. Jarrod wanted to object, knew there was something missing this time, but he couldn't as Aaren unveiled her beauty to him without shame. His eyes fell upon her breasts and his body betrayed his heart. But he craved her desperately. And she was right. He wanted it all to go away.

She saw him frown, as if to object again, until the front of her dress dropped. She didn't want to talk about anything, and she wouldn't let him, either. When he took her by the face and brought her lips to his mouth, she gasped at the crushing force behind the kiss. Aaren moaned, tasting him, reaching beneath him to grab his groin and squeeze it tight. Then he flipped her, trailing kisses along her neck, his tongue traveling south as she did battle with his belt buckle to free him. Their hurried motions robbed them both of the sweetness of lovemaking, frenzied actions that had her shoving his jeans from his hips and him forcing her panties down her thighs. He broke away to get the condom; quickly, silently, she rolled her panties the rest of the way down and slid under him. His swift entry was her reward. Her mouth gaped and her brows creased as he thrust into her. She dug her nails deep into the mounds of his ass, causing him to hiss and thrust harder. That worked. She didn't want to feel anything but him.

Moisture built behind her closed lids, tears she wouldn't spill. She let go short, quick breaths, rubbing his back where she felt his muscles tight with tension. His pace quickened, shaking the bed on its posts. He grunted, pumping in and out of her harder, faster, going deeper and deeper. The friction and the stroking had her walls clenching and toes curling. Pleasure currents built in her pelvis and radiated out, causing her hips to shake. Aaren struggled to breathe and clung to him, meeting him each time with upward thrusts of her own. She bucked and writhed, forcing him to go further. Jarrod groaned, squeezing her bottom painfully tight, as she held his. She shook through a hard orgasm that had her arching under him in a joined release.

And then it was over.

Over. That's what she wanted, what she needed. For it to be over. Jarrod laid on her crushingly hard, his breath hot on her cheek. Aaren squeezed her eyes shut in disappointment. It wasn't enough. She didn't understand what she needed, what she was doing. Not anymore. She opened her eyes, not to him, but to the room, now darkening under the twilight-purple sky.

He lifted his head and kissed her again roughly, then rolled off. She saw his face, red and strained. He still needed to heal. So did she. She rolled to her side and hugged herself. He made no move to reach for her. They laid together in silence. Aaren felt nothing—as she'd hoped—just empty.

The bed shifted. He was up and walking away, to the bathroom possibly. Leaving her was always so easy for him. Why she made the analogy now, she didn't know: this time, even she could see she'd put him on that path. It hurt nevertheless, as it always did when she thought of their love. What was the saying? Doing the same thing over, and expecting a different outcome? Aaren closed her eyes. Today had done them in, she knew it. And obviously, he felt it too. How could he not?

Jarrod stepped under the cool jets spraying from the shower head. It wasn't right, none of it. He'd been rough with her. Not on purpose, but it was as if she wanted it that way. Dropping his hands to the tiles of the shower, he let the water run over the back of his head and sluice down his spine. He'd wanted to feel it again, just a piece of the innocence they'd once had, even what he'd felt yesterday when he made love to her. He'd lost all of that today, just as she had, and he didn't know how to replace it. He lifted his head from the pour and wiped his hand down his face.

His dad bedded a married woman and lost his soul. Was his love for Noelle so consuming that he would leave his family?

Thinking of his own love for Aaren and the lengths he'd gone to preserve it, from his tattoo, to their paradise by the creek, he began to understand. What he couldn't wrap his mind around was the fact that his dad's selfish need for another man's wife drove his beloved mother to the brink of insanity. Her dying words had been a confession of jealousy and hate.

He felt sick.

Now his mother was dead and he couldn't reconcile the woman he'd known and loved from his earliest moments with the one who'd calmly confessed her sins to him just hours before. Yes, it happened long ago, but it held the power to destroy what he and Aaren should have had. That bullet had ripped through Noelle and torn far into the future, destroying the balance of right and wrong, a world that he had faith in. The world where love overcame all.

He felt the coldness of his misery blooming inside despite the warming waters of the shower. All his time in the Gulf, he'd barely been able to function in a world where sons killed other sons. He couldn't live in a world where his mother could kill another mother. He didn't know how to get past it.

Aaren rolled over, then back again. There were too many pillows. She couldn't breathe. Her eyes parted slightly, then opened. She'd fallen asleep. The last she remembered was the sound of the shower. Her sheet barely covered the raised, tender scratches on her hip. She sat up. Her thighs still ached from their lovemaking. She peered around the darkened room searching for Jarrod, though she knew he wouldn't be there.

The night had gotten cooler, so much so she was forced to pull up the front of her sundress and snap it behind her neck for cover. Throwing her legs over the side of the bed, she slipped onto the cold hardwood floors and walked out to the deck, looking out across the farm. She saw a light on at the top part of the barn, up in the hay loft.

"Jay, what are you doing?" she wondered aloud.

She nibbled her lip, conceding that she'd probably pushed him, maybe scared him a little bit, earlier. She wanted to help him through this, and told herself she could. To the back of her mind, she wondered about their future, and if past history and present lies were truly too big to overcome. Focusing on the here and now, she decided she'd make sure he didn't do what he was notorious for: running.

Aaren went to his closet and grabbed a windbreaker, then put on her sneakers. She smoothed out her dress and combed through her hair with her fingers. She raced down the stairs and out the front door. The summer night carried a wind filled with the chirping sounds of night animals. The barn loomed ahead. Set behind it was a starlit sky, one that could only be found in the open fields of the country. Even as much as she'd dreaded and loathed Penns Point, what Jarrod had created for them here was the closest thing she'd ever felt to home. For the first time, she considered what her life would be like if she chose to stay. Crazy as it was, the idea didn't totally disgust her as it had before. Even now, when it came to her future, she couldn't decide on one emotion over the other. The problem was that she was having these emotions at all. That much was clear.

The hem of her sundress blew around her knees and she slipped her hands into the pockets of his jacket. She continued to wade through the tall grass to the barn doors. Aaren pulled hard on the handle and slipped it open. The ripe smell of livestock smacked her in the face, making her eyes tear. The cows made a stir, but nothing loud enough to disturb the night. She debated calling out to him. Then she heard a loud crash above her head. Startled, she jumped. Her eyes shot upward, toward the direction of the noise, aware now of the sound of stomping feet.

"What the hell?" she mumbled.

She hurried over to the ladder that led to the loft, looking up expectantly. The crash came again and this time she recognized it. He was smashing bottles against the wall. She looked back to the open barn door, the night wind pushing against it, then up the rusty rungs of the ladder. Shaking her head, she made the climb, came to the top of the loft, and looked over the floorboards at him.

He sat on top of a crate, surrounded by empty beer bottles at his feet. She saw him turn one up and raise it in toast to the wall.

"You fucking liar!!" He upended the beer to finish the last of it, then hurled the bottle. "Who are you? Oh, that's right. You're a murderer!" he slurred, then chuckled. "Not just the head of the Women's League, but a murdering, lying witch. Pathetic, pathetic, pa-thet-ic!" He scooped up another and tossed it. Brown shards of glass cascaded everywhere from the force of the impact. He reached for another bottle. "To hell with you!"

Aaren climbed over the top of the ladder to the floor of the loft. Jarrod heard her and whirled around. They stared at each other for a moment, then she took a step toward him.

"Jay."

His face revealed hurt before his brain caught up and covered it. His eyes lowered to drunken slits as he stumbled back, shaking his head.

"Get the hell out of here!"

"What are you doing up here? What is this?" She took a step toward him, eyeing the destruction of the bottles.

"I said go away, for fuck's sake!"

Aaren's eyes narrowed on him. He wasn't the only one hurting. He wasn't the only one who'd lost something.

"Put that bottle down and let's talk."

He stared at her, his face cold and assessing. She saw rage in his bloodshot, swollen eyes. So much pain. He smirked at her, then turned and hurled the bottle with such force that its splatter shot glass shards at both of them, barely missing Aaren. She shrieked, bringing her hands defensively to her face. He was near her before she opened her eyes.

"Aaren, are you… are you… all right?"

"Get away from me!" she snapped, shoving him hard. He stumbled back and shook his head. His apology came out of him in a drunken slur.

"Look'm... I... I'm sorry."

"Is this how you deal with things?? Enough of this! Let's go!"

"NO!"

She stopped mid-turn and looked back at him, shocked by his refusal. He turned and bent for another beer bottle, a full one. He opened it, looking directly into her eyes the entire time.

"Stop it, Jay. Put it down!" She stormed over to him.

He turned it up for a drink and held her off with one hand. Aaren snatched away.

"Fine, then stay here and booze."

The moment she tried to leave, he cut her off, blocking her pass. She looked up at him, angry and frustrated.

"Why are you here?" he hissed.

"Why am I here? What does that mean?" Aaren crossed her arms.

"Why are you still here, Aaren? The truth."

"You know why I'm here, Jarrod. Now move."

He blocked her again. She stepped back, looking him up and down, suddenly not sure what she'd meant to accomplish by chasing him out here. She was barely keeping it together herself. She'd tried to be understanding. He had lost so much. But what he was doing was cowardly. And she'd already had as much of his weakness as she was prepared to take.

"She killed your mother and you're still here. But all of a sudden, you're not Aaren. You think I don't see it, that I don't feel it. What was that earlier? Who was that back there, because it sure as hell wasn't you!"

"You're drunk. Let's go back in, and you can sleep it off. We can talk about it later." She turned away from him, disgusted.

"NO! We talk about it now!" he shouted. She stopped and looked back at him. The two of them stood close together, separated by a wall of pain. He glared at her, downing another swallow of the beer, then dropped the bottle. He wiped his mouth with the back of his hand, looking her over. She didn't like the way he looked her over.

"Move, Jay." She kept her tone even, a final warning.

"You just shut down," he sneered. "Lock away the part of you that can't handle it, right? That's how you deal, give people the surface only, huh? Look at you, you didn't even want to talk about what we learned today."

"How could I!" she snapped. "You were too busy licking your wounds to talk about anything."

Jarrod nodded. "That's what it is, then? Pity? You pity me?"

"Get out of my way."

He refused to move. "That was pity back there? You felt sorry for me? You wanted to love me and then you wouldn't let me in. I felt it when I touched you, and now... now with everything... I'm... I'm losing you, aren't I?"

Aaren said absolutely nothing.

"Wait a fucking minute." He stumbled back, laughing. "I never had you, did I? Did I!"

She pushed past him and went for the ladder, ignoring his drunken shouting behind her.

"I want to know the truth! I won't sit around and wait for it to happen again! For you to leave me again!"

Aaren's head turned slowly. She couldn't believe her ears. Did he just say that *she* would leave *him*? He was the fucking coward. Always had been, and tonight, too. The runner, the scared boy that didn't know how to fight back, and he had the nerve to accuse her?

He was on the verge of collapsing but he had pushed her too far. She did love him. If nothing else, these last days with him forced her to admit she'd never stopped loving him. But part of her hated him. Hated what his cowardice had done to her, what she'd turned into. And another part of her, God help her, enjoyed his suffering. Because no one, not even him, knew how badly she'd suffered when he and her father cast her aside.

"Me, leave you? A*gain?* You don't want to go there, Jarrod. Trust me."

"I love you, Aaren. And you—"

She laughed bitterly.

He stormed over to her and snatched her by the arms. His grip was so tight, when he shook her she nearly bit into her tongue. She glared at him.

"Something's changed. I can see it in your eyes. You won't let me in!" he hissed.

"Get off me!!" She shoved him back.

Jarrod blinked at the show of rage. She trembled with fury.

"Something changed, Jarrod? Something's changed? Unfrickin-believable! You think it's *them*, don't you? The big, bad Judge and your dear, sweet mama… you think that is why I won't trust you again? Really trust you? Well, you're wrong! It's *you*!"

"Me? What have I done but spend all these years loving you!!! Take a look around here, Aaren. All for you! I couldn't even let another woman past the doors of my house 'cause of wanting for you! Wanting you back, wishing you were mine again! What have I done that—"

"You gave up, that's what! You let him drive me from this town thinking all I ever amounted to was a good lay. You were my first love and my only love and you threw that away! You threw me away! You gave up long before we even knew the real truth! So don't stand there and blame me because you were too weak to protect us!"

He blinked at her as though the beers were beginning to wear off.

"I told you, I did that because of your father! That I promised him—"

"You promised me first, you bastard! You promised me first. You promised me first!!" She shouted at him, angry tears streaking a trail down her face. "You want to know the truth Jay?" She took a step toward him, fist clenched. "That feeling you have, right now. You know the one, where you feel lost, empty, alone, betrayed, guess what Jay, it doesn't go away. No. It's like this bottomless hole in you that's spreading. All your hopes and beliefs just cave inside of it. And it just keeps consuming everything." She smiled, affording a sly, unforgiving slant to her lips. "Unless you know how to make it go away."

"How?"

"How you think?" she spat.

"How??"

She taunted him with her smirk, her stance.

"Say it, damn it! How do you make it go away?"

"Any way you can, baby," she cooed. "I found a way."

Jarrod stared at her, confused. Were they talking about the same thing? He blinked. "What does that mean? You found a way?"

"I got to college and boys liked me, Jay. They always did."

"So?" He looked away from her, swallowing.

"No, Jay, let me tell you about it. You want to know, right? Where I've been? Who I am? What I've done?" She circled him and forced him to look at her. More tears dropped. This time she refused to wipe them away.

"I want you! The real you!" he snapped back.

Aaren nodded and opened her arms. "Here I am."

"Stop it, Aaren."

"Oh no, Jay, you need to know. I figured it out, I wasn't special, and my body sure as hell wasn't. Especially after Jarrod Pennington got his way!"

"Stop it! That is not who we were."

"Sure we were. Pop saw it. He couldn't even look at me when he dropped me off at the train station. Everyone else saw it after the fair. Remember, Jay? Remember how they laughed at me? Hey! Did you know that Curtis Simmons asked me right before I left if I'd give him some of what you got? He said he didn't mind sloppy seconds."

He looked at her, heartbroken. She took a step back from his reaching hand.

"They all laughed, just like you did that day."

"You're twisting things, Aaren. I love you and always have. I gave you up to make you happy."

"You gave me up because you wanted the easy way out! Ask me how I know, Jay. Ask me! Go ahead, ask me!"

She hated everything about him and his family in that moment. Hated them and hated herself, hated her mother, hated the town, hated Pop. She was consumed by hate. The tears dried. Her heart withered. All she could do was smile, laugh, give up on feeling anything. That's what came easy.

"I know because I gave it up to any boy that wanted it. You hear that, Jay? I took the easy way out, too! Why you think I could come back to town after all these years and just give it up to you?"

Her words cut through him, filleted him down the center. She saw him pale. She saw it and felt sick and triumphant. She was disappointed to discover her triumph also made her sad.

"This was a mistake. We were always a mistake. Weren't we, Jay? We were never supposed to happen. Never." Her voice broke over the last word as her heart shuddered and wept for them, both. "Pop was right. I *am* my mother."

Jarrod watched her step calmly to the ladder. He watched her descend, then saw her walk out the open barn door without looking back. He'd never fully understood how badly he'd hurt her. Her anguished confession had finally shown him what his weakness had done, and what it had cost them both. He closed his eyes, remembering how she'd been upstairs, how desperate she was as she reached for him. That wasn't them. They weren't defined by that. That wasn't who they'd been this last week, and part of Aaren had still knew it: he'd seen it on her face.

He was to blame for the change. She'd taken his need to be alone, to recover from the day, as a rejection. To her, it was the night of the fair all over again. Her confession took on new meaning. She was trying to push him away, get there first this time.

"Aaren!" he yelled. He stumbled to the ladder and quickly down. "Aaren!"

She didn't turn or slow for him. She didn't speed up her pace, either.

"Aaren! You're wrong!"

She stopped, but didn't turn around.

"They can't touch you, Aaren. Not you. None of them could. You know why?"

Jarrod steadied himself then approached her, praying she'd heard him, that she'd believe in him, just once more. She looked back, and even in the distance he could see tears glistening on her cheeks.

"Because no one can touch you the way I do. No one knows you the way that I do, no one believes in you more. You are the love of my life."

He stepped around her. Faced her. He rubbed his thumb over her cheek. She shook her head sadly. "There's no such thing."

He wanted to laugh out loud, because all he wanted was to spend the rest of their lives proving her wrong.

"I left you once. I did. But there is nothing you can say to me that will ever make me leave you again."

Aaren broke in heavy sobs, needing to believe he spoke the truth. Finally, she came willingly into his arms. Jarrod held on tight, vowing he'd never let her go.

Chapter Fourteen

SECRETS AND LIES

Jarrod opened his eyes to searing pain. His jaw twitched, his throat constricted: it felt as dry as a desert. He reached to his side and found Aaren gone. He blinked and swallowed again, deciding to let his eyes fall closed. Then the night came back in flashes.

She'd told him her past, the awful truth. He'd felt her secret shame and pain. And he'd tried to be strong for her. He'd tried to tell her, and show her, that it didn't destroy what they had. But standing in that pasture, completely flattened by the ungodly turmoil of their day, he'd found his body swaying and his eyelids drooping. She'd leaned into him, needing him. Most of a twelve-pack and sheer exhaustion had him unprepared, and the movement almost tumbled them into the long grass. He'd barely kept them from falling.

It had been Aaren who'd turned them toward the house last night and steered him upstairs. She'd pushed him onto the mattress, then retreated to the open deck, watching him. He'd called out to her, wanting her to come to bed. She'd bitten her lip and nodded. That was the last thing he remembered.

Jarrod opened his eyes again, slowly this time. He waited for his vision to clear, then lifted his head begrudgingly from his pillow. He felt as if he wore a hat of bricks. What he needed was coffee, and an entire bottle of Tylenol.

He rolled to his side, and then immediately back. It was too soon to move. He groaned. The sleep hadn't done him much good.

"Aaren?" he called out.

In their few short days together, he'd become accustomed to the sound of her in the house. Now, the silence alarmed him. He kicked away the sheet and hurriedly brushed his teeth, then went in search of her.

The roasted smell of a fresh pot of coffee mingled with Southern breakfast, filling the air. Coming closer, he saw fried bacon and the leftovers of an egg scramble. He hit his fist to his stomach to silence the responding grumble, then managed to swallow the goofy grin forming on his face. He'd laid up in that bed so many times, fantasizing about mornings just like this.

"Mornin'." He smiled, watching her from behind.

She looked back at him, but didn't say anything. Then she turned and cracked two eggs, one-handed, into the sputtering pan.

"So you're not in a talking mood," he ventured, observing her half-eaten toast. "But you are making me breakfast."

"Something like that," she replied.

There had been a moment last night, out in the pasture, when he'd thought the worst was over and they'd simply move forward, but life was never that easy. She'd let him hold her, but the doubt in her eyes hadn't fully gone away. And though he understood why she'd done so, he'd have to come to terms with the fact that she'd kept her past from him when he'd been open about his. Even in the best of circumstances, it might take him some time. Evidently it was going to take her some time, too.

He exhaled, wondering how to right their ship. He'd tossed and turned through the night, expecting the worst. But she hadn't left. She'd stayed. And he knew her. That meant something. It gave him hope.

Jarrod walked over to the window over the kitchen sink. He stared out at his land. His stable hands were arriving and setting about the day's work. He remembered all the broken glass in the hay loft. The guys would understand, given what he'd been through yesterday, but even so, his lack of control shamed him.

"Should get out there and clean up that mess."

"Already did. I couldn't sleep."

Jarrod looked back. "How long have you been up?"

She shrugged, avoiding the question, and slid the eggs onto the plate she'd taken from the oven.

"Sit down," she said. "And don't you get used to all this domestic stuff."

"Yes, ma'am." He sat, his eyes never leaving her face. "Aaren, we okay? About last night?"

"Listen, Jarrod." She blew out a breath, then tried again. "Jay. I said things, you said things—"

"It was just the heat of the moment talking. For both of us." He caught her expression and backpedaled. "You told me the whole truth last night, and that took guts. I know that. And the things I said—"

Aaren shook her head. "No, Jay. I didn't."

Jarrod's face paled.

"I mean, every word was true. But there's more."

He nodded once, waiting. How the hell could there be *more*?

"But given… with your mom, with the circumstances, I think we should have a cooling-off period."

"Cooling-off," he repeated, uncertain.

"It's like in a divorce," she began, immediately regretting the example she'd chosen. "Between the time the papers are filed and when the hearing begins, neither party can take any further action."

"Okay…"

"And then when we're not so emotional, we come back and finish from last night."

Jarrod clenched his teeth.

"If this is it, if you're just going to dump me, then do it now."

Aaren sucked in another breath and held it. She'd been up before the sun, thinking and dealing. Her mom's affair, their fathers' parts in the cover-up of her death. She'd done her best to reconcile those actions with her own past, the choices she'd made, and her future.

"That's not what I'm saying."

"Then what?"

"I'm saying we get through the next couple of days, and then we lay our cards on the table. All of them."

"My cards already are on the table," he said. Now his stomach muscles clenched. He had to work at keeping the bitterness out of his voice. "I'm not waiting. I have waited—we have *both* waited—way too long."

"My life in New York is unfinished. I can't just walk out of it. I…"

"Hey, I get it."

He leaned forward, reaching to bring his fingertips feather-light to her face. She didn't retreat, or turn from him, and he caught the flutter of her eyes as they closed. She rubbed her cheek into his hand. He hadn't lost her yet: he saw she still ached like he did for simple touches.

"Of course you can't give up everything you've done, what you've accomplished—"

"There's more."

"Sure there is. We have to start again. Learn each other again. And that's what we will do, Aaren, without this cooling-off bullshit. Just us, one day at a time. That is my commitment to you. And all

I need to know is if you're with me. If you want me, after... after everything. That's all I need."

Aaren had to laugh. Was he kidding? He was the only thing she'd *ever* wanted. She nodded, then hugged his neck tight. She hadn't anticipated that it might hurt to believe in someone again. She almost began crying to feel him squeeze her back.

She leaned into him and began mentally rehearsing how she'd tell him about Gavin. *Long overdue*, she'd decided as Jarrod slept. Now it was only a matter of when.

"Okay, okay, can a man eat?" he choked from her neck hold.

She punched him in his stomach playfully. "Fast! Eat fast. If there's no cooling off, and if... if you're okay... then I want to go riding."

Jarrod captured her hand and squeezed.

"Got to delay it. I need to go back over to the house. You know, check on things."

"Oh, yeah, of course, Jay." She touched his shoulder. "Do you want me to go with you?"

"No, let's finish breakfast, and I'll head out. I won't be gone that long. I want that ride."

She bit her lip. "Me too. I think I might go to Pop's and make sure everything's okay. So we'll go afterwards."

"Looks like you get your time-out after all," he grumbled.

"Looks like I do."

Her family's farm was barely five minutes away. Aaren still had no idea what she wanted to do with it. Jarrod knew its value better than she did. She'd ask him. Mull over some ideas. Her car coasted from the main road onto the dirt one, a relaxing breeze blowing through her lowered windows. It helped her shake off the tension that lingered after last night's argument.

The thicket and overgrown cypress cleared and Aaren came upon her father's farmhouse. Her brow creased at the sight of a white sedan parked in front. The driver's-side door was open. She didn't recognize the car, which didn't mean much. She'd barely been in town a week. It could be anyone. Then a man emerged, turning to watch her approach. Suddenly, her eyes met Gavin's and her heart stopped.

Her foot pressed the brake pedal hard to the floorboard long after the car had come to a stop.

"Shit," she mumbled as he winked at her, removing his sunglasses.

Stunned, she just stared at him. She tried to take the keys out of the ignition but they wouldn't come. Then, realizing what she had done, she turned the car back on, threw it in park and collected herself, before pulling the key and getting out to face him.

"What are you doing here?" Her heart hammered in her ears.

"Good to see you too," he smirked, looking over the car at her.

Aaren slammed the door and narrowed her eyes at him. "Tell me you came with the papers. Tell me you're here about the divorce. Because that's all we need to discuss."

She saw him sizing her up and could hear his thoughts. Crossing her arms, she bit back her sharp tongue. The important thing was to close the door on their marriage, before Jarrod discovered it was still open.

"Can't we just talk?" he walked around the car to her. She stiffened at his approach, glancing about as if they'd be seen.

"Talk? You came here to talk?"

"I'm here because I needed to see you, to make sure you're okay," he said, reaching to take her hand.

Aaren shook her head. "You don't understand, that's not your job anymore."

"No, it's not, and you can't run from the commitment we share. Not any longer."

Aaren snatched her hand away.

"Come inside!" she snapped.

She stormed around him up the stairs to her front door. She didn't want anyone seeing him. If he had the papers with him, she could sign them and send him packing. Either way, he needed to go before Jarrod saw him. She felt sick for not telling him at breakfast when she'd had the chance.

Gavin stepped in behind her, cool and confident. It was infuriating. Even when they were fighting he wasn't one to raise his voice.

"I missed you," he said.

Aaren tensed, ignoring it. Gavin looked around her family home, openly curious, but went on as though their interaction were planned, normal. She realized in all the years they were married this was the closest he'd ever been to who she really was.

"All I could think of is your being here alone, needing me. Aaren, how are you? Really how are you?"

"I'm fine," she mumbled, a stab of guilt pierced her heart. She sat down on the sofa. Her eyes followed as he went to the mantle and stared at each picture. Smiling faces, mostly hers, peered back. Gavin was primarily interested in the one of her mother, and the few that showed her father. Aaren wondered if the Robinsons' dysfunction showed to outsiders, or only to her.

"This your mother?" He picked up the picture.

"Yes."

"She looks like you.

"You said you wanted to talk!" she snapped at him.

His eyes cut to hers and she saw them cloud with suspicion. She needed to get herself under control. She was acting guilty. Why should she be guilty? He'd kept their apartment on the Upper West Side; she'd lucked into an underpriced loft in SoHo, not that money was at all an issue. But their lives were separate: she and Gavin hadn't even lived in the same ZIP code for seven months.

SECRETS AND LIES

"What is going on with you? Where were you earlier? I've been waiting outside in that car since six this morning."

"Where are the papers?" she asked.

"Forget the papers, will you? Talk to me Aaren, tell me—"

"Tell you what? I didn't ask you to come here." She rose, then sat again, making herself crazy. She sighed. "I want my divorce!"

"Well you can't have it! I've tried it your way. I gave you space, I stayed away. Enough is enough. I want my wife back and I'm not leaving here without her!" He glared at her.

"You have to be kidding."

"You know me. I never kid. Now it's time for you to face me and figure this out."

He smiled patiently. She felt her anger flare: she hated being patronized.

"You can start by telling me who he is."

"What??"

"You heard me. Who has your head turned around like this? Something is keeping you in this one-horse town. I see it all over your face. Who the hell is he?"

Jarrod stepped out of his truck and tossed the door shut. He'd never look at his childhood home the same way again. How could either of his parents raise a family behind those walls after what happened that awful day? A cool breeze picked up, blowing through the large oaks on either side of his house. Other than the slight whistle of the wind through the branches, the neighborhood was still as death.

Death.

It was the first time he'd ever come home that his mother wasn't going to be there waiting for him. Jarrod closed his eyes and sucked in a deep breath, then exhaled and headed for the porch steps. Before he could reach them, the door was flung open and Macy came rushing out.

"Jay!" She ran straight into his arms, crying hysterically. She looked so much like their mother it made his chest constrict with pain. Jarrod hugged her tight.

"Hey! You okay?"

"No, I'm not, Jay. *Nothing* is okay," she mumbled, aghast he could even ask her that. She sniffled, then wiped at her runny nose. "Daddy's upstairs, I'm really worried. He's been smashing things—and the liquor, Jay. He won't stop drinking. You should have seen how much he hauled up to that room."

Jarrod's cheeks burned with shame. *Father like son*, he cringed to himself. Just last night he'd done the exact same thing. He cupped her face, her pain mirroring his.

"Where's Travis?"

"He couldn't take it. You just missed him. Don't know where he went."

Jarrod felt another pang of guilt. He should have made sure his brother and sister had someone with them. Their worlds were falling apart too.

"I need you to go to Pauline's and hang back there for awhile," he said.

Pauline was their second cousin, a few months younger than Travis in age, and she and Macy were very close. Jarrod didn't know what state his father was in, but Macy had just lost one parent. She didn't need to witness the other one unraveling.

"No. I want to stay with you. We have to help daddy."

"We will. I will. You trust me, Mace, don't you?"

She nodded and he cleared away the tears from her cheeks with the ball of his thumb.

"So go ahead. I'll call over there when it's clear to come back."

"And Travis?"

"Don't worry about Trav. He just needed some air. He'll be back. I'll take care of everything else."

She hugged her brother, nearly shaking with relief.

"I knew you would come back, I knew you wouldn't abandon us."

Jarrod smiled at her faith. He wanted her unchanged, it helped him decide. The Pennington family secrets would be laid to rest with his mother. Macy and Travis never need know about what happened between their parents years ago or how his mother had taken herself from their lives.

A feeling of being watched overtook him. His eyes lifted to the upper-level windows of the house. There he saw a curtain slightly parted, and behind it, his father staring down at them. He looked haggard, and for a big man, oddly fragile. The curtain fell shut as he withdrew.

"Go, Mace, go now," Jarrod pushed her gently toward the road, then headed to the house. She didn't immediately do as he asked. She stood back, arms folded, and watched him go inside. When he looked back at her once more, she nodded and walked off down the street. Pauline's house was only three blocks away. Jarrod gave a silent prayer for her as he turned away and stepped inside.

"There's no one! I'm not ending this marriage because I found someone. I'm ending it for the reason I told you when I left."

To tell him the truth about Jarrod, either the truth from back then, or the truth from now, would hurt Gavin needlessly. And besides, Gavin's jealousy over slights both real and imagined, had used up her patience long ago. His nostrils flared a bit. Aaren could see the strain in his eyes. He hated to lose. If he thought for one second she was turning to another man he'd make the divorce hell for her just for spite.

"Oh. So then you really don't love me. You're not capable of love," he said, making air-quotes and mimicking her long-ago words.

"That's right," she said, focusing on the wall over his left shoulder. She'd said it before. There was no need for them to go through this again.

He shook his head. "You can be so cold and cruel at times."

"Look, it's just—"

"Yes, you can be and you know what? I loved you just the same. Now I know that there are things, terrible things, that you keep buried, that prevent you from living. I understand you're afraid to feel—" He turned and walked calmly toward her.

"Gavin, wait—"

Aaren stepped back, her legs hitting the sofa. Her husband continued to advance on her.

"Let's try counseling."

"Please, just stop."

"Then how about Reverend Powell?"

"NO!"

"What is it? What do you need, Aaren?"

"I need a divorce, damn it! That's what I need! You agreed. You said you wanted out!"

"I lied."

"Dear God," she moaned.

"I love you."

"No, Gavin, you don't."

"I know my heart."

"Well I know mine, and you're not in it. I'm sorry if that sounds harsh, I… I never wanted to hurt you. There are things that you can't possibly understand—"

"You never gave us a chance."

"*Let go.*"

"Or?"

"Or you'll make me fight you hard and dirty. Neither one of us wants that. We can do it the easy way and just move on with our lives."

"There's no one else?"

Gavin looked around the place as if he expected to see Jarrod himself. It unnerved her how he read her heart without any telling. Through their years together, he'd mention her silent moments, her reflective moments, question if there was a some*one* instead of some*thing* keeping her heart so guarded.

And now, for the first time, there was.

When his dark eyes returned to hers, Aaren saw how much he wanted her. It made her sick to have wasted so much of both their lives on something she'd never felt.

"Gavin, our marriage died on the vine years ago. You as much as said so yourself. Let's not mourn it now. Let's let it go," she pleaded.

He reached and pulled her to him. Aaren folded her arms to prevent the embrace he sought. "I need you."

She turned her head away. "I can't."

"Damn it!" he snapped, pushing her free and stepping away. "I can't fight for you when you're so dead inside!"

Aaren winced at his once-accurate description of her. She was alive now and she welcomed that liberation. But she'd been a zombie through most of their marriage. She hated the woman she'd been with him.

Gavin reached inside his suit jacket and pulled out a thick envelope.

"You want the damn divorce? Then have it!"

He dropped it on the coffee table.

"Go ahead and sign them. Everything's there. I'll come back in the morning and if you still want out, I'll take them with me and file them."

"Why in the morning?" she asked, bending to retrieve the envelope.

"I can't get a flight till then."

"I can give them to you signed now." Her eyes searched the tables for a pen.

"That's our damn life in those papers. The least you could do is take the time to think about it!"

Aaren looked back into his face and saw him blink quickly to cover his tears. "I am sorry."

"Can you at least tell me why?"

"Why what?"

"Why you could never feel anything? Why you even married me?"

Aaren sat on the sofa. "Yes. I guess I owe you that much." She placed the envelope back on the coffee table and then rubbed the tension from her brow. "My mother died, Gavin, just before I turned five. For years, my father treated me as if I was her ghost. Then, for reasons I… can't explain, he shipped me off to NYU." She looked up at him and bit back the sob lodged in her throat. "You know the rest. I wasn't welcomed back while he was alive. Now I am back. And I've been here, facing my demons. I'm healing. It has nothing to do with you; you were a good husband. I chose you because at that time I thought I could make you happy. I know now that I was never in the position to make anyone happy the way I was—"

Aaren stopped herself abruptly.

Gavin smiled. He sat down in the chair across from her. "Then you're healing, and that's wonderful, babe."

"I've *healed*. I know my heart. I know who I am again. I'm not the woman you married. I was never really her."

He touched her leg. "Good, because I was ready to divorce her anyway."

Gavin grinned. She smiled weakly, lowering her face. He lifted her chin with his forefinger and stared into her eyes. She recognized relief in his gaze, relief that he'd learned something other than what he'd feared.

But his instincts were right. Another man did have her heart.

"Aaren, I'd like to know the new you."

"I can't," she said quietly.

"So, that's it? It's really over?" he asked.

"Yes. Gavin. It is."

He sat back up and sighed.

"Then sign the papers. I'll take them with me. I only wanted your happiness. Even at the expense of my own. That doesn't make me foolish, or a bad guy, Aaren, it just makes me a man in love. So if letting you go means your happiness then I'll do it. Contrary to what you believe, my love for you is real. So is my faith. Maybe when you're truly healed we can be more than friends some day."

"You mean it?"

"I mean it."

He spoke earnestly, his shoulders slumped. It was rare to see the defeat on her husband. He prided himself on winning every battle. Aaren reached to the end table near the sofa and pulled out the tiny drawer to get a pen. She opened the documents and flipped them over to sign the papers. Gavin watched her stoically, though his heart ached. When she was done, she folded them and gave them back. He took them and smiled sadly as he stuffed them back inside his jacket.

"I'll file them with the court when I get back. I'll have the final decree sent to your place."

"No," she decided. "Wait. Send them here."

Gavin looked up, surprised, then rose to cover it. "I'm staying at Maggie's Bed and Breakfast. I'll leave in the morning. If you change your mind, come to me."

She shook her head slowly. "I won't, Gavin. I'm sorry."

He extended his hand to her and she accepted it. He held her close, running his hands over her, smelling her hair. Aaren hugged him back, knowing she would never see him again, and regretting that her lifetime of heartache had become his.

Gavin kissed her shoulder and let her go. "If you ever need—"

"I won't. Stop worrying about me," she said, touching his cheek. "Take care of you for a change."

He kissed her forehead. "I will always love you."

"I will always carry you in my heart," she said softly.

He let her go, reluctantly, and Aaren sighed quietly. She would have her divorce and her Jarrod. Finally, something was going right for her for a change.

"Dad! Open the door!" called Jarrod, pounding on it.

"Go 'way!"

Jarrod cut his eyes. "Open the door!"

"No!"

Jarrod had spent the past five minutes trying to coax his father out of the room. Finally, giving up, he stepped back and rushed the door with his left shoulder. The lock gave, taking part of the jamb with it. He found his father off in the corner of the room holding a bottle of Evan Williams. It wasn't nearly full.

"Get the hell out!" slurred the Judge, spittle flying out of his mouth. His face was red, his eyes glazed and mean. He held himself up by the edge of the dresser.

"Have you lost your mind? What the hell are you doing?"

"What the hell do you care?"

"I don't. But Macy and Travis, they do. They need you, and once again you're behaving like a selfish asshole. Thinking of nobody but yourself."

"That's right! Blame me, Jarrod. You should be real tired of that song," he chuckled, stumbling to the overstuffed chaise under the window. Plopping down, he turned up the bottle, holding tight to the neck. His Adam's apple bobbed as he gulped down the colored poison.

"Okay, so we get it. You and I will never agree. I just don't need you making matters worse."

The Judge swayed a bit, gurgling, then stuttering.

"Wa-worse? Did you say worse? Funny... my life cain't get any worse than it is."

The Judge let go a bitter laugh and dropped his head, giving a slow shake. He shivered through a tremor as he tried to get control.

Jarrod, unnerved, frowned at the broken image of his father. He blew out the breath he was holding. His whole being was tight with indecision. What the hell was he supposed to do for the man? His eyes took a sweep of the room. It reeked of liquor. The muggy, closed-in space had the walls sweating. The destruction of mirrors and the lamps left glass and other sharp, dangerous pieces everywhere. The mattress was half off the bed and the linen was a tangled mess on top.

"Fine, your life sucks. Get over it, damn it. We've all had to bear the hardship of your selfish choices."

The Judge drank more, and more, and more. Jarrod glared.

"Do you hear me?"

"I loved them both, Jay. Your mother and Noelle. I know no one in this town believes that but it's the truth. I loved Laura Lee because she was the mother of my children. I was in love with Noelle, because we were kindred spirits. It was never a choice. It was a fact, damn it!"

The Judge looked up at him, anguished.

"I was wrong. But I never had a say in my life! I was the only child. My father paired me off with your mother without so much as a... hell. We were engaged before we'd even had a proper date. It was straight out of some damned cotillion handbook, for chrissakes. And then I was to take on the business and carry on the Pennington name with pride. I wasn't to feel anything. We Pennington men never feel anything!" he smirked.

"I didn't come here for a pity party," Jarrod hissed.

"I'm sure you didn't! Ya probly came to see how low I've sunk. Well take a look, Jay! You cain't get any lower than this!"

"Dad, enough!"

"No! I never meant for Noelle or your mother to suffer because of me. I was trying to leave this fucking town! Set your mother free and then finally be a man of my choosing. Why is that so fucking hard for anyone to grasp? I wasn't setting up a harem or trying to break taboos by screwing a black woman. I had finally found myself! I was for once in my life doing something solely for me! For once, damn it!"

Jarrod swallowed, hearing his father's pain. He'd never tried to stand in his father's shoes. Listening to him now, he saw the man's choices weren't as calculated as he'd thought.

"I destroyed them both," said James bitterly, drinking the whiskey and looking back at his son. "When Noelle died, something in your mother broke. I broke her spirit. She went through the motions, we both did, but her spirit? It was gone. Just enough for you kids, not even a little left for me. And why should she leave anything for me? I blamed *her*."

He lifted his head and looked sadly into his son's eyes. "It wasn't her fault, Jay. She was just as desperate as I was to be happy. She thought making me stay would make us happy. Instead, it sealed both our fates. See? I finally get the old Irish curse upon the Pennington men! 'Drink and be miserable,' as my old man would say!" He laughed, raising the bottle to his son with an unbalanced grin. Jarrod went to the edge of the bed and sat down.

"Mom loved you to the very end, Dad. She asked that I forgive you. She believed it was all her fault."

The Judge nodded. "Of course she did. I made her feel that way every single day. I never did one thing to free her from the guilt she carried. I wanted to make her suffer for taking my Noelle from me." The Judge dropped his shoulders. The rest came out in a broken sob. "I guess it was better than facing the ugly truth about myself."

"She did pull the trigger," Jarrod mumbled. The bitterness, like a stone in his gut, was still unmovable. He felt his father's eyes on him and was ashamed for it. The Judge put a hand to his knee and Jarrod stiffened. He looked over at his father, who shook his head *no*, slowly.

"I put the gun in her hand. I pulled that trigger by pushing her too far. Blame me."

Jarrod wanted to. It would be so easy to. But he heard his mother's voice clearly. No matter what crimes she'd committed, she'd always guided him well. She'd told him that his future with Aaren hinged on his ability to believe, and trust again. That to let go the hate, and forgive his father, would be the only way.

Easier said than done, he thought, swallowing grimly.

"I'm done with blame, Dad. What about you? What now? Drink yourself into a coma? We've got to deal with Mom's funeral. You have to be our father, her husband, again. You owe her that much."

"I do," he agreed with a deep sigh. "I do owe her that much."

Jarrod made to rise but his father grabbed his wrist. "Can you really let this go? After everything you know, can you?"

It was a valid question. One look around the room, then down at the man who had destroyed it, made Jarrod almost desperate for another path, another option.

"All I can do is try. Mom has faith in us, despite… everything. Get up. She deserves a proper burial and some respect. So pull your shit together and let's figure out how to give her at least that."

"You love Aaren, don't you?"

Jarrod bristled at the change of subject. That part of his life wasn't open for debate, especially not with his father, and especially since after last night, he and Aaren weren't a hundred percent in sync.

"Yeah, what of it?"

"Good for you son. Good for her."

The Judge pressed his palms against the mattress in a weak attempt to rise. It was too much, though. He remained slumped over as if the burdens were physically weighted to his back.

"I'll shower," he mumbled.

The Judge managed it on the second try, and Jarrod watched numbly as he headed to the door. He'd hated this man for so long. But now, it was clear. He was his father's son: the two of them were dangerously alike. And he wanted a different kind of life. He always had.

Jarrod decided. His anger, his bitterness, his hate would stop, today. He'd bury it all, deep in the ground, right next to his mother.

Chapter Fifteen

UNFINISHED BUSINESS

Aren took the last of the garbage out the side door to the large green can. She'd spent the afternoon sorting through her parents' things, evaluating what to keep and what to toss, but mostly trying to piece together the truth of the family history she'd never known.

Jarrod called hours ago and she'd understood that his family needed him more. Actually, that worked for her. She was still a little raw from the shock of Gavin standing on her father's porch. His presence, so soon on the heels of her disconnect with Jarrod, had opened wounds of regret and guilt. She'd spent the remainder of the afternoon telling herself that setting her husband free was the right thing for them both. It was the only way Gavin would find himself a love like the one she wanted with Jarrod.

She still had no idea how to tell Jarrod about her marriage, but it didn't matter any more. Gavin had *signed*. It was over.

Her cell phone rang out from the pocket of her jeans.

"Hey, Jay." She smiled widely as she walked back to the porch.

"Hey yourself," he said. "What you been up to today?"

"Just the usual pack and throw-away mission."

"Probably more fun than I had," he said.

He sounded worn-out. She sat down on the low swing, rocking herself gently back and forth with the heel of her running shoe.

"How's your family?"

A soft sigh escaped him in a quiet whistle.

"Better." His tone was low and worried. "My father was pretty much having a mental breakdown when I got there. I guess that's to be expected."

"Is he okay?"

"He is now. I got him sobered up and fed. We went to Kappel's over in Beech Grove and put the funeral in motion. It's tomorrow at eleven."

Aaren nodded. Pernell's Mortuary on the north side had closed before she'd left Penns Point. And even now, four years after the millennium, tongues would wag if Laura Lee Pennington went to Murphy Brothers on the south side of town. It wouldn't do for a Daughter of the Confederacy.

"And your sister? Brother?"

"Can't find Travis, but that's Trav. He'll be back in time. I think Macy's going to be okay. But I don't think she should be alone with my dad now. I told her she could stay with us. Just until it's time for her to go back to school."

"Of course she should," she said, squeezing the phone. Her heartbeat tripled to hear him say 'us'. The way he said it, it was almost like last night hadn't happened. Or rather, that what she'd told him last night didn't change things between them.

She looked out across her Pop's land, wanting so much to believe.

"You know something? I think I could forgive him, Aaren."

Her eyes slipped up to the starlit skies. She wanted peace for him.

"That's good, Jay."

"Can't forget what he did, Aaren. May never."

Aaren nodded in silence. Now as then, she and Jarrod Pennington understood each other better than anyone else.

"I saw into his pain today and I got it. We're more alike than I wanted to believe." Jarrod's voice trailed away, as if he were afraid to speak the rest. "Years of mourning the woman of your dreams could do a lot to a man. He loved your mother, whether it was right or wrong. He ended up destroying both of them because of it."

"My mom is a mystery to me," she said softly, looking straight ahead.

"So is mine," Jarrod acknowledged. "I know why he stayed with her: guilt. Question is, why'd she go for a gun instead of taking us and leave? I can't get my head around how she stayed."

"When you love a person so hard and so completely and then discover they don't feel the same, well Jay, it can turn you inside out."

Jarrod recalled Aaren's angry words from last night. *I took the easy way out, too, same as you. I gave it up to any boy that wanted it.* He swallowed, trying to force those echoes from his ears. It would be better all around if he didn't dwell on that. He refocused.

"But we're not them. That's not us."

"No," she agreed.

"Maybe now my mother and yours can both rest in peace. Maybe they can both forgive him for destroying their lives, and then maybe he can find a way to forgive himself. Or maybe not. All I know is that I can't hold it any longer. That hate between me and him. Mom's dead, so is your mother. It has to end."

The swing squeaked, rocking on its rusty chains. She rolled her neck, wishing he were there next to her.

"You know what I think?"

"What do you think, Aaren?" His voice, husky and low, was as good as his touch.

"I think that the power of love can cure just about anything. Your mom knew that, and she's proud of you now, Jay. This is why she wanted you to forgive your father before she died. It's why my dad wanted to bring us back together. We were all trapped by the past, but they wanted us to have another chance, a chance at a future, didn't they? You feel it?"

"Oh, I feel it."

She smiled. The inflection in his deep voice was all Jarrod, sass and strength, but true all the way through. Aaren listened to his deep breathing and felt him leave his day behind.

"So listen," his drawl continued. "Are you gonna come on home or'm I have to come over there'n fetch ya?"

She bit her lip and closed her eyes. She'd have to tell him about Gavin, but not on the phone, not after the night they'd had and the difficult day that had followed. Not now, when they were both focused on the future. Gavin was all in the past. And Jarrod was telling her the same thing: he was letting the past, right up until last night, go. He was making it easy on her.

"I'm already on my way," she said.

Gavin sat at the bar, the seat sticking to his trousers. He rolled his eyes to the rustic grime of the place. It didn't matter much. He could tolerate it until his flight left the next morning. A croony country tune played from a dollar-slot jukebox. Several locals, some in cowboy hats and boots, yukked it up over pitchers of beer. The bar seats, however, held only men like himself, those wanting little attention or service, just a shot and a bottle.

His eyes went to the television. It had been placed askew on the top shelf over the bar; it was one of the few fixtures not bolted down. A replay of last year's Derby races was on. He shook his head and lowered his eyes. Nothing about the atmosphere in this dive was going to distract him. The papers, his broken life, raged at him from his inside pocket. He was interrupted before he could pull them out.

"What-cha drinking, sugah?"

He didn't look up. "Maker's. On the rocks."

"Huh?"

He focused on the woman before him. She was munching gum hard enough that her golden locks fell over her brow. She met his eyes and stuffed her bra strap back under the shoulder of a too-tight tank top emblazoned with Haney's, the name of the place. Gavin dropped his shoulders.

"Maker's Mark. Bourbon? Hello?"

She winked and turned away. Gavin slipped out the divorce papers. Aaren was gone now, and here sat the proof. There was nothing he could do about it. He wished that she allowed herself to be loved. He wished that she had allowed him to love her.

He felt the jostle of the man sitting to his left. He hated being crowded. Gavin cut his eyes over and away, then folded the blue-covered document.

She came back, the waitress with the wide hips and the golden hair. "No Maker's Mark. We're out. How 'bout a beer?" She dropped the bottle of Bud in front of him.

"You're out of Bourbon," he frowned. "This is Kentucky, right? How is that remotely possible?"

But he took the beer. He needed it.

"Tough day?" asked the kid next to him.

"You can say that," Gavin mumbled.

"You ain't from around here?"

"Very perceptive of you. How long did it take you to figure that out?"

"Look man, don't be an ass."

Gavin shook his head. "No offense. It's just been one of those days."

"Yeah, well it's been one of those weeks for me! Name's Wesley, by the way. Wes."

Gavin drank from his bottle, not bothering to say more.

"Let me buy you a real drink. She fucking with you, saying they ain't got nothing. Carrie! Get the man something good. I know Scooter gots some Knob Creek under the bar."

Carrie walked over and smiled. Gavin frowned at the drink she poured.

"No offense hun, we keep the good stuff for the regulars. Here you go. On the house."

Gavin accepted the whiskey. They watched him in silence until he tossed it back and let it scorch the inside of his throat.

"So where you from?" asked Wes.

"New York City."

Gavin looked over, noticing the shiner around the young man's eye. Wes frowned and Carrie leaned in on the bar. Both of them had begun staring at him hard at the mention of New York.

"Funny, we have a friend from New York who just recently returned home."

"Let me guess... Aaren DuBois?"

"Aaren *DuBois*," said Carrie, shooting a silencing look at Wes. "How do you know our Aaren?"

He looked over to her and she gave him a sexy smile. Gavin shook his head, annoyed.

"She's my wife, or at least she was until today."

"Today? What happened today?" asked Wes.

"Today she signed away our life. Just like that, we're done!" Gavin snapped his fingers. "Give me another." He slid the glass back to Carrie and tipped up his half-empty bottle of beer. "My wife wants to be free. From me, hell from any man, just free."

Carrie laughed mid-pour. "Really? Is that what she told you?"

He eyed her, then the other man, who shook his head and chuckled. Gavin didn't get the joke.

"Yeah, that's exactly what she said."

The back of Gavin's head prickled as he watched Wes make eye contact with Carrie. He nodded and she winked. Then Wes turned his good eye on Gavin.

"Ole boy, I think we should tell you a story."

"A *looove* story," cooed Carrie.

Aaren grinned, taking flight. She leaned into her horse, one with the animal, as it bounded toward the western part of Jarrod's land. The small bush she jumped shot quickly into the night behind her, and glad of the moonlight, she began looking for the next obstacle. The horse knew the land better than she did, and Aaren thrilled to see him swivel an ear, or nose up the reins, communicating to her the next thicket or rise of earth, then wait for her signal before jumping again. He was an incredibly well-trained mount.

She executed a perfect barrel turn around a tree stump, then let the horse have his lead, galloping full-out across the open plain. She hadn't traveled at this speed, with the wind in her hair, for far too long. It was glorious.

"Aaren!! Slow down! It's too fast!"

Jarrod's voice carried after her but she couldn't stop. She wouldn't. The exhilaration, the freedom of the ride, was all too delicious.

Jarrod had met her at the curve in the driveway with Audrey and Dynamo, both saddled and ready to ride. Her old boots were in the trunk and she couldn't get to them fast enough. Then she'd walked straight up to Dynamo and introduced herself, before adjusting the stirrups to the length of her own arm. She'd smiled over Jarrod's worried objections. She'd wanted to ride Dynamo since the first time she'd seen him in the paddock.

The moon was her guide as she made another turn, and another, until she finally eased the animal to a canter and then a trot. Jarrod caught up behind.

"What was that?" he snapped, bringing Audrey up to Dynamo's right. "Answer me! Have you lost your mind? You could've been thrown, or broke your neck, or—"

"That was great! Great!" she panted. "Oh! It felt great! This is what I missed. This! To hell with New York, baby! This is where I want to be."

He stared at her, his nostrils flaring. Aaren didn't care. He could stare, all he wanted. She was free. She felt like living again. Starting over, doing whatever she chose. Not what was expected of her.

Pop had his rules, all her life. Even law school had been his idea. And Gavin wasn't so different. Yes, there was more room for negotiation, and she was an expert negotiator, but being his wife still held certain expectations. With Jarrod, though, here and now, she was just Aaren. With him, she felt supported. Able to do whatever she wanted.

Jarrod led his horse into a walk alongside hers. He'd suggested the night ride. He hadn't expected anything like what he'd just witnessed.

"What was that about?"

Aaren stood in the stirrups to stretch, then relaxed and twisted to face him. Her eyes were bright and wide.

"It's over, baby. The past. All of it. I mean, I know we have to deal with stuff. I think we can sell Pop's house—no. Rent it. Maybe... I can see if Sam Spence might be looking for a partner, someone to carry it on for him. I know he deals more with contract law and real estate, but law is law, right? Of course I'll have to take the bar here, get licensed in Kentucky, but—" She backed her horse into an eastward turn, then cocked her head impatiently at Jarrod. "Come on."

"Whoa... slow down," said Jarrod.

Aaren flipped her hair over her shoulder to look back at him with a grin. He expected her to break into a run again, but quickly surmised she was walking them along a beeline to the stables, instead of following the creek as they'd come. His lips twitched in appreciation: she didn't need to be told. The distance was just about a half-mile. If they walked, it meant the horses would be calmed and ready to put away for the night.

He watched her thick dark hair swing between her shoulder blades, then followed the line of her long, straight spine. He wondered what had happened to her today. The change in her was dramatic. Their disconnect had been obvious during last night's lovemaking, though he could barely call it that. Then they'd fought afterwards and she'd been furious, filled with hate. This morning, over breakfast, her behavior was tentative and withdrawn. Distant. He'd spent the day at his parents' house, worried the entire time she might bolt while he was gone. Now, she was smiling, flirting with him even, as though there had never been any argument.

And that wasn't all.

It was as though the past fourteen years, apart, hadn't happened.

For the first time since she'd come back to Penns Point, she seemed entirely like the girl he'd once known. Her wary shell was gone.

She turned them into the hardened path between the stable and the paddock. Jarrod could see a light sheen of perspiration on her bare arms.

"You cold?" he asked.

"No," she whispered, twisting to face him.

Her eyes were round and shining, and the look of them took his breath away. He'd waited to see that look his entire adult life.

She was his.

Jarrod edged Audrey ahead of Dynamo, which Dynamo didn't like. Aaren got him in line alongside the wide double-door as Jarrod dismounted, then dismounted herself. She automatically loosened the horse's girth and ran up the stirrups. Jarrod, impressed that she remembered how, watched her out of the corner of one eye as he worked through the same steps. She finished first, and when he turned, held out the bundled reins, expecting him to lead both animals inside. Instead, without a word, he led his horse past hers. Clearly, she was to follow.

Aaren bit her lip. The last time she'd been in a stable with him, it had permanently changed the course of their lives. She saw how rigid his shoulders were, how his elbows were tucked tight against his sides. It appeared to be awkward for him, too. She clucked her tongue and guided Dynamo behind Jarrod's horse. Aaren waited silently while Jarrod took over and put up the tack, attached halters, checked hooves. His movements were deliberate, deft, fast. Aaren could feel him watching her, even though he wasn't looking directly at her. She put both hands behind her back and leaned against the post, watching him work. She couldn't tear her eyes away.

It was more than just the way his muscles moved under his shirt. It was the way her body hummed whenever she was near him. It was the way she felt simultaneously supercharged and completely at peace whenever he drew near.

She'd become an expert at faking attraction, even faking love when the situation called for it. What Aaren was feeling now, though, was as real, as natural, as anything she'd ever felt. The anger she'd harbored on leaving Penns Point, the very anger that had helped her achieve her goals in life, had clouded her understanding of the truth. No one was ever going to touch her the way this man already had.

He slid the last stall door closed, then advanced the few steps back toward Aaren.

"Jarrod, we—"

He cut her off with a look and a shake of his head. "Did you mean it back there?"

Aaren's eyes went wide. She'd said a lot of things, and—

"Are you staying?"

She bit her lip and nodded mutely.

He closed the distance between them in two steps, crushing her body to his and covering her mouth with kisses. Those lips, the feel of them, had her gathering the fabric of his shirt in her hands. She returned his kisses, feeling his arms cross tight around her as he yanked his work gloves off. His hands were hot through the cotton of her shirt as he ran them up and down, kneading here and stroking there. He flicked the tip of his tongue at hers, then swept over, deepening the kiss.

Jarrod leaned them into the post. The rough column at her back matched the hard press of his arousal. Aaren felt the heat at her core thread through her body as she wrapped one long leg around him. Aching, delicious pangs of want pulsed at her center and she gasped into his mouth. Her heart felt ready to pound out of her chest.

His kisses went to her throat and her sigh turned into his name.

"Ohhhh, Jarrod... we—"

Jarrod picked her up, one hand at the back of her neck and one hand cupping the curve of her bottom. Aaren's legs wrapped automatically around his hips as he walked them around the corner from the tackroom. His kisses never ceased; she tightened her legs around him as they turned the next corner.

This room was dark. Jarrod held her up while reaching out with his other arm. Aaren thought he was turning on a light, but she heard a thump. He lowered his arm and let her slide down his legs. She could feel the flat edge of a low bunk rubbing against her calf. Aaren turned, trying to take in her surroundings.

"Where do you think you're going?" breathed Jarrod.

He pulled her back close and with practiced motions, unbuckled her belt and unbuttoned her jeans. A flurry of movements—first his shirt, then hers, next her jeans, boots—interspersed with kisses, had them panting and nearly naked.

Jarrod pulled her down to the bunk with him. She was surprised to feel a soft blanket against her bare skin. She settled into the thin but firm mattress as he slid up next to her. She felt him propped on one elbow. He hovered, brushing her windblown, tangled hair back from her face. Aaren had the notion that he was staring at her, that he could see her in the dark, even though she couldn't see him. He ran his fingertips across her collarbone and down between her breasts, over to tease her nipple, then back up to stroke her throat. Every moment, every movement, increased her arousal until she was grinding against him, nearly crazy with need.

She wondered what he was waiting for.

"What is it?" she whispered. Then she realized. "Oh."

Condom. Unlike when they were teenagers, he was so smooth with it now, she figured he'd already have it on, ready to go. The first times they'd made love, upstairs in their bed, it had been like that. She hadn't even had to mention it.

"Let me," she said, twisting over to reach for his jeans.

"Aaren." His voice had dropped in register. His hand stopped at her jawline, holding her face to his as he moved between her parted thighs. "Are you staying?"

She could feel him now positioned at her center; he rubbed the thick tip of his penis against her and the question took on new meaning.

"Yes." Aaren arched her back and moaned as he thrust inside.

"Are you mine?"

"Ooooh…" She gasped to feel him fill her, then withdraw.

"You're mine."

She locked her legs around him, heels at the rise of his ass, and hung on tight. Her eyes had adjusted to the low light. He was looking straight down at her, watching, as he brought thrust after punishing thrust.

"Say it, Aaren. Say it."

"I'm yours, baby. Yours."

The bunk groaned, creaking under the rhythmic pressure. Aaren could see now how his face was flushed with arousal, how his muscles were tight, tensed. He buried his face into the curve of her neck and kept on. He wasn't waiting for her; he wasn't holding back at all.

"Say it!"

"Yours," she panted.

"Say it."

"Jarrod, I… I'm y—" Aaren dug her fingernails into his shoulder, feeling pain and ecstasy, and guilt, wondering if her confession of last night had driven him to this. His head lifted from her neck, hot puffs of breath blown into her face as he grunted, straining against the urge to release. Their eyes locked and she was taken back to a time when her world was just this, just this simple, just him. She didn't dare look away.

"Say. It."

"Jarrod, I—I love you."

He moaned and shot his hips forward twice more. His eyes drooped closed as he came inside her, moving with his release until he could not move any more. Aaren closed her eyes and stroked him down.

She was staying. And she was his.

"What is this place?" she asked, playing with a lock of his hair.

Jarrod stroked her ankle with his big toe.

"I stay here when we're foaling."

Aaren nodded. Of course he'd be here, right beside the mare. Of course he'd stay the entire time, not willing to leave that job to one of the hired men. She could totally imagine Jarrod putting his hand on the mare's back, or not, knowing the animal so well he'd know where and how she'd want to be touched. She nestled her cheek into the hollow of his chest so she could listen to the beat of his heart. He squeezed his arms tight around her.

"You're staying here in Penns?" he whispered. He still didn't sound like he believed it. "And you're mine."

Aaren smiled, wondering how she was to reassure him if what they'd just done together didn't show him.

"Jarrod Mitchell Pennington, I have been yours since the second grade."

It was the truth at the very center of her heart. He trailed his hand up and down her arm, and rubbed the top of her head with his chin.

"I want to marry you in front of this whole town," he whispered.

"Baby. That's—" Aaren rose up and touched his cheek. She understood why he wanted to, to make up for the way he'd humiliated her that night at the fair, to make up for everything. He wanted to make it public and permanent in a way he'd not been allowed to the first time. "Baby, I don't need that. I don't want us to be this... show."

"What do you want, then?" He laid back and pulled her on top of him. Her hair hung around his face, enclosing them in a world of two.

"I want just us. Becca. Tony. Your family, if you want them. Me in a dress, and you—"

"Me in some monkey suit," he laughed.

"No, baby. That's not us." Aaren rubbed her nose to his. "Trust me?"

Jarrod smiled and rubbed her nose back. "I do."

They showered and ate supper near the television. Despite the late hour, she'd fixed him a large helping of her homemade spaghetti. It was after midnight, but they were both too wired to sleep. They talked politics and laughed at their shared views. A contradiction they both were. Him a strong Democrat and her a Republican. After dinner they sat in silence, digesting everything, the day, their love, the meal, their plans. She rested in the biggest of the chairs, waiting for him to return with the iced tea she'd made.

"Here you go," he said, handing her the glass.

"Thanks."

She smiled and sank back into the chair, crossing her feet at the ankles. Jarrod took a seat on the ottoman next to her, so he could play with her toes.

"You okay?" he asked.

She really was. She'd been dreading this moment, but if this was to be their new beginning, he deserved to know the entire truth. Especially now, now that there was nothing to fear. Not after what they'd just shared.

"Just thinking," she said softly, sipping her tea.

"About?" he pressed.

Her eyes flipped up and held his. Then she lowered her glass slowly, giving him a patient smile.

"I have something to tell you," she said, so low it was barely audible.

"Okay."

Aaren looked away. "I want you to know that I love the life you're offering me, and I love the way you've been here for me through all of this."

"It's simple. My life couldn't begin until you were in it."

Aaren sighed. "That's what I want to talk about, beginnings." She looked back at him. "I'm ready for our new beginning, but first I need to tell you about my ending."

Her courage began to slip away. She needed his faith in her. She needed him to understand, but she hadn't been open with him and there was no easy way to confess that.

Jarrod stared at her, studying her face. His smile faded. There was something in the ominous tone of her voice that alarmed him.

"What ending? What's wrong, Aaren?"

"My marriage, Jarrod."

She set her half-empty glass on the coaster. Looking back up at him, she saw the confusion on his face and struggled with her words. Aaren sat up straight, pushing her legs back so she could lean forward.

"I ended it today."

Jarrod said nothing at first, trying to process her words. The silence between them was worse than a scream. Sitting upright, he turned and planted his bare feet down on the floor to face her.

"What do you mean you ended it today?" His words were deliberate and slow, as if he'd processed each one just before he uttered it.

"I ended it, baby. I left my husband seven months ago but we never signed any divorce papers." She let that sink in for a moment, trying to ignore the look in his eyes. "Today he showed up at Pop's farm, wanting me to come home, and I told him it was definitely over. I signed the papers and ended it."

"You lied to me?"

"No. I didn't lie," she said clearly and calmly. "You made an assumption, and I didn't correct you."

"You lied to me!" he snapped again, this time more to himself than to her. The pain of a new betrayal molded his features into a grimace.

Aaren searched his eyes for an opening, a moment to clarify. The more the truth registered, the more the color drained from his face. His lips pressed into a thin angry line, and his eyes pooled with sadness. The look he gave her caused icicles to form in her belly. Then Jarrod looked away and didn't look back. A full minute passed as a slow wave of dread spread through her.

"I had every intention of divorcing him. It's—" She stuttered, failing to explain. She cleared her throat to steady herself. "It was just a technicality and now it's done."

"I asked you point-blank when you showed up on this farm about your husband. You told me you weren't married. And, what, an hour ago, you started planning a wedding with me!!" he shot up from the ottoman, flipping it to its side.

He leveled a finger at her, then clenched his fist to pull himself back, and walked away. Her worst fears were realized. Aaren rose to her feet and went after him, blocking his escape.

"We can get married. This changes nothing. It's really no big deal, we—"

"*No big deal?* How the hell could your being married be no big deal!"

"Because the marriage was over, long before I came here, long before I knew there could be an 'us' again."

"You lied to my face! After everything we've been through, you lied to my face!" he pushed her away from him, again seeking distance and space.

She would have none of it. She would make him understand. Aaren grabbed his arm and spun him toward her. "Jarrod, wait! I didn't lie, not about what's important. Not about my commitment to you."

"Commitment? For fuck's sake, you just did it again, just now!"

"Did what?"

"Fucking distract me—try to control me—with sex!" Snatching his arm away, he glared at her. "That's all it is for you? You haven't meant a damn thing you've said to me, have you?"

"Don't talk to me like that!"

"Why not? You have no respect for me or the truth! You let me take you to bed and you were married the entire time! You let me hope for a future with you and you already belonged to another man—you turned me into my father!" he shouted, grabbing her by both arms and giving her a shake. "You turned me into the same kind of liar he is!"

"No! No, it's not the same! You're twisting things—"

"It *is* the same!" He shoved her away and stormed out into the next room.

Aaren stumbled over her own feet, putting her hand over her mouth. It never occurred to her he would view it that way.

"Shit! Shit!!" She cursed herself under her breath, then followed him into the next room to face him. She saw him pacing angrily. "Jarrod, please. I'm sorry."

He turned cool, unforgiving eyes on her and they stilled her breathing. Tears formed, threatening to spill from her eyes, to see him look at her that way.

"Secrets, lies, adultery, hate, murder—all of it, Aaren. We've gone through it *all* and you stood next to me, carrying your secrets, turning our love into something like theirs."

"That's not fair. We aren't them! You said so yourself!" she said in a pleading voice, trying to check her anger and her panic. Watching him walk back and forth with his fists clenched, she felt an overwhelming sense of guilt. She'd failed him.

"The hell we aren't. Did you tell your *husband* the truth? Does he know about us? About *me*?" He slapped his chest.

"Don't call him that!" she pleaded.

Jarrod threw both hands up and turned away.

"We're divorced, baby. I told you that. You're making too much out of this," she said in a gentle voice.

She moved closer to him. He evaded her touch, but turned and narrowed his eyes on her, giving her a sardonic half-smile. "You haven't even filed papers. You're still married! Even a country hick like me knows that!" he spat. Then he turned on her with a low chuckle, glaring furiously. "*And what's the cooling-off period in New York?* Six months? How long did you plan to play house, put me off, Aaren, before we could actually marry?"

Aaren's face went ashen. She swallowed hard on the truth she didn't want to share. She'd underestimated him. Even worse than that, New York was one of the few states that did not allow no-fault divorce. An uncontested, amicable divorce where there was no property involved could take three months, but before that, she and Gavin would need to live in separate residences for one year. An entire year. And the clock didn't start to tick until the documents were filed. Her eyes dropped to the floor.

"Why are you doing this?" she asked, defeat and fear tinging her shaky voice. "Why are you making this into something ugly?"

"You did this! You did it the first time you gave yourself to me knowing you were still married! The fact that it doesn't bother you shows me I don't know you at all."

He pressed himself into the doorway of the kitchen, one palm flat against the moulding and the other to his forehead.

Aaren shook her head slowly. She stepped back from his version of the truth. His inability to believe in her stunned her, bruising an already-tender spot in her heart. She'd given herself back to him, trusted he wouldn't hurt her again. Her mouth fell open and she continued to shake her head slowly, refusing to believe they were even fighting over this. Not this. After everything, her little omission would be a deal-breaker for him? She couldn't fathom it.

"Jay, I don't know how to talk to you when you're like this."

"I don't want to talk to you, period."

"This is crazy, baby! Be angry at me, but don't just shut down. What is that? Are you serious? I told you, it's over between me and him."

Jarrod stepped into the hallway. He began to pace, turning around almost violently when he ran out of room. Aaren followed him as far as the hallway arch, unsure of what to do. His eyes were red and glistening with so much pain it siphoned the air from her lungs. He stopped near the front door.

Panic set in for Aaren. *He's going to run again*, she thought.

"It ended before I even knew there was a me and you, that there could ever be. I told you—you aren't listening to me! Jarrod, please don't go!"

He wheeled on her. His lips were pressed together so hard they were almost white.

"Jay, you said you wouldn't leave me!!"

Jarrod stomped toward Aaren. She backed up defensively, but he caught her by the elbow and half-dragged, half-lifted her down the hallway. He scooped her purse from the hall table, then twisted the front door open roughly, and Aaren found herself out on the porch without really knowing how it had happened.

"I'm not leaving," he growled. "You are."

Chapter Sixteen

FUNERAL

She felt the muscles in her back stiffening, and grimaced. Aaren often slept on the sofa in her loft; she still wasn't used to sleeping alone in her bed. But the sofa at her loft in New York was worth a small fortune, and a damn sight more comfortable.

She'd driven home from Jarrod's last night in blinding tears. Her hands shook so much she'd had trouble working the lock to her father's house. She'd had to turn the light on to get her bearings, and then she'd snapped the switch down just as quickly.

She'd slumped to the couch crying, and she'd cried until she had no more tears left. Sleep had been elusive, and when she did doze, she'd dreamed about Jarrod throwing her out. The slam of that door repeated over and over through the night.

She rolled over, trying to disentangle her legs from the tan-and-cream throw her mother had made. Funny, but she didn't remember pulling it over herself. She opened her eyes.

Aaren shrieked to see Jarrod sitting in Pop's chair, across from her. He was dressed in a dark suit, a nice one, but his eyes were cold. He gave her no smile, no hint of affection. He'd barely even

FUNERAL

responded to her scream. She put her hand to her chest, trying to still the pounding of her heart.

"How did you—"

"Your father gave me a key," he replied dryly. "Years ago."

She nodded, and bit her lip.

"Jay. Jarrod, I—"

"Here's how it's going to go down today," he said. His voice was tense and determined, and he raised his eyebrows to make sure she knew there wasn't to be any argument about his wishes. "It's half past nine. You need to get dressed. We have to be there in under an hour."

"Won't it be better for you if I'm not there? I mean—"

He shook his head impatiently. "You'll stand by my side; you'll make sure everyone knows we are together. You bat your eyelashes and you act like nothing happened last night. Like you love me. Got it?"

"But Jay—"

"I won't have the gossip. I won't let people do that to us. Only a week and look, there's trouble in paradise," he sneered. "I won't have it."

Aaren shifted uneasily.

"You can fake being apart from him, then you can fake being with me for a couple hours."

"I've never faked anything with you," she whispered.

Jarrod ignored her.

"We get through it, then after, we come back here and put our cards on the table, just like you said."

Jarrod rose abruptly and stalked toward the kitchen.

"My cards are already on the table," whispered Aaren.

Several cars began to pull out of the graveyard as the mourners who'd stayed to pay their final respects headed to the white clapboard church for the repast. Funerals and weddings were big in Penns Point. Most of the town had gathered. Aaren, seated next to the Judge, watched him out of the corner of her eye during the graveside service. He'd remained crumpled against the padding of his folding chair the entire time. He hadn't looked up once. His sons had chosen to stand, with their sister protectively between them, over their mother's open grave.

The minister made his final blessing, then shook hands with Travis, Macy, and Jarrod, one by one. He moved to stand before Judge Pennington, waiting to pay his respects. The Judge didn't respond. Aaren understood instinctively he wasn't just suffering the loss of a wife. He was grieving the life he'd never had with Noelle, too. She laid her hand gently on Reverend Whitman's arm and whispered her thanks as he left them to reflect.

It was just the family now, the family and Aaren. If it was up to her, she'd take Jarrod aside, away. They needed to talk and she didn't want to wait. But her wants didn't matter, much. He hadn't said an unnecessary word to her all morning. It was clear the first move would have to come from him.

Jarrod delivered his tearful sister into the chair next to Aaren. His stony gaze softened for a moment when Aaren wrapped her arm around Macy and pulled her close to let her sob. Then he and Travis helped Judge Pennington to the waiting limousine. The man was so weak from the constant boozing and grieving he could barely stand up straight.

Aaren glanced over the younger woman's shoulder as they moved away. She'd never been close to Jarrod's father, but watching him, her heart ached for the man. She felt he'd never find the peace he sought. She thought of her mother's love for him and wondered, again, how the two of them ever thought it could thrive. And even as it made her wonder, a part of her understood. Love could make you do things you never thought you'd do.

Jarrod returned. He reached for Macy, who didn't want to let go of Aaren.

FUNERAL

He met her eyes over the top of Macy's bowed head, and for the first time that day, Aaren saw how hard it was for him to bear the pain.

"Macy," she whispered. "It's time. Jay's going to take you back to the church." Aaren looked into Jarrod's eyes, never letting her gaze waver, as she rubbed Macy's back. "Come on, sweetie."

Aaren rose so that Macy was lifted into her brother's waiting arms. She looked on as Jarrod supported her all the way to the somber black car. Then she realized she was the last one left standing beside the earthly remains of Laura Lee Pennington and immediately tensed. Feeling sorry for the Judge and his visible pain was one thing. Being left alone with her mother's murderer was another thing entirely.

She bent to collect her jacket and purse. It was time to go home.

"Wait."

The single word cracked through the calm green of the cemetery. Jarrod closed the door of the limo and turned back toward the canopy. He'd been serious, apparently. He wanted her by his side until those last few gawkers left.

He stepped wide around her until his toes rested on the Astroturf at the edge of the grave. Aaren waited, but he didn't look back at her.

She let her purse and jacket drop back to where they'd been on the chair. Minutes ago, she'd wanted to drag him away and talk it out. Now, she knew there were words to be said; she just didn't know what those words were.

"Elizabeth did a beautiful job with *Precious Lord*," she offered. Hearing it again so soon touched her heart. Funerals for residents of the north side didn't usually include it.

"Doesn't seem like a real service without it," he replied.

As she'd suspected, he'd chosen the hymn. "And the Judge? He didn't mind?"

Jarrod smirked. "He definitely understood."

Then he went silent again, hands in his pockets, staring into the dark slash of earth that held his mother.

She stepped behind him and ran her hands over his back, then rested her face to the fine wool of his suit.

"You okay?" she asked, slipping her arms around his middle.

She felt the eyes of the few remaining attendees who'd congregated near the gate. She didn't care. And despite Jarrod's instructions earlier, she wasn't just putting on a show. She wanted the entire world to know how she loved him.

"No."

"I know."

She did know. She could feel it, and see it. The earth over Pop's grave was still new-looking, though the flowers had died. Jarrod shrugged out of her grasp.

"There's some things I have to say to you," he began.

"Me too."

His hands went back into his pockets.

"Do you want me to start?" she asked.

"No. I want to know how you could bring that into our house."

Aaren stepped back and nodded. "The way I think about it, I didn't. I barely thought about him."

Jarrod raised his chin.

"The only man I've been thinking about is you. Gavin is…" she struggled for the word. "He's… he was never… he's a part of my life that's over. Over a long time ago."

"Did you cheat on him? Before me, I mean."

Aaren nearly had to stop herself from laughing. Jarrod was worried she'd be faithful to him? Her marriage had failed largely because Gavin in real life couldn't compete with the memories of Jarrod in her head.

"Never."

"Why'd you lie—"

"I did not *lie* to you."

FUNERAL

"Fine. But you didn't tell me the truth, either."

"Gavin was *over*. And I didn't think *he* would bother you more than... the others."

"I really don't know which one of those things bothers me more," laughed Jarrod bitterly.

Aaren hoped her face didn't show the shame she felt. She let his remark go unchallenged.

"Are any of the rest of them going to show up here?"

"No," she shot back, anger coiling at the center of her chest. Half of them, they didn't even know her name. More than half. Way more.

"What else am I going to find out about you?"

"There's nothing else."

"Do you have kids?"

"No!"

He looked away from her. She cut her eyes at the back of his head and he drew in a deep breath.

"Have you ever been pregnant?"

"No."

Jarrod turned sidewise to face her, his hands still in his pockets and his eyes glassy with tightly-held tears.

"Not ever?"

"*Never.*"

She'd played that scenario out in her head, over and over. Her period was late when Pops had put her on the train out of Penns Point, but it had been stress, not a pregnancy. Not Jarrod's baby, which would have rendered all the arguing and separation moot. Even Abraham Robinson would have wanted them married before a baby came. She'd spent orientation week at NYU lying in bed in her dorm room, mourning what never was.

He looked down, embarrassed, and stepped back from the edge of the grave.

"Is that it? Jarrod?"

He nodded.

She bit her lip, remembering the many times she'd stopped to wonder where Jarrod was at that precise moment, what he was doing, if he was happy. If he missed her. Aaren moved so she could see his face.

"You knew where I was. You could have found me any time."

She pressed her lips together, thinking of the fight she'd had with Gavin after she'd told him she wasn't changing her name when they got married. She'd insisted it was because she'd already established herself professionally. Aaren could admit now why it had been so important to her, why she'd refused Gavin that reasonable request.

"Yeah? What would you have done if I'd have shown up?"

"I'd have given it to you with both barrels." She'd played that one out in her head many times, too. "Did you ever try to find me? Call me?"

"No."

"Mmhmm. And there were others for you, too. Carrie Benson. Did you turn to her right away, or was that night of the fair just for show?"

"Naw. She went off to college same time as you just about. Stayed up there after graduation. Got a job up there, got married to some fella worked at Ford. She came home when it didn't work out."

"And the two of you?"

"I'd been back a couple years, and she kept coming by."

"And you've been together how long?"

"We're not together. I mean, it was never a thing."

"Relationship. The word you want is *relationship*."

"Well it never was."

"She seems to think otherwise."

"She always did."

"And you always let her."

"Look, the only reason I was with her was… Jesus! If I was with anyone else, they'd have been after me to…"

FUNERAL

"Get married?"

Jarrod frowned. "It wouldn't have been fair to be with someone, not like that. With Carrie? It was never going to go anywhere. And I told her that. I outright told her that."

"And you told her this for how long? Five *years*?" Aaren watched with satisfaction as Jarrod's mouth fell open. The blush rose to his cheeks. She wished he'd look at her.

"Still wasn't never going to happen."

Aaren crossed her arms over her chest and waited until he met her eyes.

"I know *exactly* what you mean."

Jarrod exhaled, closing his eyes. "Next you're going to say we're even."

"Are we?" she asked.

He opened his eyes to search hers. He looked exhausted, ready to break. Aaren stepped directly into him, wrapping her arms tight around his chest. Jarrod nodded heavily into her shoulder. She held him, kissed his jaw and stroked his hair.

"Do you want me to say it?" she whispered. "It's always been you. Always."

He squeezed her tighter. Aaren closed her eyes, letting her heart fill with him.

"So much time," she whispered. "Just wasted."

"Too much."

"So? Can we put it all down, and go forward? Can you do that?"

Jarrod exhaled, low and long, then straightened enough to touch his forehead to hers. "I can do that."

All she wanted was to take him home and be able to leave this day behind.

"Come on," said Aaren. "Let me get you to the repast."

"No." He held out his key ring between them. "Take the truck. I'm going to walk over."

"Baby, I... you shouldn't be alone."

"Won't be." Jarrod tipped his head behind them, to where his mother lay. "There's some things I have to say to her, too."

Aaren parked in back and walked the long way around to the front of Memorial, debating if she should go inside by herself, or wait for Jarrod. She turned the corner and nearly bumped into Antonio, who was leaning up against the white clapboards near the side door, drawing on a hand-rolled cigarette.

"Bec's been looking for you."

"Hi, Tony."

"Where is he?'

"He wanted to stay at the cemetery for a bit," she replied. "It's been... hard on him. I wish there was something, you know? Something I could do to make it better."

Antonio nodded. He usually let his silences do the talking. "Having you back makes it better for him."

She smiled her first real smile of the day and let him pull her under his arm for a hug. Antonio gave her a quick squeeze, then released her and laid back up against the wall, exactly where he'd been the moment before.

"Don't blow it," said Antonio.

Her smile vanished. She crossed her arms, willing herself to stay calm and wondering what the hell had brought that comment on. Becca burst through the door, letting the aluminum screen slam back into place behind her.

"Where you been? I mean, how're you doing and all? Okay?"

Aaren nodded and opened her mouth, but Becca went on.

"Okay. Good. Is Jarrod with you?" She looked over Aaren's shoulder expectantly; Aaren shook her head. "Where's he at?"

"Over at the cemetery still."

Becca slipped another furtive look, this time in Antonio's direction.

"Tony, you keep a good eye out for him? Stay with 'im? And Aaren, come with me." Becca took Aaren's arm and pulled, hard.

"Listen, Becca—I should go inside."

"No, probly you shouldn't. Not yet."

They rounded the front of the building and Becca yanked her back behind a poplar tree.

"Did he invite *her*?" Becca's face was flushed with indignation, and for a moment, Aaren was transported back to high school.

Aaren looked across the church lawn, putting her hand up to shield her eyes from the sun. Even from this far away, she could recognize Carrie. Her heart started to pound.

"And who-all is that with her?" demanded Becca.

The well-dressed man next to Carrie turned around. Aaren pressed her lips into a thin line. *Gavin.*

"He was supposed to be gone! I don't believe this! How dare he show up here?" She stalked off toward the pair, leaving Becca staring after her.

Aaren felt her heels sink into the grass. She ignored the smug look of satisfaction on Carrie's long face, and kept her eyes locked on those of her smiling husband. She went straight to him.

"What are you doing here?"

Carrie smirked at her. "We came to pay our respects, of course."

"Do not speak to me!" Aaren snapped.

Carrie sneered. "How is he, Aaren? Does he know your husband is in town?"

Aaren ignored her and looked at Gavin. "Answer me. Why are you here?"

"I came to see for myself. See if it was true. Meet the man that you compared me to for our entire marriage."

Aaren swallowed, not enjoying the way he was hurting. She might not have been in love with him, but he had been a good husband to her all these years. The last thing she ever wanted to do was punish him any further. And it was obvious that Carrie had filled his ears with some distorted version of her love affair with Jarrod. She could only imagine what Gavin was going through. She ran her hand through her hair and sighed, defeated. There would be no turning this around now.

"Please. Just leave. This is not the place for this. Have some respect, Gavin. He just buried his mother."

"Respect? You mean like the way you respected me enough to tell me you were leaving me for another man?" In her peripheral vision, Aaren saw people slowing down to stare at them. "Maybe the respect, the decency, to tell me that you've been down here screwing your brains out instead of burying your dead father!!"

Aaren flinched.

"Go, Gavin. I mean it. Now."

She turned to walk away but he snatched her up quickly by both her arms and shook her violently. She was so shocked by the force that she choked on her protests.

"Damn it! You won't treat me like this anymore! I'm not some doormat for you to wipe your feet on! I loved you, and God help me, I still do!!"

Aaren's brain couldn't handle that he'd laid hands on her. He'd never been violent with her, not once, and she was truly afraid. Before she could respond, she felt herself being ripped from Gavin's grasp.

"Don't you fucking touch her! Don't you *ever* touch her!"

Once clear of him, she saw Jarrod lunge at Gavin, throwing him to the hood of a parked car. Jarrod had him in a choke-hold. Gavin was turning purple. Aaren stumbled out of the way as Antonio and Travis jumped on Jarrod, fighting to get him off Gavin. Becca, finally making it over to Aaren's side, touched her arm.

"Sweetie, my Lord, are you okay?"

Carrie moved in close, unable to hide her glee over her handiwork. "Yes, Aaren, are you okay?"

"You think you've won something here? The only thing you have succeeded in doing is royally pissing me off!" she shot back.

FUNERAL

Becca grabbed Aaren to prevent another scene.

"Aaren, don't! For heaven's sake, we're burying Jarrod's mother. Look at how this is affecting her!" Becca pointed over to Macy, who had come out of the church and was crying loudly. "What's wrong with all of you??"

To Aaren's embarrassment, a small crowd had formed. She softened, feeling guilty for bringing this ugly scene into Macy's world. Jarrod kept shouting the things he planned to do to Gavin, taking his grief and anger out on the man. Antonio finally got a good hold of him and dragged him away. Travis turned to help Gavin, who pushed away the assistance and bent to pick up his cracked glasses. He looked over to Jarrod who was furious, glaring, his hair in his face.

"She's my wife! My damn wife! Do you hear me, country boy?"

Everyone looked at Aaren, shocked, as Carrie snickered. Aaren spoke up quickly.

"I'm not married to you any longer, Gavin! Do you hear me? We signed the papers and it's over!"

Gavin laughed. "You mean these papers?"

He pulled them out of his pocket and held them up in front of everyone. Aaren looked at him, horrified, but before she could say a word, he began to tear the pages up neatly, then toss them up in the air. "You're mine, and that redneck can't do a damn thing about it!!"

"Redneck, hunh?" Jarrod sneered at him. Antonio, not liking the taunt, let his boy go and Jarrod went for Gavin again.

"I'll show you redneck, chump. You think I give a shit about those papers? She's home, home with me, and there isn't a damn thing you can do about it! It's time this country boy gave you a good country ass-kicking!"

Travis got in front of Jarrod, stopping him. "Not here, Jay!! Think of Macy. Think of Mom, damn it!"

Gavin nodded toward his car and pointed his finger at Aaren. "I'll leave, but you are coming with me!"

"The hell she is!!" Jarrod shouted, his face beet-red.

Aaren's heart was just as torn apart as the tattered pieces of her divorce on the pavement. She looked back up at Gavin so he could see the tears in her eyes.

"Don't do this, Gavin. You said you wanted me to be happy," she stammered.

"You said you would honor me and forsake all others. I guess we are both liars, huh? You come home to hillbilly land and forget about our life together. The vows you made!! You take another man to bed? You been doing this all along, and I knew it! What type of lowly slut are you?" His anger had him shaking.

"Don't talk to her! Don't you fucking look at her!! Another word and I'm cracking your fucking skull!!" Jarrod shouted, trying to get at him again; Travis and Antonio began to shove him further back off the grass onto the paved road.

Aaren went to Gavin. "You can't stop this divorce and you know that. I'll just file myself."

"No you won't. Not after I hit the courts with your adultery and this betrayal. Plus, I hear you have property here. It looks to me like you were trying to conceal your assets. I'll drag your ass into court for everything and anything I can think of!"

"Why? What do you possibly gain?"

"Because its time you feel what I feel. It's time for you to want something so bad, too long for it, and then have it denied to you over and over again!"

Aaren stared at him in disbelief. "You have no idea what my life has been like and who I am. If you did, you would know that I paid that price a long time ago."

"How would I know? You've pushed me away throughout our entire marriage. You never let me in!"

"Then why do this? It won't bring me back to you. It won't make a difference!" she said her voice cracking.

"Aaren!" Jarrod shouted. "Let's go! Now!"

FUNERAL

Aaren turned to look at Jarrod, who had been dragged further away from her. Travis and Antonio blocked him from coming after Gavin again. She turned back to her husband. For Jarrod, she would beg.

"Please don't do this. I know I handled things badly with us, but Gavin, you have to want out. Just as much as I do."

"You know what I want and you didn't care. You never cared! So why should I care about you and your wants now?"

She smiled sweetly at him. "Because you aren't me. You aren't full of bitterness and anger. Stop this. Please," she said. She touched his hand, squeezed it gently. "Let me go, please." Aaren looked into his eyes, then turned on her heels and strode back to Jarrod. Gavin could do nothing but watch her, holding his broken glasses in his hands, as Jarrod pulled her into his arms. She blocked out all the stares, placed her hands up to Jarrod's face, and nodded to him that they were okay.

Nothing and no one would separate them again. Aaren slipped her hand into Jarrod's and they walked away.

Chapter Seventeen

STARTING AGAIN

Jarrod muttered something unintelligible and rolled toward her. They'd come home from the altercation at the repast and gone inside and straight upstairs. Without a word between them, they'd shed their clothes, dropping them piece by piece over the hardwood floor, before crawling into bed together. Aaren had managed to keep herself awake only a minute or two longer than Jarrod, and they'd slept out the remainder of the afternoon. She'd awakened first, and now she could tell he was on his way to waking up, too.

He snaked his hand around to her belly and pulled her close, bending himself to fit the curve of her back. She could feel him, hard, through his boxers.

"'kay?" she whispered, her voice catching. She tried again, stronger. "You okay?"

"Mmm."

His fingers splayed tight against the vee of her abdomen, pressing her to him. She felt her nipples tighten against the thin cotton of her camisole as she pushed back against him. His other hand reached underneath, insistent, to cup the weight of her breast.

Jarrod trailed kisses from the back of her neck to her shoulder, and she moaned.

"Wait—" She closed her eyes in frustration and covered his seeking hand with hers. "We can't. I have to go."

Jarrod exhaled sharply and flopped back against the mattress. Aaren couldn't tell if it was anger or the same frustration she was feeling, or both. But this time, sex would only get in the way. She didn't want Jarrod to be able to say she was trying to distract him, again.

"Why?" he asked.

"He's not going to just go away. I'm going to go over there, and—"

"Fine."

"Just... fine? That's it?"

"You're right," he said, rolling back to press himself against her again. "After. Not before."

Aaren twisted within his grasp, trying to see his face in the dim light. "You're so calm. You okay with this?"

"I don't know about okay."

"Jarrod, I—"

"It has to happen." She raised her eyebrows so he'd continue. "We have to be together on this, right? You did it my way this morning. Now we do this your way."

Her heart was pounding. She couldn't believe it was that easy.

"When I get back, I will tell you everything that happens. No secrets."

"Aaren, you do whatever you need to do to get yourself out of this. Whatever you need to do. Beyond that, I don't ever want to talk about him."

He held her tight, kissing the curve of her neck as though there had been no interruption. "The sooner you go, the sooner you're back. Right?"

Aaren stepped out of her car and faced the only hotel located in Penns Point. She could see his rental still parked in the lot. She walked up the sidewalk, slowly, to prepare herself. Carrie barreled through the double front doors, her Haney's tee shirt pulled tight across her ample chest. Aaren realized she must work here. Had she known, she'd have used the back entrance.

Carrie looked up and met her eyes dead on, a wicked smile crossing her lips. "Well, didn't take you long to dump Jay and come over here on bended knee."

Aaren put her purse on her shoulder, considering the bait. "Being my substitute the past few years couldn't have been easy for you."

"Get over yourself!" hissed Carrie.

"I know that somewhere in that barren cold chest of yours a heart beats, one that genuinely loves Jay. If that's true, stop with the shenanigans and grow the hell up, Carrie. It's time we all move on."

"You don't know a damn thing about me!"

Aaren stepped around her. Carrie reached and grabbed her arm, but dropped it immediately when Aaren leveled her with a threatening glare.

"I've loved him, Aaren. I've been here, while you were out living the high life in New York. Let him go. Take your husband and leave this town in peace. It's not enough your mother destroyed two men in this town, now you want to do it, too?"

Aaren eyes widened. It wasn't the revelation: her mother's affair had been discovered by Carrie's mother. The shock was that Carrie was bold enough to say it to her face.

"That's the only free pass you'll have on speaking to me about my family," she said through clenched teeth, then stepped away.

Carrie watched her go. "He won't let you leave him! I told him everything!" Carrie shouted after her.

Aaren ignored her and went through the door. She saw Gavin on his cell phone, pacing at the opposite end of the lobby. He turned when he saw her and ended the call.

"Can we talk?" she asked, meeting him halfway.

"Sure. Come to my room."

"No. Over there," she said, pointing to some chairs arranged around a low table.

"I won't discuss this with you in the open," he said abruptly. "Besides, after some of the things I've learned, you'll want privacy too."

"Fine," she said, heading past him, holding onto her purse.

She saw a wolf's grin on his face as she swept by. This thing between them would end here. She waited as he pushed the button on the elevator and kept her eyes trained ahead as the elevator lifted. She followed him to his suite, all in silence. When he opened the door for her to enter, she straightened her back and strode in without hesitation.

Gavin's bags were packed and on the bed. She looked back at him and half-smiled.

"So you were leaving?"

"I was, until I learned the truth."

"Which truth?"

"The one where this town covered up the murder of your mother," he said, stepping toward her.

"That's not what happened, Gavin." Aaren tossed her purse to the bed.

"Oh, I've already placed some calls. We'll see exactly what happened and how your lover's family played a role in it!"

Aaren frowned. "You did what?"

Gavin got in her space. "I can stop it. I can keep the skeletons buried if—"

"If what?" Aaren moved back out of his reach and shook her head.

"If you come back to me. If you come home with me. Because if not, your lover's daddy and several others are going to prison!"

Aaren stared at him in disbelief. "You would try to blackmail me into being with you?"

"I'll do anything to have you."

"Oh, Gavin," she whispered, combing her hands through her hair. Had she done this to him, made him so desperate? It sickened her to think so.

He grabbed her hand and brought her palm to his lips. "I need you Aaren. If you can give yourself to him, then I know you can try again with me!"

"Stop it!!" she snapped, snatching her hand away.

"Why? Why him and not me!!"

"I love him. I've loved him since I was sixteen, and honestly? Since years before that. He's been the sole reason I've slept through our marriage. He's why you and I never could get there. I'm so sorry. I didn't want to tell you this, have you hear it this way. I made vows and Gavin, you know I tried, but… I just… I'm just not her. The woman you thought you married. Forcing me won't bring us back together. It won't make me stop loving him."

"So I'm supposed to walk away? Let him have you? I won't do that! I can't do that!" Gavin pulled her into him. He tried to plant a kiss on her but she twisted free.

"Stop it, damn it! It's not going to happen!"

"Do you hear yourself? His parents murdered your mother and the whole town conspired to cover it up."

"You don't have the facts."

"I have plenty. What is going on with you? You need to come home with me!"

"No!! You call off your people and leave Penns. If you don't, I swear…"

"What? If I don't, then what?"

"You want to talk about skeletons? What about the Simon case?"

Gavin didn't even blink. "What about it?"

"You know that I know where your skeletons are buried. Don't make me get out my shovel."

Gavin shook his head, unnerved by her threat. "Do you hate me that much?"

"I love Jarrod that much."

"You would destroy everything I've built just to have him?"

"You did that when you destroyed evidence for nothing more than a couple hundred shares. I'll go straight to the prosecutor's office and bring the firm down." She was annoyed to hear her voice shaking.

"Don't forget, you'll bring yourself down, too. You'll be disbarred."

She saw his retreat, saw his mind considering all the dirty little deeds she knew about through the firm. She stepped in closer, nodding.

"I didn't forget," she smiled. "I don't care about the firm. And being disbarred? I plan to stay in this 'hillbilly town' as you so eloquently put it."

"You heartless bitch!" he snapped. "All I ever did was want to love you."

"No, if you loved me then you would have set me free. That's what Jarrod did for me fourteen years ago. That's what true love is. You overplayed your hand with this stunt you pulled today. So make your choice. Either go back and get me my divorce papers down here, signed and ready to file, or we start a war, and I learned how to fight from you. Be very careful which you choose."

She grabbed her purse and headed for the door.

Gavin turned to watch her leave.

"Aaren?"

"Yes?" She turned to look back at him.

"I will never stop wanting you," he said sadly.

"And I'll never stop loving him," she said, walking out and closing the door behind her.

Leaning against the hotel room door, Aaren let out the breath she'd been holding. She'd called his bluff. Now the outcome was up to him.

She'd never been sure if he'd destroyed that evidence but his reaction let her know that her suspicions were true. She was saddened by that realization and it dawned on her that she hadn't known Gavin any better than he knew her. She looked back at the door with disgust.

"Good bye, Gavin," she said softly. Then she lifted her frame from the door and walked away.

Walking down the stairs in nothing but his drawstring pajama pants, Jarrod headed to the kitchen to get something to drink. He smiled. Aaren was upstairs sleeping: *after* had definitely been the right choice. It was just after ten and too early for him to retire with her. Walking through the house, stretching, he began to think of all the things he would need to develop with Abraham's farm. Maybe he'd grow corn over there as well. Bright light beams swept through the front windows of the house. He stopped in his tracks. Figuring it to be Macy or his brother, he headed to the front door barefoot.

He opened it to see Gavin step out of his rental car. Narrowing his eyes, Jarrod flung open the screen door and came out on the porch.

"Why are you here?" Jarrod asked menacingly.

Gavin threw his hand up immediately. "I didn't come to make trouble."

"Then why *did* you come?"

"To say goodbye to her." Gavin looked past him to the door.

Jarrod wiped his jaw and checked himself. "She's asleep."

"Asleep? Right. Of course she'd be able to sleep now, she's with you," he said bitterly. Gavin shook his head. "Can I ask you a question?"

Jarrod folded his arms. Gavin took that for *yes*.

"Does she smile when she's with you? Does she... does she laugh?"

"What kind of question is that?"

Gavin sighed. "Then I guess she does."

Running his hand through his untamed hair, Jarrod looked past Gavin into the night. He didn't know what the man's life with Aaren was like. He couldn't imagine a life without her laughter or seductive smiles. He couldn't fathom how this man had been with her all this time and not really experienced her. It explained the man's desperation. He began to feel sorry for him. Gavin picked up on the question in Jarrod's eyes.

"I love her. You may not think so after what happened today, but I do. I think in all the time I've known her I've seen her happy maybe on three different occasions and that's not counting our wedding." He shook his head. "Tell her that I'm giving her the divorce, because I love her, not because of her threats. If you can make her smile, then I say it's worth it. I only wanted to make her happy." Gavin turned and headed to his car.

"Hey man, wait." Jarrod came down the steps.

Gavin stopped to watch warily as Jarrod approached him, unsure if he'd take a swing at him again, or not. Jarrod stuck out his hand, offering a handshake. Gavin looked at his hand for a moment then up into the eyes of the man who'd always had the love he wanted. It took him a moment to accept the gesture.

"I don't know you, but I appreciate the fact that you love her." Jarrod hesitated, not wanting to rub the other man's nose in his loss. "She's going to be happy here. She's home."

Gavin nodded and let go of Jarrod's hand. "Take care of her. She's special. It's about time she knew that," he said, getting in to his car. He stared straight through the windshield, but spoke loud enough so his voice would carry out the open window. "Tell her to file here. 180 days residency, 30 days for a decree. I won't contest it."

Jarrod watched him back away and then pull off. Turning on his heel, he headed back to the house. Suddenly, all he wanted to do was lie next to his Aaren and drift into a comfortable sleep.

Epilogue

"Baby, guess what I have here!" shouted Aaren, waving him over to the side of the ring with the envelopes she carried in each hand.

Jarrod tied the horse's lead around the aluminum rail and pulled his gloves off.

"Which one first?" She held out the envelopes, the fat one and the really thin one.

"That one," he pointed.

Aaren smiled broadly. "That one says that I'm officially single, as of last Tuesday."

"That only took 203 days," he grumbled.

"196," she shot back.

"Have it your way." Jarrod looked at his boots. "Are you finally gonna tell me how you got him to give us that divorce?"

She raised her eyebrow at the word *us*.

"Finally? I thought you didn't want to know anything about it."

Jarrod looked up, right into her face.

"Gavin's a man of reason," she shrugged. "I just gave him the best reason to play nice with us. Self-preservation. I always had suspicions about the way one of our cases just went away. I called his bluff, told him I'd bring the firm down and him with it." She

EPILOGUE

shrugged, pulling the edges of her puffy coat closer together. It was almost as cold inside the work ring as it was outside.

"You'd have implicated yourself, too, right?"

"Yes. Funny, he mentioned that as well."

"Why would you risk that?"

"Same reason I told him, Jay. I was staying in Kentucky. Being a lawyer in New York wasn't that high on my list any more."

Jarrod fell silent.

"Any more questions?"

"Nope."

"I got one, then." Aaren waited until he met her gaze. "I was wondering if maybe you still wanted to marry me."

Jarrod pursed his lips, holding back a smile, then reached through the aluminum bars of the enclosure, pushing her coat aside, pulling her to him. The tip of his tongue swept gently past her lips, then deeper, urgent, wanting more. Aaren kissed him back, laughing at the fence, which was the only thing keeping them from going further. She pushed at his chest.

"Wait! Don't you want to know what's in the other envelope?"

Jarrod's brow furrowed. Already he didn't like that envelope, since it had caused Aaren to interrupt their kiss. But he couldn't resist her bright smile, and played along.

"What's in the other envelope?"

"It's my ballot application. For this spring."

"Ballot? For what??"

"Special Election. For Judge. Bullitt County."

He craned his neck back and looked down into her face.

"Apparently the sitting judge has decided to retire. His term's not even up."

Jarrod tucked his chin down.

"And I think being the youngest-ever district judge elected to the Bullitt County bench is... well, I wouldn't call it my destiny. But with my qualifications, it seems like a no-brainer. Wouldn't you agree?"

Jarrod didn't say a word.

"I'll have your support, right? Maybe even your vote?"

"On one condition."

"What's that?"

"You take my name."

"Oh, I'm counting on that. It's the centerpiece of my campaign platform."

"Really?"

"Absolutely. I'm told no Pennington has ever lost an election in Bullitt County history."

"Actually, that's true." Jarrod laughed, seeking her lips again. Each kiss was sweeter to Aaren than the last. "You win and you'll make history, you know."

"What, you don't think Penns Point is ready for its first black judge?"

Jarrod shook his head.

"Oh, do not even think about telling me it's because I'm female."

"No, ma'am. But what I'm about to do to you? A pregnant judge is gonna make their heads explode."